'Her gallery of personages is huge, her scene painting superb, her pathos controlled, her humour quiet and civilised.'
ANTHON

'A fantastically tart an
in eastern Europe
SARA

D1458439

'Magnificent . . . full of wit, sharp insight and vivid description.'
THE TIMES

'So glittering is the overall parade . . . and so entertaining the surface that the trilogy remains excitingly vivid; it amuses, it diverts and it informs, and to do these things so elegantly is no small achievement.'
SUNDAY TIMES

'Glittering characterisation, sharp and eloquent writing.'
SUNDAY TELEGRAPH

'A delicate, tough, mesmerising epic that grabs you by the hand and takes you straight into war, flight, and a complex and vulnerable young marriage.'
LOUISA YOUNG

'I shall be surprised, and, I must admit, dismayed if the whole work is not recognised as a major achievement in the English novel since the war. Certainly it is an astonishing recreation.'
NEW YORK TIMES

'Dramatic, comic and entirely absorbing.'
CARMEN CALLIL

OLIVIA MANNING

Olivia Manning, OBE, was born in Portsmouth, Hampshire, spent much of her youth in Ireland and, as she put it, had 'the usual Anglo-Irish sense of belonging nowhere'. She married just before the War and went abroad with her husband, R.D. Smith, a British Council lecturer in Bucharest. Her experiences there formed the basis of the work which makes up *The Balkan Trilogy*. As the Germans approached Athens, she and her husband evacuated to Egypt and ended up in Jerusalem, where her husband was put in charge of the Palestine Broadcasting Station. They returned to London in 1946 and lived there until her death in 1980.

ALSO BY OLIVIA MANNING

NOVELS

Artist for the Missing
School for Love
A Different Face
The Doves of Venus
The Play Room
The Rain Forest

THE BALKAN TRILOGY

The Great Fortune
The Spoilt City
Friends and Heroes

THE LEVANT TRILOGY

The Danger Tree
The Battle Lost and Won
The Sum of Things

SHORT STORIES

Growing Up
A Romantic Hero

Friends and Heroes

Olivia Manning

WINDMILL

1 3 5 7 9 10 8 6 4 2

Windmill Books
20 Vauxhall Bridge Road
London SW1V 2SA

Windmill Books is part of the Penguin Random House group of companies
whose addresses can be found at global.penguinrandomhouse.com.

Penguin
Random House
UK

First published in Great Britain by William Heinemann in 1965
First published in paperback by Mandarin Paperbacks in 1990
This edition published by Windmill Books in 2021

www.penguin.co.uk

A CIP catalogue record for this book is available from the British Library.

ISBN 9781786091543

Typeset by Palimpsest Book Production Ltd, Polmont Stirlingshire
Printed and bound in Great Britain by Clays Ltd, Elcograf S.p.A.

The authorised representative in the EEA is Penguin Random House Ireland,
Morrison Chambers, 32 Nassau Street, Dublin D02 YH68

To
Dwye and Daphne Evans

THE BALKAN TRILOGY
VOLUME THREE

Friends and Heroes

PART ONE

The Antagonists

I

When the hotel porter rang to say a gentleman awaited her in the hall, Harriet Pringle dropped the receiver and ran from the room without putting on her shoes.

She had sat by the telephone for two days. Her last three nights in Athens had been sleepless with anxiety and expectation. She had left her husband in Rumania, a country since occupied by the enemy. He might get away. The man in the hall could be Guy himself. Turning the corner of the stair, she saw it was only Yakimov. She went back for her shoes, but quickly. Even Yakimov might have news.

When she came down again, he was drooping like an old horse under his brim-broken panama and the sight roused her worst apprehensions. Unable to speak, she touched his arm. He lifted his sad, vague face and, seeing her, smiled.

'It's all right,' he said. 'The dear boy's on his way.' So eager was he to reassure her that his large, grape-green eyes seemed to overflow their sockets: 'Got a message. Got it on me somewhere. Must be here. Someone in Bucharest phoned the Legation. One of our chaps said to me: "You know this Mrs Pringle, don't you? Drop this in on her when you're passing."' His fingers were dipping like antennae into the pockets of his shantung suit: 'Bit of paper, y'know. Just a bit of paper.'

He tried his breast pocket. As he lifted his long bone of an

3

arm, she saw the violet silk of his shirt showing through the tattered shantung of his jacket, and the blue-white hairless hollow of his arm-pit showing through his tattered shirt. The pockets were so frayed, the message could have fallen out. Watching him, she scarcely dared to breathe, knowing that any show of impatience would alarm him.

Their relationship was happy enough now, but it had not always been like that. Yakimov – Prince Yakimov – had installed himself in the Pringles' flat and would not be dislodged until Bucharest became too dangerous for him. She had disliked him and he had feared her, but when they met again in Athens, they became reconciled. He was the only person here who understood her fears and his sympathy had been her only consolation.

'Ah!' he gave a gasp of satisfaction: 'Here we are! Here it is! Got it safe, you see!'

She took the paper and read: '*Coming your route. See you this evening.*'

The message must have been received hours before. It was now late afternoon. Guy would already have touched down at Sofia to find, as she found, that the Rumanian plane would go no farther and he must continue on the Lufthansa. The German line had agreed to carry allied passengers over neutral territory, but she had heard of planes being diverted to Vienna so that British subjects could be seized as enemy aliens. Harriet herself had not been at risk but Guy, a man of military age, might be a different matter.

Seeing her face change, Yakimov said, abashed: 'Aren't you pleased? Isn't it good news?'

She nodded. Sinking down on the hall seat, she whispered: 'Wonderful,' then doubled over and buried her face in her hands.

'Dear girl!'

She lifted her head, her eyes wet, and laughed: 'Guy will be here at sunset.'

'There you are! I told you he could look after himself.'

Confused by exhaustion and relief, she remained where she

4

was, knowing the suspense was not over yet. She had still to live until sunset.

Yakimov looked uneasily at her, then said: 'Why not come out a bit? Get a breath of air. Do you good, y'know.'

'Yes. Yes, I'd like to.'

'Then get y'r bonnet on, dear girl.'

She entered the daylight as though released after an illness. The street was in shadow but at the end she could see a dazzle of sunlight. As Yakimov turned the other way, she said, 'Could we go down there?'

'There!' he seemed disconcerted: 'That's Constitution Square. Like to stroll through it? Adds a bit to the walk, though.'

'But are we going anywhere in particular?'

Yakimov did not reply. They entered the square where there was a little garden, formal and dusty, with faded oranges upon orange-trees. The buildings, Yakimov said, were hotels and important offices. Some were faced with marble and some with rose-brown stucco. At the top of the square was the parliament house that had once been a palace and still had the flourish of a palace. Beside it were the public gardens, a jungle of sensitive bushy trees from which rose the feathered tops of palms. Four immense palms with silvery satin trunks stood across the garden entrance. Buildings, trees, palms, traffic, people – all were aquiver in the fluid heat of the autumn afternoon.

'Athens,' Harriet thought: 'The longed-for city.'

Bucharest had been enclosed by Europe, but here she had reached the Mediterranean. In Bucharest, the winter was beginning. In Athens, it seemed, the summer would go on for ever.

If they could survive till evening, she and Guy would be here together. She imagined his plane where it would be now: in the empyrean, above the peacock blue and green of the Aegean. She willed it to stay on course. He had left the unhappy capital and the maniac minions of the New Order, and now she had only to wait for his safe arrival. Trying to keep her mind on this, her imagination eluded her control.

She thought of those who had been left behind. She thought of Sasha.

Yakimov, acting as host and guide, was pointing out places of interest. Modestly conscious of being in a position of vantage, his manner had a touch of the grandiose.

'Nice town,' he said: 'Always liked it. Old stamping ground of your Yak, of course.'

He had left his debts behind and none of his new friends had had time to learn about them. He had found employment. Though his clothes were past mending, they had been cleaned and pressed, and he wore them with an air that proclaimed his sumptuous past. He nodded towards an ornate corner building and said:

'The G.B.'

'What happens there?'

'*Dear girl!* The G.B.'s the best hotel. The Grande Bretagne you know. Where Yaki used to wash his socks. Intend moving back there when'm a bit more lush.'

Turning into the main road, his steps faltered, his tall, slender body sagged. They had covered perhaps a couple of hundred yards but as he made his way through the crowd, he began to grumble: 'Long walk, this. Hard on your Yak. Feet not what they used to be. Tiring place, this: uphill, downhill, hot and dusty. Constant need for refreshment.'

They had come in sight of a large café and, giving a sigh of relief, he said: 'Zonar's. Their new café. Very nice. In fact, Yaki's favourite haunt.'

Everything about the café – a corner of great glass windows, striped awnings, outdoor chairs and tables – had a brilliant freshness. The patrons were still dressed for summer, the women in silks, the men in suits of silver-grey; the waiters wore white coats and their trays and coffee pots glittered in the sun. Behind the windows Harriet could see counters offering extravagant chocolate boxes and luscious cakes.

'It looks expensive,' she said.

'Bit pricey,' Yakimov agreed: 'But convenient. After all, one has to go somewhere.' They crossed the side-road and reaching

6

the café pavement, Yakimov came to a stop: 'If I'd a bit of the ready, I'd invite you to take a little something.'

So this had been his objective when they set out! Harriet understood his form of invitation. He had delivered the message and now she was expected to make repayment. She said: 'They changed some Rumanian money for me at the hotel, so let me buy a drink.'

'Dear girl, certainly. If you feel the need of one, I'll join you with pleasure,' he sank into the nearest basket-chair and asked impressively: 'What will you take?'

Harriet said she would have tea.

'Think I'll have a drop of cognac, myself. Find it dries me up, too much tea.'

When the order came, the waiter put a chit beside his glass. Yakimov slid it over to Harriet then, sipping his brandy, his affability returned. He said:

'Big Russian colony here, y'know. Charming people; the best families. And there's a Russian club with Russian food. Delicious. One of the members said to me: "Distinguished name, Yakimov. Wasn't your father courier to the Czar?"'

'Was your father courier to the Czar?'

'Don't ask me, dear girl. All a long time ago. Yaki was only a young thing then. But m'old dad was part of the entourage. No doubt about that. That coat of mine, the sable-lined coat, was given him by the Czar. But perhaps I told you?'

'You've mentioned it once or twice.'

''Spose you know m'old mum's dead?'

'No. I am sorry.'

'No remittance for Yaki now. Good sort, the old mum, kind to her poor boy, but didn't leave a cent. Had an annuity. All went with her. *Bad* idea, an annuity.'

He emptied his glass and looked expectantly at Harriet. She nodded and he called the waiter again.

In the past she had been resentful of Yakimov's greed, now she was indifferent to everything but the passing of time. Time was an obstacle to be overcome. She wanted nothing so much as to see the airport bus stop at the corner opposite.

'Look at that chap!' said Yakimov: 'The one hung over with rugs. Turk, he is. I knew one of those in Paris once. Friend of mine, an American, bought his entire stock. Poor chap walked home without a rug on him. Caught pneumonia and died.'

She smiled, knowing he was trying to entertain her, but she could not keep her mind on his chatter. She glanced about her, bewildered by her safety, unable to believe in a city so becalmed in security and comfort. Her nerves reacted still to the confusion of their last months in Rumania. As Yakimov talked, the splendid café faded from her view and she saw instead the Bucharest flat as it had been the night before she left, when the Pringles returned to find the doors open, the lights on, the beds stripped, pictures smashed, carpets ripped up and books thrown down and trampled over the floor.

She and Guy had hidden Sasha, a young Jewish deserter from the army. The louts of the Iron Guard, searching for evidence against Guy, had found the boy. Sasha was gone. That was all they knew, and probably all they would ever know.

Yakimov recalled her with a cough. His glass was empty again but at that moment the airport bus drew up and she searched in her bag to pay the bill. 'I must go,' she said.

'Don't go, dear girl. Plenty of time for another one. That bus waits twenty minutes or more. It's *always* there. Just one more . . . just one more,' he wailed as she sped off.

Bleakly, he watched her as she crossed the road and boarded the bus. Had he known she would desert him like this, he would not have finished his cognac so quickly.

She took her seat, prepared to wait, she did not care how long. Simply to be on the bus meant another inroad upon time. It seemed to her that when the plane arrived she would have conquered anxiety altogether.

2

Harriet's plane had been punctual. It had swept down between the hills at a sublime moment – the moment acclaimed by Pindar – when the marble city and all its hills glowed rosy amethyst in the evening light.

Standing on the withered tufts of airfield grass, awaiting the moment as harbinger of Guy's arrival, Harriet saw the refulgence as a gift for him. But it touched perfection and began to darken; for a little while the glow remained like wine on the hills, then she was left with nothing but her own suspense. Nearly an hour passed before the Lufthansa came winking its landing-lights over Parnes.

At last it was down. She saw Guy on the steps. Short-sighted and lost in the beams of the ground lights, he knew he would never be able to find her, so stood there: a large, untidy, bespectacled man with a book in one hand and an old rucksack in the other, waiting for her to find him. She stared a moment, amazed by reality; then ran to him. When she reached him, she was weeping helplessly.

'Whatever is the matter?' he asked.

'What do you think? I was worried, of course.'

'Not about me, surely,' he laughed at her, frowning to hide his concern, and gave her elbow a shake: 'You knew I'd be all right.' In his humility, he was surprised that his danger had so affected her. Putting an arm round her, he said: 'Silly,' and she clung to him and led him through the shadows to the customs shed.

When the luggage came from the plane, Guy's suitcase came

with it. He had been back to the flat and filled the case and rucksack full of books.

'What about your clothes?' Harriet asked.

'I've a change of underwear in the rucksack. I didn't bother about the other things. One can get clothes anywhere.'

'And books,' she said, but it was no time to argue: 'Had anyone been to the flat?'

'No, it was just as we left it.'

'And no news of Sasha?'

'No news.'

When the bus stopped at the corner opposite Zonar's, Harriet pointed to the large, brilliant windows with the fringe of basket-chairs, and said: 'Yakimov's here. That's his favourite haunt.'

'Yaki's here! How splendid! Let's get rid of this luggage and go and find him.'

'Have you any money?'

'No drachma. But you must have some?'

'Not much. And I'm dead tired.'

Though impatient to gather this new world to him, Guy had to agree he, too, was tired. The fact bewildered him but on reflection, he said: 'I didn't go to bed last night. That may have something to do with it.'

'How did you spend the night?'

'David and I sat up playing chess. I wanted to sleep at the flat but David said it'd be a damnfool thing to do, so we went to his room.'

'Did you leave him in Bucharest?'

'No. His job doesn't carry diplomatic privilege, so he was ordered to Belgrade. We travelled together as far as Sofia.' Guy smiled, thinking they had parted like comrades, for they had, as David said, seen the *bouleversement* through to the end: 'When we had dinner,' he said, 'there were German officers sitting all round us. I'm afraid we were a bit hysterical. I'd made up my mind that, come what may, I would stay on, and David was calling me the Steadfast Tin Soldier. We couldn't stop laughing. The Germans kept turning round to look at us. I think they thought we were crazy.'

'If you wanted to stay in Rumania, then you were crazy.'

'Oh, I don't know! I hadn't been ordered to go; but next morning the Legation got on to me and said we were all being turned out. No reprieve this time. David was just leaving for the airport, so I went with him. Young Fitzsimon promised to try to get a message to you.'

'Yes, someone rang through. Yakimov brought it. You know, he's terribly important, or so he says. He's employed at the Information Office.'

'Dear old Yakimov. I *do* look forward to seeing him.'

In the dim light of the hotel's basement dining-room, Guy's face, usually fresh-coloured, was grey and taut. As they ate, he sighed with weariness and joy, but he had no intention of going to bed. It was early yet and there was no knowing what life might still have up its sleeve.

He said: 'Let's go out and see the town.'

They went to Zonar's, but Yakimov was not there. They walked around for half an hour without meeting anyone known to them – a fact that seemed to baffle Guy – then, at last, he admitted he was exhausted and ready to go back to the hotel.

At breakfast, on his first morning in Athens, Guy said: 'I must see the Director and get myself a job. Have you discovered anything about him?'

'Only that he's called Gracey. Yakimov doesn't know him and I was too worried to think about anything like that.'

'We'll go to the Organization,' Guy said. 'We'll report our arrival and ask for an interview with Gracey.'

'Yes, but not this morning, our first morning here. I thought we could go and see the Parthenon.'

'The Parthenon!' Guy was astonished by the suggestion but realizing the excursion was important to her, he promised: 'We will go, but not today. For one thing, there wouldn't be time.'

'I thought of it as a celebration of your arrival. I wanted it to be the first thing we did together.'

11

Guy had to laugh. 'Surely there's no hurry? The Parthenon's been there for two thousand years, and it'll be there tomorrow. It may even be there next week.'

'So will the Organization office.'

'Be reasonable, darling. I'm not on holiday. The order was that all displaced men must report to the Cairo office. I'm not supposed to be here. I took a risk in coming here, and it won't improve matters if I go off sightseeing the minute I arrive.'

'No one knows you're here. We could have one morning to ourselves.' Harriet argued, but faintly, knowing he was, as usual, right. Cairo had become a limbo for Organization employees thrown out of Europe by the German advance and Guy, hoping to avoid its workless muddle, had come here against orders. He could justify himself only by finding employment.

Seeing her disappointment, he squeezed her hand and said: 'We will have a morning together; I promise. Just as soon as things are fixed up. And if you want to go to the Parthenon – well, all right, we'll go.'

Harriet found that Guy had already asked the porter the whereabouts of the Organization office and, breakfast over, they must set out without delay. The office was in the School, and the School was in the old district near the Museum. As the porter had recommended, they took the tramway-car which passed the hotel and, seated on the upper deck, they looked down on the pavements crowded in the radiance of morning. Sliding her fingers into Guy's hand, Harriet said: 'We are here together. Whatever happens, no one can take that from us.'

'No one will take it from us,' Guy said. 'We are here to stay.'

Harriet was impressed. The fact that Guy was by nature tolerant and uncomplaining gave to his occasional demands on circumstances a supernatural power. She was at once convinced that they would stay.

The streets in the Omonia Square area were unfashionable

and decayed, but the School – a large house that stood in a corner site – had been restored to its nineteenth-century grandeur, and there were beds of zinnias and geraniums in the sanded forecourt. The double front-door had elaborate brass-work and glass panels engraved with irises. The inside stairway, carpeted in red, ran up to a main floor where there was another door with glass panels. This was marked 'Lecture Room'. Looking in through the glass, Harriet saw a man on a platform addressing a roomful of students.

'Who do you think is lecturing in there?' she asked in a low voice. Too short-sighted to see for himself, Guy asked: 'Who?'

'Toby Lush.'

'I don't believe it.'

'Yes. Toby – pipe and all.'

Guy caught her arm and pulled her away from the door: 'Do you think they're both here? Toby Lush and Dubedat?' he asked.

'Probably. I remember now that Yakimov said something about Toby being in an influential position.'

Guy was silent a moment before he said firmly: 'That's a good thing.'

'Why is it a good thing?'

'They can put in a word for me.'

'But will they?'

'Why not? I helped them when they needed help.'

'Yes, but when you most needed help, they bolted from Rumania and left you to manage on your own.'

They were standing in a passage where the doors were marked 'Director', 'Chief Instructor', 'Library' and 'Teachers' Common Room'. Before Harriet could make any further indictment of Lush and Dubedat, Guy opened the door marked 'Library' and said: 'We can wait in here.'

A Greek girl sat at the Library desk. She welcomed them pleasantly but seemed shocked when Guy asked if he could see the Director.

'The Director is not here,' she said.

'Where can we find him?' Harriet asked.

The girl dropped her gaze and shook her head as though the Director were too august a figure to be lightly discussed. 'If you wait,' she said to Guy, 'you may be able to see Mr Lush.'

Guy said: 'I would rather make an appointment to see Mr Gracey.'

'I don't think it is possible. You would have to consult Mr Lush. But I could make an appointment for you to see Mr Dubedat.'

'Is Mr Dubedat here now?'

'Oh, no. Not at the moment. He's very busy. He's working at home.'

'I see.'

Harriet murmured: 'Let's go.'

Guy looked nonplussed: 'If we go,' he said, 'we'll only have to come back. As we're here, we might as well wait and see Toby.'

Guy wandered off round the shelves, but Harriet remained near the door, waiting to see how Toby Lush would behave when he caught sight of them. The two men, Lush and Dubedat, had come to Bucharest from different occupied countries and Guy had employed each in turn. They had become close friends and without consulting Guy or anyone else, they had left together, secretly, fearful of the threatened German advance.

Harriet could hear Toby scuffing in the passage before he entered. He blundered against the door and fell in with it, his hair in his eyes, his arms full of books. He bumped against Harriet, stared at her and recognized her in dismay. He looked round suspiciously, saw Guy and dropped the books in order to grip his pipe. He sucked on it violently, then managed to gasp: 'Well, well, well!'

Guy turned, smiling with such innocent friendliness that Toby, restored, rushed forward and seized him by the hand.

'Miraculous,' gasped Toby, his big fluffy moustache blowing in and out as he spoke. 'Miraculous! And Harriet, too.'

He swung round as though he had just become aware of her. 'When did you get here, you wonderful people?'

As Guy was about to reply, Toby shouted: 'Into the office,' and rushed them from the Library before they could speak again. Inside the room marked 'Chief Instructor', Toby placed them in chairs and seated himself behind a large desk. 'Now then,' he said, satisfied, and he examined them, his eyes protruding with the joviality of shock.

'Who'd've thought it!' he spoke as though doubtful of their corporeality. 'So you got away, after all?'

'After all what?' Harriet asked.

Toby treated that as a joke. While he whoofed with laughter, his coarse-featured, putty-coloured face slipped about like something too soft to hold its shape, and he clutched at his pipe, the only stronghold in a world where anything might happen. He was still dressed in his old leather-patched jacket, the shapeless flannels which he called his 'bags' and his heavy brogues, but, in spite of his dress, his manner suggested that he had become a person of consequence. The first greetings over, he sat back importantly in his chair and said to Guy:

'So you're on your way to the mystic east, eh? The mystic Middle East, I should say?'

'No, we want to stay here. Can you arrange for me to see Gracey?'

'Oh!' Toby looked down at his desk. 'Um.' His head dropped lower and lower while he gave thought to Guy's request, then he said in an awed tone: 'Mr Gracey's a sick man. He doesn't see anyone in the ordinary way.'

'What about the *extra*-ordinary way?' Harriet asked.

Toby cocked up an eye, took his pipe from his mouth, and said solemnly: 'Mr Gracey's injured his spine.'

He pushed his pipe back through his moustache and started to relight it.

'Who is doing his work while he is unwell?' Guy asked.

'Um, um, um, um.' Toby, sucking and gasping, was forced to abandon one match and light another. 'No one,' he said at last and added, '*really*'.

'Who is in charge then?'

'It's difficult to say. Mr Gracey doesn't do any work but he likes to feel he's in control. *You* understand!'

Guy nodded. He did understand. 'But,' he said, 'he must have a deputy. He could never run this place on his own.'

'Well, no,' Toby struck another match and there was a long delay while the pipe lighting went on. At last, amazingly, a thread of smoke hovered out of the bowl and, shaking out the match, he leant forward confidingly: 'Fact is, when we arrived here, Mr Gracey was in a bit of a fix. His two assistants had beetled off leaving him . . . well . . .' Toby gave Harriet a nervous glance before he completed his sentence: '. . . in the lurch.'

'Why?'

'It was one of those things. I don't know the details, but you know what it's like: a misunderstanding, a few heated words. . . . Such things happen! Anyway, they took themselves off.'

'How did they manage it? The Organization is a reserved occupation.'

'They were transferred. One of them had influence – his father was an M.P. or something. Bit of dirty work, if you ask me. They wanted to go home but they were sent to the Far East. Mr Gracey applied for two new assistants; the London office had no one to send. They'd had their quota. He was told he'd have to wait and keep things going with locally employed teachers. He had two or three Greeks and a Maltese chap, but no one who could give a lecture. That's how it was when we turned up.

'You saved the day in fact?' said Harriet.

'In a manner of speaking, we did just that.'

Guy asked: 'Who gives the lectures now?'

'Dubedat gives some. As a matter of fact . . .' Toby guffed and after a pause said with triumphant coyness: 'I give the odd lecture myself.'

'On what?'

'Eng. Lit. of course.'

Guy seemed at a loss for comment and Harriet said: 'It looks as though Gracey will be glad to have Guy.'

Toby's face tautened in a wary way: 'Don't know about that. Can't say.' He stared down at the desk and mumbled: 'Numbers've been dropping off . . . not much work for anyone these days . . . local teachers had to be sacked . . . very quiet here . . .'

Harriet broke in: 'It's pretty obvious from what you say that someone's needed to pull the place together.'

'That's for Mr Gracey to decide.' Toby sat up and gave Harriet a severe look. In an attempt to exclude her from the conversation, he turned in his seat and stared directly at Guy. 'Mr Gracey had this accident but he won't admit defeat. You've got to admire him. He's doing his best to run the place from his sick-bed, if you know what I mean. You can't just say to a man like that: "You aren't up to it. You need someone to pull the place together." Now, can you?' He frowned his emotion and Guy, touched by the appeal, nodded in sympathetic understanding. There was a long condoling pause broken by Harriet.

She wanted to know: 'When can Guy see Mr Gracey?'

Toby straightened up and put his hands on the table as though forced by Harriet's lack of tact to demonstrate his authority: 'I could . . .' He hesitated and gave a last suck at his pipe before committing himself: 'I could get you an interview with Dubedat.'

'Are you serious?' Harriet asked.

Toby ignored her and spoke directly to Guy: 'I can't say exactly *when* he can see you. It mightn't be for a day or two. He's up to his eyes. He's practically running things here, you know! But I'm sure he *will* see you.' Toby nodded assuringly, then got to his feet. 'Where are you staying?' He noted down the name of the hotel, then shot out a large, soft hand. 'We'll keep in touch.' He paused, sucked, and added: 'And I'll do what I can for you. I promise.'

Returning to the dusty heat of mid-morning, the Pringles walked as far as Omonia Square before either spoke, then

Harriet burst out: 'An interview with Dubedat! Have we come to that?'

Guy, giving a brief, shocked laugh, had to admit: 'It was pretty cool.'

He looked pale so Harriet did not tell him it was her belief he had created the whole situation by his indiscriminate generosity. Toby was unqualified; Dubedat's qualifications were mediocre. Neither had much ability. Guy could have managed without them and, in the end, had to manage without them. Had he not employed them, they would have been sent to Egypt and probably conscripted. As it was, they had become resentful of the fact that Guy would not let them do anything more than teach. Toby had wanted to lecture but Guy would not hear of it. Remembering the tone in which Toby had said: 'I give the odd lecture myself,' Harriet knew he had never forgiven Guy for standing between him and his ambition. She could see that Guy had his own methods of arousing enmity. He did not give too little, he gave too much. Those who give too much are always expected to give more, and blamed when they reach the point of refusal.

She said: 'If I were you, I'd insist on seeing Gracey. And don't take "No" for an answer.'

'I'll certainly insist on seeing Gracey. I'll tell Dubedat . . .'

'Surely you won't see Dubedat? If you're wise, you'll have nothing to do with him.'

'Why not? He's a pal.'

'Just as Toby Lush is a pal.'

'Toby is an ass, but Dubedat is different. He's no fool. He'll be much easier to deal with.'

'We'll see.'

Guy's faith, even his unjustified faith, had its own dynamism, and she would not weaken it. Their position was weak enough as it was. She contented herself by saying: 'Toby thinks he has only discouraged us and we'll take ourselves off. He knows we haven't much money. Without money, no one can hang around a foreign capital for long.'

'We'll hang around as long as we can.' Guy said, and in

18

Stadium Street he found a bureau that gave him drachma for his Rumanian *lei*. The exchange was made reluctantly and the rate was low, but Guy was delighted to get anything at all. As soon as he had money in his pocket, he wanted to spend it. He said: 'Let's go to the café you showed me: Yakimov's favourite haunt.'

'Zonar's. It's not cheap.'

'Never mind.'

They found seats in the sun and sat amid the affluent, leisured Greeks who were reading an English newspaper with the headline: '*Seven German Submarines Sunk.*' The headline filled the Pringles with wonder, for in Rumania they had come to believe, like everyone else, that the only ships sunk were British ships.

As soon as he saw the English couple, a gentle, quivering, old Greek came to Guy and held a copy of the paper before him. When Guy handed over a note, the old man neither bolted with it nor begged for more, but carefully counted the change on to the table and began to move on. When Guy pushed some of the coins back to him, he bowed and gathered them up.

Guy read his paper while Harriet watched the men moving between the chairs, selling nougat, peanuts and sponges. One of them, catching her eye, offered her an enormous melon-yellow sponge. She tilted up her chin in the Greek fashion and murmured: 'Oxi.' The man offered other sponges, cream, golden, fawn and brown; at each Harriet gave a smaller tilt of the chin and her 'Oxi' became scarcely audible. The man did not become angry like the terrible beggars of Bucharest, but smiled, amused by her performance, and moved on. Relaxed in her chair, she felt a subsidence of tension as though some burden, carried for too long a time, was gradually losing weight. How different life would be here, in this indolent sunshine where the fate of Rumania was a minor fracas, too far away to mean anything!

Here one had only to be English to be approved. It was not only that the Greeks and the English shared a common cause, but she felt a sympathy between them. If they could stay here, she and Guy would never have reason to worry again. Wanting him to acknowledge the peace they had found, she said: 'It's marvellous!'

Looking up from the paper, he turned his face to the sun and nodded.

'To feel safe!' she said. 'Simply to feel safe! It's marvellous to be among people who are on your side.' Having come from a country that had sold itself in fear, she was conscious of the ease of the Greeks. They had the right to be at ease; their dignity was unassailed.

When he had read the little two-page paper, he began to watch the passers-by with an eager, inquiring look, wanting to know and be known. While Harriet was content to observe people, Guy longed to communicate with them and she wished someone would appear to whom he could talk. Someone did appear: Toby Lush.

She said: 'Good Heavens! Look!'

Guy looked and his face fell. Toby, getting out of a taxi, seemed anxious and, as he pushed between the people on the pavement, his movements were so discordant, he appeared deranged. Seeing the Pringles, he threw up his arms and shouted: 'There you are! I thought I'd find you here!' He fell into a chair and slapped at the sweat which ran down the runnels of his face. 'Must have a drink. What about you two?' He swung out his arm at a passing waiter and knocked the man's tray to the ground.

The Pringles sat suspended while Toby ordered himself an ouzo; then he said: '*Now!*' as though about to produce a solution of Guy's predicament. After a pause, he added firmly: 'I've had a word with himself.'

'With the Director?' Guy asked.

'No, no. With Dubedat. And he told me to tell you: "We'll do what we can."' Toby stared at Guy, expecting gratitude, but Guy said nothing. Disconcerted, Toby went on: 'After all, you did what you could for us.'

'What do you think you can do?'

The question seemed to reassure Toby, who sagged down in his chair and got out his pipe. An air of importance came over him as he said: 'The old soul thinks we might get you a spot of teaching.'

'What a cheek!' said Harriet.

Toby let out his breath in a laugh and turned to Guy as though to suggest life would be easier if there were no women around. Enraged further, Harriet went on: 'Guy is a member of the Organization. He was appointed in London and sent out under contract. Gracey is Director here. If Guy wants to see him, he's bound to see Guy.'

'I don't think so,' said Toby, speaking as one who had the upper hand. 'Your hubby's got no right to be here.'

'He has a right, if there's a job here. You said that Gracey had asked the London office for lecturers.'

'That was a year ago. Things have changed since then. No more chaps are being sent to Europe. Europe's a write-off.'

'Greece isn't a write-off.'

'Not at the moment, but who knows what's going to happen? It's tricky here. Since August, it's been very tricky.'

'Why? What happened in August?'

'The Italians torpedoed a Greek ship. There was a lot of feeling about it. Any day, things could go up in flames.'

'Oh!' Harriet had nothing to say. This was a world in which only the ignorant could be happy.

Seeing he had deflated her, Toby gave her hand a small admonitory pat and grinned. His masculine superiority established, he drank his ouzo neat, like a man, and said: 'It's like this! We'll speak to Mr Gracey. We'll be seeing him tomorrow. Might even drop in on him tonight. Why not? Anyway, you can rely on us. We'll put in a word for you. We'll say you're a decent chap, good teacher, good mixer, reliable. One of the best, in fact.'

Guy listened blank-faced to his listed virtues and at the end, said only: 'We'll need some money.'

'Must go into that,' Toby examined the chit beside his glass and brought out a handful of small change.

'Leave that to me.' Guy said.

'Oh, all right. Must get back to the School; have a busy day. Got to lecture again at twelve. Now, don't worry. Just wait till you hear from us.' Toby called a taxi and was gone.

'He was sent after us,' Harriet said. 'He rang Dubedat and Dubedat said: "Go after them, you damned fool. Keep them sweet. Stop them making a move on their own." They don't want us to see Gracey, that's clear. But why?'

'Really, darling!' Guy deplored her suspicion of her fellow-men. 'They're not conspirators. They *do* owe me something, and Dubedat probably saw it that way.'

'They don't want us here.'

'Why shouldn't they want us here?'

'For several reasons. If Gracey can get you, he might not want them. There is also the fact you know too much.'

Guy laughed: 'What do I know?'

'You know they bolted from Rumania in a funk.'

'They lost their nerve. It could happen to anyone. They couldn't possibly think we would mention that. They know they can trust us.'

'But can we trust them? I don't think we should wait to hear from them. We should find out where Gracey is and go to see him.'

'Do we know anyone who knows Gracey?'

She shook her head and slid her hand into Guy's hand. 'Apart from Yakimov, we have no friends.'

They sat for some moments, hand in hand, reflecting upon their position, then Harriet, glancing in through the café window gave a laugh: 'There is another person here who's known to us; someone, what's more, who might know Gracey.'

'Who is it?'

'He's inside there, eating cakes.'

Guy looked round to see a little man seated at an indoor corner table. The collar of his greatcoat was up round his ears, his trilby hat was pulled down to his eyes; his shoulders were raised as though against a draught. His hands were gloved. Using a silver fork, he was putting pieces of *mille feuille* in through his collar to his mouth. Nothing of his person was visible but a blunt, lizard-grey nose: the nose of Professor Lord Pinkrose who had also bolted from the dangers of Bucharest.

'Pinkrose,' Guy said without enthusiasm.

Sent out to lecture in Rumania at a disastrous time, Pinkrose had blamed Guy, as much as anyone, for what he found there. The Pringles could hope for little from him.

Suddenly a familiar voice called: 'Dear boy!' and Pinkrose was forgotten. Guy, giving a cry, jumped up and extended his arms to Yakimov, who tottered into them.

'What a glad sight!' Yakimov sang on a note of tender rapture. '*What* a glad sight! The dear boy well and safely here among us!'

They now suffered idleness. With the air growing cooler and more delicate each day, Harriet refused to sit around waiting for word from Dubedat, and said: 'Let's see the sights while we have the chance.'

Guy, uneasy at being taken outside the area of communication, paid a brief visit to the Museum. Next day he agreed, unwillingly, to go up to the Parthenon. Climbing the steps between the ramshackle houses of the Plaka, he could take no pleasure in their character, their coloured shutters, the scraps of gardens and the unknown trees. Several times he came to a stop and, like Lot's wife, gazed back towards the centre of the town where a message might be arriving for him. He was, whether he liked it or not, a non-combatant in the midst of war and he felt that only work could excuse his civilian status. Now even his work had been taken from him.

Unhappy for him, Harriet said: 'If we don't hear from those two by tomorrow, you must go to the Legation and ask to be put into touch with Gracey. That should settle things one way or the other.'

'It could settle them the worst possible way. If Gracey does not want to see me, I'd be told to take the first boat to Alexandria. We'd just have to go. As it is, Dubedat may do something for us. We have to trust him,' Guy said, though there was no trust on his face.

Seeing him held against the blade of reality, forced to deduce that belief in human goodness was one thing, dependence upon it quite another, Harriet felt an acute pity for him. When he paused again, she said: 'Would you rather go back?' She had brought him up here against his inclination and had lost her pleasure in the expedition because he could not share it.

He said: 'No. You want to see the Parthenon. Let's get it over.'

He plodded on in the growing heat. They walked without speaking round the base of the Acropolis hill and climbed up to the entrance. As they passed through the Propylaea into sight of the Parthenon, Guy stopped in amazement and gave a murmur of wonder. Harriet, with her long sight, had seen the temple clearly enough while wandering in Athens. Set on its hill, it was always surprising the eye, like a half-risen moon. Guy, myopic, saw it now for the first time.

He pulled down his glasses, trying to elongate his sight by peering through the oblique lenses, then he began making his way cautiously over the rough ground. She ran ahead, transported as though on the verge of a supernatural experience. Imagining there was some magical property in the placement of the columns against the cobalt sky, she went from one to another of them, pressing the palms of her hands upon the sun-warmed marble. From a distance the columns had a luminous whiteness; now she saw that on the seaward side they were bloomed with an apricot colour. In a state of wonder, she moved from column to column, touching each as though it were a friend. When Guy reached her, she pointed towards the haze of the Piraeus and said: 'Can you see the sea?'

She watched him pull down his glasses again and was moved, remembering he had told her that when he was a little boy he dared not let his parents know that he was short-sighted because the cost of glasses would have caused a crisis in the household. At school he had not been able to see the

blackboard and had been regarded as a dull boy until a percep-
tive master discovered what the trouble was.

'With the sea so near, we can escape,' she said. 'There's
always a boat of some sort.'

After a long look in the direction of the sea, Guy said: 'I
can't swim.'

'You can't?'

'I didn't even see the sea until I was eighteen.'

'But wasn't there a swimming-bath?'

'Yes, but it frightened me – the echo and that strange smell.'

'Chlorine. A very sinister shade of yellow, that smell. I don't
like it either.'

They sat on the top step facing the Piraeus and the distant
shadow of the Peloponnesus, and Harriet thought with dismay
of the fact that Guy could not swim. There was no safety in
the world. Here, on the summit of the Acropolis, she saw
them shipwrecked in the Mediterranean and pondered the
problem of keeping Guy afloat.

As for Guy, he sat still for four minutes then looked at his
watch and said: 'I think we should go back. There *might* be
something.'

When they reached the hotel, the porter handed Guy an
envelope. Inside there was a card on which the words 'At
Home' were engraved. Mr Dubedat and Mr Lush invited Mr
and Mrs Guy Pringle that evening to take a drink at an address
in Kolonaki.

The flat occupied by Dubedat and Toby hung high on the
slopes above Kolonaki Square. The Pringles, admitted by a
housekeeper and left on a terrace to await their hosts, looked
across the housetops and saw Hymettos. The terrace, marble-
tiled, with an inlaid marble table, wrought-iron chairs and
trained creepers covering the overhead lattice, impressed
Harriet who, looking to where the wash of pink-cream houses
broke against the pine-speckled hillside, thought that Toby
and Dubedat had done very well for themselves. The district
had an air of wealth without ostentation: the most expensive
sort of wealth.

25

'Those two seem to be pretty well off,' she said.

Guy said: 'Shut up.'

'I suppose I can say that this is where I would like to live myself?'

Toby Lush, walking silently on spongy soles, overheard her. He gulped and spluttered in gratification but, deferring to Guy's egalitarian principles, said: 'Nothing too good for the working classes, eh?'

There was no democratic nonsense about Dubedat, who came out five minutes later. He had the aggressive assurance of a man who had seen bad times but had come into his own, and none too soon. He advanced on Harriet as though she were the final challenge. He swung his hand out to her, and when he spoke she noted he was trying to drop his north-country accent.

'Well,' he said, 'this is very pleasant.' He smiled and she saw that his teeth had been scaled. His fingernails had been cleaned. The scurf had been brushed from his hair. His gestures were languid and dramatic.

Guy moved expectantly forward but Dubedat merely waved him to a chair. 'Do sit down,' he begged in his new social manner. His eyes and smiles were for Harriet, and Guy might have been no more than her appendage. Knowing he disliked her as much as she disliked him, Harriet supposed his belief was that if he could charm her, he could charm anyone. For Guy's sake she responded as he wished her to respond.

The housekeeper wheeled in a trolley laden with bottles and glasses. 'What are we all going to drink?' Dubedat asked.

'What is there?' Harriet asked, impressed and modest.

'Oh, everything,' said Dubedat.

And, indeed, there was everything.

'Shall I pour out?' Toby asked.

'*No*,' said Dubedat sharply. 'Go and sit down.'

As he poured the drinks, there was a rattle of glass against glass. His face, with its prominent beak and tiny chin, was set as tensely as the face of a foraging rat. He became very red and at one point dropped a decanter stopper.

'Can I give a hand, old soul?' Toby solicitously asked.

'You can *not*,' Dubedat fiercely replied and Toby dodged back, pretending he had received a blow.

He said: 'Crumbs!' and looked at the Pringles, but there was no laughter. Both Guy and Harriet were nervous, and everyone felt the delicate nature of the occasion.

The drinks dispensed, Dubedat sat himself down briskly. 'I've seen Mr Gracey.' There was a pause while he placed his glass on the table and took out a handkerchief to wipe his fingertips. The pause having taken effect, he went on: 'I regret to say I've no very good news for you.'

The Pringles said nothing. Dubedat frowned at Toby, who was moving about the party like an anxious old sheep-dog. 'Do sit down, Lush,' he said, an edge on his voice. Toby obeyed at once.

As though an impediment were out of the way, Dubedat cleared his throat and said impressively: 'I've approached Mr Gracey on your behalf. He would see you, he would like very much to see you, but he's not up to it.'

'He's really ill, then?' Harriet asked.

'He had an accident. He's been unwell for some time. He has his ups and downs. At the moment he doesn't feel he can see anyone. He says you're to proceed to Cairo.'

'Suppose we wait a few days . . .' Guy began.

'No,' Dubedat interrupted with placid severity. 'He can't keep you hanging round here . . . can't accept the responsibility. He wants you to take the next boat to Alex.'

'But wherever I am,' Guy said reasonably, 'I'll have to hang around. Egypt's full of Organization men, refugees from Europe, all waiting for jobs. The Cairo office doesn't know what to do with them. They're trying to cook up all sorts of miserable little appointments in the Delta and Upper Egypt. The work's minimal: just a waste of time. If I have to wait for work, I'd rather wait here.'

'No doubt. But Mr Gracey doesn't want you to wait. You're to proceed. It's an order, Pringle.'

There was a pause, then Guy spoke with mild decision:

'Mr Gracey will have to tell me that himself. I'll stay until I see him.'

Dubedat, flushed again, took on his old expression of peevish rancour. His voice grew shrill and lost its quality. 'But you can't stay. You're not supposed to be here, and Mr Gracey doesn't want you here. You're expected in Egypt. So far as the Cairo office is concerned, you're a missing person. That's why Mr Gracey can't *let* you stay. And he's doing the right thing – yes, he's doing the right thing! You ought to know that!' Dubedat ended on the hectoring note with which he had once condemned everyone whom fortune had favoured above himself.

Guy, who had been worried by Dubedat's earlier effusion, now said with composure: 'I intend to stay.'

Dubedat gave an exasperated laugh. A frantic sucking noise came from Toby in the background. No one spoke for some moments; then, gathering himself together, Dubedat began to reason with Guy: 'Look, there's no job for you here. What with the war and one thing and another, the School isn't what it was. Mr Gracey hasn't been well enough to see to things. Numbers have dropped off. That's the long and the short of it. *The work just isn't there.*'

'So, as Harriet said, someone is needed to get the place back on its feet.'

'Mr Gracey's in charge.'

'Exactly,' Guy agreed. 'And I'm not prepared to leave Athens before I've seen him.'

Dubedat let out his breath, suggesting that Guy's total lack of good sense was making things difficult for all of them, and said with the gesture of one throwing down a last card: 'Your salary's paid in Cairo.'

'I can cable the London office.'

'This is Mr Gracey's territory. The London office can only refer you to him.'

'I'm not so sure of that.'

Dubedat, agape between surprise and anger, shifted in his seat. It had never occurred to him that Guy, the most accommodating of men, could prove so unaccommodating. Now, as he met Guy's obstinacy for the first time, something malign came into his gaze. He put his hand into his inner pocket and brought out a letter. 'I'd hoped we could discuss things in a friendly way, I didn't think I'd need to produce this. Still, here it is. Better take a dekko.'

When Guy had read the letter, he passed it to Harriet. It was a typewritten statement informing anyone whom it might concern that Mr Gracey, during the term of his disablement, appointed Mr Dubedat as his official representative. Harriet returned it to Guy, who sat studying it in silence, his expression bland.

'So you see,' Dubedat shifted about in his excitement, saying in a tone of finality: 'What I say, goes. Mr Gracey can't see you. He won't see you and he won't be responsible for you here. So if you're wise, you'll take yourself off on the first boat from the Piraeus.' He snatched the letter from Guy and, folding it with shaking fingers, replaced it in his inner pocket.

Guy looked up but said nothing.

Beginning to relent a little, Dubedat leant towards him and spoke with an earnest, almost entreating, compliance. 'If I were you, I'd go. Really, I would. For your own sake.'

Guy still said nothing. He maintained his bland expression but it was wan, and Harriet could scarcely bear his mortification. Unassuming though he was, he was conscious of a natural authority, the authority of the upright man. He believed in people. He had always supposed that his generosity would give rise to generosity. Helping others, he would, when the need came, be helped in his turn. It was not easy for him to accept that Dubedat, a mediocrity whom he had employed out of charity, would try to run him out of Athens. And the astonishing fact was that Dubedat was in a position to do it.

There was nothing more to be said. The sun had gone down while they were talking. Watching the distant hill stained rich with the afterglow of evening, Harriet seemed to see, like something sighted from a speeding train, an enchantment they could not share. So Athens was not for them! But what was there for them in this disordered world? Where could they find a home?

Dubedat had also observed the changing light. 'Oh, dear,' he said, 'we'll have to go. What a pity! Another night you might have stayed to supper.'

Toby explained: 'We've been asked to Major Cookson's. Sort of royal command. He likes everyone to be on time.'

The Pringles did not ask who Major Cookson was. It did not matter. They were not likely to receive his royal command. Guy emptied his beer and they left with scarcely another word.

The lights were coming on in the small shops and cafés in the square of Kolonaki. The central garden was dark. Pepper trees grew along the pavements, their fern-fine foliage clouding in the air like smoke. A smell of dill pickle came from the shops.

Harriet said: '*Will* you cable the London office?'

'Yes.'

His decision disturbed her. Because of their insecurity, the streets seemed hostile and she began to see Cairo as a refuge. 'Perhaps we'd better take the next boat,' she said.

Guy said: 'No,' his face fixed with his resolution: 'I don't want to go to Egypt. There's a job here, and I intend to stay.'

Their money had almost run out. They could not afford Zonar's, so walked the length of Stadium Street and sat at a café in Omonia Square where, drinking a cheap, sweet, sleepy, black wine, Harriet thought of Yakimov and wondered how he had survived his years of beggary in foreign capitals. She, with Guy beside her, knowing the worst anyone could do was send them to Egypt, felt very near weeping.

3

The hotel in which the Pringles were staying had been recommended to Harriet as the most central of the cheap hotels. It was gloomy and uncomfortable but favoured by the English because of its position and its extreme respectability. Athens had been absorbing refugees since 1939 and, even before the Poles arrived, there had been a backlog of Smyrna Greeks and White Russians seeking some sort of permanent home. Hotel rooms were scarce; flats and houses even scarcer.

The Pringles, packed together into a single room, had been promised a larger room should one fall vacant. When Harriet reminded the porter of this promise, he told her that rooms never fell vacant. People stayed at the hotel for months. Some had made it their home. Mrs Brett, for instance, had lived there for over a year.

Harriet knew Mrs Brett, a gaunt-faced Englishwoman who eyed her accusingly whenever they met on the stair. One day, a week after Guy's arrival, Mrs Brett stopped her and said: 'So your husband did arrive, after all?'

As Harriet tried to edge past, Mrs Brett stood her ground, saying: 'Perhaps you don't remember me?'

Harriet did remember her. When alone in Athens and distracted by the news from Rumania, Harriet had approached this fellow Englishwoman and confided the fact she had left her husband in Bucharest. Mrs Brett had replied: 'He'll be put into a prison-camp. You'll have him back after the war. My husband's dead.'

This may have been meant as condolence, but it did not console Harriet who now wanted only to avoid the woman.

'I'd like to meet your husband,' Mrs Brett said. 'Bring him to tea on Saturday. I live here in the hotel: room 3, first floor Come at four o'clock,' and without waiting for acceptance or refusal, she was off.

Harriet hurried to tell Guy: 'That God-awful woman's invited us to tea.'

'Why, how kind!' said Guy, to whom any social contact was better than no contact at all.

'But it's the woman who said you'd be put in a prison-camp.'

'I'm sure she meant no harm,' Guy confidently replied.

The Pringles, on the top floor of the hotel, were in a slice of room overlooking a china-bricked well and containing two single beds, end to end, a wardrobe and a dressing-table. Mrs Brett's room, at the front, was a bed-sitting room and was crowded with an armchair and table, as well as a large bed. Mrs Brett had hung up two paintings, one of anemones and one of lily-of-the-valley, and she had set out her china on the table beside a large chocolate cake.

Guy, delighted that someone had made them a gesture of friendship, met Mrs Brett with such warm enthusiasm, she became excited at once and dodged around them, shouting: 'Sit down. Sit down.' Another visitor was in the room. This was a square-built man who was growing heavy in middle age.

'Really!' Mrs Brett complained. 'You two big men! What am I to do with you both? And,' she turned to the middle-aged man with amused horror, 'Alison Jay says she'll be dropping in.'

'Dear me!' the man murmured.

'We'll manage. We've managed before. Mrs Pringle can take the little chair – she's a lightweight; and I'll give Miss Jay the armchair when she comes. Now, you two! Here.' She placed the two men side by side on the edge of the bed. 'Sit down,' she ordered them. 'I don't need any help.'

A hotel waiter brought in a pot of tea and while Mrs Brett

was filling cups and asking each guest several times whether he took milk and sugar, the man beside Guy spoke below the commotion. 'My name is Alan Frewen.'

'Didn't I introduce you?' Mrs Brett shouted, pushing cups at her guests. 'That's me all over; I never introduce anyone.'

Alan Frewen, whose large head was set on massive shoulders, had a face that seemed to be made of brown rock, not carved but worn to its present shape by the action of water. His eyes, light in colour and seeming lighter in their dark setting, had a poignant expression; and as he sat on the bed edge stirring his cup of tea, his air was one of patient suffering. Having given his name, he had nothing to say but kept looking uneasily at Mrs Brett because she was on her feet while he was sitting down.

She said to Guy: 'So you're just out of Rumania? Tell us, are the Germans there or *not*?'

While Guy was answering her, Alan Frewen observed him and the large, dark face softened as though something in Guy's appearance and manner was allaying his sorrows. He leant forward to speak but Mrs Brett did not give him a chance. She said to Guy:

'You're an Organization man, aren't you? Yes, Prince Yakimov mentioned it. I could tell you a few things about the Organization. You knew my husband, of course? You knew what they did to him here?'

As Guy said, 'No,' Alan Frewen gave a slight moan, anticipating a story he had heard before and dreaded hearing again.

Ignoring Frewen, Mrs Brett stared at Guy: 'I suppose you know my husband was Director of the School?'

'Was he? I didn't know.'

'Aha!' said Mrs Brett, preparing the Pringles for a grim tale. She kept them in anticipation while she handed round the cups. Alan Frewen watched her with an expression pained and fascinated. She sat down at last and began.

'My husband was Director, but he was displaced. Very meanly displaced, what's more. You must have heard of it?'

'We know very few people here,' Guy said.

33

'It was a scandal, and there was a lot of talk. It got around much farther than Athens. My husband was a scholar, a very gifted man.' She stopped and fixed Guy accusingly. 'But you must have heard of him? He wrote a history of the Venetian Republic.'

Guy said soothingly: 'Yes, of course,' and she went on:

'You know this fellow Gracey, I suppose?'

'I . . .'

'It was Gracey got him out. Gracey and that louse Cookson.'

Harriet said: 'We've heard of Cookson. He seems to be important here.'

'He's rich, not important. Leastways, not what *I* call important. He calls himself "Major". He may have been in the army at some time, but I have my doubts. He lives in style at Phaleron. He's one of those people who don't need to work but want to have a finger in every pie. He wants power; wants to influence people.'

'And he's a friend of Gracey?'

'Yes, Gracey's one of that set. When we first came here, Cookson asked us out to Phaleron but Percy wouldn't go. He was doing his own work *and* running the School. No time for junketing, I can tell you.'

'How long ago was this?'

'Just when the war started. We knew the old Director: a fine man, a scholar, too. He retired when war broke out and offered the job to Percy. I told Percy he ought to take it. It was war work. He wasn't a young man, of course, but he had to do his bit. I think I was right.'

Mrs Brett paused and Alan Frewen stirred at his tea as though again bringing himself to the point of speech, but again Mrs Brett thwarted him. 'Well, Percy took over here and everything was going swimmingly when that Gracey turned up.'

'Where did he come from?'

'Italy. He'd been living near Naples tutoring some rich little Italian boy and doing a bit of writing and so on; having a grand time, I imagine, but he knew it couldn't go on. He got nervous. He decided to come here, worse luck; then, when he got here, he wanted a job and Percy took him on as Chief Instructor. Oh, what a foolish fellow! Percy, I mean.' She shook her head and clicked her tongue against the back of her teeth.

'He could scarcely have known,' Alan Frewen said.

Mrs Brett agreed as though the thought had only just occurred to her. 'No, that's right, he couldn't.'

'Wasn't Gracey qualified?' Guy asked.

'Too well qualified. That was the trouble. He wasn't willing to work under Percy. No, he didn't want to play second fiddle – he wanted Percy's job. He went to see Cookson and buttered him up, and said: "You can see for yourself that Percy Brett isn't fit to run the School," and I can tell you there's nothing Cookson likes better than to be in the middle of an intrigue. Those two began plotting and planning and telling everyone that Percy was too old and not trained for the work. And Gracey got Cookson to write to the London office . . .'

'Do you really know all this?' Alan Frewen mildly protested.

'Oh, yes.' Mrs Brett looked fiercely at him. 'I've got my spies, too. And the next thing, the London office flew out an inspector to inquire into the running of the School. Just think of it! An inspector poking his nose into Percy's affairs. . . . And *then* what do you think happened?'

Mrs Brett's voice had become shrill in tragic inquiry, and as Alan Frewen caught Harriet's eye, his pitying expression told her that Mrs Brett's aggression covered nothing worse than unhappiness.

Sombre and weary, he dropped his gaze and Harriet, who had hoped to learn something about Gracey, began to wonder if they were listening to anything more than the fantasies of lunacy. Guy evidently thought so. His face pink with concern, he waited intently to know what happened next.

'Percy fell ill,' Mrs Brett said. 'He fell ill just as the inspector arrived. Imagine what it was like for me with an inspector nosing around, and Gracey and Cookson telling him just anything they liked, and my poor Percy too ill to defend himself.

'He said to me: "Girlie" – he always called me Girlie – "I never thought they'd treat me like this!" He'd worked like a Trojan, you know. Unremitting, I called him. He improved the School. All Gracey did was take over a going concern and let it run down. And poor Percy! He was ill for weeks; nine, ten weeks. . . . He had typhoid.' She was gasping with the effort and emotion of the story, and her voice began losing its strength. 'And they got rid of him. Yes, they got rid of him. A report was sent in and then a cable came: Gracey was to take over here; Percy was to go to a temporary job at Beirut. But he never knew any of this. He died. Yes he died you know!' She looked at Guy and said hoarsely: 'I blame myself.' She clenched one of her ungainly hands and pressed the knuckles against her mouth, her eyes on Guy as though he alone understood what she was talking about. After some moments she dropped her hands to her lap. 'He never wanted to come here. I made him. I worked it . . . yes, I worked it, really. I wrote and suggested Percy for the job, and that's why it was offered to him. We lived at Kotor, you know. I got so tired of it. Those narrow streets, that awful gulf. I felt shut in. I wanted to go to a big city. Yes, it was me. It was my fault. I brought him here, and he got typhoid.'

Guy put his hand over her hand and said: 'He could have got typhoid anywhere – even in England. Certainly anywhere on the Mediterranean. You've read *Death in Venice*?'

Mrs Brett looked at him bleakly, puzzled by the question, and to distract her he began telling her the story of Mann's novella. Approaching the crisis of the plot, he paused dramatically and Mrs Brett, thinking he had finished or ought to have finished, broke in to say: 'When Gracey took over, Percy was still alive. They didn't even wait for him to die.'

Harriet asked: 'Is this why the two lecturers asked to be transferred?'

'You've heard about that, have you?' Mrs Brett jerked round to look at Harriet: 'I wonder who told you?'

'Dubedat and Lush mentioned it.'

'*Them!*' said Mrs Brett in disgust: 'They're a pretty pair!'

'They are a pretty pair,' Harriet said, and she would have said more, but was interrupted by a loud rat-tat on the door.

'Here she is! Here she is!' Mrs Brett cried and jumping up with the alacrity of a child, she threw open the door so it crashed against the bed: 'Come in! Come in!' she shouted uproariously and a very large woman came in.

The woman's size was increased by her white silk draperies and a cape which, caught in a draught between door and window, billowed behind her like a spinnaker. Her legs were in Turkish trousers, her great breasts jutted against a jerkin from which hung a yard of fringe. As she stood filling the middle of the room, her fat swayed around her like a barrel slung from her shoulders.

'Well,' she demanded. 'Where do you want me to sit, Bretty?'

'The arm-chair, the arm-chair.' Delighted by the arrival of this new guest, Mrs Brett told the Pringles: 'Miss Jay rules the English Colony.'

'Do I?' Miss Jay complacently asked. She sank into the arm-chair and looked down at her big raffia shoes.

When she had introduced the Pringles, Mrs Brett said: 'I was just telling them how Gracey treated Percy.'

'Um,' said Miss Jay. 'I thought I'd let you get that over before I turned up.'

'I haven't finished yet.' Mrs Brett swung round on Guy: 'And what do you think they did *after* Percy died?'

In an attempt to distract her, Alan Frewen said: 'Could I have some more of that delicious tea?'

'When the water comes, not before,' said Mrs Brett and she continued with determined crossness: 'After Percy died, I decided to give a little party . . . a little evening of remembrance. . . .'

The waiter came to the door with hot water. Mrs Brett took the pot from him, slammed the door in his face and added firmly: 'A little evening of remembrance.'

Miss Jay said: 'How about giving me a cup before you start again?'

Mrs Brett attended to her guests in an exasperated way, then, the tea dispensed, faced Guy again: 'You understand why I'm telling you this, don't you? I felt you ought to know something about the people who infest this lovely place. There's not only Cookson and Gracey; there's that Archie Callard, too.'

Alan Frewen said: 'Archie can be tiresome. He has the wrong sort of sense of humour.'

'Do you think what they did to me was intended as humour?'

'I don't know.' Alan Frewen looked confused. 'It could have been – of a macabre kind.'

'Macabre? Yes, indeed, "macabre" is the word! What do you think they did?' Mrs Brett turned on Guy: 'When Cookson heard that I was giving my little party at the King George, he arranged to give a party himself on the same evening. A very grand party. What do you think of that? Of course they all had a hand in it: the Major, Callard and Gracey . . .'

Miss Jay said: 'I really doubt whether Gracey . . .'

'Oh, I'm sure he had. Three clever fellows plotting against a poor old woman! Everyone was invited to Cookson's party – except me, of course. It was the biggest party Cookson's ever given.'

'And your party was spoilt?' Guy asked.

'I had no party. No one turned up. Some of my best friends deserted me in order to go to Phaleron. I've never spoken to them since.'

'It really was most unkind,' Alan Frewen murmured.

'You weren't here; you'd gone to Delphi,' Mrs Brett exonerated him. 'And you . . .' she nodded to Miss Jay. 'You were on Corfu.' She smiled at the two who had not been in Athens to take part in her betrayal, then suddenly remembered Harriet and turned on her, asking: 'What do you think of all this, eh? What do you think of the sort of people we've got here?'

Harriet, glancing aside, saw Miss Jay watching her with a keen, critical eye and knew that whatever she said would be repeated, probably with disapproval. She said: 'I do not know them, and we've been living so differently. Our experiences didn't give us much time to have social worries.'

'You were lucky. I'd rather have experiences,' said Mrs Brett. 'We all envy you.'

Looking into her weathered old face, Harriet saw there a flicker of kindness, but Miss Jay said pettishly: 'Experiences! Heaven keep us from experiences.'

'The Pringles have just come from Bucharest,' Mrs Brett said. 'They saw the Germans come in.'

'Oh, did they!' Miss Jay eyed the Pringles as though they might have brought the Germans with them. 'We don't want anything of that sort here.'

Alan Frewen, looking at Guy with interest, asked Guy how long he intended to stay.

Guy said: 'As long as we can. But it depends on Gracey. I came here in the hope he would employ me.'

'And won't he?' Frewen asked.

'It doesn't look like it. The trouble is, I can't get him to see me. They say he's too ill to see anyone.'

Mrs Brett broke in: 'Whoever told you that?'

'Toby Lush and Dubedat.'

'How very odd!' Alan Frewen looked at Mrs Brett, then at Miss Jay, his face crumpled like the face of a small boy trying to smile while being caned. 'I don't think there's much wrong with Gracey, do you?'

'It's him all over,' Mrs Brett said. 'He can't be bothered; he doesn't want to be bothered. He leaves everything to those two louts. It's disgraceful the way the School's gone down.'

Still smiling his curious smile, Alan Frewen said: 'I know Colin Gracey quite well. We were at King's together. I could say a word . . .'

'I wouldn't interefere,' Miss Jay interrupted with such decision that Frewen seemed to retreat. His smile disappeared and he looked so forlorn that Guy, whose hopes had been raised and then thrown down, felt it necessary to justify him.

'I suppose we must leave it to Dubedat,' Guy said. 'After all, he is Gracey's representative.'

39

Mrs Brett began to protest but Miss Jay had had enough of the conversation. Gripping her friend by the arm, she said: 'I've heard about a flat that might suit you.'

'*No?*' Mrs Brett cried out in excitement; and Guy's troubles were forgotten.

'On Lycabettos. Two American girls have it at the moment. They're going on the next boat. They'll let it furnished. They're looking for someone who'll keep an eye on their bits and pieces, someone reliable. They're not asking much for it.'

'Suit me down to the ground.'

While Mrs Brett discussed the flat, Alan Frewen looked at his watch and Harriet raised a brow at Guy. The three rose. Miss Jay glanced at them brightly, glad to see them go, but Mrs Brett scarcely noticed their departure.

Frewen paused on the landing and looked at the Pringles as though he had something to say. When he said nothing, Guy decided to go down and ask at the desk if there was a message for him. They all descended the stairs together. At the bottom, a black retriever, tied to the banister post, leapt up in a furore of greeting.

At this, Frewen managed to break silence: 'This is Diocletian.' He untied the lead, then put on a pair of dark glasses preparatory to entering the twilit street, but he did not go. Holding his dog close, he stood with his face half obliterated by the black glass, and still could not say what he wanted to say.

Watching him, Harriet thought: 'An enigmatic, secretive man.'

There was nothing for Guy at the desk and as the Pringles said their good-byes, Alan Frewen said at last: 'Do you know the Academy? It used to be the American Academy of Classical Studies, but the Americans went home when the war started. Now it's a pension for solitary chaps like me. I was wondering, could you find your way there one day and have tea?'

'Why, yes,' Guy said.

'What about Thursday? It's a working day but I'm not very busy. I needn't get back to the office till six.'

'What do you do?' Harriet asked.

'I'm the Information Officer.'

'Yakimov's boss?'

'Yes, Yakimov's boss.' Alan Frewen gave his smiling grimace and, the invitation safely conveyed, he let the dog pull him away.

4

Harriet was usually wakened by the early tram-car. On Thursday morning she was wakened instead by a funeral wail which rose and fell, rose and fell, and at last brought even Guy out of sleep. Lifting his face from the pillow, he said: 'What on earth is that?'

By now Harriet had remembered what it was. She had heard it on news films. It was an air-raid siren.

She put on her dressing-gown and went to the landing where the window overlooked the street. The shops were beginning to open and shopkeepers had come out to their doors. Men and girls going to work had stopped to speak to each other and everyone was making gestures of inquiry or alarm. People were running down the hotel stairs. Harriet wanted to ask what was happening, but no one gave her time. As the siren note sank and faded on a sob, a batch of police came running from the direction of the square. They were bawling as they came and some had taken out their revolvers and were waving them as though revolt were imminent. In a minute all the innocent, wondering bystanders had been pushed into shops and doorways. Cars were brought to a stop and their occupants sent indoors like the rest. The police sped on, making all possible noise, and leaving the street empty behind them.

It was a fine, mild morning. Harriet pulled up the window and leant out but saw only imprisoned faces, deserted pavements, abandoned cars.

Guy, getting into an emergency rig of trousers and pullover, shouted from the room: 'Is anything happening down there?'

'The police have cleared the street.'

'It must be a raid.'

'Let's go down and find out.' Harriet spoke with the calm of an old campaigner. Conditioned to disorder, she dressed with the sense that she was returning to reality, and when they ran down the stairs to the hall, she knew what to expect. She could have described the scene before she reached it, for she had seen it before on an evening of crisis in an hotel hall in Bucharest.

But here there was someone known to her. Mrs Brett, in a dressing-gown, her face flushed, was talking to everyone, her grey-brown pigtail whipping about as she jerked her head from side to side.

The porter was on the telephone, speaking Greek with occasional words of English, and his free hand was thumping the desk to emphasize what he said. The other guests, English, Polish, Russian and French, were chattering shrilly, while from outside there rose the high swell of the 'All Clear'.

Seeing the Pringles, Mrs Brett shouted: 'We're at war. We're at war.' As she did so, the porter dropped the receiver on to the desk and throwing out his arms as though to embrace everyone in sight, said: 'We are your allies. We fight beside you.'

'Isn't that splendid!' said Mrs Brett.

The sense of splendour possessed the hall so it seemed that in secret everyone had been longing to live actively within the war and now felt fulfilment. The Pringles, because they were English, were congratulated by people who had not given them a glance before. They heard over and over again how the Greek Prime Minister had been wakened at three in the morning by the Italian Minister who said he had brought an ultimatum. 'Can't it wait till the honest light of day?' Metaxas asked; then, seeing it was a demand that Greece accept Italian occupation, he at once, without an instant's hesitation, said: 'No.'

'*Oxi*,' said the porter. 'He said "*Oxi*".'

Mrs Brett explained that Mussolini also wanted his triumphs. He had chosen a small country, supposing a small country was a weak country, thinking he had only to make a demand and the Greeks would submit. But Metaxas had said 'No' and so, in the middle of the night, while the Athenians slept, Greece had entered the war.

'Well, well, well!' Mrs Brett sighed, exhausted by happiness and excitement, and turning accusingly on the Pringles, said: 'You see, you're not the only ones who have adventures. Things happen here, too.' She started to go upstairs, then turned and shouted: 'Anything yet from Gracey?'

'Nothing, I'm afraid,' said Guy.

'Well, don't go. You be like Metaxas. You stand firm. Tell him he's got to give you a job. If I were on speaking terms, I'd tell him myself.'

Guy mentioned that they were going that afternoon to tea with Alan Frewen. Mrs Brett said she, too, had been invited but Miss Jay was taking her to see the promised flat.

'You go,' she urged Guy. 'He'll introduce you to Gracey.'

'I don't think so. He said nothing about Gracey.'

'Oh, he will; Gracey's up there. He lives at the Academy. Alan'll do something – you'll see! Cookson thinks he can fix everything, but he's not the only fixer. A lot of things happen in my little room that he knows nothing about.' Giving a high squawk of laughter, she shouted over her shoulder: 'Oh yes, I'm a fixer, too.'

The Pringles had almost exhausted their money. They had just enough to pay their hotel bill and buy steerage berths on the boat that would sail on Saturday; but, caught up in the afflatus of events, they could not face the hotel breakfast and when ready to go out, decided to take coffee in the sunlight. The streets were crowded with people exchanging felicitations as though it were the first day of holiday rather than of war. It seemed an occasion for rejoicing until the Pringles met Yakimov, who was wheeling his bicycle uphill, a look of gloom lengthening his lofty camel face.

In the past he had gone through every crisis with the optimism of the uninformed. Now, working in the Information Office, nothing was hidden from him.

44

'Greeks won't last ten days,' he said.

'Is it as bad at that?' Guy asked.

'Worse. No army. No air-force. Only one ship to speak of. And the I-ties say they'll bomb us flat. What's going to happen to us, I'd like to know? They starve you in these prison-camps.'

'Surely we'll be evacuated?' Harriet said.

'Don't know. Can't say. All depends.'

Having reached the level of University Street, he ran his bicycle along, leapt at it, somehow landed on the saddle and, high perched in precarious dignity, he weaved away.

The Pringles, knowing Yakimov, could not rely on anything he said. They bought the English newspaper, which took an inspiriting view of the new front and made much of the fact the British had promised aid.

Harriet said: 'Whatever happens, I want to stay. Don't you?' She felt confident of his answer and was dismayed when he replied: 'I want to stay more than ever, but . . .'

'But what?'

'I can't work for a man like Gracey.'

She realized the trouble was Mrs Brett. When, after the tea-party, she had asked Guy what he thought of Mrs Brett's stories, he would not discuss them. Caught up in a conflict between his desire to remain here and the fact he could remain only by Gracey's favour, he had to reflect upon them.

'So you believe all she said?' said Harriet.

'I can't imagine she invented it.'

'There might be a basis of truth, but I felt she was pretty dotty. I'm sure if we knew the whole of it, we'd find it was quite different.'

'I don't know. She may have exaggerated, but the others didn't defend Gracey. He seems to be quite despicable.' Guy looked angry and defiant at the very thought of Gracey and Harriet knew that in this mood he would make no attempt to win him. Guy's persuasive force could function only with people for whom he had respect. He was incapable of dissimulation. Once he had accepted the dictates of his morality, he could be inflexible. If he despised Gracey, or had cause to doubt his own personal probity in the matter, their cause was as good as lost.

She began to fear they would be on the Egyptian boat when it sailed in two days' time.

By midday the first plaudits of war were over. By the time the Pringles set out to find the Academy, there had been news of a raid on the factories at Eleusis, and a rumour that Patras had been bombed. Athens, so far untouched, was sunken into the somnolence of afternoon.

Following the directions given by the hotel porter, the Pringles took the main road towards Kifissia. They were alone on the long, wide, sun-white pavement when a convoy of lorries, full of conscripts, passed on their way to the station. As the Pringles waved and shouted 'Good luck', the young men, recognizing them as English, shouted back 'Zito the British navy' and 'Zito Hellas' and, as Harriet called out to them, one of the young men bent down and caught her hands and said in English: 'We are friends.' Gazing into his dark ardent eyes, she was transported by the glory of war and threw herself on Guy, crying: 'It's wonderful!'

Guy hurried her along, saying: 'Don't be silly. They may all be dead in a week.'

'I don't want to go to Egypt,' she said, but Guy refused to discuss it.

The Academy came into view: a large Italianate building painted ochre and white and set in grounds that had been dried to an even buff colour by the long summer heat.

Alan Frewen was waiting for them in the common-room. He hurried towards them, his dog at his heels, his manner stimulated by the day's events, saying: 'I'm glad you're early, I may get called back, but probably not. At the moment the Information Service is little more than a joke, but if the Greeks make any sort of a stand, then we'll have to pull up our socks.'

'Can the Greeks make a stand?' Guy asked. 'Have they anything to make a stand with?'

'Not much, but they have valour; and that's kept them going through worse times than these.'

While Alan talked, Harriet glanced about her. Agitated by the fact she was in Gracey's ambiance, she wanted to see the other occupants of the vast room who, seated on the faded armchairs and sofas, gave a sense of being intimately unrelated in the manner of people who exist together and live apart. The room itself had been bleached like the garden, by the fervour of the light. Even the books in the pitch-pine bookcases were all one colour, and the busts that looked down from the bookcase tops were filmed with dust and as sallow as the rest. She made a move towards one of them but Alan stopped her, saying: 'All locked. We are in the Academy, but not of it. The students left their *materiel* behind but we, of course, must not touch.'

He led them out to the terrace where seats and deck-chairs, blanched like everything else, were splintering in the sun. Stone steps led down to a garden where nothing remained of the flower-beds but a tangle of dry sticks. The lawn beyond, brick-baked and cracked in the kiln of summer, was an acre of clay tufted over with pinkish grass. The tennis courts were screened behind olives, pines and citrus trees. The wind that played over the terrace was full of a gummy scent, unique and provocative, that came from the pines, and from the foliage that had dried and fallen into powder.

'That is the smell of Greece,' Harriet said.

Alan Frewen nodded slowly: 'I suppose it is.'

'Can we have tea out here?'

'I am afraid it is not allowed. Miss Dunne – who decides things here – says it makes too much work for the girls. The girls say they don't mind, but Miss Dunne says "No".' A bell rang and they went inside and sat near the french windows. A plate of cakes came in with Alan's tea-tray and he said: 'I'm glad you're here to help me eat these. When I heard the last boat had gone, I was afraid you might be on it.'

'The last boat? Do you mean the boat that was going on Saturday?'

'Yes. There won't be another. The Egyptians won't risk their ships, and who can blame them? The boat went this morning and the shipping clerks closed the office and went with her. I'm told that a few wide-awake people managed to get on board, though I don't know who could have warned them.'

Guy said: 'Surely there are Greek boats?'

'No. Anyway, not for civilians. Greece is on a war-time basis now.'

'And no air-service?'

'There never was an air-service to Egypt.'

Looking at Guy, Harriet laughed and said: 'Freedom is the recognition of necessity.'

'What about Salonika?' Guy persisted. 'There must be a train to Istanbul?'

'That's a war zone, or soon will be. Anyway, there's an order out: foreigners are not allowed to leave Athens. You might be refused an exeat to Salonika.'

'Is that likely?'

'Anything's likely here during an emergency. Greek officials are very suspicious.'

'So we can't get away? In fact, no one can get away?'

'There may be an evacuation boat of some sort. The Legation think they ought to send away the English women with children. I don't know. Nothing's been arranged yet. If Mrs Pringle wants to go, I could probably get her a passage.'

Harriet said: 'I'm staying here, if I can.'

'That's the spirit. Anyway, what's this talk of trains to Istanbul? I thought you both wanted to stay?'

'It's Mrs Brett's stories. Guy doesn't like the idea of working for Gracey now.'

'Oh!' Alan Frewen rubbed the toe of his shoe up and down the dog's spine and smiled in apparent pain as the dog stretched in pleasure. He reflected for some moments, then said: 'Mrs B.'s obsessional. She's always telling stories about the Cookson set. I think Brett was treated meanly, but he was an old fuddy-duddy; quite incapable of running the School. All the work

48

was done by the two lecturers, who liked him. They left when Gracey took over, as I think you know.'

Harriet said: 'What about the business of the memorial party?'

'It was unkind, but she provoked it. She has been inexcusably rude to Cookson at different times. She practically accused him of murdering her husband. She's a bit hysterical. You saw it yourself.'

'If you'd been here, would you have gone to Cookson's party?'

Frewen raised his eyebrows slightly at Harriet's question, but smiled again: 'I might, you know. It would have been a difficult choice. Cookson's parties are rather grand.'

Guy said with conviction: 'I am sure you would not have gone. No decent person would treat a lonely, ageing woman in that way.'

Frewen's smile faded. He gave Guy a long, quizzical look, but before he could say anything a middle-aged woman in shorts, tennis racquet under arm, came in through the french windows. Lumpish, bespectacled, with untidy fox-red hair, she was hot and damp and breathing heavily. She acknowledged one or two of the men with sidelong grimaces, then, catching sight of the strangers, she rolled up her eyes in appalled self-consciousness and sped from the room.

'Who?' Harriet whispered.

'That's Miss Dunne, the terrible sportsgirl.'

'Is she at the Legation? What does she do?'

'Oh, something so very hush-hush, I'm told she's led to it blindfolded. But I wouldn't know, and I wouldn't dare to ask. She's the genuine thing, sent out by the Foreign Office. Most of us are only temporary, so she's a cut above the rest.'

Harriet said under her breath: 'Pinkrose.' Guy looked up quickly. They watched as Pinkrose came across the room with a cake carton in his hand. He sat down, placed the carton very carefully on his table and opened it. When his tea arrived, he took out three ornamental cakes, disposed them on a plate and studied them. He chose one, transferred it to a smaller plate, then, on reflection, returned it to the big plate and studied the three again.

Harriet asked Alan Frewen: 'Do you know him?'

'Indeed I do. He's by way of being a colleague of mine.'

'You mean he's found a job already?'

'Yes, though job is no name to call it by. He got into the Information Office somehow. I gave him a desk in the News Room and he potters about. That enables him to live here. He told them at the Legation he couldn't afford an hotel.'

'You're joking?'

'I'm not. He could have gone back to England. There was a ship going from Alex round the Cape, but he wouldn't risk it. He said he had a delicate constitution and would be less of a burden to others in a comfortable climate.'

'He may be regretting that now.'

'If he is, it's not affecting his appetite.'

After tea they strolled with the dog about the garden and coming back through the lemon trees that shaded the drive, Alan said diffidently: 'I mentioned to Gracey that you would be here this afternoon. He suggested you might go and see him about six. Of course, if you don't want to, I can make your excuses.'

Guy grew red and after a moment said: 'This is very kind of you.'

'Oh, no. I made the merest mention, I assure you. It was his idea.'

'I will go, of course. I'm very grateful.'

'I'll take you up to Gracey's room, but I can't stay. I'm due back at the office.'

Gracey's door was at the end of the long, broad, upstairs passage. Alan knocked. The voice that called him to enter was firm, musical and beautifully pitched.

The room inside was a corner room with windows overlooking the gardens to north and east. Between the two windows Gracey was stretched out on a long chair, a table nearby and a circle of chairs about him.

He welcomed them on a high note: 'Ah, *do* come in! Do

sit down! How nice to meet you two young people at last! Alan, be a good chap; pour us some sherry! It's on the chest-of-drawers.'

When he had handed round the glasses, Frewen said he would have to go.

'So soon?' Gracey sounded very disappointed. 'Are you so terribly busy?'

'Not busy at all, I'm afraid. I wish we were. The situation demands action, and we don't know what to do. Still, one must put up a show. I feel I ought to get back.'

Gracey protracted the good-byes as though he could not bear to part with Alan; then, the parting over, he leant earnestly towards Guy: 'You must tell me all about your escape from Bucharest. I want to know every detail.'

He spoke as though their safe arrival had been a profound relief to him and the bewildered Pringles did not know what to say. Their 'escape' was over and done with, the 'details' were losing importance. No one could tell what was happening in Rumania now. A door had shut behind them and they had other things to worry about.

Awkward in his distrust of Gracey, Guy did his best to give an account of the Rumanian break-up, while Harriet observed the man who had been, they were told, too ill to see them. His long, graceful body lay in an attitude of invalidism, but the impression he gave was of perfect health, almost of perfect youth. There was, she felt, something almost shocking about his fair, handsome head. It was some minutes before the effect began to crumble. There were lines about his eyes, his cheeks were too full for the structure of his face and his hair was blanched not by sun, but by age. He must be forty or more; perhaps even fifty. She began to see him as mummified. He might be immensely old; someone in whom the process of ageing was almost, but not quite arrested. As he gazed at Guy and listened, the smile became congealed on his face.

Guy's constraint was making things difficult. Even if he had not heard Mrs Brett's stories, he would not have been at his best. He was a man whose charm and vitality were most evident when he was himself the giver. Now, dependent upon Gracey's bounty, his spirit shrank.

Gracey let him struggle on a little longer, then asked: 'You knew Lord Pinkrose, of course?'

'Yes.'

'He may look in this evening, I'm sure he'll be delighted to see you. My friends are so kind. Major Cookson has been particularly kind. They all come to cheer me up after supper. Sometimes there's quite a crowd here.'

Gracey sipped at his sherry, then, as though the moment had come, he asked, laying the question like a trap: 'What exactly were you doing in Bucharest?'

Guy looked surprised, but answered mildly: 'I assisted Professor Inchcape who was in charge of the English Department. When war started, he became Director of Propaganda for the Balkans and I ran the department. It was rather reduced, of course.'

'Of course. And our friend Dubedat? What part did he play in all this?' Gracey was again leaning towards Guy and his smile encouraged confidences.

Guy answered stiffly: 'Surely Dubedat told you what he did?'

Gracey lay back, not answering the question but apparently reflecting upon it, then said: 'I am grateful to Dubedat; and to Lush, too, for that matter. They've proved invaluable. When I had my accident, they took over and thus enabled me to recoup in peace and quiet. You may have heard there had been a little trouble here? Two lecturers left. They had been fond of Brett. He was hopeless as Director, but a nice enough old fellow and his men resented me. So off they went and I was left to cope alone. The London office couldn't replace them. When Dubedat and friend turned up, I didn't inquire too closely into their teaching experience being thankful to get them.'

Gracey's tone implied that he was inquiring now. He looked expectantly at Guy, but Guy merely said: 'I understand.'

His tone a little sharper, Gracey said: 'I've never regretted the association; I've only wondered why you let them go.'

'They chose to go,' Guy said.

'Ah?' Gracey regarded Guy with a warm interest. 'I gather there had been jealousy. Dubedat and Lush are active fellows; apt, perhaps, to take too much upon themselves. After all, they were not officially appointed. Someone may have wanted them out of the way? Most likely Professor Inchcape?'

Guy said: 'Professor Inchcape barely knew them. They were employed by me.'

Still holding Guy with his warm, smiling regard, Gracey said: 'Anyway, the story seems to be: they received the usual order to leave the country and no one made a move on their behalf. They were just let go.'

'They told you that?'

Gracey looked perplexed. 'Someone told me. It's so long ago: I've quite forgotten the details.'

'May I ask,' Guy asked, 'did Dubedat mention that I came to Athens in the hope that the Organization could use me here?'

'Yes. Oh, yes, Dubedat let me know you were keen to stay.' Gracey sat up and stared, as though entranced, from the window to where the sun had dropped down behind the olive trees and the light came broken through the small grey-silver leaves. 'I have no wish to criticize,' he said. 'You were answerable to your professor, of course; no doubt he approved. But don't you think there was a lack of – what? *Seriousness*, shall we say? . . . Well, to put it another way: wasn't it a tiny, a very tiny, bit frivolous to put on a theatre production during the blackest days of the fall of France?'

Guy, startled by this criticism, flushed and began to say: 'No, I—' But Gracey went on: '*And* when your students needed elementary English in order to get to English-speaking countries?'

'I suppose Dubedat told you that he took a part in the play?' Harriet said.

Guy moved a hand to silence her. Dubedat's part in the play was a point beside the point, and one he would not make. Willing to do more work than most, conscious of his own integrity, he had, over the years, become unused to criticism and tended to see himself as above it. But he was ready to accept the justice of Gracey's criticism and said only: 'Am I to take it that this is why you do not choose to employ me?'

'Good gracious me, no,' Gracey laughed. 'That is merely a private opinion. The question of your employment doesn't rest with me any longer. I'm *hors de combat*. I've delegated authority, and, I may say, I'm preparing to leave Greece. A friend, a very generous friend, feels I must have proper treatment. He has offered to send me to the Lebanon where there is an excellent clinic.'

Harriet said: 'Mr Frewen says there are no ships. The Egyptian line has come to a stop.'

'That won't affect me. I'm hoping to get a priority flight, but it's all hush-hush, of course.'

'So Dubedat is in charge?' said Guy.

'Someone has to be,' Gracey said. 'But I cannot say who will take over when I'm gone. There are several candidates for the post.'

'I suppose the London office knows . . .'

'Oh, dear me, yes. Cables have gone forth and back. It all takes so long nowadays.'

'Is there any likelihood of Dubedat being appointed?'

'Dubedat's name had been mentioned, but it does not rest with me. The London office will make the appointment.'

Guy stared into his glass, his eyebrows raised, his lips slightly pursed. He had had his interview with Gracey; he now had no cause for suspicion or complaint. He looked towards Harriet and put down his glass, preparing to go. He said: 'If there's no transport, we'll have to stay in Athens – anyway for the time being. I don't suppose you want me to be around doing nothing?'

'Oh!' Gracey made a gesture that suggested the matter was too trivial to be discussed further. 'Argue it out with Dubedat. He's in charge of the School now. If you don't try to high-hat him, you'll find him quite helpful. Go and be nice to him.'

The Pringles started to rise.

'Stay a while. Have another drink.'

The command was cordial, but it was a command. Guy and Harriet settled back in their seats unwillingly, but not without hope. They had nowhere else to go. They might as well stay and perhaps, by staying, something could be gained.

Gracey now lay back as though the interview had wearied him. The Pringles, despondent, were not much company and they felt he was waiting in the hope of better.

Harriet said: 'This is a pleasant room.'

Gracey looked at it doubtfully: 'Rather comfortless, wouldn't you say? A student's room. This was a hostel for the young, of course. So cold in winter. And the cooking's dreadful.'

Gracey's complaints went on while Harriet looked round the vast, bare room in envy. The sun was low and the windows were in shadow, but outside the sunlight still trickled, like an amber cordial, beneath the olive trees. The distant glow was refracted into the room so the twilight about them was as tawny as the glitter in apatite.

This, she thought, was the room for her. The unpolished floorboards, the dusty herbal scent and the space, made more spacious by the vistas of garden, seemed familiar. For a moment she knew where she had encountered it before, then the knowledge was gone. As she pursued it through memories of childhood books, a noise recalled her.

Someone opened the door. Gracey, revivified at once, sat up and cried: 'Archie, what a joy!'

A young man entered the room with a shy aloof smile, sidling in as though he knew himself more than welcome and wanted to counter the fact by apparent diffidence.

Gracey said to Harriet: 'This is Archie Callard,' then, seeing there was a second visitor following the first, added in a tone of anti-climax: 'And this is Ben Phipps.'

Both men noted the Pringles as they might note people whom they had heard discussed. Ben Phipps stared with frank curiosity, but Callard gave no more than an appraising glance hidden at once in a show of indifference.

'Where is the Major?' Gracey eagerly asked.

Callard murmured in an off-hand way: 'Gone to a party. He'll come later.'

It was clear to the Pringles that they had been detained on view for Gracey's friend. Once introduced, they could take a back seat and they were in no mood to do much else. Guy, usually stimulated by new acquaintances, sat silent, his glass held like a mask at the level of his lips. Harriet tried to accept the situation by detaching herself from it and watching the company as she would watch a play.

At first sight she could see no more reason for Callard's welcome than Phipps's lack of it. Callard was the better looking, of course, but Phipps had vitality and a readiness to please. When asked to pour drinks 'like a good fellow', he went at the task with a will. Perhaps he was over-ready. If that were a fault, it was not one of which Callard was guilty. He threw himself at full length on one of the two beds and when Gracey questioned him further about the Major's whereabouts, did not trouble to reply.

Phipps gave the answers, only too eager to be heard. When the drinks had been handed round, he placed himself in the middle of the room, somehow extruding his personality, prepared to talk.

Addressing him as someone who knew, Gracey asked: 'What's the news from the front? Is anything happening up there?'

Phipps, short, thick-boned, with mongrel features and a black bristle of hair, sat forward on his strong, thick haunches and said in a decided voice: 'Not much news. Town's full of rumours, but no one knows anything.'

Archie Callard, muffled by the pillow, said: 'The Italians'll be here tomorrow – and that's no rumour.'

Gracey jerked his head round and said reproachfully: 'That's not funny, Archie.'

'It's not meant to be funny. They crossed the frontier at six a.m. They're making for Athens. What's to stop them coming straight down?'

Gracey turned in appeal to Phipps: 'Surely there'll be some resistance? Metaxas said they would resist.'

Phipps, staring at his host, had an air of obliging good humour that came from the fact his gaze was neutralized by a pair of very thick, black-rimmed glasses. Harriet, viewing him from the side, could see, behind the pebbled lens, an observant eye that was black and hard as coal.

'Oh, they'll resist, all right,' said Phipps. 'Submission is all against the Greek tradition. They're a defiant people and they'll resist to the end, but . . .' Having started out with the intention of reassuring Gracey, he was now led by his informed volubility into a far from reassuring truth. 'They've got no arms. Old Musso's been preparing for months, but the Government here's done damn all. They saw the war coming and they just sat back and let it come. Half of them are pro-German, of course. They want things over quickly. They want a Greek collapse and an Axis victory . . .'

Guy, his attention caught by this criticism of the Metaxas Government, watched him with an intent interest, but Gracey, more mindful of the particular than the general, moved uneasily in his chair and at last broke in to protest:

'Really, Ben! You're trying to frighten me. You both are. I know you're just being naughty, but it's too bad. I'm an invalid. I'm in great pain when I walk. I couldn't get any distance without help. If the Italians march in, you can take to your heels. But what can I do?'

Phipps gave a guff of laughter. 'We're all in the same boat,' he said. 'If there's a ship of some sort, we'll see you get away all right. If there isn't, none of us'll get far. The Italians will blow up the Corinth Canal bridge and here we'll be – *stuck*!'

'Why worry?' Callard sat up, laughing. With auburn hair too long, mouth too full, eyes too large, he looked spoilt and entrancing, and conscious of being both. 'The Italians are charming and they've always been very nice to me.'

'I don't doubt,' Gracey said in a petulant tone. 'But times have changed. They're Fascists now, and they're the enemy. They're not going to be very nice to a crowd of civilian prisoners.' The reality of war, touching him for the first time, was shattering his urbanity. He frowned at Ben Phipps, who may have been aware of his fears but too roused by the situation to be impeded by them.

'I must say,' said Phipps, 'I like the idea of Metaxas coming down to see Grazzi in a bath-robe. It was about three-thirty. The ultimatum gave the Greeks about two and a half hours to hand over lock, stock and barrel. Metaxas said: "I couldn't hand over my house in that time, much less my country." I've never had much use for him but I must admit he's put up a good show this time.'

'Yes, but what am I to do?' Gracey asked impatiently. 'I've got to get to Beirut for treatment.'

The boasted 'priority flight' forgotten, he was twitching with so much nervous misery that Harriet could not but feel sorry for him. She said: 'I've heard there's to be an evacuation boat. It's for women and children but I'm sure . . .'

'Women, children and invalids,' Archie Callard interrupted. 'Don't worry, Colin. The Major will get you safely away. He'll fix it.'

Gracey subsided and his smile returned. 'One certainly can rely on the Major.' As a tap came on the door, he added happily: 'And here's the man himself. *Entrez, Entrez.*'

Pinkrose entered.

'Oh, it's Lord Pinkrose.' Gracey greeted him without enthusiasm.

Pinkrose did not notice how he was greeted. Trotting across the room, he nodded to Callard and Phipps, ignored the Pringles, and began at once: 'I'm worried, Gracey; I'm extremely worried. We're at war – but perhaps you know? You do? Well, I went up to the Legation to ask about my repatriation. I could have spoken to Frewen, but I thought it better to deal with the higher powers.'

'Who did you see?' Gracey asked.

'Young Bird.'

'Good God!' Archie Callard sobbed his laughter into the pillow. 'Is that your idea of higher power?'

'What did they say?' Gracey asked.

'Not very much. Not very much. No, not very much. There may be a boat.'

Gracey seemed displeased that Pinkrose knew about the boat and said reprovingly: 'If there's a boat, it'll be for women and children, not for *men*. You can't force your way on. It would never do.'

'Indeed?' Pinkrose gave Gracey a look of startled annoyance while Gracey faced him indignantly. The two men eyed one another in a fury of self-concern.

The light had almost faded. In the spectral glimmer of late dusk, Gracey's desiccated youth looked deathly while Pinkrose's cheeks were as grey and withered as lizard skin. Seeing Pinkrose glaring like a wraith in the gloom of hell, Gracey pulled himself together and said with strained amiability:

'Be a good fellow, Ben, and switch on the lights.'

As the light restored him, Gracey leant back and said: '*I* may *have* to go on the boat; but, given the choice, I would not dream of it. The Mediterranean is full of enemy shipping: submarines, U-boats, mines, and so on. It's a perilous sea.'

'Oh!' said Pinkrose, faltering.

Archie Callard, who was sitting up in amusement, agreed. 'I wouldn't dream of it either. Any British ship is "fair game" on the Med., and there'll be no convoy. The navy can't spare a cruiser.'

'Oh!' said Pinkrose again and he looked about with fearful eyes.

He was about to speak when another tap came on the door and Gracey brought him to a stop by saying joyfully: 'The Major, at last!'

They all watched as the door crept open and a hand, pushed through, waved at them. A head appeared. Smiling widely, Major Cookson inquired in a small, comic voice: 'May I come in?'

'Come in, come in; bless you,' Gracey cried.

The Major was carrying several prettily wrapped parcels which he brought across and dropped on Gracey's table. 'A few goodies,' he said, then stepped back to examine the invalid with an admiring affection. 'How are we today?'

Querulous in a playful way, Gracey said: 'Those tiresome Italians! Such a worry.'

'Not for you. *You're* not to worry. Leave that to your friends.'

Middle-aged, of middle height, with a neat unremarkable face and bleared blue eyes, the Major held himself tightly together, hands clasped at the bottom edge of a neat, dark, closely buttoned jacket. When he sat, he sat with a concise movement and, unclasping a hand which held a tightly rolled handkerchief, dabbed at his nostrils.

Archie Callard jumped up from the bed with a sudden show of energy and, coming to the table, began to sniff at the parcels and put his nose into bags.

'Naughty!' The Major gave him a surprisingly sharp slap and he jumped aside like a ballet dancer. Gracey giggled helplessly.

There was a sense of union between the three who seemed to be hinting at a game that was not played in public. Pinkrose watched perplexed but it was Ben Phipps who seemed to be the real outsider here.

Gracey wanted to have news of the party at which the Major had been detained. While he talked with Cookson and Callard, Phipps made several attempts to join in and each time was ignored. On edge at this treatment, he pushed himself to the fore, talking too much and too loudly, and the others looked at him in exasperation.

Discomforted by his behaviour, Harriet saw that the over-cultivated voice and over-large glasses were blazonry intended to disguise his own plainness of person. She suspected that he rode a rough sea of moneyless uncertainty and was a man who would always demand from life more than life was likely to give.

The Major began opening the parcels, saying: 'I thought as I could not get here until supper time, it would be nice if we all took a little bite together.'

60

'What a charming idea!' Gracey said.

He had not troubled to introduce the Pringles to Cookson and they knew they were now required to take themselves off. As they got to their feet, Gracey sped them with a smile.

'Do come again some time,' he said.

The parcels were being opened before they left the room.

Down in the hall the supper bell rang. The Academy food might be indifferent, the lights cheerless, the rooms under-furnished, but Harriet longed to be sheltered here, one of a community, fed, companioned and protected.

The streets were unlit. The authorities had imposed a black-out. The Pringles clung together in the darkness of the un-familiar district where pavements were uneven and areas unrailed. Guy, quite blind under these conditions, fell over some steps and groaned with pain.

Savagely, Harriet said: 'Bloody Dubedat!' and Guy had to laugh: 'You can't blame him for the black-out.'

'No, but I blame him for a lot of other things. I'd like to know what he told Gracey about you.'

'So would I; but what does it matter? Dubedat wanted to do something more than teach. He asked me if he could give an occasional lecture. I refused. I must have hurt his pride.'

Harriet, feeling for the first time that she had had enough of Guy's forbearance, said: 'Dubedat is nothing but a conceited nonentity. The pity is that you ever employed him at all. I hope you don't intend to ask him for any favours.'

'No. We'll wait and see who gets Gracey's job.'

'Could the London office appoint Dubedat? Is it possible?'

'Anything's possible. All they know is what Gracey cares to tell them. He said there were several candidates. The choice will really be Gracey's choice because they will choose the person he recommends. It's as simple at that.'

'He couldn't recommend Dubedat.'

'He could recommend worse . . . I suppose.'

'I doubt it. But we'll see. Meanwhile, what are we going to do about money?'

'Don't worry. The Organization won't let us starve.'

'You'll speak to Gracey?'

'No. I'll cable the Cairo office.'

'You might have done that days ago.'

'If I had, we'd've been ordered to Cairo. Now we're stranded here. They'll have to let me have my salary.'

She was suddenly exhilarated. Their hopeless and moneyless condition had filled her with fear, but suddenly her fear was gone. She threw her arms round Guy, feeling that his human presence was a solution of all life's difficulties, and said: 'What would I do without you?'

Perhaps he was not as confident as he wished her to think, for he returned her embrace as though lost himself in the darkness of this city that had nothing to offer him. They stood for some minutes wrapped together, each thankful for the other, and then guided each other down through the main square to the hotel. There they went to supper in the basement, the only place where they could get a meal without making an immediate payment.

5

The young men were disappearing from the city. The porter left the Pringles' hotel, first saying an emotional farewell to everyone, and his place was taken by an old man moustached like the great Venizelos.

Each day lorry-loads of conscripts were driven through the streets to the station and the girls threw flowers to them. Farmers came into Athens leading horses that were needed for the army. But there was no sight of the Italians.

Mussolini had told Hitler that he would take Greece in ten days, just as the Germans had taken France. At the end of the ten days his troops were still on the Kalamas River, at the spot where they had found the Greeks waiting for them.

The Italian radio complained of their reception. It said that the Duce had offered to occupy Greece in a friendly, protective spirit and had not been prepared for this resistance. It would take the Italians a day or two to get over the shock.

The Italian Minister had not left Athens and was pained when he found his telephone had been cut off. He rang Metaxas to ask why he was being treated in such a fashion. Greece and Italy were not at war.

'Sir,' Metaxas replied, 'this is no time for philological discussion,' and he put down his receiver.

The war was, in its way, comic, but no one imagined it would remain comic for long. The Italians had behind them the weight of Axis armour. Beneath all the humour was the fear that the Greek line would break suddenly and the enemy arrive overnight.

An order had gone out from the Legation that British

subjects must be prepared to leave Greece at an hour's notice. Each person could take a suitcase, and the suitcase should be kept ready packed. When Guy presented himself at the Legation and asked for his salary to be diverted from Cairo, he saw a junior secretary who said: 'If that's how you want it, I'll pop a note in the jolly old bag; but my guess is: while the transfer is winging its way here, you'll be off to where it came from. Do you want to take the risk? Righteo, then! You know the drill? You chaps draw from Legation funds. If you like, you can have a small advance to settle your hotel bill.'

The bill was settled, to Harriet's relief, but there would be no money to spend until the transfer arrived.

The Pringles heard nothing more from Gracey. No word came from Dubedat, but a few days after their visit to the Academy, the porter rang to say a visitor was on his way up.

Harriet opened the door. Toby Lush, outside, said with ponderous gravity: 'I'd like a word with himself.'

Guy was sorting out his books. Greeting him with unusual sobriety, Toby sat on the edge of the bed and contemplated his pipe. The Pringles waited. He spoke at last:

'We hear you went and saw Mr Gracey?'

Guy said: 'Yes.'

'Well, it's like this . . .' Toby stuck the empty pipe into his mouth and sucked it thoughtfully. 'When we came here, the old soul and me, we had to find work. After all, we had to *eat*. So when we met Mr Gracey, we laid it on thick. Anyone would under the circumstances.'

'What did you tell him, exactly?'

'Oh, this and that. We said we'd done a spot of lecturing up in Bucharest . . . a few other things. You don't want the gory details, do you? Just a bit of hornswoggle. *You* understand. But the thing is, the old soul's moidered; hopes you didn't give us away.'

'I didn't give anything away.'

'That's all right then. But . . .' an expression of inquisitorial cunning came over Toby's features and he pointed the

64

pipe stem at Guy: 'Supposing Mr Gracey asks you direct what we did?'

Formal with annoyance, Guy replied: 'I would tell him I do not discuss my friends' affairs.'

'Oh, good enough! Good enough!' Toby whoofed with relief: 'And you didn't mention we'd done a bolt?'

'Certainly not.'

'Fine. Splendid. I said you wouldn't.' Much heartened, Toby leant back against the wall and, taking out his tobacco and matches, prepared himself for a chat.

Harriet was having none of this. 'Now,' she said, 'I'd like to ask you something. What did *you* tell Gracey? Did you say that Guy wasted his time producing *Troilus and Cressida*?'

Toby jerked up with a pained frown. 'Me? I never did.'

'What about Dubedat?'

Toby sat up. Scrambling his equipment together with agitated hands, he said: 'How do I know? He sees Mr Gracey in private. He doesn't tell me everything.' He got to his feet. 'Have to scarper. The old soul's a bit carked. I'll let him know you didn't sneak. He'll appreciate it.'

'He ought to.'

Toby made off with the gait of a guilty fox. When he had gone, Harriet said to Guy: 'Dubedat means to be Director. He's afraid you might have queered his pitch.'

'It certainly looks like it,' Guy was forced to agree. Pale and unhappy, he returned to his books, wanting to hear no more. Harriet pitied his disillusionment, but had no patience with it. Reality was not to be altered by an inability to recognize fact.

She had remained with Guy, imprisoned in the room, but now, uplifted by a sense of being the stronger of the two, she said: 'Come on, let's go for a walk.'

He did not move. 'You go. I don't want to go.'

'But what will you do, shut up here alone?'

'Work.'

'Have you any work?'

'I'm getting quotations for a lecture on Coleridge.'

'Surely you could do that any time? You might not lecture again for months.'

He shook his head. Bent over his books, he whistled softly to himself: a sign of stress. Harriet stood at the door, longing to go out, not knowing what to say. During past crises – the fall of France, the final break-up in Bucharest – he had found escape, first by producing *Troilus and Cressida*, then by organizing a summer school. Throwing himself into one occupation or another, he had managed to keep anxiety on the periphery of consciousness; now, without employment, without friends, without money, he was trying to follow his old escape pattern. But there was no route open to him. All he could do was sit here in this dark, narrow room and try to lose himself in work.

'Wouldn't you be better at the School library?' she asked.

'I'd rather not go there.'

One afternoon, while wandering about alone, Harriet met Yakimov and, strolling with him up University Street, took the opportunity to ask about some of the people they had seen in Athens.

'Who is Major Cookson?'

Yakimov answered at once. 'Very important and distinguished.'

'Yes, but what does he *do*?'

That was more difficult. '*Do*, dear girl?' Yakimov pondered the question heavily, then brightened: 'Believe . . . indeed, have inside information to the effect: he's something big in the S.S.'

'Good heavens, the German S.S.?'

'No. The Secret Service.'

As there was little point in pursuing that fantasy, Harriet went on to inquire about Callard and Phipps. Sighing at being forced into intellectual activity, Yakimov dismissed them as 'both very distinguished'.

'What about Mrs Brett and Miss Jay?' Harriet persisted.

'Don't ask me, dear girl. Town's full of those old tits.'

'Yes, but what are they all *doing* here?'

'Nothing much. They live here.'

The English who lived in Bucharest had gone there to work. The English in Athens were clearly of a different order. Encountering for the first time people who lived abroad unoccupied, she was amazed by their inactivity and, learning nothing from Yakimov, decided to take her curiosity to Alan Frewen. He had asked them if they would go with him on Sunday morning when he exercised Diocletian in the National Gardens.

He called for them as agreed and Guy said to Harriet, as he had said before: 'You go.'

She pleaded: 'Do come darling. He doesn't want me alone. Why not bring your work and sit in the gardens while we walk round!'

Resolute in his revolt against circumstances, Guy said: 'No, I'm all right here. Go on down. Alan'll love having you to himself.'

Harriet could not believe it. She descended diffidently to the hall where Alan waited, his face so obscured by his glasses it was impossible to tell how he felt. He was as shy as she was and they said nothing until they reached the square.

He was limping and several times when the dog pulled on the lead, he had difficulty in keeping his footing. He apologized, explaining that he had had an attack of gout.

'I had to stay home for a couple of days,' he said. 'Not that it mattered. Things are still slack at the office. There's not much to do except get out the News Sheet.'

'What does Yakimov do?' she asked.

'Oh, his job is to deliver it.'

'Is that all?'

Alan gave a laugh and did not reply.

There had been a shower of rain, the first of the autumn. It had scarcely moistened the ground but the sky, broken with mauve and blue clouds, had taken on the fresh expectancy of spring. Harriet longed for Guy to be with them, not only to ease their constraint but to enjoy, as she enjoyed, the changing season.

She suddenly burst out: 'Guy's very unhappy. What can we do for him?'

'You had no luck with Gracey, then?'

'None at all. He said he had delegated his authority. He suggested Guy go and ask Dubedat for work.'

Alan stared down frowning, considering what she had said, then started to speak with some force: 'I really feel this can't go on. The School's becoming a laughing-stock. There are all sorts of stories going round about the lectures. Apparently Lush suggested that Dante and Milton might have met in the streets of Florence. When one of the students pointed out that there was about three hundred years between them, Lush said: "Crumbs! Have I made a clanger?" Cookson's protected the lot of them for some time, but there've been complaints. I know Mrs Brett has written home. I'm sure a responsible person will be appointed when Gracey goes. My advice is: wait.'

'Guy would agree, but I'm afraid he finds it a strain.'

'I know. I know,' Alan nodded his sympathy, and after this she felt there was harmony between them.

It occurred to her that Alan was the first friend she and Guy had made on equal terms. In Bucharest the people she knew had been the people known to Guy before his marriage and she imagined herself accepted because she was Guy's wife, a state of affairs the more disjunctive because she was unused to being a wife. It had seemed to her then that she had left behind not only her own friends but her individuality. Now she began to feel the absurdity of this. Why, after all, should Alan Frewen not be as content with her as he would be with Guy?

They passed the Washingtonia Robusta palms that stood with their great silvery satin trunks across the entrance to the gardens. Inside, the sandy walks curved and flowed beneath sprays of small, tremulous leaves. The sun came and went. Moving soundlessly, they entered a tropical dampness filled with the scents of earth. Alan released Diocletian, who was off at once prospecting beneath the bushy trees that sifted the

68

sun on to the dark, soft, powdery ground. The paths were all much alike. The foliage was all light, a peppering of dry, rustling greenery that dappled the sand with light and shade. Then a vista opened. There was a drive lined with greyish, rubbery trees.

'Judas trees,' Alan said. 'You must see them in the spring.'

'Is that when they flower?'

'They flower for Easter.'

And where would they be at Easter? Alan had said 'Wait', but he said nothing more. And what could he say? By coming here, Guy and she had created their own problem, and they must solve it for themselves.

She had thought they need only reach a friendly country and their lives could begin; but here they were, and their lives were still in abeyance. In Bucharest they had had employment and a home. They had had Sasha. Guy might find employment here, they might even find a home but Sasha, she feared, was lost for ever. Even his memory was disappearing into the past. For the last week or more she had not given him a thought, though there always remained, like a shadow on her mind, the hollow darkness into which he had disappeared. He was dead, she supposed, like her loved red kitten that had fallen from the balcony of the flat. If one could not bear the memory of the dead, then they must be shut out of memory. There was no other action anyone could take against the bafflement of grief.

She was recalled from her thoughts by the squawks of water-birds and the cries of children. They were walking through a coppice where the air was jaundiced with the weedy, muddy smell of lake water.

Alan said: 'Where's Diocletian? I'd better put him on the lead.'

He held the dog close as they emerged from under the trees and came to a sunlit clearing where small iron seats stood round the sandy lake edge. The lake was small. A bridge spanned the water that now, in the last days of the dry season, was scarcely water at all, but a glossy, greenish film in which ducks, geese and swans were squelching about. The children were feeding the birds and the birds, snatching and quarrelling, were making all the noise in the world.

Limping towards a couple of vacant chairs, Alan said he must sit down. He lowered his large backside on to the little iron seat and with a sigh let his bulk settle down. When they were both seated, an attendant came and stood at a distance, respectfully awaiting the sum that was payable in fee. When Alan handed over the money, the old man counted back some coins so small they now bought nothing but the right to sit for a while beside the lake. Alan talked in Greek with the attendant and afterwards told Harriet they had been discussing the war. The old man said he had two sons at the front but he was not at all disturbed because the English had promised to aid the Greeks and everyone said the English were the strongest people in the world.

'He knows me,' Alan said. 'I come here often to read Cavafy. I suppose you know Cavafy? No? I'll translate "The Barbarians" for you one day. It fits our times.'

'Are the English going to send aid?'

'I wish I knew. They haven't much to send. I've heard the Greeks aren't interested in half-measures and I don't think we could rise to a full-scale campaign.'

There was not much to be said about the war and when they had said it all, they sat for a long time in the sunlight while Harriet considered how she might put to him the questions that Yakimov could not answer. She at last overcame her own reticence and asked:

'Have you known Cookson long?'

'I've been seeing him on and off, over the years.'

'You've lived here a long time, then? Before the war, were you one of these people who live abroad and do nothing?'

Alan laughed at her disapproving tone and said: 'Indeed I was not. I had to earn my living. I came here as a photographer. I had a studio on Lycabettos and I went to stay in places like Mycenae, Nauplia, Delphi and Olympus. When I settled in a place, I'd try to absorb it and then record it. I wrote a few introductory pieces to albums of photographs, nothing much, the pictures were the thing. I'd like to record the whole of Greece.'

'And when you have, what will you do?'

'Begin at the beginning again.'

'And Diocletian goes with you?'

'Of course. Diocletian is a Grecophil like me. I brought him from England when I was last there, five years ago – partly for his own sake and partly so I need not go back.' When he saw her look of inquiry, he smiled. 'If I took him back he would have to go into quarantine. We would be separated for six months, which is unthinkable. He is my safeguard. When my relatives write reproachful letters, I reply: "I would love to come and see you, but there is the problem of Diocletian."'

'But supposing you have to leave? I mean, if we all have to leave? What will you do?'

'Let us consider that when the time comes.'

She took the chance to return to Cookson. 'He seems to be very influential,' she said.

'He is, I suppose. He's lived here a long time and knows a great many influential people. He's liked. He's rather a charming old thing; he has this house at Phaleron – by the sea, very pleasant in summer. He's hospitable. His parties are famous and no one wants to be left out.'

'Is he married?'

'He was once, I think.'

'And now?'

Alan laughed. 'Now? I really can't say. He invited me once to "a ra-ther small and ra-ther curious party". I'm afraid I left early; I could see it was going to get curiouser and curiouser.'

'He seems to have been extremely kind to Gracey.'

'Yes, they're great friends. Gracey played up to him. They all play up to him. That's all that's necessary.'

'I wish Guy could do that,' Harriet said. 'But he never plays up to the right people.'

'I imagine that's the nice thing about him?'

'Perhaps, but I don't suppose it will get us anywhere.'

Alan laughed and when he said nothing, she went on to ask about Gracey. Was he really an invalid?

'Who can say? He certainly slipped on Pendeli and hurt his back. A good many people have done that but I've never known anyone before who had to spend months lying in a chair. Still, he seems determined to get to the Lebanon clinic for a cure.'

'My belief is, he's tired of the whole game.'

'Really?' Alan looked round, his face alive with amused interest: 'You mean the injury? You think it's a game, do you?'

'Yes. Mrs Brett says he's bone lazy. I'm sure he never wanted to run the School, he wanted to be an elegant figurehead; but the lecturers went off leaving the place on his hands. He must have been thankful when Toby and Dubedat turned up; and the accident was a godsend. It excused his idleness, but now the pretence has been going on too long. He's stuck with it till he can get away.'

'You may be right.' Alan edged himself off the seat and managed to stand up. Rejecting Gracey as an enigma of little importance, he said: 'It looks as though we're in for another shower.'

The sun had gone in. The grown-ups were calling the children from the lake and a few drops of rain made small mooncraters around the fluttering water-birds.

Walking back under the trees, Alan stared ahead and did not speak. Unless stimulated by questions, he seemed to feel no need for conversation and Harriet wondered why a man so withdrawn and silent should seek out company at all. As there was little else to be said, she might as well continue to ask her questions. What about Archie Callard? He was, of course, a friend of the Major, but was he anything more than that?

'He's a clever young man,' Alan said. 'No fool I assure you, but he's handicapped by having a rich father. He is not forced to work but is always complaining that he doesn't get enough to spend. He occasionally starts out on some project that he hopes will bring in money. He went to Lemnos to look for a labyrinth that probably never existed. Recently he's been staying on Patmos with some idea of writing a life of St John. Of course he gets bored, and back he comes and that, for the moment, is that.'

'And Ben Phipps? I shouldn't have thought he had a rich father.'

'Indeed he hasn't. He's been working here as a journalist and he's published a few things. I haven't read any, but I believe he has some reputation.'

'What's he doing in that set?'

'Hanging on hopefully.'

'But what is he likely to get?'

'Preferment. He's sick of scraping a living with his bits of journalism. He'd like an easy, steady, well-paid job; a job that would place him right in the front of the social picture.'

'You mean: Gracey's job?'

'That would do as well as another.'

'I see. If he got it, do you think he'd employ Guy?'

'He very well might. I know he doesn't think much of Rosencrantz and Guildenstern.'

'Lush and Dubedat? The betrayers who served the king. What rewards, I wonder, for those who have served Gracey?'

'We'll know soon enough.'

They were now back at Harriet's hotel and as she paused, Alan said: 'I'm meeting Yakimov at Zonar's. Won't you join us?'

She said: 'I'd love to. I'll see if I can get Guy out,' and she ran upstairs to persuade him.

She half-expected to find him gone, for restless, gregarious, eager to entertain and influence, he was not one to spend two hours alone in their little room, yet he was still there lying on the bed, propped up with pillows, his glasses pushed to his brow, a pencil stuck in his hair and books all around him.

She scolded him: 'You've been here long enough. You need a drink. Come on.'

73

'I'd rather not.'

'What's the matter with you, for heaven's sake? Are you ill?'

'No,' he pulled down the glasses in order to see her. 'We haven't any money.'

'Let Yakimov buy you a drink. You bought him plenty when he was hard up.'

'I can't go to cafés in the hope someone else will pay for me.'

'Do come. I'll pay for you.'

'No, don't worry about me.'

'Then come down to the dining-room and have something to eat.'

He followed her and took his meal without saying much. She had hoped that, alone here, dependent upon each other, they would be closer than they had ever been. Now it seemed to her she had been nearer to him when he was not here; nearest, probably, when she had imagined him in the Lufthansa above the Aegean. He had only to arrive to take a step away from her.

He was not to be shut up in intimacy. The world was his chief relationship and she wondered whether he really understood any other. His quarrel now was not with her, but with defaulting humanity and he was in retreat from it. And here they were with leisure and freedom – things they had not had before in the year of marriage – and Guy was closeted with his dilemma while she went for walks with a stranger.

6

Next morning, called to the telephone while at breakfast, Guy returned transformed. He took the dining-room steps at a run, his face alight, his whole person animated, and called to Harriet: 'Hurry up. We're going to the Legation.'

'Really? Why?'

'The Cairo office has approved my presence here. Apparently they've got all the chaps they can deal with in Egypt. They don't want any more. The Legation say I can have some money.'

Harriet walked up with him and waited in the Chancellory while Guy saw the accountant and was permitted to draw on Legation funds. She could hear his voice raised happily in the office and when he came out he was pushing his drachma notes into an old two-penny cash-book which he kept in his breast pocket. He expressed by his action his indifference to money but he was not, Harriet now knew, indifferent to the lack of it.

'And what do you think?' he said: 'Our old friend Dobbie Dobson is being sent here from Bucharest. We'll have a friend at Court.'

'Will we?' Harriet doubtfully asked.

'Of course.' Guy was confident of it and walking down-hill to the main road, he said: 'I like Dobson. I do like Dobson. He's so unaffected and amiable.'

Guy, too, was unaffected and amiable which, considering the poverty in which he had grown up, was a more surprising thing. He had seemed to Harriet to have a unique atti-tude to life, an attitude that was a product of confidence and simplicity, but she had seen that the simplicity was not as unified as it seemed, the confidence could be shaken. Moneyless, he had remained under cover and now, emerging, he emerged for her in a slightly different guise.

She said: 'I'm never quite sure with you where showmanship ends and reality begins.'

'Don't bother about that,' he said. 'Where do you want to eat tonight?'

'Anywhere but the hotel crypt.'

'Let's ask Frewen to supper. He'll say where we should go.'

At midday they found Alan at Zonar's, in his usual place. When he received their invitation, he grew red and his face strained into its painful smile with a gratitude that was almost emotional. They could see how deeply he wished for friends. And how odd, Harriet thought, that he had so few and, after all his years in Greece, should be dependent upon newcomers like Yakimov and the Pringles. Was it that he approached people, instigated friendship, but could go no further? She could imagine him with many acquaintances but known by none of them.

He suggested that they go to a taverna where they might see some Greek dancing. He knew one beyond the Roman agora and that evening called for them in a taxi. He handed Harriet a bunch of little mauve-pink flowers.

She said: 'Cyclamen, already!'

'Yes, they begin early. In fact, things here begin almost before they stop.'

'Do you mean the winter stops before it starts?'

'Alas, no. The winter can be bitter, and it's likely to come down on us any day now. The weather's broken in the mountains. Reports from the front say "torrents of rain". I only hope the Italians and their heavy gear get stuck in the mud.'

They were put down in a wide, dark road where the wind blew cold. Alan led them between black-out curtains into a small taverna where there was only the proprietor, sitting as though he despaired of custom. At the sight of Alan, he leapt up and began offering them a choice of tables set round an open space. The space was for dancing, but there was no one to dance.

When they sat down, he stood for some time talking to Alan, his voice full of sorrow, his hands tragically raised, so the Pringles were prepared for unhappy news long before Alan was free to interpret it. The proprietor had two sons who, being themselves skilled dancers, had drawn in rival performers from the neighbourhood. But now his sons and all the other young men had gone to the war and here he was, alone. But even if the boys were home, there would be no dancing, for the Greeks had given up dancing. No one would dance while friends and brothers and lovers were at the war. No, no one would dance again until every single enemy had been driven from the soil of Greece. Still, the taverna was open and the proprietor was happy to see Alan and Alan's companions. When introduced to Guy and Harriet, he shook each by the hand and said there was some ewe cooked with tomatoes and onions, and, pray heavens, there always would be good wine, both white and black.

He went to the kitchen and Alan apologized for the gloom and quiet. Seeing him crestfallen, Harriet began asking him about the boys who used to dance here. How did they dance? Where did they learn?

Stimulated at once, Alan began to talk, saying: 'Oh, all the Greek boys can dance. Dancing is a natural form of self-expression here. If there's music, someone runs on to the floor and stretches out his hand, and someone else joins him and the dance begins. And then there's the *Zebeikiko*! The dance they do with their arms round each other's shoulders. First there may be only two or three, then another joins and another; and the women clap and . . . oh dear me! The whole place seems to be thudding with excitement. It stirs the blood, I can tell you.'

'I would love to see it.'

'Perhaps you will. The war won't go on for ever.'

When the wine was brought, Alan invited the proprietor to drink to a speedy victory. The old man held up his glass, saying: 'Niki, niki, niki,' then told them the Italians would be on their knees before the month was out. He had no doubt of it.

When he left them, the room was silent except for the purr of the lamps that hung just below the prints pinned on the walls. One print showed the Virgin done in the Byzantine manner; another was a coloured war-poster in which the women of Epirus, barefooted, their skirts girded above their knees, were helping their men haul the guns up the mountainside.

After he had brought in the food, the proprietor retired tactfully and sat at his own table, apparently preoccupied until Alan called to him: 'Where are all the customers?'

The proprietor sprang up again to reply. He explained that in these times people were not inclined to go out. They would not seek merriment while their young men were fighting and losing their lives.

When the man returned to his seat, Alan gazed after him with a reminiscent tenderness and Harriet said: 'You love Greece, don't you?'

'Yes. I love the country and I love the people. They have a wonderful vitality and friendliness. They want to be liked, of course: but that does not detract from their individuality and independence. Have you ever heard about the Greek carpenter who was asked to make six dining-room chairs?'

'No. Tell us.'

'The customer wanted them all alike and the carpenter named an extremely high figure. "Out of the question," said the customer. "Well," said the carpenter, "if I can make them all different, I'd do them for half that price."'

Alan talked for some time about the Greeks and the country-side: 'an idyllic, unspoilt countryside'. Guy, interested in more practical aspects of Greek life, here broke in to ask if by 'unspoilt' Alan did not mean undeveloped, and by 'idyllic', simply conditions that had not changed since the days of the Ottoman Empire. How was it possible to enjoy the beauty of a country when the inhabitants lived in privation and misery?

Alan was startled by Guy's implied criticism. His great

78

sombre face grew dark and he seemed incapable of speech. After some moments he said, as though his vanity had been touched:

'I've seen a great deal of the country. I have not noticed that the people are unhappy.'

There was a defensive irritation in his tone and Harriet would, if she could, have stopped the subject at once, but Guy was not easily checked. Certain that Alan, a humane and intelligent man, could be made to share his opinions, he asked with expectant interest:

'But are they happy? Can people be happy under a dictatorship?'

'A dictatorship!' Alan started in surprise, then laughed. 'You *could* call it a dictatorship, but a very benevolent one. I suppose you've been talking to members of the K.K.E.? What would they have done if they'd got power? Before Metaxas took over there'd been an attempt to impose a modern political system on what was virtually a primitive society. The result was chaos. In the old days there'd been the usual semi-oriental graft but as soon as there was a measure of democratic freedom, graft ran riot. The only thing Metaxas could do was suspend the system. The experiment was brought to a stop. A temporary stop, of course.'

'When do you think it will start again?'

'When the country's fit to govern itself.'

'And when will that be? What's being done to bring Greece into line with more advanced countries? I mean, of course, industrially advanced countries?'

'Nothing, I hope.' Alan spoke with a tartness that surprised both Guy and Harriet. 'Greece is all right as it is. Metaxas is not personally ambitious. He's a sort of paternal despot, like the despots of the classical world; and, all things considered, I think he's doing very well.'

Guy, assessing and criticizing Alan's limitations, said: 'You prefer the peasants to remain in picturesque poverty, I suppose?'

'I prefer that they remain as they are: courteous, generous, honourable and courageous. Athens is not what it was, I admit. There used to be a time when any stranger in the city was treated as a guest. As more and more strangers came here, naturally that couldn't go on; yet something remains. The great tradition of *philoxenia* – of friendship towards a stranger – still exists in the country and on the islands. It exists here, in a little café like this!' Alan's voice sank with emotion; he had to pause a moment before he could say:

'A noble people! Why should anyone wish to change them?'

Guy nodded appreciatively. 'A noble people, yes. They deserve something better than subsistence at starvation level.'

'Man does not live by bread alone. You young radicals want to turn the world into a mass-producing factory, and you expect to do it overnight. You make no allowance for the fact different countries are at different stages of development.'

'It's not only a question of development, but a question of freedom; especially freedom of thought. There are political prisoners in Greece. Isn't that true?'

'I'm sure I don't know. There may be, but if people are intent on making a nuisance of themselves, then prison is the best place for them.'

'They're intent on improving the conditions of their fellow men.'

'Aren't we all?' said Alan, with the asperity of a docile man attacked through his ideals. He took his dark glasses out and sat fingering them.

Seeing that his hands were trembling, Harriet said: 'Darling, let's talk of something else,' but Guy was absorbed in his own subject. As he spoke at length of good schools, clinics, antenatal care, child-welfare centres, collective farms and industries communally owned, Alan's face grew more and more sombre. At last he broke in, protesting:

'You come from an industrial area. You can only see progress in terms of industry. Greece has never been an industrial country and I hope it never will be.'

'Can Greece support its people without industry?'

Without attempting to answer, Alan said: 'I love Greece. I love the Greeks. I do not want to see any change here.'

'You speak like a tourist. A country *must* support its populace.'

'It does support them. No one dies of starvation.'

'How do you know? Starvation can be a slow process. How many Greeks have to emigrate each year?'

There was a sense of deadlock at the table. Alan put his glasses down, stared at them, then gave a laugh. 'You'll have to have a talk with Ben Phipps,' he said. 'I think you'd see eye to eye.'

'Really?' Harriet asked in surprise.

'Oh, yes. Ben prides himself on being a progressive.'

'Surely Cookson wouldn't approve of that?'

'He's not taken seriously at Phaleron. It's fashionable to be left wing these days, as you know. Phipps is accepted as a sort of court jester. He can believe what he likes so long as he doesn't try to change anything.'

'I'd like to meet him again,' Guy said.

'I think it can be arranged.'

'Let's have another bottle.'

Alan had lost possibility for Guy, but unaware of this, he looked like a boy let out of school and returned to the beauties of Greece, talking at length about his travels on the mainland and to the islands. Guy, sitting back out of the conversation, attended with a smiling interest, viewing him no more seriously than Cookson viewed Phipps.

When they left, the proprietor took their hands and held to them as though he could scarcely bear to be left alone again in the empty silence that had once been alive with music and dancing youths.

There was little traffic outside and no hope of a taxi. Alan, walking ahead, led them through the narrow streets to the Plaka Square which they reached as the air-raid warning sounded. Police regulations required everyone to go under cover during an alert, but the raids, that came every day, were over the Piraeus, and Athenians avoided the regulation if they could. Alan suggested they should sit on the chairs outside the café in the square. They could hurry inside if the police appeared.

The moon, that shone fitfully through drifting cloud, touched the old houses and trees, and the plaque that said Byron had lived somewhere near. The strands of the pepper trees in the central garden moved like seaweed in the wind. It was too cold now to sit out after dark, but the outdoor chill was preferable to the hot, smoky air behind the curtain of the little café.

The café owner, hearing voices outside, looked through the curtains and asked if they would like coffee. Alan explained that they were only waiting for the raid to end. The owner said they might wait a long time and he invited them to take coffee as his guests. The coffee, hot and sweet, came in little cups, and the waiter left the curtain open slightly as a gesture of welcome while someone with a concertina inside began to play 'Tipperary' in their honour. They drank down their coffee and ordered some more. The moon disappeared behind cloud and there was darkness except for the crack of light between the café curtains.

Alan said: '"They are daring beyond their power and they risk beyond reason and they never lose hope in suffering."'

'Thucydides?' asked Guy. Alan nodded and Harriet begged him: 'Repeat some of your translations of Cavafy.'

He reflected for a while then began: 'Why are we waiting, gathered in the market place? It's the barbarians who are coming today . . .' He stopped. 'It is a long poem; too long.'

'We have nothing to do but listen,' said Harriet, and she suddenly realized how happy she was here with Guy, come out of his seclusion to be a companion of this freedom that, having neither past nor future, was a lacuna in time; a gift of leisure that need only be accepted and enjoyed.

Alan was about to start his recitation again when the all clear sounded. 'Another time,' he said. 'Now I must go back and feed my poor Diocletian.'

7

Alan had asked Harriet if she would join him again when he went to the greens and, being told there was a visitor in the hall, she said to Guy: 'Won't you come, too?'

Guy, restored to all his old desire for contact with life, said: 'I'd like to come,' but running down the stairs, he stopped and whispered: 'I don't want to see him.'

'Who?'

'It's Toby Lush again.'

Guy's expression, injured and apprehensive, roused her to fury. 'I'll deal with him,' she said. 'You stay there.'

Toby, in his leather-bound jacket, with his wrack of moustache and hair in eyes, looked like some harmless old sheepdog. He grinned at Harriet as though he had come on a pleasing errand and seemed startled by her tone when she asked:

'What do *you* want?'

'The old lad. Is he about?'

'No.'

'When can I see him? It's urgent.'

'You can't see him. You can leave a message.'

'No. Have orders to see Guy in person.'

'He refuses to see you. If you have anything to say, you can say it to me.'

Toby spluttered and shifted his feet, but in the end had to speak. 'There's going to be an evacuation ship. It's all arranged. Dubedat told me to tell you he's wangled berths on it for the pair of you.'

'Has he? Why?'

83

'It's your chance, don't you see? There's nothing here for you: no job, no money, nowhere to live, and now the Italians invading. You're jolly lucky to be getting away.'

'And is Gracey going?'

'Yes, we're losing him, sad to say.'

'And you and Dubedat?'

'No, we'd go if we could, but we've got to hold the fort. The ship's not for us chaps. The old soul used his influence and they stretched a point because he said you're stranded.' Laughing nervously, his moustache stirring, damp, beneath his nose, Toby added; 'I'd rather go than stay.'

'You surprise me. The news is unusually good. I've been told the Italians are putting up no fight at all. There's a whole division trapped in a gorge of the Pindus mountains and they're not even trying to fight their way out.'

'Oh, you can't believe those stories. The Greeks'll say anything. The I-ties may be stopped for the moment, but they're bound to break through. They've got tanks, lorries, big guns, the lot. Once the break comes, they'll be down here in a brace of shakes. We don't want to stay here, but we've got a job to do.'

'You had a job to do in Bucharest, but you bolted just the same.'

'Oh, I say!' Toby had been searching his pockets and now, finding a match, he began digging about in the bowl of his pipe. 'Play fair!' he said. 'The old soul's put himself out for you. And you're lucky to be going.'

'But we're not going.'

Toby's eyes bulged at her. 'You are, you know. It's orders. You saw that letter. Dubedat's boss here now and if Guy's sensible he won't make trouble. If he reports for work in Cairo, we'll stay mum. Not a word about his coming here against orders. The old soul promises. Now be sensible. It's the only boat. The last boat. So hand over your passports and we'll do the necessary.'

Harriet repeated: 'We're not going,' and went upstairs while Toby shouted: 'We'll ring the Cairo office. We'll complain . . .'

Guy had gone to the room where Harriet found him sprawled on the bed, a book in his hand, an air of detachment hiding his anticipation of a new betrayal.

'We're ordered on to the evacuation boat. Dubedat's command.'

'Is that all?' Guy laughed and dropped the book.

'It's the last boat. If we don't go, we're stuck.'

'We couldn't be stuck in a better place.'

8

The night before the ship sailed, Cookson gave a farewell party for Gracey. Yakimov was among the invited.

'Who was there?' Harriet asked him next day.

'Everyone,' said Yakimov.

Harriet felt excluded because she had imagined herself and Guy to be part of English life here; now it seemed they were not. But when the ship had sailed a different atmosphere began to prevail. Uncertain who had gone and who had not, the survivors met one another with congratulations and, like veterans left behind to stem an enemy advance, they felt a new warmth towards one another.

At the same time, the situation had changed. The ship had no sooner gone than the streets were jubilant with the news that the Alpini Division trapped in the Pindus had surrendered to a man. The Greeks had taken five thousand prisoners. People said to one another: 'Even Musso can't make the I-ties fight.' The Greeks, who had fought but imagined the fight was hopeless, now began to see the enemy as a pantomime giant that collapses when the hero strikes a blow.

On top of all this excitement, British airmen began to arrive at Tatoi and Eleusis and appeared in the streets just when the Greeks were buoyant with triumph and hope.

Guy and Harriet, invited to Zonar's by Alan, saw the young Englishmen, pink-faced, and sheepish, pursued and cheered by admirers in every street. Walking up to the café, they met a crowd running down the road with a bearded English pilot on their shoulders. As he was carried towards Hermes Street, the Greeks shouted the evzone challenge of 'Aera! Aera!' and the pilot, his arms in the air, shouted back: 'Yo-ho-ho and a bottle of rum.'

A woman on the pavement told everyone that that was the very pilot who had shot down an Italian bomber over the Piraeus. The statement was accepted as fact and there was applause among the Greeks seated outside Zonar's. When the Pringles joined Alan, a man nearby, hearing them speak English, asked: 'What is the "yo-ho-ho and a bottle of rum"?'

'It is an old English battle-cry,' Alan replied and as his words were repeated around, the applause renewed itself.

The pilot was now out of sight, but before enthusiasm could die down, a lorry-load of Greek soldiers stopped on the corner. The men were perched on bales of blankets and heavy clothing donated by the Athenians who were giving all they could give to the troops now fighting in rain and sleet. At the sight of the lorry, people went out to seize the soldiers by their hands. Harriet, carried away by the ferment, lifted Alan's glass and ran with it to the road, where she held it up to the men. One of them, smiling, took it and put it to his lips, but before he could drink, the lorry drove off taking both man and glass.

Harriet said: 'I'm sorry.'

'You could have done nothing more fitting,' Alan assured her. 'The Greeks love gestures of that sort,' and added: 'As this is our first meeting since the ship sailed, let's drink to the fact you've stayed in spite of everything. And, I think, wisely. It's my belief we'll see the weak overcome the strong, the victims overcome the despoilers.'

They drank and Harriet said: 'Now, I suppose, Dubedat really is in charge?'

'No,' said Alan. 'There was an interesting little incident at the party. With everyone watching, Gracey required Dubedat to return the letter that appointed him Acting-Director, having decided the School should close until a new Director be appointed.'

'Still, Dubedat might be appointed Director.'

'He might. Who can say? And here's another contender for the title. Guy said he would like to meet him again.'

Ben Phipps, crossing University Street, had lost his cheerful air but, seeing Alan, he waved and hurried to the table. He looked over the company with an alert gaiety, but the disguise was carelessly assumed and the man himself seemed to be a long way behind his manner.

He said: ''Fraid I can't stay long. I'm dining at Phaleron and I've had trouble with the car. Had to leave it at Psychico.'

'I suppose you'll have time for a drink,' Alan said with an ironical sharpness that caused Phipps to try to connect with his genial mask. 'Hey,' he said, 'don't get shirty. I'm none too bright. I've still got a bit of a hangover as a result of the great Farewell.'

The two men were talking about Cookson's party when Mrs Brett passed on her way into the café with her friend Miss Jay. She stopped to say she had just moved from the hotel.

'I've a flat of my own now. I'll be giving parties, you wait and see! Splendid parties. You'll come, won't you?' she demanded of Alan, then jerked her head round to the Pringles: 'And you two?' She ignored Ben Phipps, who gazed over her head as though she were unknown to him. When she had finished describing the wonders of the new flat, she gave him a venomous glance and said: 'So we've got rid of Gracey! I hear there were great rejoicings down at Phaleron! Obviously I wasn't the only one glad to see the back of him.'

Taking this to himself, Phipps now turned to Miss Jay and asked smoothly: 'How did you enjoy the Major's party? I saw you having a good tuck-in at the buffet.'

For answer, Miss Jay and her white spinnaker swept ahead into the café, but Mrs Brett stood her ground and, stimulated by the presence of an enemy, talked with more than her usual excitement. 'What about Lord Pinkrose?' she asked. 'I hope he didn't go?'

Alan, standing unsteadily on his gouty foot, smiled in

pain and embarrassment. 'No, he didn't go. He was a doubtful starter right up to the last, then he decided to stay in Athens. I think the news from the front was a deciding factor.'

'Good for him.' Mrs Brett spoke as though Pinkrose had shown some unusual courage in staying. 'I'm told he's in the running for the Directorship, and I hope he gets it. A scholar and a gentleman, that's what's needed here. There aren't many of them. It'll be a nice change to get one.'

She went at last and as the other men sat down, Phipps sank as though winded into his chair. His voice had grown weak. 'I didn't know Pinkrose was a candidate?'

'He is, indeed.'

'A *likely* candidate?'

'Who knows? But he certainly courted Gracey. I was always seeing him slipping into the room with little gifts: a bottle of sherry, chocolates, a few flowers . . .'

'Good heavens,' said Harriet.

Alan laughed. 'I shall never forget the sight of Pinkrose, smirking like a lover, with two tuberoses in his hand.'

Ben Phipps did not laugh, but looked at his watch.

Alan said: 'I really asked you along because Pringle here would like to meet some of your young Greek friends: the left-wing group.'

'Oh?' Ben Phipps did not look at Guy. His black eye-dots dodged about behind his glasses as he said, with a glance at Alan: 'I don't see much of them nowadays.'

Eager for information, Guy asked: 'I suppose they're mostly students?'

'Mostly, yes,' Phipps said. 'The older chaps'll be in the army now.' There was a pause while Guy looked expectant and Phipps, forced to make some concession, lifted a brow at Alan. He said: 'You could take him to Aleko's. They're always there. Introduce him to Spiro, the fellow behind the bar; he'll put him in touch.'

'I could, I suppose,' Alan reluctantly agreed.

Phipps looked at Guy for the first time and said by way

of explanation: 'I haven't been there for some time,' then seeing a bus draw up, he jumped to his feet saying: 'My bus. Goodbye for now,' and hastened to catch it.

Looking after him, Alan said: 'The Major usually sends his Delahaye in for favoured friends. I think poor Ben has reason to be nervous. And he seems to be shuffling off his left-wing affiliations.'

Turning on Guy, Harriet said suddenly: 'Why shouldn't you be Director?'

He looked at her in astonishment, then laughed as though she had made a joke.

'Well, why not? You're the only member of the Organization left in Athens. Pinkrose is a Cambridge don. He has no knowledge of Organization work.'

'Darling, it's out of the question.' Guy spoke firmly, hoping to crush the suggestion at its inception.

'But why?'

He explained impatiently: 'I have not had the experience to be a Director. I was appointed as a junior lecturer. If I can get a lectureship here, I'll be doing very well.'

'You've had more experience than Phipps or Dubedat.'

'If either were appointed – and I'm pretty sure neither will be – it would be a piece of disgraceful log-rolling. I'm having no part in it. I'm certainly not using this situation to get more than my due.' Turning away from her, Guy spoke to Alan: 'I'd like to go to that place Phipps mentioned.'

'Aleko's? We might go later, but . . .' Alan looked for the waiter.

Twilight was falling; a cold wind had sprung up and people were leaving the outdoor tables. Alan said: 'I was hoping you'd take supper with me?' When Harriet smiled her agreement, he asked: 'Is there any place you would like to go?'

'Could we go to the Russian Club?'

Alan laughed. This, apparently, was a modest request and he said: 'I'm sure we can. It's called a club but no one is ever turned away.'

The club, a single room, had been decorated early in the

'twenties and never redecorated. As they entered, Alan said: 'We might see Yakimov,' and they saw him at once, seated at a small table, a plate of pancakes in front of him.

He lifted an eye and murmured affectionately: 'Dear girl! Dear boys! Lovely to see you,' but he did not really want to see them. While they stood beside him, he spread red caviare between the pancakes then gazed at the great sandwich with an absorbed and dedicated smile before pouring over it a jugful of sour cream.

'You're doing yourself proud,' Alan said.

'A little celebration!' Yakimov explained. 'Sold m'car, m'dear old Hispano-Suiza. German officer bought it in Bucharest. Thought I'd never get the money, but m'old friend Dobson brought me down a bundle of notes. Your Yak's in funds, for once. Small funds, of course. Just a bit of Ready. Have to make it last a long time.' He waited for them to move on. In funds, he had no need of friends. When he could buy his own food, he ate well and ate alone.

Alan and the Pringles sat in a bay window, looking out at the Acropolis fading into the last shadowy purple of twilight. They, too, had pancakes with red caviare and cream, and Harriet said: 'Delicious.'

Guy was tolerant of the Russian Club. He was also tolerant of Alan Frewen. He could accept the fact that some of his friends were what he called 'a-political' just as some might be colour-blind. He would not blame Alan for his disability, but his slightly distracted manner made it clear that his mind was elsewhere. Harriet knew he was simply marking time until he could get to Aleko's and meet those who thought as he did, but Alan had forgotten Aleko's. Having invited them here, he was relaxed happily in his chair and wanted to make much of the meal. He looked as though he were settled there for the evening.

Guy, on edge to be gone, took it all patiently. Harriet took it with pleasure. Something about the place stirred an old, buried dream of security, a dream she had despised when she went to earn her living with the other unconventional young in London. Then she would have repudiated with derision the idea of an orderly married life. She married for adventure.

In Bucharest once she had been amused when Yakimov said: 'We're in a nice little backwater here. We should get through the war here very comfortably,' for she and Guy had set out expecting danger and not unprepared to die. Now after the perturbed months, the subterfuges and the long uncertainty, she knew she would be thankful to find a refuge anywhere. But the uncertainty was not over yet.

She said: '*Are* the Italians going to break through?'

'Why?' Alan laughed. 'Do you want them to break through?'

'No, but if we're going to spend the winter here, we'll have to get some heavy clothing. I left all mine in Bucharest and Guy brought nothing but books.'

'You'll certainly need a coat of some sort.'

Guy said: 'Harriet can get a coat if she wants one, but I never feel the cold.'

'*And*,' said Harriet, 'we'll have to find somewhere to live.'

'Nonsense,' Guy said: 'The hotel's cheap and convenient.' He would not waste time discussing clothes and homes; the important thing was to get the meal over. As Alan lifted the menu again, he said: 'I don't want anything more. If we're going to Aleko's, I think we ought to go.'

Still resistant, Alan looked at Harriet: 'How would you like some baklava? I'm sure you would. I must say, I'd like some myself.'

Guy smiled while they ate their baklava, but Harriet, aware of his hidden longing to be gone, could not enjoy it. When Alan suggested coffee, she said: 'Perhaps we ought to go. It's getting late.'

'Oh, very well.' Alan eased himself up, groaning, and as he balanced on his feet, he gave a slow, dejected salute to the sideboard on which the coffee cona stood. Seeing the disappointment beneath the humour, Harriet, who had felt the need to indulge Guy, now felt resentful of his impatience to be elsewhere. She decided she would not go to Aleko's. Bored by politics, she was becoming less willing to accept Guy's chosen companions in order to gain Guy's company.

Yakimov had also finished supper. Lounging in an old basket-chair, over which he had spread his sable-lined great-coat, he was sipping a glass of Kümmel.

'Whither away?' he asked, more alive to their departure than he had been to their arrival.

Alan said: 'We're going to Aleko's.'

'Indeed, dear boy! And where is that?'

'Behind Omonia Square. A little café, patronized by progressives. Like to come?'

'Think not. Not quite *simpatico*. Not quite the place for your poor old Yak.'

They had to walk to Constitution Square in search of a taxi and, as he limped along, Alan suggested more than once that Aleko's might be left for another night. Guy would not hear of it. Seeing a taxi pass the top of the square, he pursued and caught it and brought it back.

Giving him no time to over-persuade her, Harriet now said: 'I won't come. I'm going back to the hotel to bed.'

'Just as you like. I won't be late.' Guy, bouncing to be off, caught Alan's arm and pulled him into the taxi before he, too, could excuse himself; then, slamming the door shut, he shouted: 'Aleko's. Omonia Square.'

Watching the taxi drive off, Harriet marvelled at Guy's vigour and determination in the pursuit of his political inter-ests. Why could he not bring as much to the furtherance of his own career. He was eager – too eager, she sometimes thought – to give, to assist, to sympathize, to work for others, but he had little ambition for himself.

When she first met him, she had imagined he needed noth-ing but opportunity; now she began to suspect he did not want opportunity. He did not want to be drawn into rivalry. He wanted amusement. He also wanted his own way, and, to get it, could be as selfish as the next man. But he was always justified. Yes, he was always justified. If he had no other justification, he could always fall back on some morality of his own.

She walked despondently back to the hotel, beginning to fear that he was a man who in the end would achieve little. He would simply waste himself.

PART TWO

The Victors

9

One evening, in the steel-blue chill of the November twilight, the church bells began to ring. They had been silent for nearly a month. No bell in Greece would sound while one single foreign invader remained on Greek soil. Now the whole of Athens was vibrant with bells. People came running into the streets, crying aloud in their joy, and when Harriet went out to the landing, she heard the chambermaids shouting to one another from floor to floor.

The Italians had been driven back. The Greeks had crossed the Albanian frontier. Greek guns were trained on the Albanian town of Koritza and Greek shells were falling in the streets. All that had happened, but the bells had not rung. What could have caused them to ring now?

Harriet threw up the landing window and looked out in search of an answer. One of the chambermaids, seeing her there, shouted to her in Greek. When Harriet shook her head to show she did not understand, the girl lifted a hand and slapped it down on the window-sill: 'Koritza,' she shouted. 'Koritza.'

So Koritza had fallen. It was a victory. The first Greek victory of the war. As Harriet laughed and clapped her hands, the girl caught her about the waist and swung her round in a near hysteria of delight.

Outside it was almost dark but the black-out was forgotten. The Italians were much too busy now to take advantage of a few lighted windows. Someone began speaking on the wireless. The voice, rapid, emotional, pitched in triumph, began coming from all the lighted windows and doorways, and people in the streets cheered whenever the word 'Koritza' was spoken. Another voice came very loud from the square, speaking over an uproar of shouting, music, applause, with the bells pealing above it all. Harriet could not bear to stay in, but was afraid to go out for fear that Guy would return for her.

The winter was setting in. There were still bright days, but mostly the sky was white with cold and a wind, high, sharp and gritty, swept the dust along the pavements. The night before it had poured with rain. When Harriet went to the gardens she saw the palm fronds blown from side to side like shocks of hair. The paths, that a week before had been warm and quiet, were now draughty channels, so cold that she realized if she did not get a coat, she would soon have to stay indoors.

Having left Guy with his books, contemplating a lecture on Ben Jonson, she hurried back to get him out to the shops and found him gone. He had left no message. She knew he had gone to Aleko's.

Guy had taken her there once but the visit had depressed her. She liked the Greek boys but was shy with them – being so constituted she could cope with only one or two people at a time; but Guy, she saw, was having the time of his life. He was an adolescent among adolescents, and they were all elevated by the belief that, together, they would reform the world. She was made uneasy by their faith in certain political leaders, their condemnation of others, the atmosphere of conspiracy and her own guilty self-doubt. She was an individual and as such had no hope of reforming the world. The stories that inspired them – stories of injustice and misery – merely roused in her a sense of personal failure.

'But you must sacrifice your individuality,' Guy told her.

'It's nothing but egoism. You must unite with other right-thinking, self-abnegating people – then you can achieve anything.'

The idea filled her with gloom.

Guy, who was learning demotic Greek, could already discuss abstract ideas with the students in their own language. He amazed them.

One of the boys said to Harriet: 'He is wonderful – so warm, cordial and un-English! We have elected him an honorary Greek.' As an honorary Greek, admired and made much of, Guy was at Aleko's all the time.

Harriet, out of it and a little jealous, refused to go to the café again. Guy told her she was 'a-political'. Alan Frewen had been similarly condemned. He was, Guy said, the sort of man who thinks the best government is the one that causes him least inconvenience. So much for Alan; but Alan, unaware that his epitaph had been spoken, continued to invite them as though he saw himself the friend of both.

When the telephone rang in the bedroom, it was Alan, calling from his office: 'I've heard that Athens is *en fête*. No night for cold mutton at the Academy. How about coming to Babayannis'? If there's anything to celebrate, that's where everyone goes.'

'I'm worried about Guy,' Harriet said. 'I think he must be at Aleko's.'

'I'll call with a taxi. We'll roust out the old bolshie on the way.'

When she joined Alan in the taxi, he told the driver to go through the Plaka. 'I want you to see something,' he said to Harriet. They turned into the square where the loudspeaker was singing out: 'Anathema, anathema . . .' The curse, of course, was on those who said that love is sweet: 'I've tried it,' said the song. 'And found it poison.' But the curse was also on those who had imagined Greece was there for the taking. The Italians had tried it and they, too, had found it poison.

As they went through the narrow Plaka streets, the

Parthenon appeared. It was flood-lit, a temple of white fire hanging upon the blackness of the sky.

Harriet, catching her breath, said: 'I've never seen anything more beautiful.'

'Is there anything more beautiful to be seen?' Alan asked.

In the Plaka Square, where they had sat during the raid, the café had pulled aside its black-out curtains. The light, streaming greenish pale through the bleared window, lit the men dancing in the road.

'It's the *Zebeikiko*,' Harriet cried, wildly exhilarated by all the rejoicings.

Alan, amused that she had remembered the name, told the taximan to stop and they watched the dancers, arms about one another's shoulders, moving through the light, beneath the pepper trees. The music changed. A man standing on a chair against the window took a leap into the middle of the road. He shouted. The others shouted back. Someone threw him a handkerchief and he stood poised, holding the handkerchief by one corner at arm's length. Another man ran out to take the opposite corner. Both men were grey-haired, with the dark, lined faces of out-door labourers, but they danced like youths.

The city was intoxicated. In the narrow streets the taxi crawled through a mass of moving shadows. There were mouth-organs and accordions; and between great outbursts of laughter people sang popular songs to which they fitted new words about the behaviour of Mussolini and his ridiculous army.

When they reached Aleko's, Harriet sent Alan in, saying: 'If we both go, Guy will only persuade us to stay.'

Alan stayed inside for several minutes, then came out and said with a shrug: 'He says he'll join us at Babayannis'.'

Bitterly disappointed, Harriet said: 'But I want him to come with us. I want him to see everything. I want him to enjoy it, too.'

Alan climbed with a sigh back into the taxi. 'You must accept him as he is,' he said. 'After all, his virtues far outweigh his faults.'

At the taverna called Babayannis', the curtains had been looped back and the smell of cooking came out like a welcome. The entrance light had been dimmed but there was enough to show the big stone-flagged hallway where there was a range on which the food was displayed in copper pots. The chef in attendance knew Alan. He spoke in English and said he had once worked in Soho. He was sad there was so little to offer the English guests but, as was fitting, the best of the meat went to the fighting-men and restaurants had to take what they could get.

Looking down into the brown cream of the moussaka, the red-brown stews with pimentos, tomatoes, aubergines and little white onions, Harriet said: 'Don't worry. This is good enough for me.'

The inner room was crowded. The lights were not very bright but the whole taverna seemed a-dazzle with vivacious life. Almost as soon as Alan and Harriet were seated, Costa, the singer, came out to sing. He was laughing as he appeared and went on laughing as though he could not repress his high spirits. At once, responding to his gaiety, the audience began a frantic clapping and shouting, demanding songs they had not heard since the invasion began. In the past, the songs had been sad, telling of the need to fight and die, of lovers separated and loved ones who would not return. But all that, they seemed to think, was over and done with. Now they need do nothing but rejoice.

In the midst of this uproar, Costa stood laughing, turning from side to side, his teeth brilliant in his long, dark, folded face; then he held up a hand and the noise died out. People sat intently silent, scarcely breathing for fear of missing a word.

He said: 'The invaders have fled. But there are still Italians on our soil; a great many Italians, several thousand. However, they are all prisoners.'

In the furore that followed, people wept with joy and leapt up, laughing while the tears streamed down their cheeks. Costa asked: 'What shall I sing?' and sang 'Yalo, yalo' and 'Down by the seaside' and every other song for which they asked. There could be no doubt of it: the mourning days were over and people were free to live again.

Harriet murmured several times: 'If only Guy were here!'

Alan's face crumpled into its tragic smile: 'Don't worry,' he said. 'Costa will sing again later.'

When the singer retired, people who had waited at the entrance began to move in to their tables. Among them Harriet saw Dobson who had been Cultural Attaché in Bucharest and was now in Athens. She did not share Guy's faith in Dobson's essential good-nature but as soon as he caught sight of her, he captivated her at once.

He seized her shoulder with affectionate familiarity: 'What fun!' he said. 'We're all here together. How naughty, you two, choosing Greece instead of the heat, dirt, flies, disease and all the other delights of the Middle East! But who cares? Not the London office, I'm sure.' He rubbed his hand happily over his baby-soft puffs of hair and rocked his soft, plump body to and fro. 'You're well out of Bucharest. Not much "Paris-of-the-East" these days. *And* what do you think has happened on top of everything else? The most terrible earthquake. You know that block you lived in, the Blocul Cazacul? It collapsed in a heap. Went down like a dropped towel with all the tenants buried beneath it.'

Harriet stared at him, shocked by this resolution of their year in Bucharest, then said: 'I hope our landlord went down with it.'

Dobson opened his blue baby eyes and laughed as though she had been extremely witty. 'I expect he did. I expect he did,' he said in delight as he moved off.

Harriet laughed too. Bucharest had become a shadow and its devastation had little reality for her, but as she put the past back where it belonged, she suddenly saw Sasha dead among the ruins. For a second she caught his exact image, then it was gone. Sasha, too, had become a shadow. As she searched for his face in her mind, she found herself looking into another face. A young man was watching her. When their eyes met, he turned his head away. His action was self-conscious. He looked young enough to be a schoolboy but he was wearing the uniform of an English second-lieutenant. She noticed that the men with whom he sat were Cookson, Archie Callard and Ben Phipps.

'Who is the English officer at Cookson's table?' she whispered to Alan.

'English officer? Oh yes, Charles Warden. He's just come here from Crete.'

'But I thought the Greeks wouldn't have British troops on the mainland?'

'He's in the Military Attaché's office. You know we're going to have a Military Mission? Well, I think he's being groomed to act as liaison officer.'

Harriet observed the young officer for a moment and said: 'He's very good-looking.'

'Is he?' Alan gave him a wry, dismissive glance and said: 'Yes, I suppose he is.'

Sasha had not been good-looking, but he had had a gentle face like that of a tamed and sensitive animal. There was nothing gentle about Charles Warden. He had been caught looking at her once and would not be caught again. He looked away from her and his profile, raised with something like arrogance, suggested a difficult and dangerous nature. Alan had shown that he did not like Warden, and he was probably right.

'Not a pleasant young man,' she thought.

When they were served with wine, Harriet caught Dobson's smiling eye and said to Alan: 'Do you think we might move to the Academy? Perhaps Dobson could put in a word for us.'

'You'd hate the place,' Alan said. 'It's like a dreadful girls' school. That bossy red-headed virgin Dunne won't even let poor old Diocletian sleep on the chairs.'

Sitting among the hilarious Greeks, Harriet did not want to hear about Miss Dunne, but Alan had started a long story about Miss Dunne's taking all the hot water for a bath then blaming him when he used what remained because she wanted to wash her stockings.

Harriet laughed but Alan did not laugh. She could see how intolerable it was for him, after his year of solitary freedom, to live a sort of conventional life beneath a female tyrant, but his complaints did not discourage her. She remembered Gracey's spacious, shabby room and could imagine their days there, planned, coherent and beautiful. She had had enough of disorder and had seen that in war there was anxiety instead of expectation, exhaustion instead of profit, and one burnt one's emotions to extract from life nothing but the waste products: insecurity and fear.

She said: 'For a while, I'd love to live in an ordered community. You can have too much of confusion. In no time, you begin to think that war is real and life is not.'

'Or that war is life?'

She nodded. 'I couldn't believe in the peace-time society here. It was almost a relief when the air-raid siren sounded. I felt at once that I knew my way around.'

Alan laughed and some minutes later asked her: 'Would you take a job, if there was one?'

'I certainly would.'

'We'll have to expand when the Mission arrives. Nothing definite yet, but I may be able to offer you something. We'll see. Ah!' On a rising note of satisfaction Alan added: 'Here's our man at last.'

Guy, making his way round the restaurant, was not alone. He was talking boisterously and his voice told Harriet that he had had more than enough to drink. He was followed by a train of young men in air-force uniform, among them the bearded pilot whom they had seen carried shoulder high past Zonar's.

The procession arrested the whole room. Even Cookson's party paused to gaze. Guy, leading his prize in, waved to Dobson and Dobson, not over-sober himself, stood up and embraced Guy fervently.

'Welcome,' said Alan. 'Welcome.'

Guy's introductions were wordy but vague, for he had found the airmen wandering aimlessly through the narrow lane of the Plaka and did not know what they were called.

The waiter, flustered and important because the British aircrew had come to his table, seized chairs wherever he could find them and seated the men down with a proprietary firmness. He insisted that the pilot sit on one side of Harriet and the rear-gunner on the other. As this was being arranged, she glanced over at Charles Warden and found him watching her. He gave her a smile of quizzical inquiry, but now it was her turn to look away, and with an expression that told him she had enough young men and could manage very well without him.

She wanted to know what the pilot was called.

'Surprise,' he said. Surprise what? Nothing – just Surprise. But he must have another name? He shook his head, smiling. If he had, he had forgotten it.

'Why are you called Surprise?'

He laughed, not telling. Sprawled in his chair, his eyes half-closed in sleepy amusement, he treated her questions as a joke. He seemed not to know the answer to anything. He simply laughed.

Harriet turned to the rear-gunner, an older man, who said he was called Zipper Cohen. She asked: 'Tell me why he's called Surprise.'

Cohen said: 'When the Group Captain saw him, he was so surprised he fell off his chair.'

'Why?'

'Because he was wearing a beard.'

'They're not worn in the air force, are they? How can he get away with it?'

'He can get away with anything.'

The navigator, Chew Buckle, was a small, thin, sharp-nosed boy who, in normal times, would probably be morose and unsociable. He still had nothing to say, but he laughed without ceasing.

Guy was drunk enough but the airmen were more drunk

and evaded any sort of serious topic as a blind man evades obstacles. Only Zipper Cohen was ready to talk. He took out a cigarette-case, opened it and, showing Harriet a photograph tucked into the lid, watched her keenly as she looked at the face of a young woman holding a child.

'My wife and little girl,' he said. He seemed the only one whose feet were on earth and when Harriet handed back the cigarette-case, he sat staring at the picture which attached him to the real world. But this incident did not last long. In a moment he shut the case, put it away and began asking what was wrong with the girls in this place. Harriet was the only girl who had given him a smile since he got here.

'The Greek girls won't look at us,' he complained.

'It's their way of being loyal to their men at the front.'

Zipper gave a howl of laughter. 'I hope my old woman's being as loyal as that.'

Alan, drawn into the rantipole merriment of the young men, tried to talk to Chew Buckle who sat beside him. Why were they stationed so far behind the lines? he asked.

Chew Buckle giggled. He was a man used by events but not involved with them. When asked a direct question, he knew something was expected of him, but could scarcely tell what.

The war had plucked him out of his own nature but given him nothing to take its place. He giggled and shook his head and giggled.

Zipper explained that the Greeks, fearful of provoking the Axis, kept them well behind the lines with some idea that the Germans would not notice them. 'We just about managed to get to Albania and back. When we landed last night, there wasn't a pint in the tank.'

'Suppose you're forced down?' asked Alan.

Zipper laughed. 'It's a friendly country. Not like Hellfire Pass.'

The mention of Hellfire renewed the laughter and Chew Buckle, speaking in a deep, harsh voice, said: 'They cut y'r bollocks off there.' The others collapsed.

It was some time before the three civilians could discover that, if the Arabs of Hellfire Pass caught a pilot, they held him to ransom and, as proof of his existence, sent his expendable parts to Bomber Command.

When Costa came out to sing again, the enjoyment had a second focal point, and Costa, acknowledging applause, waved at the aircrew to show they were as much part of the entertainment as he was. Glasses of wine were sent over to the young men and, as a special honour, apples were sliced and put into the glasses. More bottles were ordered by Guy and Alan so these compliments could be repaid, and glasses passed to and fro, and were sent to Costa, then to the proprietor and the waiters, and soon the tables all around were covered with glasses, some empty, some half full and some waiting to be drunk. The restaurant swayed with drink, and the air quivered with admiration, affection and the triumph of the day.

Suddenly one of the waiters, a middle-aged man as thin as a whippet, ran into the middle of the floor, and began to dance, and the audience clapped in time for him. Cookson and his friends watched, not clapping but indulgently approving.

Guy was in a jubilant state. He suffered from his own frustrated energy and the challenge of other men's activity, but now it seemed nothing could daunt him. A sort of electricity went out from him and infected the neighbouring tables, and even the airmen began to talk. They told, in terms of riotous humour, how they were sent out every morning over Valona at exactly the same time. It was intended as a double bluff. The Italians were expected to think such tactics impossible and so be unprepared.

'But the bastards are expecting us every time,' shouted Zipper Cohen, and Surprise, shaking in his chair, said: 'Thank God for the Greek air force. They'll fly anything. They go up on tea-trays tied with string.'

The wine was as much for Guy as for the air-crew. Among the Greeks he was an honorary Greek, among the fighting-men, he was an honorary fighting man. Aware that she could not, for the life of her, attract so much enthusiasm, Harriet was moved with pride in him.

Now there were six men out dancing and the clapping had settled into a rhythmic accompaniment that filled the room. Unfortunately, while things were at their height, Major Cookson felt he must take his party away. He said to those around that it was all very pleasurable but, alas, he had invited friends to drop in after dinner and must be at Phaleron to greet them. Those with him rose, but not very willingly. Harriet felt Charles Warden look at her as he went, but she kept her eyes on Zipper Cohen.

The departure of Cookson brought the dancing to a stop. In the silence that came down, Chew Buckle threw back his head and sang to the tune of 'Clementine':

'In a Blenheim, o'er Valona,
Every morning, just at nine;
Same old crew and same old aircraft,
Same old target, same old time.
"Bomb the runway," says Group Captain,
"And make every one a hit."
If you do, you'll go to heaven;
If you don't, you're in the . . . whatd'ycallit . . . ?'

Amidst the applause, Buckle climbed slowly and deliberately up on his chair, then to the table where he bowed on every side before sinking down, as slowly as he had risen, and going to sleep among the bottles.

Alan said it was time to get the boys back to Tatoi. He went out to order a taxi while Guy roused Chew Buckle and got them moving. As they left the room, Dobson called to the Pringles:

'Hey, you two! There's a special film show. You've got to come. It's in aid of the Greek war effort. After the show, we're holding a reception.'

Guy looked at Harriet and said: 'Would you like to go?'

'I'd love to go,' she said.

'Then you shall.' In elated mood, he flung an arm round her shoulder and said: 'You know if you want to go, you've only got to say so. Whatever you want to do, you've only got to let me know. You know that, don't you?' He spoke so convincingly, that Harriet could only reply: 'Darling, yes, of course.'

10

Every day now there was something to celebrate. There might not be a decisive victory like Koritza, but there was always an advance and always stories of Greek prowess and heroism. People queued to give food and clothing to the men who, having quelled the invaders, were now driving them into the sea.

The snow was falling in the Pindus mountains. As it blocked the passes and disguised the hazards of the wild, roadless regions, the retreating Italians abandoned their guns and heavy armaments. It was said the mere sight of an unarmed Greek would put a whole Italian division to flight. Posters showed the Greeks in pursuit, with nothing to abandon, leaping like chamois from crag to crag. The Italian radio called them savages who not only pitched their enemies over precipices but threw after them the splendid equipment which the Italian people had bought at such sacrifice to themselves.

While it snowed in Albania, it rained in Athens. The wind blew cold. The houses were unheated. People went to cafés and crowding for warmth behind the black-out curtains, told one another if it were not victory by Christmas, it would be victory by spring.

Guy could be idle no more. He went to Aleko's and announced his intention of starting an English class. Would any student lend a living-room in his house? The boys, made exuberant by his exuberance, all offered living-rooms.

When Guy turned up for the first class, expecting perhaps a dozen pupils, he found the room packed to the door with young people who acclaimed him not merely as a teacher but as a representative of Britain. Some of them had attended the

School before it closed, but the majority knew only a little English. They felt if they were too young to fight, they could at least learn the language of their great ally. Guy, greatly stimulated by their response, began to plan a course of study. He would divide up the students into grades and hold a class every night. But where? The householder, a widow, treating the invasion of her living-room as a joke, said: 'Tonight, yes. Very good. Other nights, some other place. Yes?' The classes were moved from house to house, but no room was large enough and everyone hoped that soon some permanent meeting-place would be found.

Guy, pressed by obligations, was now in the condition he most enjoyed. He wanted to do more and more. One night, coming back to the hotel-room, he told Harriet that the students were eager to do a Shakespeare play. He was thinking of producing *Othello* or *Macbeth*.

'But then I'll never see you at all,' Harriet said in dismay.

'Darling, I have to work. You wouldn't have me hanging around doing nothing while other men are fighting?'

'No, but I can't spend my life doing nothing, either; and certainly not in this miserable little room.'

'You can always go to a café.'

'Alone?'

'Alan would be glad to have you with him.' Guy had relegated Alan to the position of Harriet's friend.

'I don't always want to be with Alan. Besides, people talk.'

'Good heavens, what does that matter?'

'I'm sure if you spoke to Dobson, he could get us into the Academy. We might even have Gracey's room.'

Eventually persuaded, Guy approached Dobson, but his approach was not successful. Dobson explained – 'quite nicely', Guy said – that the rooms had to be kept in case Foreign Office employees turned up.

'Fact is,' Dobson had said: 'Gracey had no right to be there. Don't know how he worked it, but I suspect the Major's influence. Anyway, if he'd stayed on, he'd've been told to find "alternative accommo", so you can see it's a case of "no can do".'

'And that's that,' Guy said to Harriet, glad that his onerous task was over.

Harriet had to accept it: the Academy was not for them. She said: 'At least he's sent us tickets for the film-show.'

'What film-show?'

'The one he told us about. A new English film has been flown out. It'll be the first new film we've seen since Paris fell.' She handed him the tickets that would admit them to a showing of a film called *Pygmalion*. Guy handed them back.

'Sorry. Can't manage it. That's the evening I promised to address a gathering of students on the state of left-wing politics in England.'

'But you promised to take me. You said when we were at Babayannis' that we would go.'

'I'm afraid I forgot. Anyway, the meeting's much more important. I can't let the students down.'

'But you can let me down?'

'Don't be silly. What does a film-show matter?'

'But I've been looking forward to it. I haven't seen a new English film for months.'

'You can get someone else to take you. Give my ticket to Alan.'

'He doesn't need your ticket. He's going with Greek friends.'

'Then ask Dobson to take you.'

'I wouldn't dream of asking Dobson to take me.'

'It's only a cinema. Why not go by yourself?'

'There's a reception as well; and I won't go by myself. I should hate it by myself. You ought to understand that. You promised to take me, and I want you to take me. I've been looking forward. So you must ask the students to change the day of the meeting.'

'I can't do that. I can't put them off. It's not possible. If you break an appointment with English people, you can explain. But it's different with foreigners. They would think there was more to it. They wouldn't understand.'

'You expect me to understand?'

'Of course.'

To Guy, the discussion had been light and Harriet's disappointment was of so little moment that he scarcely paused to consider it. To her it was shattering. She could not believe it. She was certain that when Guy had reflected upon it all, he would arrange to change the day of the meeting and, this accomplished, would present the change to her as a token of their importance to each other; but he did nothing of the kind.

The days passed. She began to wonder whether he had given the film-show another thought. He had not; and he was surprised when, at the last minute, she mentioned it again.

'But we have discussed all this,' he said. 'I told you I had to go to the meeting. There was no question of putting it off. If it's a choice of a film-show or a political meeting, naturally the meeting must come first.'

To Harriet it seemed a choice between much more than that. She said: 'You promised to take me.'

'I told you to get someone else to take you.'

'Wherever I go, I have to get someone else to take me. Why? Being married to you is much the same as not being married at all. You ought to understand my feelings. I want you to take me; just to show you understand. You're my husband.'

'My husband!' he echoed her. 'The trouble is, you cling too much to things. You cried your eyes out when that kitten died. You couldn't have made more fuss if it'd been a baby.'

'Well, it wasn't a baby.'

Ignoring this, he went on: '*My* husband! *My* kitten! You promised *me*. What an attitude!' His face shut off in a mask of obstinacy, he began collecting his books together, eager to get away before she spoke again.

She did not try to speak again. Instead, she told herself that the meeting was important to him not because of his political ideals, but because it would accord him what he wanted most: attention. He was simply longing to be on view again. Lecturing or teaching, producing plays or giving advice to students, he was what he most wanted to be – the centre of attention. That meant more to him than she did.

As he made off, his face blank with purpose, she felt angry, but more than that, she felt abandoned. She sat for a long time on the bed, stunned and yet acutely lonely. The mention of the kitten had renewed in her a sense of loss. She had lost the kitten, she had lost Sasha, she had lost faith in Guy. Collapsing suddenly, she lay on the bed and wept helplessly.

She might have asked someone to take her to the reception but to do so, she felt, would be a public admission that Guy had failed her. She imagined herself being taken out of charity, an object of pity, a creature wronged and humiliated. If she went alone, it would be the same. Guy, in the past, had laughed at what he called the female 'zenana-complex', no intelligent woman could possibly be restricted by such feelings. Yet something in her upbringing put an absolute check on the possibility of going alone.

It was an evening of full moon. With nothing else to do, she went out, and, drawn to the occasion, made her way up through Kolonaki past the hall where the film was to be shown. She may have hoped that someone she knew would see her and persuade her in; but she walked so quickly and purposefully that anyone who did see her would have supposed she was hurrying to another engagement.

And someone did see her. Charles Warden was standing outside the hall and as she gave a glance, fleet and longing, at the open door, she saw his face white in the white light of the moon. Safely past, hidden by shadow, she looked back. He was watching after her, regretfully; and she went regretfully on.

Energetic in unhappiness, she made her way uphill until she reached the final peak of the town where the old houses, crowded together among trees and shrubs, made a little village on their own. It was here that Alan had had his Athens studio. A path ran away into the rough, open ground of the hilltop. Following it, she found herself in a deserted waste-land, passing further and further out of human existence; the moon her only companion. Hanging oddly near, just above her shoulder, the great white uncommunicating face, blank in a blank grey-azure sky, increased her sense of solitude.

Athens, stretched below, was a map of silver. As she rounded the hill and came in sight of the Piraeus, the air-raid sirens began. At this height their hysterical rise and fall was faint and seemed not to relate to the city that in the blue-white light might have been a toy city, an object of crystal and moonstone.

From habit, she looked for shelter. Ahead there was a hut where refreshments were sold in summer. Standing against it, she watched the bombers coming in from the sea. The guns opened up but the aircraft came on, untouched. One bomber dropped a star of light that hung, incongruous and theatrical, in the moon-hazed distance. Apart from the distant thud-thud of the guns, the whole spectacle appeared to be in dumb-show until an explosion startled the air. A fire sprang up.

All the time the white, unharming city lay like a victim, bound and gagged, unable to strike back. The raid was brief. In a moment the raiders had turned. They flashed in the moon-light and were gone. The fire burnt steadily, the only thing alive among the white toy houses.

The all-clear did not sound and at last, bored and cold, she started to walk again. The path brought her to the top terrace of houses. The releasing blast of the all-clear rose as she made her way down to University Street. After the empty hill-top even Toby Lush, when she met him, seemed a friend. She told him where she had been and he spluttered and guffed and said: 'Crumbs! I wouldn't do that walk alone at night for a lot of money.'

'But surely it's not dangerous?'

'Don't know about that. There're bad types in most cities. I'm told it's not safe to go on the Areopagus after dark.'

'Oh dear!' She was unnerved at having taken a risk from ignorance and, remembering the cinderous hill-brow in the ghastly light, it seemed to her there had been menace everywhere. She went back to the hotel, amazed at having survived the longest and loneliest walk of her life.

I I

The bells rang again for the capture of Muskopolje. They rang
again for Konispolis. And on the first day of December, while
the rain teemed down on Athens, they rang for the great
victory of Pogradets. This battle, that lasted seven days, was
fought in a snowstorm. The old porter, who waited in the
hall with the news, enacted for the Pringles and other foreigners the drama of the encounter. He stumbled about to show
how the Italians had been blinded by snow then, drawing
himself up, eyes fixed, expression stern, he showed how the
Greeks had been granted miraculous penetration of vision by
Our Lady of Tenos.

'Why Our Lady of Tenos?' someone asked.

Because, explained the porter, his wife, who came from
Tenos, had sent their son a Tenos medallion only two days
before the battle began.

Now victory followed victory. When the bells started up,
strangers laughed and shouted to each other: 'What, another
one!' The Athenians danced in the streets. Elderly men danced
like boys and the women on the pavements clapped their
hands. People said the Greeks had taken prisoner half of
Mussolini's army. As for the war materials captured, they
could challenge the world with it.

When someone came into a café and shouted a name that
no one had heard before, there was no need to ask what it
was. It was a victory. In no time it was familiar. Everyone
repeated it: it was the most repeated name in Athens. Then,
overnight, it became yesterday's victory, and another name
took its place.

After Pogrodets, there came the capture of Mt Oztrovitz; then Premeti, Santa Quaranta, Argyrokastro and Delvino. The evzoni captured the heights of Ochrida in a snowstorm. The attack lasted four hours and the Greek women, who had followed their men, climbed barefooted up the mountainside to take them food and ammunition.

For every victory the bells rang. People asked gleefully: 'What now?' The Greeks had captured a little town that no one could find on the map. Then came a halt. The Greeks had advanced along the whole Albanian frontier and, unprepared for such success, they were outdistancing their supply lines. This was a breakthrough on a grand scale. They must treat it seriously.

On the morning when news came of the capture of Santa Quaranta – an important capture for the Greeks needed a port at which to unload supplies – Guy returned early for luncheon. He had heard, quite casually, from a student, that the new Director had been appointed. The School was to reopen. The students, weary of tramping around from one house to another, sent one of their number to tell Guy: 'We have been grateful, sir, but now we must work at the School. There is no longer a room for teaching in any house. Our parents order us to enrol where there is space to learn.'

'And who is the Director?' Harriet asked. 'Not Dubedat?'

'No.'

'Pinkrose?'

'No.'

'So it's Ben Phipps?'

'No.'

'There's no one else.'

'Archie Callard.'

Electrified, Harriet said: 'But this is much better than we expected. We had nothing to gain from Dubedat and Pinkrose, but with Archie Callard, there's no knowing. He might do something for you.'

'Yes.'

They went to the hotel dining-room that nowadays, with food becoming scarce, was no worse than anywhere else. Guy behaved as though nothing singular had happened but there was something distraught in his appearance and he could not keep his mind on the meal.

Harriet said: 'When do you suppose Callard heard?'

'Yesterday, I should think.'

'Then he may still contact you.'

'Oh yes, I'm not worrying.'

'If he doesn't, what will you do?'

'I don't know. I haven't thought.'

'You have every right to contact him. He's now your Director.'

'Yes,' Guy said doubtfully, disturbed by the possibility of having just such a move forced on him. Harriet, observing his timidity when it was a question of fighting his own battle, thought how little they had known each other when they married, hurriedly, under the shadow of war. The shadow, of course, had been there for years; but during the warm, dusty summer days when they first met, it had been the shadow of an avalanche about to drop. Having nowhere else to turn, people turned to each other. Guy had seemed all confidence. Had he grown up under the protection of wealth, he could not have displayed more insouciance, good-humour and generous responsibility towards life. Offering himself, he seemed to offer the protection of human warmth, good sense and reliability. And, in a sense, those qualities were his, but in another sense, he was a complex of unexpected follies, fears and irresolutions.

She said: 'He *must* appoint you Chief Instructor. There's no one else capable of doing the job. Pinkrose or Ben Phipps might have done as Director; but when it comes to teaching, who is there?'

'Dubedat.'

'Don't be ridiculous, darling.'

The only heat in the hotel came from the oil-stove in the restaurant. The tables were set round it and guests were slow to take themselves up to their rooms. The Pringles were still

116

sitting over their little cups of grey, washy coffee when the porter came down with a hand-delivered letter. He gave it to Guy, who, opening it, laughed and said casually: 'It's from Callard. An invitation to tea at Phaleron where he's staying with Cookson. You're to come, too.'

'But this is wonderful, darling.'

'Perhaps. We don't know what he wants.'

'Oh yes, we do. He's got the directorship; now he wants someone to do the work.'

'Come on. I'll buy you some real coffee at the Braziliana.'

In the little bar, that was so small there was nowhere to sit, people stood elbow to elbow drinking the strong, black coffee that was rare enough at the best of times but was now a luxury. Looking between the crowded faces, Harriet saw Ben Phipps. Thrust into a corner beside the door, he stood by himself, staring into the street with an air of bitter dejection. Could the directorship have meant so much to him?

If she had liked him better, she would have pointed him out to Guy and Guy, of course, would have hurried over to console him. As it was, Guy was too short-sighted to see him and she too nervous to give him a second thought.

It was a sepia day. When the bus left them on the front at Phaleron, they saw a yellowish sea indolently spreading its frills of foam like a bored bridge player displaying a useless hand. The shore was as empty as an arctic shore, and almost as cold. The esplanade, stretching into the remote distance, was grey and bare, but there were palms.

'The Mediterranean,' said Harriet.

Guy adjusted his glasses to look at it: 'Not exactly the sea of dreams,' he said, but that afternoon they had something else to think about.

Passing the villas where no one seemed to be at home, he hummed to express confidence in the interview ahead, and walked too quickly. Harriet, trotting beside him, kept up without comment. They hurried to meet the moment when their equivocal position would be resolved at last.

Cookson's villa was easily found. It was the largest of the seaside villas and its name, 'Porphyry Pillars', was written in roman letters. The villa was of white marble. The pillars – mentioned in Baedeker, Alan had said – were not at their best in this light.

Harriet whispered: 'They look like corned beef,' and Guy frowned her to silence.

A butler admitted them to a circular hall where there were more pillars, not porphyry but white marble, and on to an immense drawing-room filled with Corfu furniture and hung with amber satin.

Out of the prevailing glimmer of gold, the Major rose and shifted his rolled handkerchief so he might extend a hand.

'How delightful to meet you again,' he said, though they had scarcely met before. He placed Harriet on an amber satin sofa as in a position of honour and apologized to Guy: 'So sorry Archie isn't here. He had a luncheon appointment in Athens and hasn't got back yet.'

Guy blamed himself for being early, but the Major protested: 'Oh, no, it's Archie who is late. Such a naughty boy! A little fey, I'm afraid. But never mind. For a tiny while I have you to myself, so you must tell me about Bucharest. I was there once and met dozens of princes and princesses; all delightful, needless to say. I hope no harm will come to them. *What* a débâcle! How *do* you account for it?'

Guy talked more readily to Cookson than he had talked to Gracey. As he analysed the Rumanian catastrophe, Cookson gave exclamations of wonder and horror, then insisted on being told how the Pringles managed to make their escape. 'And you,' he asked Harriet with deep concern, 'weren't you most terribly worried by it all? Even, perhaps, a little frightened? And when you left, were you very, *very* sad?'

The Major, looking from Harriet to Guy, from Guy to Harriet, exuded so attentive a sympathy that Harriet was completely won by him. His attitude was that of a courteous and benevolent host welcoming newcomers into the circle of his friends. And how privileged, these friends! She could well understand why, in the social contest, poor Mrs Brett had scarcely made a showing.

But Guy was less easily beguiled and less ready to desert Mrs Brett. Though he responded to the Major – being quite incapable of not responding – it was not his usual whole-hearted response to a show of friendship. Once or twice when there was some noise in the house, he glanced round, hoping for Archie Callard's arrival. The Major, apparently unaware of such moments of inattention, said: 'Do tell me . . .' asking one question and another, doing his best to distract them from their unease. But too much depended on the interview ahead. The atmosphere was amiable but Guy's thoughts wandered and the Major murmured, 'Where *can* Archie be?'

At last the door opened and Callard appeared. Though the light was failing, the Pringles saw from his face that he had forgotten them. He was not alone. Charles Warden was with him.

Harriet and Warden exchanged a startled glance, and Harriet felt her temperature fall. It was as though some trick had been played upon the pair of them.

Callard had dropped his old air of jocular indifference to life and, conscious of responsibility, was sober and constrained. 'How kind of you to come,' he said. 'You do all know each other, don't you?'

Accepting this as introduction, Harriet and Warden bowed distantly to each other and waited to see what would happen next.

The Major, who seemed flustered by Callard's new impor-tance, rose and said:

'Archie dear, I think I'll take Mrs Pringle and Charles into the garden while you have your little talk. There's just light enough to see our way around. Now, don't be long. I'm sure we're all dying for our tea.'

He opened the french windows and led the young people outside. Harriet went with some excitement but, looking back as the door closed, she saw Guy inside, his face creased with strain. Guilty at having gone so willingly, she hurried ahead to join the Major, behaving as though he and she were the only people in the garden. He conducted her round the beds, describing the flowers that would appear after the spring rains, and though there was not much to admire, she exclaimed over everything. Flattered by her vivacious interest, he said: 'You must see it in April: but, of course, I hope you'll come many times before that.'

The lawn was set with citrus trees that stood about in solitary poses like dancers waiting to open a ballet. Harriet kept her back turned to Charles Warden but, pausing to examine some small green lemons, she glanced round in spite of herself and saw him watching her behaviour with an ironical smile. She was gone at once. Catching up with the Major, she defiantly renewed her enthusiasm.

As they rounded the house and came in sight of the sea, the clouds were split by streaks of cherry pink. The sun was setting in a refulgence hidden from human eye. For an instant, the garden was touched with an autumnal glow, then the clouds closed and there was nothing but the wintry twilight.

'Yes,' said the Major regretfully, 'we must go in; but you will come again, won't you? You *really* will? I give a few little parties during the winter, just to help me pass the gloomy weeks. There's always a shortage of pretty girls – I mean, of course, pretty English girls. Plenty of lovely Greeks, and how lovely they can be! Still, English girls are a thing apart: so slender, so pink and white, so *natural*! Do promise you will come?'

Smiling modestly, Harriet promised.

The chandeliers had been lit inside the golden drawing-room. The Major tinkled on the glass, at the same time opening the door and saying: 'May we join you?'

'Yes, of course,' said Callard, as though he could not understand what they were doing out there.

Apparently the talk inside the room had finished some time before. Harriet had entered in high spirits but, meeting Guy's eye, she lost her buoyancy. He gave her a warning glance, then stared down heavily at the floor. Now, she only wanted to leave this treacherous company, but the Major was saying: 'Come along. You've got your business over, so let's have a jolly tea.'

The dining-room was on the other side of the hall. Tea was served on a table with rococo gilt legs and a surface of coloured marbles. The marbles formed a composition of fruits and game entitled in letters of gold: 'The Pleasures of Plenty'. Placed on the centre of the picture was a plate of very small cakes. The Major said:

'Dear me, look at them! As cakes increase in price, they decrease in size. One day, I fear, they'll vanish altogether.'

As though he found these remarks frivolous or vulgar, Archie Callard said: 'Then you won't have to pay for them.'

The Major laughed, knowing himself reproved, and went on in a pleading tone: 'But, Archie, such absurd little cakes! Do look at this one! Who would have the heart to eat it? Really, I'm ashamed, but . . .' He turned to Harriet: 'It's not easy to get any these days, even at the Xenia. Don't you find shopping *terribly* difficult?'

'We live in an hotel,' she said.

'How wise! But not, I hope, at the G.B.? I hear the Military Mission has taken possession of our darling G.B. and all our friends have been turned out. So sad to be turned out of one's suite at a time like this! Dear knows where they've all gone. And no more cocktail parties in that pretty lounge! Not that there have been many since the evacuation ship took the ladies away. Still,' he added quickly: 'We mustn't complain. Others have come in their place.'

'Really!' said Archie Callard, 'you seem to suggest that the ship took the rightful occupants of Athens and left behind nothing but wartime flotsam.'

'Archie, that's quite enough!'

Delighted at having shocked the Major, Callard gave his attention to Charles Warden. He wanted to know *all* about the Mission. What was its function? How many officers were there? What position would Charles himself hold?

Speaking stiffly and briefly, the young man said he knew

nothing. The Mission had only just arrived.

There was, Harriet thought, a hint of self-importance in his tone and she condemned him not only as an unpleasant young man but as one who took himself too seriously.

The telephone rang somewhere in the house. A servant came to say that Mr Callard was wanted.

Archie Callard, tilting his head back with a fretful air, asked who was on the line. When told the British Legation, he said: 'Oh, dear!' The Major sighed as though to say that this was what life was like these days.

When Callard went off, the others waited in silence. Glancing at Charles Warden, Harriet found his gaze fixed on her and she turned her head away. He said to Cookson: 'I'm afraid I must get back to the office.'

'But *you* don't have to go, do you?' the Major smiled on Guy and Harriet. '*Please* stay and have a glass of sherry!'

Before they could reply, Archie Callard returned with a rapid step, his manner dramatically changed. Both his fraudulent gravity and his irony were gone. Now he was not playing a part. With face fixed in the hauteur of rage, he ignored the guests and demanded of Cookson: 'Did you know Bedlington was in Cairo?'

'Bedlington in Cairo? No, no. I didn't.' Bewildered and alarmed, the Major dabbed at his nostrils. 'But what of it? What has happened?'

'You should have known.'

'Perhaps I should, but no one told me. People are too busy to keep me posted and, living down here, I'm a bit out of things. Why are you so annoyed? What's the matter?'

'I'll tell you later.' Callard made off again, slamming the door as he went.

'What can it be?' said the unhappy Major. 'Archie's such a temperamental boy! It's probably something quite trivial.'

The invitation to sherry was not repeated. The Major's anxiety was such he scarcely noticed that the guests left together.

A staff car was waiting outside for Charles Warden and he

offered the Pringles a lift. Heartened by this kindness, Guy rapidly regained his spirits and as they drove up the dark Piraeus road, was voluble about an entertainment which he planned to put on for the airmen at Tatoi. He may only just have thought of it – certainly Harriet had heard nothing about it – but now as he talked, the idea developed and inspired him. The Phaleron interview was forgotten. If he had been depressed, he was depressed no longer; and Harriet marvelled at his powers of recuperation.

If he had been offered nothing, if his future was (as she feared) vacant, he was already filling the vacancy with projects. The entertainment at Tatoi was only one thing. He discussed the possibility of producing *Othello* or *Macbeth*. And why should he not restage *Troilus and Cressida*?

Was there ever any need to pity him! He was never, as she too often was, disabled by disappointment. He simply turned his back on it.

Harriet noticed that Charles Warden laughed with Guy, not at him. Listening to Guy's schemes, he murmured as though Guy and Guy's vitality were things he had seldom, if ever, encountered before. She realized now that his restraint when replying to Callard had shown not self-importance but a disapproval of Callard's insolent wit. She had to admit the young man was by no means as unpleasant as she had wished to believe.

The car stopped outside the main entrance to the Grande Bretagne.

'Let's meet again soon,' said Guy.

'Yes, we must,' Charles Warden agreed.

Walking back to their hotel, Guy could talk of nothing but this new friendship until Harriet broke in: 'Darling, tell me what Callard had to offer.'

'Oh!' Guy did not want any intrusion upon his felicity. In an offhand way, as though the whole matter were of no consequence, he said: 'Not much. In fact, he wasn't able to promise anything.'

'But he must have had some reason for sending for you?'

'He wanted to see me, that's all.'

'Didn't he tell you anything?'

'Well, yes. He told me . . . he felt he ought to tell me personally – which was, after all, very decent of him – that he had been forced to make Dubedat his Chief Instructor. He had no choice. Gracey made him promise.'

'I see.' For some minutes her disappointment was such she could not say anything more.

Guy talked on, doing all he could to justify Callard. Knowing that what he said was a measure of his own disappointment, Harriet listened and grew angry for his sake. She said at the end:

'So Archie Callard was appointed on the understanding that he rewarded Dubedat for Dubedat's services to Gracey?'

'It looks like that. I will say Callard was rather apologetic. He said: "I'm sorry about this. I hope you won't refuse to work under Dubedat?"'

'He expects you to work under Dubedat? He must be mad.'

'He said there would be work, but not immediately. He hopes to fit me in when things get under way. I must say, I rather liked Callard. He's not at all a bad chap.'

'Perhaps he isn't. But here you are, the best English instructor in the place, expected to hang around in the hope that Dubedat will offer you a few hours' teaching. It's monstrous!'

'I came here against orders. I'll have to take any work I can get.'

'What's this about Lord Bedlington being in Cairo? Couldn't you write to him or cable him? You have a London appointment. You've a right to state your case.'

'Perhaps, but what good would it do? Bedlington knows nothing about me. Gracey, Callard and, I suppose, Cookson have all backed Dubedat. There's no one to back me. I'm merely an interloper here. The fact that I was appointed in London doesn't give me a divine right to a plum job. I could make trouble – but if I do that and gain nothing by it, I'm in wrong with the Organization for the rest of my career.' Guy put his arm round Harriet's disconsolate shoulder and squeezed it: 'Don't worry. Dubedat's got the job and good luck to him. We'll work together all right.'

'You *won't* work together. You'll do the work, and Dubedat will throw his weight around.'

Guy's tolerance of the situation annoyed Harriet more than the situation itself. He had achieved education and now, she suspected, his ambition had come to a stop. In his spiritual indolence, he would be the prey of those with more ambition; and he would not worry. It was, after all, easier to be used than to use.

She asked bitterly: 'Will it be like this all our lives?'

'Like what?'

'You doing the work while other people get the importance.'

'For heaven's sake, darling, what do you want? Would you prefer that I became an administrator: a smart Alec battening on other men's talents?'

'Why not, if there's more money in it? Why should you be paid less for your talents than other men are for the lack of them? Why do you encourage such a situation?'

'I don't. It's the nature of things under this social system. When we have a people's government, we'll change all that.'

'I wonder.'

They had reached the hotel. Her hands were clenched and Guy, picking them up and folding them into his own hands, smiled into her small, pale, angry face, saying, as he had said many times before: '"Oh, stand between her and her fighting soul."'

'Someone has to fight,' she said. Repeating a remark she had heard as a child, she added: 'If you don't fight, they'll trample you into the ground.'

Guy laughed at her: 'Who are "they"?'

'People. Life. The world.'

'You don't really believe that?'

She did not reply. She was more hurt for him than he was for himself. She had imagined because he was amiable, he must be fortunate, and now she saw others, neither able nor amiable, put in front of him. She felt cheated but tried to reconcile herself to things. 'I suppose we are lucky to be here; and we're lucky to be together. If you're prepared to work under Dubedat, well, there's no more to be said.'

'I'm prepared to work. It doesn't matter whom I work under. I'm lucky to be employed. My father was unemployed half his life and I saw what it did to him. We've nothing to complain of. Other men are fighting and getting killed for people like us.'

'Yes,' she said and embraced him because he was with her and alive.

An announcement in the English newspaper stated that the School would open under the Directorship of Mr Archibald Callard. Mr Dubedat was to be Chief Instructor and Mr Lush would assist him. But, for some reason, there was a delay.

The students returned to the School and waited about in the library and the lecture-room but Mr Callard, Mr Dubedat and Mr Lush did not appear. The librarian-secretary said they were not in the building. There was no one to enrol students. The offices were locked and remained locked for the next couple of weeks.

12

It was a dull December. The Greek advance had come to a stop. The papers explained that this was a necessary remission: the supply line must be strengthened, supplies brought up and forces rearranged. There was no cause to be downcast. But the victories, the bell-ringing, the dancing, the comradeship of triumph – these things were missing, and the city became limp in anti-climax. Even the spectacle of the Italian prisoners did little to distract people in a hard winter when it was as cold indoors as out and food was disappearing from the shops.

The prisoners were marshalled through the main streets: a straggle of men in tattered uniforms, hatless, heads bent so that the rain could drip from their hair. They were defeated men yet in every batch there were some who seemed untroubled by their plight, or who glanced at the bystanders with furtive and conciliatory smiles, or gave the impression that the whole thing was a farce.

'Where are they going?' people asked, fearful that there would be more mouths to feed, but the prisoners were not to stay in Greece. They were taken to the Piraeus and shipped to camps in the western desert.

No wonder there were some who smiled. They would eat better than the Greeks and a camp in the sun was more comfortable than the Albanian mountains where men bivouacked waist deep in the snow.

At the canteen started for British servicemen, Guy washed dishes and Harriet worked as a waitress. The men were mostly airmen, but a few sappers and members of the R.A.S.C. had arrived. Food and fuel were supplied by the Naafi and the civilians were thankful these winter nights not only for occupation, but for warmth.

The wives of the English diplomats organized the work and agreed among themselves that the food should be for the servicemen and only for them. They were honour bound not to touch a mouthful themselves. In the first throes of unaccustomed hunger, the women fried bacon, sausages, eggs and tomatoes and served men who accepted their plates casually and took it for granted that the civilians ate as much as they did.

One night, Harriet, carrying two fried sausages to a table, nearly burst into tears. A soldier, observing her with an experienced eye, said: 'You look fair clemmed. Don't she look clemmed?' he asked his friends: 'Ev'nt seen no one so clemmed since my old man mowed a grass-pitch for a tanner and lost his sick benefit.'

Harriet laughed, but the men were concerned for her and asked: 'You get your grub here, don't you?'

She explained the rules of the canteen and the first man said: 'That's fair silly. There's lashings more where this comes from. Here,' he pushed his plate at her, 'have a good tuck-in.'

She laughed again and shook her head and made off for fear she might succumb. The rule had been made and no one had the courage to break it, least of all Harriet who was shy among the diplomatic set.

A few nights later the same group of sappers arrived with a parcel which they put into Harriet's arms: 'We won it,' they said. 'It's for you.'

When she opened it in the kitchen, she found a leg of Canterbury lamb. The other women looked at it with some disapproval, and Harriet explained: 'They won it.'

Only Mrs Brett, on duty at the gas-stove, had anything to say: 'And I expect they did,' she said. 'There's always a raffle or a draw or some game of that sort going on in these camps.'

Eyeing the meat, she remarked confidentially to Harriet: 'That's a nice piece of lamb.'

'Yes, but what can I do with it?'

'Not much use to you, is it? Where could you cook it? I should have been the one to get it.'

Presented with the meat, Mrs Brett parcelled it up in a businesslike way and put it with her outdoor clothing. When she came back, she nudged against Harriet and said with fiercely threatening sympathy: 'So that Archie Callard's the new Director? What's he going to do for Guy?'

'Very little. He says he promised Gracey he'd put Dubedat in charge.'

'It's sickening.' Mrs Brett stared for some moments at Harriet, then seemed to come to a decision: 'You want to get away from the hotel, don't you? Well, I know a Greek couple who are thinking of letting their villa. It's not much of a place, mind you, but you've got to be glad of anything these days.'

When Harriet began to thank her, Mrs Brett interrupted sternly: 'Don't thank me. You gave me the joint, didn't you? You go and see about the villa before someone else gets wind of it.'

The villa was on the outskirts, between the Piraeus and Phaleron roads, and so likely to be cheap. Guy let himself be taken to see it but would make no comment on the two rooms and their bare functional furniture. The hotel was enough for him. Before he married he had lived for months at a time with no room of any sort, keeping his possessions in a rucksack and sleeping in the houses of friends, often on the floor. He resisted the extravagance of the villa, but resisted more the bus or metro journeys in which it would involve him.

The owner of the villa, Kyrios Dhiamandopoulos, was an artist – *très moderne*, said his wife – and had designed the villa himself. Kyria Dhiamandopoulou went up on to the roof-terrace and left the Pringles alone to make their decision.

'Can we take it?' Harriet asked.

'Do you really want to take it?'

'It's the best we're likely to get.'

'Why not stay where we are?'

'Because we can have a house of our own. A home. In fact, our first home.'

'Our first home? What about the flat in Bucharest?'

'That was different. A house is a home, a flat isn't.'

'Why?'

'A house is good for the soul.' She was excited by the thought of their own house, even this house, and Guy said: 'Very well; take it.' He accepted Harriet's eccentricities as symptoms of immaturity. He usually ignored them but this was one he felt he must indulge.

13

As Christmas approached Guy said: 'I've been unemployed for three months. I'm beginning to deteriorate.' All unemployment, even unemployment with pay, seemed to him a rebuttal of a basic human right. In desperation, he called at the School library, hoping the sight of him would remind Archie Callard of his need for work. But Archie Callard was not at the School. The secretaries said they had never seen Mr Callard. The students had given up and gone away. The librarian, won to sympathy by Guy's mildness of manner, admitted that it was 'all very odd'. In fact, if things went on like this, there would be *un scandale*.

When another letter came for Guy, it was not from Archie Callard or Dubedat but from Professor Lord Pinkrose. Pinkrose, describing himself as Director of the English School, summoned Guy to appear at the Academy. Harriet telephoned Alan and asked: 'What has happened now?'

He said: 'All I know is: Archie's out and Pinkrose is in. As to how it happened, I'd be glad if you could tell me.'

The Pringles were not cheered by the change. Archie had shown some goodwill but they could expect nothing from Pinkrose who, whenever he met them, behaved as though they did not exist.

They walked up to the Academy between the rain showers. As the Academy building appeared, flashing its ochre colour beneath the heavy sky, they saw a Greek soldier moving painfully towards them. His left foot was bandaged but fitted into an unlaced boot, the right was too heavily bandaged to wear anything. He had a crutch under his right arm and paused every few yards to rest with his free hand against the wall.

Everyone had heard of the glory of the Greek advance, but it was not all glory. The truth was coming out now. There were terrible stories of the suffering that had been caused by unpreparedness. Many of the men had been crippled by long marches in boots that did not fit, while others, who had no boots at all, fought barefoot in the snow. Struggling through the mountain blizzards, they were soaked for days. Their ragged uniforms froze upon them. Their hands and feet became frost-bitten and infected for lack of sulpha drugs. Their wounds were neglected. There were thousands of cases of gangrene and thousands of amputations.

The Pringles, as they approached the soldier, gazed at him with awe and compassion. He met their pity with indifference. His gaunt face was morose with pain. He was intent on nothing but making the next move.

On the other side of the road there was a hospital. Other wounded were making their way round the tarmac quadrangle.

As they looked across, Guy raged against the pro-German ministers who, knowing the war would come, had prevented the stock-piling of medical supplies, but Harriet said nothing, knowing if she tried to speak she would burst into tears.

The Academy door stood ajar. They went through to the common-room where the air was dank with cold. There was no one to meet them. At that hour the inmates were at work and the whole building was silent. Not knowing what else to do, they sat down to wait. Pinkrose must have been watching for them. He let them linger in suspense for ten minutes, then they heard the trip of his little feet coming down the stairs and along the tiled passage.

'Ah, there you are!' he said. His tone surprised them. It was not a friendly tone but it suggested he might have something to offer.

Guy stood up. Pinkrose gave him a rapid, oblique glance then gazed at the empty fireplace. He was wearing his great-coat and scarves and though he had no hat, his flattened dog-brown hair showed a ring where his hat had been.

He took a letter from his coat pocket and slowly unfolded it, saying: 'I sent for you . . . Yes, I sent for you. Lord Bedlington . . . by the way, are you known to him?'

Guy said: 'No.'

'Well, strangely enough . . . he's chosen you to be Chief Instructor. You're to be appointed. It's a definite order. I could say, you've already *been* appointed. It's in this letter here. You may read it, if you wish. Yes, yes, if you wish, you may read it.' He pushed the letter at Guy as though disclaiming any part in it.

Embarrassed by his discourtesy, Guy said: 'May I ask what has happened? I was recently called out to Phaleron to see Mr Callard.'

'I know you were. Yes, I know you were. Mr Callard heard from the Cairo office that he was to be Director, but the appointment was not confirmed. No, it was not confirmed. In fact, it was rescinded. Mr Callard's announcement was premature *and* a trifle unwise, I think. Lord Bedlington decided that the position called for an older man. *I* am to be Director and have asked Mr Callard to act as Social Secretary, a position more suited to his particular gifts.'

Guy extruded unspoken inquiry as to how this had come about. Pinkrose, after a reflective pause, chose to explain: 'I contacted Lord Bedlington . . . I made it my business to contact him. We were at Cambridge together. He was unaware that I was in Athens. I fear that Mr Gracey had failed . . . had failed to mention me. An oversight, I have no doubt. Never mind, the matter has been put right; and in accordance with Bedlington's wishes, I am appointing you Chief Instructor.'

'May I ask if you were kind enough to recommend me?'

'No. No, I can't say that I did. I recommended no one. You are Lord Bedlington's choice.'

'And what about Dubedat and Toby Lush? Am I to employ them?'

Pinkrose gave no sign that he had ever heard of Dubedat and Lush. 'You may employ whom you please,' he said.

'When will the school reopen?'

'I suggest the first of January. Yes, the first of January will be an excellent date.'

'And may I start enrolments?'

'You may do what you like.' Pinkrose walked out of the room without a good-day and Guy and Harriet were left to find their way out. They took the steps down to the garden where the new green was pushing through the straw tangle of dead plants. Once they were safely away from the house, Harriet said: 'That was interesting. It looks as though Pinkrose, when pushed, is tougher than we thought.'

Grinning in exultation, Guy said: 'We know how he got his job; but heaven knows how I got mine.'

'You've got it. That's all that matters.' Harriet was as exultant as he: 'In spite of your follies, luck is on your side.'

14

Two days before Christmas, the bells started up again. The Greeks on the Albanian coast road had taken Himarra. So the advance continued and the hope of a conclusive victory lightened the winter. Everyone was certain that in a few weeks, in a month or less, the enemy would be asking for terms. The war was as good as over.

Still, it was a sparse Christmas. There was little enough for sale in the shops that did their best, decking the windows with palm and bay in honour of the Greek heroes, and olive for the expected peace.

There were candles and ribbons – blue and white ribbons, and red, white and blue ribbons – and, for the short space of twilight, the shops were allowed to shine for the festival. Everyone came out to see the brilliance of the streets, but when darkness was complete, the black-out came down and those who could afford it crowded into the cafés. The others went home.

Harriet went shopping to celebrate another victory: the conquest of a city that was on no map but their own. Guy was employed. They had found a home. They could remain where they most wanted to be. She bought Guy a length of raw silk to be made into a summer jacket, one of the last silk lengths left in a shop which had been opened by an Englishwoman to encourage the arts of Greece. The woman had gone back to England, and no one had time now to weave silk or make goatskin rugs or pottery jars for honey.

The Pringles were asked to two Christmas parties, one to be given by Mrs Brett and one by Major Cookson. The Major's invitation came in first but Guy thought they should accept Mrs Brett's. 'We owe it to her,' he said. 'She would never forgive us if we went to Cookson.'

'Why do we owe it to her?' asked Harriet, who was drawn to the idea of the Phaleron party.

'She's been so badly treated.'

'She probably deserved it. I would much rather go to Cookson's.'

'It's out of the question. She'd be deeply hurt.'

In the end Harriet was over-ridden, as she always seemed to be, and the argument came to an end.

On Christmas Day the sky was overcast. The parties did not begin until 8 o'clock and they had to get through the day that was a sad and empty day of the homeless.

When they went out to walk in the shuttered streets, the Pringles met Alan Frewen who was wandering about with his dog. He joined them and they went together towards Zonar's where Ben Phipps sat staring into vacancy. At the sight of them, he jumped up, asking eagerly: 'Where are you off to?' They did not know.

University Street stretched away, long, straight and harshly grey, with only one figure in sight – Yakimov, his tall, fragile body stooped beneath the weight of his fur-lined coat. Seeing four persons known to him, he began to hurry, several times tripping over his fallen hem, and came to them smiling a smile of great sweetness, and singing out:

'How heartwarming to see your nice familiar faces! What can one do on this day of comfort and joy? Where, oh where, can poor Yaki get a bite to eat?'

Alan said he had promised to give Diocletian a Christmas present of a real walk. Why should they not take the bus down to the sea-front and stroll along the beach?

Yakimov looked discouraged by this suggestion but when the others moved towards the bus stop, he followed with a sigh.

They were alone on the shore. The air was moist but there was no wind, and the cold, instead of blowing into their faces, seeped down from the yellowish folds of cloud above their heads.

The sea was fixed like a jelly in bands of sombre colour: neutral at the edge, a heavy violet in mid-distance, indigo where it touched the horizon.

In the jaundiced light the esplanade was grey but the pink and yellow houses shone with an unnatural clarity, while the Major's villa was as white as a skull within a circlet of palms and fur-dark pines.

The dog, released, had taken off like a projectile and now dashed back and forwards, sending up flurries of sand and barking its joy in freedom. Alan, chiding it with a doting smile, made matters worse by throwing stones for it.

Ben Phipps, who on the bus had been silent as though unsure of his welcome in this company, frowned as the dog chased about him. When the uproar tailed off, he said: 'I heard a bit of news yesterday evening.'

'Good news, I hope,' Guy said.

'Not very. It might even be bloody bad news.'

That put a stop to Alan's activity and when everyone was attending him, Phipps went on: 'One of our chaps, out on a reccy over the Bulgarian front, thought he saw something in the snow. Something fishy. He dropped down to have a dekko and nearly had kittens. What d'you think? Jerry's got a mass of stuff there – tanks, guns, lorries, every sort of heavy armament. All camouflaged. *White.*'

'You mean it hadn't been there long?' Harriet said. 'But it could have been painted on the spot.'

Phipps gave her a look, surprised by her grasp of his point and not over-pleased by it. 'Unlikely,' he said. 'That sort of stuff isn't painted, it's sprayed. A factory job.'

'Couldn't it be sprayed on the spot?'

'Perhaps it could.' A repository of information in Athens, he seemed more annoyed than not by the fact Harriet's suggestions made sense.

'Where did you hear all this?' Alan wanted to know.

'In the mess at Tatoi. I've been doing a piece on British

intervention in Greece. It may be hush-hush but when I was there the place was buzzing with it. The pilot had just come in. No one had had time to clamp down on his report and the chaps were talking.'

'You think the Germans are preparing an invasion?'

'Your guess is as good as mine. You might even say it's as good as D'Albiac's. No one knows anything. But you'd better keep it under your hat.' Feeling he may have said too much, Ben Phipps looked sternly at the Pringles and turned to warn Yakimov, but Yakimov was dawdling far behind.

The party, oppressed by the day, became more oppressed as they contemplated the possibility of a German move. And how possible it now seemed! Why should the stronger partner of the Axis stand by inactive while the weaker suffered ignominious defeat? Yet who could bear to think the Greeks had suffered in vain?

Guy said: 'The Bulgarian roads are the worst in Europe. There's only one bridge over the Danube. How could all this heavy stuff get to the frontier? Don't you think it's some cock-and-bull story?'

'Well . . .' Having blown up his sensation, Ben Phipps saw fit to deflate it: 'The pilot saw something all right, but perhaps it wasn't what it seemed. It could have been a sham – something set up to scare the Greeks or, for that matter, the Jugs. There's this tricky situation in Yugoslavia: Peter and Paul. Which one's going to fly away? The pro-German faction's behind the Regent; the others are behind the King. If Paul's allowed a free hand, then the Germans'll let things ride. Their troops are spread thin enough as it is. They don't want to hold down more unproductive territory.'

Alan murmured his agreement. It was not much of a hope, but these days they existed off just such a hope as this one. And there was the persisting human belief that nothing could be as sinister as it seemed. They began to rise out of their consternation and as they did so, found that Yakimov, hurrying to catch them up, had caught a sentence or two of Phipps's talk.

'What's this, dear boy? The Nasties coming here?'

Looking into Yakimov's great, frightened eyes, Ben Phipps could only laugh: 'I didn't say so.'

'But if they do: what'll happen to us?'

'What, indeed!'

Harriet said: 'We have the sea. It makes me feel safe.'

'This great ridiculous mass of useless water!' Ben Phipps peered at it: 'I'd feel a lot safer if it weren't there.'

Guy said: 'I'm inclined to agree,' and the two men laughed as though they shared a joke.

Phipps' manner towards Guy suggested understanding and incipient intimacy while Guy, aware of the interest they held in common, behaved as though their concurrence were only a matter of time. Harriet was disturbed, feeling that the atmosphere between them was like the onset of a love-affair. She became more critical of Phipps, suspecting he was the sort of man who, though sexually normal, prefers his own sex. He disliked her and probably disliked women. He had about him the reek of the trouble-maker, the natural enemy of married life; the sort of man who observes, or seems to observe, the conventions while leading husbands astray and undermining the authority of wives.

She walked between them but when they reached the point at Edam, they turned and Phipps placed himself beside Guy, saying: 'I heard you'd been appointed Chief Instructor, and I was jolly glad. I never had any use for that twit Dubedat. And what about Callard? I bet he's had some little *douceur* slipped into his hand?'

'He's to be Social Secretary.'

'Social Secretary!' Phipps's tone was hollow with disgust. 'The rest of us work our balls off for a living while he lies around at Phaleron and gets paid for it.'

Guy laughed. This exchange confirmed the understanding between them. Their unfortunate introduction at Zonar's was forgotten and Guy's manner lost a last hint of restraint.

Phipps became confidential: 'I won't pretend I wasn't after the directorship. I *was*. I need something more than free-lance journalism to keep me going, but it was Gracey who led me to believe I might get it. He humbugged me. And Pinkrose and Dubedat. We were all after it, *you* know that. He had us all running errands and taking him gifts and circling round him like planets round the sun. If he spoke we listened open-mouthed. We were all waiting for the crown to drop from his nerveless fingers; each one thought he'd get it when it fell.'

'Did you know Callard was in the running?'

'No. That was a secret between Archie and Colin Gracey. *And* the Major, of course. The rest of us poor mutts were just led up the garden. I have a reputation – you may have heard that I scribble a bit. I had a book published by the Left Book Club. I'm not unknown. I got friends at home to do a bit of lobbying. Then, if you please, word comes from Cairo that Archie's got the job. Gracey had fooled me. I was mad. In fact, I was hopping mad.'

'But why did Gracey choose Callard?'

'A matter of friendship. Gracey liked to move in the right circles.'

'And had Callard any sort of qualifications?'

'He'd a degree of sorts; third in History or something. It's quite fashionable to get a third, of course. One of his Oxford admirers described him as "frittering away an intellectual fortune". The fortune, if it exists, is kept well under lock and key. I've seen nothing of it. Have you?' Phipps spoke in a tone of breathless inquiry as though a sense of injustice were at last bursting free. 'I could do the job better; you could do the job better; even Dubedat could do it better. Yet it was simply handed to Callard as though he had some natural right to it.'

Guy nodded in understanding of Phipps's indignation. 'He probably thought he had a natural right to it,' Guy said. 'A class right. There's a certain sort of rich, privileged young man who imagines he is born to be in the front rank of everything; even the arts. If he chooses to write or paint, he must be a genius. There are some who feel quite a sense of grievance when proved wrong. Really, believe it or not, there were those who felt it monstrous that D. H. Lawrence, a miner's son, should have so much talent. Some of them remain dilettante, believing that if they chose to apply their talents, they'd be remarkable; but they don't choose.'

Ben Phipps's laughter stopped him in his tracks. He threw back his head, shouting: 'You're right. That's Archie: a genius by right of birth who has chosen to be a dilettante. The great "might have been".' Phipps's laughter came to an abrupt stop. He said: 'I can tell you this: if his appointment had been confirmed, I intended to institute an inquiry.'

'I think Pinkrose did institute an inquiry.'

'Did he? Good for him. Still, I can't see him making a go as director here. He's too narrow, too much the don. It's a position for a younger man. I should have got it.'

'I think so, too,' Guy spoke a firm declaration of faith in Phipps and Harriet, looking at Phipps, said:

'You'd better not pass that on to Pinkrose.'

'What do you think I am?' Phipps stared angrily at her and she stared back, offering no conciliation. If Guy chose to make a declaration of faith, she was just as ready to make a declaration of war. Phipps turned his back on her and said to Guy: 'Pinkrose's own appointment was a bit of a wangle, I bet? How did he fix it?'

'He's a friend of Lord Bedlington. They knew one another at Cambridge.'

'Hah!' said Phipps, needing to be told no more, and the two walked just a little quicker, drawing ahead and dropping their voices in a privacy of agreement. Catching a word here and there, Harriet knew they were discussing in an atmosphere of scandalized conspiracy, the suppression in different countries of the left wing opposition, which was for both of them the suppression of desirable life.

'Look at them!' Harriet said to Alan. 'They're like a couple of schoolgirls discovering sex.'

Alan smiled. Sensing her jealousy but refusing to become involved with it, he started hunting for flat stones which he sent skimming over the sea for the entertainment of Diocletian. As the dog ran about, Harriet saw that its vertebra was visible and its haunches stood out from its skin, but, galvanized by the game, it tore about the beach, splashing in and out of the water, and panting in anticipation whenever Alan felt need for a rest.

Yakimov said confidentially to Harriet: 'I expect, dear girl. you're feeling a trifle peckish. I know I am. Where are we going to eat? We ought to give our mind to the problem, don't you think?'

'Yes, I think we should.'

They had hoped to eat in one of the sea-side restaurants, which before the war had been noted for their crayfish and mullet, but now they were all shut, not from a shortage of fish but a shortage of fishermen.

She said: 'We could try the Piraeus. There must be some sort of eating place for the men employed about the harbour.'

'You think that's the best we can do?' Yakimov looked glum. 'I know, dear girl, one mustn't complain. Not the done thing. Must think of the fighting men; but it comes a bit rough on your poor old Yak. I'm doing an important job, too. I need nourishment. Don't get paid much, but it's regular. For the first time in years your Yak can lay his hands on the Ready, and he can't get a decent meal for love nor money.'

'It's hard,' Harriet agreed: 'But, remember, you're going to the Major's party.'

'Oh yes. Get a bite there all right.' He turned to Alan: 'What about you, dear boy?'

Alan, like the Pringles, had been invited to both parties. He had, he said, decided to support Mrs Brett.

Harriet looked to where Guy and Phipps walked with their heads together: 'Why don't we ditch Mrs Brett?' she said.

Alan said, shocked: 'No. No, we couldn't do that.'

The rain began to fall in a gentle film, chilling their faces like powdered ice. Someone was coming towards them along the esplanade: a man with a fish basket, the first human being they had met since they left the bus. They were all hungry with a hunger that had not yet touched starvation but caused an habitual unease. As the man approached, Harriet, though talking of something else, watched him in expectation, certain he was there on their behalf. He had fish in the basket and would open his restaurant for no purpose but to feed them. Impelled by her faith, or so it seemed, he made for a wooden cabin, unlocked the padlock and went inside.

Alan grunted as though he had shared Harriet's dream, and said: 'It looks as though we may get something after all.'

The cabin, of clinker board, was built out to form a verandah over the shore. A stairway led up from the beach.

Recalled by the same excitement that possessed the others, Ben Phipps and Guy went up the stair and knocked on the door. Alan, Harriet and Yakimov watched hopefully from below. The man came out, surprised to have custom, but when Phipps explained their need, he smiled and said he had come from Tourkolimano where he had been able to buy some red mullet. He waved them to the verandah tables, for the cabin itself was nothing but a cook-house.

The verandah had a roof and there were rush-screens at either end so that the party would be protected from the rain if not from cold.

As the smell of frying mullet came from the kitchen, Yakimov hunched his shoulders and clasped his hands to his breast as though in prayer. The others swallowed down their impatience and stared out at the sea that had lost its violet and green. The band of indigo still lay along the horizon but the rest was a glaucous yellow pocked by rain-drops. The rain, gathering strength, bounced on the glossy sand and hit the roof above their heads. Diocletian had remained on the shore, but soon had had enough of it and came up in search of his master. Finding Alan, he shook himself violently then eagerly sniffed the air. 'Lie down,' said Alan and he lay, head on paws, but with eyes restless, on edge with hunger like the rest of them.

The talk had lapsed. Harriet asked Yakimov if he could still get *blinis* at the Russian Club. He sighed: '*Hélas!* No caviare, no cream, no *blinis*. But sometimes they have octopus. Do you like octopus?'

'Not much.' She had an innate horror of eight-legged

creatures, but was glad enough to eat anything for now not only the flesh of beasts, but the hearts, kidneys and livers went to the army, and the civilians ate the intestines. Grey, slippery and bound up like shoelaces, these had brought about an epidemic of dysentery.

The mullet was ready. The proprietor hurried out to set the table and Alan asked if he had anything to spare for the dog. The man bent down and ruffled Diocletian about the ears then, shaking his head in compassion, he described the dog's condition with sad gestures. When he brought out the mullet, he placed three squid before the dog. Diocletian opened his mouth and they were gone. The company watched open-eyed, but they had been small squid and the fish also were small. They disappeared as quickly as the squid. Guy said: 'We've had our Christmas dinner, after all.'

'I wish we could have it again,' said Yakimov. 'D'you think he'd fry a few more?'

'We have had our share.'

The man came out and said he was leaving but the guests were to remain seated until the rain grew less. He refused payment for the squid which were a present for the dog, and charged very little for the mullet. After they had settled their bill, he remained for a while talking to Alan with so much vitality and laughter that Harriet and Yakimov, who knew no Greek, thought he was telling some entertaining story. When he had shaken hands with them all and gone off, still carrying his fish basket, Alan said: 'He said he didn't intend opening today. He went to Tourkolimano at dawn and waited all morning to get the fish. It was for his own family. He came here merely to get his knife, but seeing we were English, he could not refuse us.'

'So we've eaten his food?' said Harriet.

Phipps said: 'I expect he's got more in the basket.'

Guy, overwhelmed, praised the generosity of the Greeks and their tradition of hospitality. He talked for a long time and at the end Harriet said: 'And they are poor. If you are really poor, you can't refuse to sell anything.'

'He did not sell Diocletian's food. It was a gift.'

'Yes, if you are poor you sell things or you give them away. What you cannot do is keep them.'

Guy regarded her with quizzical wonder before he said: 'Why aren't you a Progressive? You recognize the truth yet don't subscribe to it.'

'I disagree. Truth is more complex than politics.'

Guy looked to Ben Phipps but Ben was not taking on Harriet. Instead, he bawled out:

> 'A petty bourgeois philistine,
> He didn't know the party line.
> Although his sentiments were right,
> He was a bloomin' Trotskyite.
> Despite great mental perturbation,
> Persistent left-wing deviation
> Dogged his foot-steps till at last,
> Discouraged by his awful past
> And taking it too much to heart, he
> Went and joined the Labour Party.
> The moral of this tale is when in
> Doubt consult the works of Lenin.'

Thinking he was having a sly dig at her, Harriet was not much pleased by this song, but Guy was delighted. Phipps, encouraged, passed into a gay, satirical mood and began to entertain the company. He lifted the edge of Yakimov's coat and after examining the lining, whistled and said: 'Sable, by Jove! Always thought it was rabbit.'

In no way offended, Yakimov smiled and said: 'Fine coat. Once belonged to the Czar. Czar give it to m'poor old dad.'

'Thought you were English?'

'Certainly I am. Typical Englishman, you might say. Mother Irish.'

'And your father?'

'Russian. White Russian, of course.'

'So you're against the present lot? The Soviets?'

A wary look came over Yakimov's face. 'Don't know about that, dear boy. Lot to be said for both lots.'

Phipps stared at Yakimov with mock severity then said: 'This story about you doing undercover work? I suppose there's no truth in it?'

Gratified by Phipps's interest, Yakimov murmured: 'Not in a position to say.'

'Um. Well, if I were you, I'd issue a denial.'

'Really, dear boy? Why?'

'I just would, that's all. British Intelligence isn't popular here. The Italians took exception to their activities. It's my belief, if those goofs had kept out, there'd've been no attack.'

Yakimov's eyes grew moist with disquiet. He said: 'Wish you'd elucidate, dear boy,' but Phipps merely nodded with the threatening air of one who knows much but will say nothing. Yakimov sniffed with fear.

'Don't tease him,' said Alan.

Bored and dispirited, they watched the rain plop heavily into the sand and the sea, jaundiced and viscous, move an inch forward and inch back. With the same viscous and inane slowness the afternoon crawled by. Cold and bored, they remained on the rickety verandah chairs because there was nothing else to do, nowhere to go. Yakimov said suddenly: 'Athens, the Edinburgh of the south!'

It was so long since he had roused himself sufficiently to exercise his wit that the others looked at him in astonishment. He smiled and subsided and for a long time no one spoke.

Alan broke the silence to say that his friend Vourakis had told him a curious thing. The Greek people were saying that someone had run to Athens with the news of the victory of Koritza and, crying 'Nenikiamen', had fallen down dead.

'I've heard that before,' said Ben Phipps.

'We've all heard it before,' said Alan. 'After the victory of Marathon the runner Phidipides ran with the news to Athens and, crying "Nenikiamen", fell dead.'

'It is possible,' Guy said, 'that the Marathon story had no more truth than the Koritza story.'

'It is possible,' Alan nodded. 'But it is not a question of truth. This war, like other wars, is collecting its legends.'

The rain drummed on the slats above their heads, its rhythm breaking every few minutes when an overflow pipe released a gush of water. At last the fall slackened. The light was failing and they had to get to their feet and go.

As they reached the bus stop, a car came hooting behind them.

The car, a Delahaye, slowed down by the kerb and a head covered with wild, straw-coloured hair, shouted: 'Hello, there!'

The car stopped and Toby Lush jumped out. 'What brings you all to Phaleron?' He ran at Guy, slipping on the wet road, almost falling headlong in his eagerness to clinch the meeting. 'What a bit of luck, meeting you! Come on. Get in. Room for everyone.'

Yakimov and Ben Phipps, needing no second invitation, got themselves into the back seat, but Guy, though he found it impossible to snub Toby, had no wish to be driven by him.

Alan said: 'There isn't room for the dog. I'll take the bus.' He limped off, and Guy looked after him.

'Get in. Get in.' Toby seized Guy's arm and manoeuvred him into the front seat. 'Three in front,' he shouted, then caught Harriet's elbow: 'Come along now. In there beside Guy.'

He was more than usually excited and, when under way, told them he had been helping to prepare the villa for the Major's party. 'They're laying out the buffet. Gosh! Wait till you've had a dekko! You're all coming, aren't you?' He was hilarious as though he had won a prize which, in a way, he had. The prize was Guy, and Toby had not captured him without reason.

'Jolly glad you got that job,' he said. 'No one better fitted for it. *Jolly* glad. We're both jolly glad. I don't mean the old soul wasn't put out. He was a bit, you know! Stands to reason; but what he said was: "If it's not to be me then I'm glad it's old Pringle."'

Guy gave an ironical: 'Oh!' but it was an amused and good-natured irony, and Toby, encouraged, went on: 'You're opening in the new year aren't you? You'll be needing teachers? Well, what I wanted to say is: you can rely on the pair of us. We'll help you out.' His tone of open-hearted friendliness suggested that all was forgotten and forgiven.

Guy said 'Oh!' again and laughed. Harriet thought it likely enough that Dubedat and Toby Lush, when the School re-opened, would be installed there as senior teachers.

'Perhaps you think we behaved like a couple of Bs,' Toby said. 'Well, we didn't. I'd like you to know that. We'd've done what we could for you but Gracey was dead against you. So we couldn't do a thing.'

'Even though Dubedat was in charge?' Harriet asked.

'That was all my eye.' Toby blew out his moustache in disgust: 'The old soul was hamstrung. He daren't make a move without consulting Gracey.'

'And why was Gracey dead against Guy? Because somebody told him that Guy neglected his work in order to produce a play?'

'Look here!' Toby Lush exploded in an injured way. 'We told him the play was a smash hit. We said H.E. was in the royal box and every seat was sold. It was Gracey who disapproved – and I can tell you why! He was jealous. He couldn't bear someone to do something he hadn't done himself.'

'Couldn't he produce a play?' Guy asked.

'He'd be terrified to take the risk. Suppose it didn't succeed! Besides, he was too damned lazy.'

'Why didn't you tell us this before?' Harriet asked.

'There's such a thing as loyalty.'

'Then why mention it now?'

'Oh, I say!' Toby now was both injured and indignant. 'You can't blame us. Look how the old soul's been treated. He worked like a black doing Gracey's job for him and what's he got to show? We're loyal. We're loyal all right but . . .'

'You weren't loyal to Guy.' Harriet broke in but Guy had had enough enmity and he talked her down, assuring Toby that both he and Dubedat would get all the work they wanted when the School re-opened.

When he dropped Guy and Harriet at their hotel, Toby shot out his hand in a large liberal gesture that bestrode all the disagreements of the past. 'See you tonight,' he said.

Guy explained that they could not go to the Major's party because they had committed themselves to Mrs Brett.

'Why not go to both?' said Toby and as Ben Phipps and Yakimov joined in persuading him, Guy said: 'I suppose we could.'

'Right. I'll pick you up,' Toby said, gasping with importance. "Fraid I won't be able to take you to old Ma Brett's. This is the Major's car. Got the loan of it to run a few errands for him. See you later, then.'

Guy was surprised that Harriet showed no particular pleasure at this change of plan.

'You're not going to please me,' she said. 'You're going to please Toby Lush and horrid little Phipps.'

He had to laugh: 'Darling,' he pleaded: 'Don't be so unreasonable.'

When Toby returned for the Pringles, Dubedat was sitting in the front seat. Guy, to reassure him, greeted him affably, but Dubedat sat with his shoulders hunched and did not even grunt. He had renounced his fine social manner and was as sullen as he had ever been. He made no attempt to talk in the car and the Pringles, when they came into the lighted hall at Phaleron, saw his face set again in lines of discontent. Toby, who had been chatting happily with Guy, wanted to stay with the Pringles but Dubedat was having none of that. Calling Toby to heel, he marched him off to another room and Harriet said: 'You didn't get much change out of that one.'

'I certainly didn't. I'm afraid he thinks I've somehow done him out of a job.'

'He probably thought it was his by rights. He thinks everything is his by rights. If he doesn't get it, he's been done out of it. That accounts for his resentful expression.'

Guy laughed and squeezed her arm. 'You're a terrible girl!' he said.

The Pringles were early but the rooms were already

crowded. Yakimov came pushing through to them with a dejected air. 'Nice state of affairs,' he complained. 'First here, I was. First on the green, and the butler said no one's to touch a sliver till the Major gives the word. He's standing guard over the grub. Not like the Major at all. If we wait for the whole mob to arrive, there won't be enough to go round.' He had left the dining-room in disgust but could not stay away for long. 'Come and have a look,' he said to Harriet. 'Must say, it's a splendid spread.'

Guy had found Ben Phipps, so Harriet went willingly to the dining-room where the hungry guests, packed about the buffet, were doing their best to hide their hunger.

Yakimov, crushed against Harriet, whispered: 'Most of them were here on the dot. Usually it's a case of first come, first served, but last time they'd wolfed the lot in the first fifteen minutes. S'pose there've been complaints. I recommend standing here beside the plates. Soon as we get the nod, grab one and lay about you.'

'Where does it all come from?' Harriet asked in wonder.

'Mustn't ask that, dear girl. Eat and be thankful. My God, look at that! *Cream*.'

As more people came in, those at the centre were so pressed against the buffet they could scarcely keep their feet.

Trembling in an agony of anticipation, Yakimov said to the butler: 'Dear boy, there'll be a riot soon.' The butler began to look for the Major.

Harriet noticed Guy beckoning her to join him in the doorway. As she moved, Yakimov said: 'Don't go. Don't go. They're just about to give the word.'

'I'll come straight back.'

Guy gripped her wrist and said in fierce indignation: 'Who do you think is here?'

'I've no idea.'

'The Japanese consul.'

'How do you know?'

'Ben pointed him out.'

Ben Phipps, standing behind Guy, looking more amused

than indignant, said: 'Last Christmas the Major invited the German minister, an old pal of his. He went round saying "What's a war between friends?" The British diplomats were furious and Cookson got his knuckles rapped.'

Pulling Harriet from the room, Guy said: 'Come on. We're going.'

'Not yet. Let's eat first. And we haven't seen anything.' She looked round at the sumptuous dresses of the rich Greek women, the hot-house flowers, the laurel swags decorating the marble pillars and said: 'I don't want to go yet.' As she spoke, she saw Charles Warden. He was looking at her and, catching her eye, took a step towards her. Impulsively, she moved away from Guy, who held to her, saying: 'Get your coat. I'm not staying here.'

'But we're not at war with Japan.'

'I won't remain in the room with the representative of a Fascist Government. Besides, we're due at Mrs Brett's.'

Ben Phipps was looking the other way. Before Harriet could say more, Guy led her firmly to the alcove where she had left her coat. The Major, still welcoming the incoming guests, looked perplexed by the departure of the Pringles. 'Surely you are not going so soon?' he protested.

'I am afraid we must,' said Guy. 'Mrs Brett has invited us to supper.'

'Oh!' The Major caught his breath in a snigger at the mention of Mrs Brett, but it was a peevish snigger. He could not bear that anyone, not even young people like Guy and Harriet, should leave his party to go to another.

They had scarcely entered the house when they were outside it again. Harriet, feeling as peevish as the Major, said: 'Mr Facing-both-ways stayed on.'

'Who?'

'Your friend Phipps.'

'You're always wrong about people.'

'I don't think so. I never liked Dubedat and I was right. I was doubtful of Toby Lush . . .'

'You're doubtful of everyone.'

'Well, you do pick up with the most doubtful sort of people.'

Guy made no reply to this but, keeping his hold on her, hurried her to the bus stop where a bus was preparing to depart. The bus carried them away but Harriet's thoughts remained with the radiant dresses, the splendid villa – and with Charles Warden.

Mrs Brett's flat on the slopes of Lycabettos was equipped with two small electric fires. Electric fires had become valuable possessions, not to be bought at any price now. The guests, delighted to find the rooms warm, were still discussing the fires when the Pringles arrived.

Mrs Brett was shouting in self-congratulation: 'Aren't I lucky! Yes, aren't I lucky! The girls left them behind. I opened a cupboard and there they were. I thought: "What sensible girls to spend their pennies on things like this instead of silly fripperies."'

Spreading her large-boned hands in front of one of the fires, she was shaking all over and nearly deranged at being the centre of so much attention. When the Pringles tried to speak to her, she pushed them aside and went to the kitchen where something was cooking.

The room was full of middle-aged and elderly guests, mostly women who had remained in Athens because they had no reason to go anywhere else. Harriet, seeing no one she knew, thought: 'If we hadn't come, we would not have been missed.' They remained unwelcomed until Mrs Brett returned to the room. Becoming aware of them, she seized hold of Guy as though his arrival were a long-awaited event. 'Attention,' she called. 'Attention. Now! I want you all to meet the new Chief Instructor at the English School: Mr Guy Pringle.' This announcement was made with such impressement that there was a flutter of clapping before anyone had time to reflect and ask what it was all about. Mrs Brett, hand raised, stood for some moments rejoicing in their bewilderment, then decided to enlighten them. She said:

'You all saw the announcement that Archie Callard was to

be the new Director at the School! Perhaps you don't all know that he isn't the new Director after all? The appointment wasn't confirmed. No. Lord Bedlington decided that Lord Pinkrose was better fitted to take charge in an important cultural centre like this, and I'm sure you all agree with him. Lord Pinkrose is *somebody*, not like . . . well, naming no names. Anyway, Lord Pinkrose was told to appoint Guy Pringle here as Chief Instructor; and do you know why?' She grinned at the circle of blank faces, then turned on Guy: 'Do you know why?' Guy shook his head.

'Does Lord Pinkrose know why?'

'I don't think he does,' Guy said.

'I'll tell you why. I'll tell you all why. I had a hand in it. Oh, yes, I had. My Percy had friends in high places. We knew a lot of people. The poor old widow's still got influence. We knew Lord Bedlington years ago when he was just young Bobby Fisher, travelling around, and he used to stay with us at Kotor. He's just been made Chairman of the Organization, and when I heard he was in Cairo, I sent him a letter. It was a strong letter, I can tell you. I let him know what's been going on here. I let him know about Gracey and Callard and Cookson. I said we were all disgusted at the way the School had gone down; and I said things would be no better under Callard. I said Callard couldn't run a whelk-stall. Yes, I said that. I don't mince matters. And I said there was this nice young chap here, this Guy Pringle, and he was being discriminated against. I opened Bobby Fisher's eyes, I can tell you. And the long and the short of it is, our friend Guy Pringle's got the job he deserves.' She lifted her hands above her head and applauded herself.

'What an *éclaircissement*!' said Miss Jay acidly. 'Just like the last act of a pantomime.' But whatever doubts she raised were dispelled by Guy who flung his arms round Mrs Brett saying: 'Thank you. Thank you. You're a great woman!' He kissed her resolutely on either cheek.

Flushed, bright-eyed, gasping from her oration, Mrs Brett, not a little drunk, danced up and down in his arms, snapping her fingers to right and left, and shouting: 'That for Gracey; and that for Callard! And that for the hidden hand of Phaleron! You can go and tell Cookson there's life in the old girl yet!'

If she had caused embarrassment, Guy's spontaneous and artless good nature had won the guests and the embarrassment went down in laughter. Everyone, even Miss Jay, joined Mrs Brett as she banged her hands together. Harriet, observant in the background watched the room converge round Guy while he looked to her, smiling, and held out his hand. He might have said: 'You see how right I was to come here,' but he said nothing. He merely wanted to include her in the fun.

The rumpus subsided when Mrs Brett shouted: 'The hotpot! The hot-pot!' and ran back to the kitchen.

'About time,' said Miss Jay whose heavy cream wool dress with all its fringes hung lank upon her.

The lean times were telling on Miss Jay and her monstrous face had drooped into the sad, dew-lapped muzzle of a bloodhound. It was not only her flesh that had collapsed. Her malicious self-assertion had lost its force and her remarks made no impact at all.

Harriet knew now she could, if she wished, say anything she liked about English society in Athens. Miss Jay counted for little. Local soceity had shrunk like a balloon losing air and Miss Jay had shrunk with it. Harriet was free to speak as she pleased.

During the excitement of Mrs Brett's speech, she had noticed Alan Frewen among the guests. Moving over to him, she asked: 'Is Miss Jay a rich woman?'

Amused by this direct question, Alan said: 'I believe she has a modest competence, as Miss Austen would say.'

'A modest competence' seemed to disclose Miss Jay. Harriet saw her with her modest competence, tackling the world and getting it under control; but the world had changed about her and now, an obsolete fortress, with weapons all out of date, there was not much due to her but pity.

Alan suggested that Harriet meet the painter Papazoglou who, young and bearded, in a private's uniform, was spread against the wall as though he would, if he could, sink through it and out of sight. Alan said that as everyone was doing something to enhance the Greek cause, Mrs Brett had proclaimed herself a patron of the arts and had placed the young man's canvases round the room, calling attention to them with such vehemence that several people present were still under the impression she had painted them herself.

Papazoglou spoke no English so Harriet went round peering into the little paintings of red earth, dark foliage and figures scattered among the pillars and capitals of fallen temples. Much moved, she came back and said to Alan: 'What can I do? Isn't there any work for me?'

'We've been given an office in the Grande Bretagne,' he told her. 'Now that we have more room, I'll find you a job.'

A scent of stewed meat drifted out from the kitchen where Mrs Brett had been unpacking a case of borrowed plates. She came out shouting: 'Supper's ready,' then explained how she had hired a taxi the day before and gone to Kifissia, having heard that a small landowner, taking advantage of the high prices, was killing off his goats for the festival. She could not find the landowner but she had been passed from one person to another and in the end had managed to buy a whole leg of kid. 'And what do you think I've made? A real Lancashire hot-pot. I come from Lancashire, you know . . .'

While Mrs Brett talked, the smell of the hot-pot grew richer until Miss Jay broke in with: 'Cut it short, Bretty. I'll help you dish up.'

Miss Jay's expression was avid as she spooned out the hot-pot. The plates were quickly emptied and Mrs Brett went round urging everyone to eat, saying: 'Who's for second helpings? Plenty more in the pot.'

Miss Jay was catching the last of the gravy in the spoon when a ring came at the front-door. Three women who had been detained at the bandage-rolling circle, walked in bright-faced, cold, hungry and ready to eat.

'I forgot all about you,' Mrs Brett said, 'But never mind! There are some jolly nice buns for afters.'

Guy, appreciative of everything, handed back his plate with the remark that the hot-pot had been the best he had ever eaten.

The hungry ladies, taking it in good part, munched their buns and made jokes about not getting Mrs Brett's goat.

'Wasn't that a good party!' Guy's voice rang through the empty darkness of the streets as they went home: 'You wouldn't have enjoyed the Major's half so much.'

Blind in the black-out, he clung to Harriet as they slipped on and off the narrow pavement, and slid over the wet and treacherous gutter stones: 'Isn't Mrs Brett magnificent? Thanks to her, I have the job in the place where I most want to be.'

Harriet pressed Guy's arm, happy to rejoice with him, and said: 'Alan thinks the war might end this year.'

'It might, I suppose. The Germans have most of Europe. We are alone. We may be forced into some sort of truce.'

'But *could* the war end that way?'

'No; and don't let us deceive ourselves. It wouldn't be the end. There would be an interval of shame and misery, then we would have to return to the fight.'

'In fact, the real enemy is untouched. The real war hasn't even begun.'

'It could last another twenty years,' said Guy.

The excitement of the party was wearing off. The warmth of the wine was passing from them and as they turned into the wet wind blast of the main street, they held to each other. knowing they might never see the end of hostility and confusion. The war could devour their lives.

Next day Yakimov was full of the fact that by leaving the Major's party, the Pringles had missed 'no end of a dust up'. Everyone was talking about it. Late in the evening, Phipps, described by Yakimov as a 'a trifle oiled', had attacked the Major for supporting Archie Callard's appointment and deceiving Phipps himself about his chances.

'Callard's never done a day's work in his life,' he told Cookson and an attentive company. 'What good did you think he'd be as Director? He'd've been a figurehead and a poor one, at that! He's a playboy and a poseur with nothing but his neuroses to recommend him.'

'And so on and so on,' said Yakimov, aghast and delighted by such plain speaking.

Callard, listening, had put up a show of indifference, but the Major had been much upset. He had sniffed and dabbed his nose and tried to hush Phipps, but in the end he had turned and 'told Ben P. a thing or two'. He had said that Gracey, when asked for his opinion, had cabled the London office to say that Phipps, as a result of his politics, his past association with undesirable persons and his generally facetious attitude towards the reigning authorities, was totally unsuited to be in any sort of authoritative position.

Having revealed this, the Major, in a state near hysteria, had shouted shrilly: 'And I agree. I agree. I agree.'

'Then you know what you can do,' Phipps had told him and raging out of the house, had crashed the front door so violently the glass had fallen out and broken in pieces all over the hall.

Guy said: 'We were fortunate to miss that.' An opinion Harriet did not share.

PART THREE

The Romantics

15

In the New Year, when the move to the villa was imminent, Guy was too busy even to discuss it. He had returned to work like a reformed drunkard returning to the bottle. He was exuberantly busy.

Some mornings he would not wait for breakfast. When Harriet asked what he did all day, he said he was arranging schedules, laying out lecture courses, enrolling students and reorganizing the library. And what on earth kept him so late at the School each night? He interviewed students and advised which course of study was more suitable for each. Soon he would be even more busy, for he was about to rehearse the entertainment he had promised the airmen at Tatoi.

'Is that still going on?'

'Certainly.'

'There seems to be no end to it.'

'Of course there's no end to it,' Guy cheerfully replied. 'That's what teaching is.'

When she asked if he would help move their stuff to the villa, he could only laugh.

'Lunch time, or evening, would do,' Harriet said.

'Darling, it's impossible.'

She took the baggage in a taxi. The taxi could not get down the narrow lane to the villa. Kyria Dhiamandopoulou, seeing her carrying the cases to the door, asked playfully: 'Where is that nice Mr Pringle?'

'Working.'

'Ah, the poor man!'

Kyria Dhiamandopoulou was ready to leave but had to wait for her husband who had driven into Athens on some piece of business. She was a small, handsome woman who, in spite of the food shortage, had managed to stay plump. When they first met, she had been off-hand and seemed harassed; now, on the point of departure, she was in high spirits.

She insisted that Harriet must come up to the roof where the mid-day sun was warm. 'See how nice,' she said. 'In spring you will see it is very nice.' A marble table was set beneath a pergola over which a plant had been trained. Kyria Dhiamandopoulou touched the branches that flaked like an old cigar. 'My pretty plant,' she sighed. 'How sad that I must leave it! Here, here, sit here! It is not so cold, I think? We will take coffee till my husband come.'

She sped off to fetch a tray with cups like egg-cups and a brass beaker of Turkish coffee. While they sipped at the little cups of sweet, black coffee, she pointed out the distant Piraeus road and the rocky hill that protected the roof from the sea wind. 'On the other side there is a river. Now not much, but when there is more rain there will be more river. It is the Ilissus. You have heard of it? No? The classical writers speak of it. It is a classical site, you know. Before the invasion, they were building here, but now they have stopped. It is quiet like the country,' she sighed again. 'How sad that we must leave!'

'But why are you leaving?' Harriet asked.

Kyria Dhiamandopoulou gave her a searching glance before deciding to let her know the truth.

'I dream true.'

'Do you?'

'I will tell you. You know, *par exemple*, that old woman who begs in Stadiou? In black, with fingers bound in such a way?'

Harriet nodded. 'I'm frightened of her. They say she's a leper, but I suppose she can't be?'

'I don't know, but I don't like. Now, I'll tell you. I had a dream. I dreamt she came running at me in Stadiou. I ran from her . . . I ran to a shop, a pharmacy; she ran after me. I scream, she scream. What horror! She has turned crazy. Well, next day, I forgot. One forgets, you know! I went to Stadiou and there was the woman and when she saw me, she rush at me . . . "My dream!" I cry and I run to a shop. It is a pharmacy – the same pharmacy, mind you! The people inside, alarmed that I scream – the same! The very same! "Help me, she's mad!" I cry and someone slams the door. The proprietor telephones the police. I sit in a chair and shake my body. It was unspeakable!'

'Yes, indeed! But surely you are not leaving because of that!'

'No. That was one dream only. I have many. Some I forget, some I remember. I dreamt the Germans came here.'

'You mean to this house?'

'Yes, to this house. When I wake, I say to my husband: "Now is the time to leave. I have a brother in Sparta. We will go to him."'

'Are you sure they were Germans? They might have been Italians.'

'They were Germans. I saw the little swastika. They came down the lane. They struck upon the door.'

'Then what happened?'

'I saw no more.'

'But Greece is not at war with Germany.'

'That is true. Still, we go to Sparta.'

'If the Germans come here, won't they go to Sparta?'

'I have no indication.'

Harriet, easily touched by the supernatural, was dismayed by Kyria Dhiamandopoulou's dream, but Kyria Dhiamandopoulou, mistaking her fearful immobility for phlegm, said: 'You English have strong nerfs!'

Before Harriet could disclaim this compliment, a hooting

came from the unmade road at the top of the lane and Kyria Dhiamandopoulou leapt up delightedly, crying: 'My husband. Now we can go,' and she ran down to join Kyrios Dhiamandopoulos who had already started loading up the car.

Joining in the bustle and laughter of the departure, Harriet forgot the dream, but then, all in a moment, the Dhiamandopoulaioi were gone and she was alone in the unfamiliar silence.

When she had unpacked the clothing, she went out to look at the Ilissus. The lane led over the hill through the damp, grey clay from which flints protruded like bones. On the other side a trickle of water made its way between high clay banks overhung by a wood of wind-bent pines. It looked a sad little river to have engaged the classical writers and survived so long. Half-built houses stood about amid heaps of cement and sand, but the district seemed deserted.

The memory of Kyria Dhiamandopoulou's dream came down on her and she knew she had made a mistake. She had brought Guy here against his will. They had no telephone. They were too far away from things. They would be forgotten and one day wake to find the Germans knocking at the door.

Cold with fear, she went back to the villa and found Guy in the living-room. Gleefully, she cried: 'How wonderful. But why are you here?'

She ran at him and flung her arms round him but he was unresponsive. He had been unpacking his books and had a book in his hand. He stared at it with his lower lip thrust out.

'What's the matter?'

He did not answer for a minute, then said: 'They've closed down the School?'

'Who? Who did it? Cookson?'

'Cookson? Don't be silly. The authorities did it. They didn't realize we intended opening again. When they found we were enrolling students, they ordered an immediate closure.'

'But why?'

'Oh, the old fear of provoking the Germans. I suppose British cultural activities could be regarded as provocation!'

'I'm sorry,' she held to him but in his despondency he simply

162

waited for her to release him. When she dropped her arms, he returned to his books.

'What will you do?'

'Oh,' he reflected, then began to rouse himself: 'I'll find plenty to do. I'm organizing this air-force revue, for one thing. Now I can start rehearsals at once.' As he arranged his books, he became cheerful and said: 'Coming here wasn't such a bad idea, after all.'

'You think so? You really think so?' She was relieved, for in the twilight the villa, bare, functional and very cold, had seemed worse than a mistake; it had seemed a disaster.

'Oh yes. It's splendid having a bathroom and kitchen, and two rooms of our own. We can give a party.'

'Yes, we can.'

She had not intended telling Kyria Dhiamandopoulou's dream but could not suppress it.

Guy said: 'Surely you don't believe her?'

'You mean, you think she made it all up? Why should she?'

'People will say anything to appear interesting.'

Unable to accept this, Harriet said: 'You think there's nothing in the world that can't be explained in material terms?'

'Well, don't you?'

'I don't,' she laughed at him. 'The trouble is, you're afraid of what you can't understand so you say it doesn't exist.'

As they worked together, putting their possessions straight, Harriet felt a sense of holiday and said: 'Let's do something tonight! Let's go and eat at Babayannis'!'

He said: 'Well!' In the face of her excitement, he could not disagree at once but she saw there was an impediment. It turned out that he had arranged to go to Tatoi. Ben Phipps was driving him out and they had been invited to drinks in the Officers' Mess.

'We've got to discuss arrangements for the revue,' he said.

Inclined, unreasonably, to blame Phipps for Guy's engagement, she said crossly: 'I don't know what you see in him. He's taken up with you simply because he's fallen out with Cookson.'

'Don't you want me to have a friend?'

'Not that friend. Surely you could find someone better. What about Alan Frewen?'

'Alan? He's a nice enough fellow, but he's a hopeless reactionary.'

'You mean he doesn't agree with you? At least, he's honest. He's not a crook like Phipps.'

'Ben is a bit of a crook, I suppose,' Guy laughed. 'But he's amusing and intelligent. In a small society like this, if you're over-critical of the people you know, you'll soon find you don't know anyone.'

'Then why were you so critical of Cookson?'

'That Fascist! Whatever you may say about Ben, he has always been a progressive. He has the right ideas.'

'Would he go to the stake for them?'

'Who knows? Worse men than Ben Phipps have gone to the stake for worse ideas.'

'You think the occasion makes the man?'

'Sometimes the man makes the occasion.'

She said bitterly: 'I'm surprised you bothered to come home at all.'

'You said you wanted me to help you move in.'

'Well, don't let me keep you now.'

Untroubled, he agreed that it was time for him to get the bus into Athens.

Late that night Harriet, tensed by the unfamiliar noiselessness outside, lay awake and listened for him.

Some time after midnight he came down the lane singing contentedly:

> 'If your engine cuts out over Hellfire Pass
> You can stick your twin Browning guns right
> up your arse.'

He had been privileged to see a squadron set out on a raid over the Dodecanese ports. Ben Phipps had gone home to write a 'think piece' based on this experience and Guy would show his appreciation, too, by putting on the best entertainment the Royal Air Force had ever seen.

Early next morning the Pringles were awakened by the sound of someone moving about in the villa. They found an old woman like a skeleton bird, with body bound up in a black cotton dress, head bound in a black handkerchief, setting the table for breakfast. At the sight of the Pringles, she stood grinning, her mouth open so they saw she did not possess a single tooth. She pointed to her breastbone and said: 'Anastea.'

Guy did his best to question her in Greek. The master and mistress had forgotten to tell her they were leaving, but she was not much concerned. One employer had gone, another had come. She said that in the mornings she did the housework and shopping; in the evening she came in to cook a meal. Guy said: 'Let her stay. We can afford her.' Harriet was doubtful, but said: 'We could afford her if I got a job.'

While the Pringles conversed in their strange foreign tongue, Anastea stood with hands modestly clasped before her, confident that the great ones of the world would provide for her. When Guy nodded, she grinned again and continued her work without more ado.

16

The information office, which had once been an unimportant appendage of the Legation, now had independent status within the domain of the Military Mission. Harriet found 'Information Office (Billiard Room)' signposted right through the Grande Bretagne but when she came to the Billiard Room, which was at the rear of the hotel, she saw it could have been reached directly by the side entrance. There was no sound behind the Billiard Room door. She imagined Alan Frewen and Yakimov at work there, but when she opened the door she met the stare of two elderly women whom she had never seen before.

The women sat opposite each other at desks placed back to back in a greyish fog of light that fell through a ceiling-dome. There was no other light. The room, with its dark panelling, stretched away into shadow. From where Harriet stood at the door the two old corpse-white faces looked identical, but when she reached them, Harriet saw that one, who looked the elder, was bemused, while the younger had the awareness of a guardian cockatrice.

'Yes, what is it?' the younger demanded.

'I'm looking for Mr Frewen.'

'Not here.'

'Prince Yakimov?'

'No.'

Both women were paused in their work. The elder hung over a typewriter, her bulbous puce-purple lips wet, tremulous and agape; the brown of her eye had faded until nothing remained but a blur of sepia, lacking comprehension; but the younger sister – they could only be sisters – still had a dark, sharp gaze which she centred on Harriet's chest.

'When will Mr Frewen be back?' Harriet asked.

The younger sister seemed to quiver with rage. 'I really can't tell you,' she said, her quivering sending out such a dispelling force Harriet felt as though she were being thrust out of the room. The women suspected her purpose in coming to the office and would tell her nothing. Defeated, she moved away and as she did so, the elder dropped her head over her machine and began to strike the keys slowly, producing a measured thump like a passing bell.

Alan and Yakimov were often at Zonar's. When Harriet went there, she found only Yakimov. He was inside and had just been served with some unusual shell-fish which were set out on a silver dish with quarters of lemon and triangles of thin brown bread. When she approached, he looked flustered as though he might have to share this elegant meal, and said: 'Nearly fainted this morning. Lack of nourishment, y'know All right for you young people, but poor Yaki is feeling his years. Like to try one.'

'Oh, no, thank you. I'm looking for Alan Frewen.'

'Gone back to feed his dog.'

'When can I find him in his office?'

'Not before five. The dear boy seems upset. If you ask me, Lord Pinkrose upset him. The School's been closed down – 'spose you know? – so Lord P.s' landed back on us.'

'And Alan doesn't want him?'

'Don't quote me, dear girl. Alan's a discreet chap; soul of discretion, you might say. And I've nothing against Lord P. Very distinguished man, doing important work . . .'

'What sort of important work?'

'*Secret* work, dear girl. And he has influential friends. This morning he said there was need here for a Director of Propaganda, so he's cabled a friend in Cairo – an extremely influential friend . . .'

'Lord Bedlington?'

'Could be. Bedlington! Sounds familiar. Anyway, it looks

as though Lord P.'ll be promoted. Sad for Alan. He didn't say a thing, not a thing, but I thought he looked a trifle huffed.'

'Understandably,' said Harriet.

'Ummm.' Fearful of committing himself, Yakimov made a neutral murmur. In recognition of Harriet's presence, he had lifted himself a few inches out of his chair but now cried out piteously: 'Do sit down. I'd offer you an ouzo but I'm not even sure I can pay for this little lot.'

Harriet sat and Yakimov relaxed into his chair and squeezed lemon over the shell-fish. 'Why don't you order some? Give yourself a treat?'

Harriet, convinced she had only to eat a single shell-fish to be laid out with typhoid, asked: 'What are they?'

'Sea-urchins. Used to get them along the front at Naples. Quite a delicacy. I suggested them to the head waiter here and he said: "People wouldn't eat them." I said: "Good heavens, dear boy, when you think what people *do* eat these days."' Tackling the urchins with avidity, he spoke between sucks and gulps. 'Try them; try them,' he urged her, but Harriet, who feared strange meats, ordered a cheese sandwich.

'Who are those women in the Billiard Room?' she asked.

'The Twocurrys. Gladys and Mabel. Mabel's the batty one. Just a pair of old trouts.'

'What do they do?'

'Unsolved mystery, dear girl.'

'Alan thought he could give me a job in the office.'

'Why not?' Yakimov, having downed the urchins as rapidly as Diocletian had downed the squid, mopped the remaining juices with the corners of bread. 'Excellent idea!'

'But I wouldn't want to work for Pinkrose.'

'War on, dear girl,' Yakimov dismissed her qualms in a lofty way. 'Can't pick and choose who you'll work for, y'know. Look at me. Must do one's bit.'

Having eaten, he sat for a while with eyelids drooping, then slipped down inside his great-coat. 'Time for beddy-byes,' he said and began to doze.

Harriet, uncertain whether to remain or go, looked round

for the waiter and saw Charles Warden descending from the balcony restaurant. He was looking in a speculative way in her direction and came straight to Yakimov's side. Yakimov opened an eye and Charles Warden said: 'I have a permit to visit the Parthenon. Why don't you come with me?' He turned to include Harriet: 'Both of you,' he added.

Roused out of sleep, Yakimov sighed: 'Not me, dear boy. Your Yak's not fit . . . overwork and underfeeding . . . the years tell . . .' He resettled himself and slept again.

Charles Warden looked to Harriet with a smile that seemed a challenge and she got to her feet.

They walked without a word through the Plaka. While each waited for the other to speak first, Harriet observed him from the corner of her eye, seeing his firm and regular profile lifted slightly, as though he were preoccupied with some solemn matter; but she was aware of his awareness. She wanted to say something that would startle him out of his caution, but could think of nothing.

She noticed as they went through the narrow, confusing streets, that he led her with unhesitating directness to the steps that climbed the Acropolis hill. On the way up, he asked abruptly: 'Where do you live in Athens?'

'Beside the Ilissus. It's a classical site.'

This remark amused him and he said: 'The Ilissus runs right through Athens.'

'It doesn't!'

'I assure you. Most of it's underground, of course.'

'We are a long way out. Half-way to the Piraeus. A rather deserted area, but not so deserted as I thought at first. You can see a few little houses on the other side of the river and, of course, people live near the Piraeus Road. They're quite friendly; they recognize us because we employ Anastea. I like it better now. It's home of sorts.'

He said: 'I'd be quite happy to have a home of any sort.' He told her he had stayed, when he first came, at the Grande Bretagne, but had been crowded out when the Mission arrived. They had had to find him a room at the Corinthian.

'That's nothing to complain about.' From nervousness, she spoke rather sharply and he looked disconcerted, supposing she intended some reflection on young military men who manage to get themselves billeted in the best hotels. He stared into the distance, and she knew they would return to their difficult silence if she could not think of something to say. She said: 'You seem to know Athens quite well.'

'I was here before the war.'

'Did you know Cookson then?'

'He was a friend of my people. I was staying with him when the war started.'

'It must be pleasant there in summer?'

'Yes, but we had the war hanging over us.'

'I know. And it was a beautiful summer. Were you on holiday?'

'Not altogether. I came to learn demotic.'

'You did languages?'

'Classics.'

'You've got a classics degree?'

'No. I hadn't time. I'll go back after the war.'

She realized he must be two, even three, years younger than she, and not much older than Sasha. His youth had an untouched brilliance like something newly minted. She felt he had done nothing; experienced nothing. The whole of his life lay ahead. To keep him talking, she said: 'I suppose you were posted here because you speak Greek?'

'Yes.' He gave a laugh. She wondered if he found her questions inapposite or naïve? He looked at her, smiling, expectant of more, but she refused to say more.

Walking round the base of the Acropolis, they were conscious of tension that could, in a moment, spark into misunderstanding.

Since Harriet had last climbed up, a change had come over the rocky flank of the hill. The first rains had been enough to bring the earth to life. Every patch of ground was becoming overlaid with a nap of tiny shoots, so tender that to tread on them was to destroy them.

Seen from this height the green spreading over the Areopagus seemed not a composite of yellow and blue but a primary colour, lucid and elemental.

When they turned the corner and came in sight of the sea, Harriet was struck by the immense structure of cumulus cloud rising out of the Peloponnese. The sky visible between the Plaka roofs had shown only a meaningless patching of grey and white. At this height, the cloud capes of pearl and slate and thunderous purple could be seen swelling upwards like a cosmic explosion, while to the east a luminous undercloud, floating out like a detached lining, lay peach-golden against the blue.

Observing this spectacle, yet oddly removed from it, Harriet felt she should stop and appreciate it; but Charles went on, behaving as though he were rather more displeased than not by such a distraction. Indeed, when they reached the Beulé gate, he bounded up the stones ahead of her as though enraged by the whole outing.

The evzone sentry examined Charles's permit, then looked Harriet over approvingly. When he returned the permit, he presented arms with as much exertion and clatter as his equipment allowed.

This performance broke down Harriet's nervous restraint. Laughing, she asked: 'Are you entitled to a salute like that?'

Charles flushed, then burst into laughter himself: 'They lay it on a bit if you're with a girl,' he said.

She was enchanted. Detached from limiting reality, lifted into a realm of poetic concepts, she saw Charles not as an ordinary young man – she had, after all, known dozens of ordinary young men, some of whom had been quite as handsome as he – but a man-at-arms to whom was due both deference and privilege. She was her own symbol – the girl whose presence heightened and complimented the myth. Enchanted, she was almost immediately disenchanted; was, indeed, amazed at finding herself dazzled by the cantrips of war. She was against war and its trappings. She was thankful to be married to a man who, whether he liked it or not, was exempt from service. She was not to be taken in by the game of destruction – a game in which Charles Warden was a very unimportant figure. Giving him a sidelong glance, she was prepared to ridicule him; instead, as she found his eyes on her, she felt warmed and excited, and the air about them was filled with promise.

They had the plateau to themselves. The wind blew fresh, singing between the columns, and the distances, sharpened by winter, were deeply coloured. The paving inside the Parthenon was brilliant. Again and again during the last weeks the slabs had been washed by rain and dried by wind until now the whole great floor, reflecting the gold and blue and silver of the sky, seemed to be made of mother-of-pearl.

Harriet wandered about, amazed by the lustre of the marble which held, in its hollows, small pools of rain left by the morning showers, and when she returned to Charles she said: 'If you hadn't brought me, I would never have known it could be like this.'

He was pleased by her pleasure, and for the first time she saw his simplicity. She had thought him vain and critical, and now she thought he was not only young but artless, almost as artless as Sasha. They moved around the Acropolis contained in a contentment like a crystal, that both excluded and burnished the outside world. Harriet exclaimed about everything. The view that in autumn had been flattened by dust and sun, now fell back to the remotest rises of the Argolid with the hills blue-black and violet, the gulf waters an ashy blue and stained with shadows as with ink.

She said: 'Why must they close the Acropolis to visitors?'

Charles did not know. In the seventeenth century the Parthenon had been hit by a Venetian cannon ball and he thought perhaps the Greeks feared more destruction.

She spoke of the golden patina on the columns and asked why he supposed it was darkest on the seaward side. She watched him while he examined the marble. His expression grave and inquiring, he placed his hand on the surface as though he could divine by touch the nature of the marble's

172

disorder. His hand was square, the fingers no longer than the palm, an intelligent and practical, but not a visionary, hand. Her dislike had changed – and changed suddenly – to a sense of affinity. She was amazed and worried as though by something supernatural.

With his hand starred out on the column, he said he thought the salt wind had drawn some mineral from the marble. 'Iron, I should think. It's a sort of rust, in fact. The marble has been oxidized by time.'

She watched him, not really listening. When he turned and found her eyes fixed so intently on him, he smiled in surprise; and she saw how this sudden, unselfconscious smile transformed his face. As they looked at each other, a voice said: 'Love me.'

Harriet did not know whether he had spoken or whether the words had formed themselves in her mind, but there they were, hanging on the air between them, and conscious of them, they were moved and disquieted.

She said: 'I must get back. I'm seeing Alan Frewen at five.'

'I must go, too.'

They returned as they had come, without speaking, but now their silence was luminous and unnervingly fragile. A sentence could corroborate their expectations, if it were the right sentence. Neither would take the risk of speaking; anyway, not then, not at that moment.

As they approached the centre of the town, Harriet felt this suspended anticipation more than she could bear. In Hermes Street, fearing to be caught in further, she planned her escape. She would buy – what? She thought of writing-paper, but before they reached the stationer's shop, she felt the vibration that preceded the air-raid warning. She stopped. Charles paused in inquiry. They were held an instant as though the tremor were some tangible assertion of their nervousness, then the sirens broke out.

She said: 'I'm supposed to take cover.'

Charles, though exempt from the order, caught her arm and looked round for shelter. The street was clearing. They followed the others into the basement of an office block that had been left unfinished when war began. They went down a flight of steps and through a swing door. On the other side, they were in darkness.

Though they could see nothing, they could feel the breathing presence of people and, uncertain what was ahead, came to a stop just inside the door. As a precaution against panic, it was forbidden to speak during a raid, but the whole shelter was alive with small noises, as though the floor ran with mice. The traffic had been stopped and the city was still. The noise, when it came, was shocking. One explosion followed another, each uproarious so it seemed that bombs were bursting overhead. The concrete shuddered and a moan of terror passed over the crowded basement. Harriet felt a movement and, afraid of a possible stampede, she put out her hand and met Charles's hand outstretched to touch her.

He whispered: 'It's nothing. Only the guns on Lycabettos.'

'Are there guns on Lycabettos?'

'Yes, there's a new anti-aircraft emplacement.'

The raid was a long one. The air grew hot. Whenever the Lycabettos guns opened up, the same curious moan filled the shelter and fear, like a breeze, passed over it, rustling the crowd. As Harriet pressed against the door, it opened an inch and, seeing the twilight outside, she whispered: 'Couldn't we stand out there?' They slipped quietly out.

Two other people were on the basement stair: a woman and a small boy. The woman, not young, was seated with the boy on her knee. She was pressing the child's cheek to her bosom and her own cheek rested on the crown of his head. Her eyes were shut and she did not open them when Harriet and Charles came out. Aware of nothing but the child, she enfolded him with fervent tenderness, as though trying to protect him with her whole body.

Not wishing to intrude on their intimacy, Harriet turned away, but her gaze was drawn back to them. Transported by the sight of these two human creatures wrapped in love, she caught her breath and her eyes filled with tears.

She had forgotten Charles. When he said: 'What is the matter?' his lightly quizzical tone affronted her. She said: 'Nothing.' He put a hand to her elbow, she moved away, but the all clear was sounding and they were free to leave.

Outside in the street, he said again: 'What's the matter?' and added with an embarrassed attempt at sympathy: 'Aren't you happy?'

'I don't know. I haven't thought about it. Is one required to be happy?'

'I didn't mean that. "Happy" isn't the word. I don't know what I meant.'

She knew what he meant but said nothing.

'Guy is a wonderful person,' he said at last. 'Don't you feel you're lucky to be married to him?'

'You scarcely know him.'

'I know people who know him. Everyone seems to know him, and speak highly of him. Eleko Vourakis said: "Guy Pringle will do anything to help anyone."'

'Yes, he will. That's true.'

Not enlightened by her agreement, Charles gave a laugh – the brief, exasperated laugh of a man who suspects he is being swindled. It occurred to her that her first impression of him had had some justification. Whatever he might be, he was not simple. She was relieved when they reached the Grande Bretagne.

'Are you seeing Frewen now?' he asked.

'Yes. I may get a job in the Information Office.'

'Then you'll be next door to me.'

'It's not settled yet.'

'Have tea with me tomorrow?'

'Not tomorrow.'

'Then, when?'

'Thursday is possible. I'll have to see what Guy is doing.'

He opened the hotel door and as the interior light fell on his face, she saw he was chagrined. 'Perhaps you'll let me know,' he said.

'Yes, I'll let you know.' She went off, scarcely knowing why she felt elated, and made her way back to the Billiard Room. This time the Misses Twocurry did not give her a look. The desks were overhung by two green-shaded bulbs pulled down so low there was nothing to be seen but the desk-tops and the outline of the women. Harriet asked for Mr Frewen and, as though too occupied to speak, the younger waved her towards a door.

Alan and Yakimov were in a room marked News Room. Filled with elegant little escritoires and gilt, tapestry-seated chairs, it had once been the hotel writing room. Every piece of furniture was hung with news-sheets Roneoed over with blocks of information that had either been marked as important or heavily crossed out.

Alan was seated behind a massive desk that might have come from the manager's office. He was working on the sheets with a charcoal pencil, scoring out or underlining information, then handing them to Yakimov who sat, with negligent humility, in front of the desk. Although, as a military establishment, the hotel was heated, Yakimov still had his coat about him. At the sight of Harriet, he struggled to his feet, delighted that she should not only see him working but interrupt his work.

Alan was less sociable. He seemed ill at ease in the position of employer, but he was prepared for her arrival. He had books, maps, depositions and newspaper cuttings stacked ready, and started at once to explain how she must correlate the material in order to make a handbook for the troops who were preparing to invade Dodecanese. He was in the midst of this when Miss Gladys Twocurry entered and started to sort the letters in a tray. Alan stopped speaking and when Harriet began to question him, he lifted a hand to silence her. When at last it became evident that Miss Twocurry would hear nothing, she took herself off.

Alan made no comment on this sally but said to Harriet: 'I had hoped to put you in here with Yakimov, but apparently we are to have a Director of Propaganda.'

'Lord Pinkrose?'

'Yes. The Legation says his appointment is imminent. He has decided he must have my office, so I've had to move in here. There'll be more space for you in the outer office. Don't let anyone quiz you about your work. Simply say you're not allowed to discuss it.'

He gathered up Harriet's impedimenta and led her back to the Billiard Room where he switched on a central light, disclosing a confusion usually hidden beneath the gloom of day or the shadows of night.

As though scandalized by this, Miss Gladys Twocurry clicked her tongue.

Alan passed her without a glance. The billiard tables, with their stout legs and little crocheted ball-traps, had been pushed against the walls and covered with dust-sheets. The sheets, intended to protect the baize, had fallen awry. Unfiled papers were heaped on the green surface which was growing grey with dust. Beside the billiard tables there were dining tables, bureaux, military trestle-tables and card tables; and every surface was covered with letters, reports, news sheets, newspapers, maps and posters, all thrown pell-mell together and growing écru with age. An open bureau was filled with rolls of cartridge paper, made brittle by the summer heat, and as Alan swept them to the floor, they cracked like crockery and Miss Gladys clicked again, more loudly.

Alan said: 'You can work here. If you need anything, let me know.' He left the room.

Harriet, arranging her books and papers, was conscious of the Twocurrys behind her. Miss Mabel's typewriter was still. Miss Gladys seemed not to breathe. Then, suddenly, Miss Gladys crossed the room and her personal smell, a smell like old mutton fat, filled the neighbourhood of Harriet's desk. She was peering down at a copy of the *Mediterranean Pilot* which Harriet had opened on the table.

She asked severely: 'What are you doing here?'

'I'm working. I've been employed.'

'Indeed! And what are you working at, may I ask?'

'I'm afraid I can't tell you.'

'*Indeed!*' Miss Gladys's head quivered with indignation. 'Who employed you? Lord Pinkrose?'

'I was taken on by Mr Frewen.'

'Ah!' Miss Gladys seemed to think she had uncovered a fault and, turning, went purposefully from the room.

Harriet waited apprehensively, knowing her apprehensions were absurd. If Pinkrose disapproved her, he could do no more than dismiss her. As he was not yet Director of Propaganda, he could not, as yet, do even that.

The door opened again. She could hear Pinkrose's grunts and coughs and, glancing over her shoulder, she saw he had stopped at a safe distance from her and was viewing her as though to confirm whatever Miss Gladys had said.

'Good evening, Lord Pinkrose,' Harriet said.

He coughed and muttered: 'Yes, yes,' then went to a bookcase where he took down a book, opened it, fluttered the pages, clapped it to and returned it. He muttered several times: 'Yes, yes,' while Miss Gladys stood by hopefully and watched. Harriet returned to her work. Having dealt with several other books, Pinkrose left the bookcase and began rustling among the papers, several times saying: 'Yes, yes,' in an urgent tone, then suddenly he sped away. Miss Gladys let out her breath in an aggravated way. For the first time it occurred to Harriet that Pinkrose was as nervous of her as she was of him.

Next morning, soon after she arrived in the office, a military messenger rapped the door and came in with a note.

'Bring it over here,' Miss Gladys pointed imperiously to a spot on the floor beside her.

The messenger said: 'It's for Mrs Pringle.'

Harriet took the note and read: 'Will you have lunch today?' There was no signature. In the space for a reply, she wrote 'Yes' and handed back the paper. Miss Mabel thumped on unawares, but Miss Gladys watched with the incredulity of one who wonders how far insolence can go.

Charles Warden was at the side entrance, standing casually as though he had merely paused to reflect and would, in a moment, move away. When Harriet said: 'Hello,' he appeared surprised and she said: 'Someone invited me to lunch. I thought it might be you.'

'You weren't sure? It could be someone else?'

'I do know other people.'

'Of course,' he agreed but his serious, speculative expression seemed critical of the fact. She laughed and his manner changed. He seemed to laugh at himself, and asked: 'Where shall we go? Zonar's?'

She said: 'Yes,' but she did not want to go to Zonar's. It was the restaurant where Alan ate at mid-day, usually taking Yakimov with him. Ben Phipps also went there. Because of Charles's good-looks and the current of understanding between them, she knew their friendship could be misunderstood. There was disloyalty to Guy in inviting such misunderstanding. But this was not easy to explain. Also, Guy had said he cared nothing for the suspicions of others, so why should she hesitate and shift and evade, and have guilt imposed upon her?

When Zonar's came into view, it was Charles who hesitated: 'Do you want to go there?' he said. 'We'll probably run into people we know. Let's go to the Xenia! The food's still tolerable there.'

'Yes, I'd like to see the Xenia.'

No one known to Guy ever went there. Harriet was stimulated by the thought of this expensive restaurant and when she found it dingy, the walls decorated in shades of brown with peacocks and women in ancient Egyptian poses, and hung with lamps of Lalique glass, she was disappointed.

The tables not already taken were reserved and Charles had to wait while the Head Waiter, unwilling to turn away an English officer, consulted his list and decided what could be done for them. In the end an extra table was set up close to the curtain that separated the restaurant from the famous Xenia *confiserie* where Major Cookson had bought his very small cakes.

Harriet said: 'This place is a relic of the 'twenties.'

'The wine is good,' Charles said defensively.

Most of those present were businessmen but there were some officers, Greeks on leave or Englishmen from the Mission. The atmosphere was dull and though the wine was, as Charles said, good, the food, which imitated French food, seemed to Harriet much worse than the taverna stews.

To avoid Charles's fixed regard, Harriet watched the comings and goings on the other side of the coffee-coloured chiffon curtains. The people who entered the shop, some furtively, some with nonchalance or aggressive rapidity, chose cakes which were handed to them on a plate with a little fork. However chosen, the cakes would be devoured with the greed of chronic deprivation. Harriet, brought to a state of nervous nausea by Charles's proximity, had no appetite herself and she began to wonder what she was doing, fomenting a situation that reduced her to such a state.

She sat with a hand on the table and, feeling a touch, found Charles had stretched out his little finger and was pulling his fingernail along the edge of her palm.

'Tell me why you were crying yesterday.'

'I don't know. Not for any reason, really. I suppose I was frightened.'

'Of the raid? You know Athens hasn't been bombed.'

'The guns startled me.'

He gave his laugh, the laugh of a swindled man, that she now began to see was characteristic of him. He would not even pretend to accept her explanation. Her original dislike was roused again and she began to wish herself away. Once away, she would see no more of him.

An apathetic sense of failure came down between them. Charles looked sullen. She felt he was reproaching her for attracting him, then telling him nothing. He fixed her with his cold light-coloured eyes and asked: 'How long have you been married?'

'We married just before the war. Guy was home on leave.'

'Had you known one another long?'

'Only a few weeks.'

'You married in haste?'

The questions were asked mockingly, almost derisively, and she gave her answers with the intention of annoying him: 'Not really. I felt I had known him all my life.'

'But did you? Did you know him?'

'Yes, in a way.'

'But not in every way?'

Knowing he was taking revenge for her refusal to confide in him, she felt her own power and answered composedly: 'Not in every way. There are always things to be discovered about every human being.'

'But you still think him wonderful?'

'Yes. Too wonderful, perhaps. He imagines he can do everything for everyone.'

'But not for you?'

'He sees me as part of himself. He feels he does not need to do things for me.'

'Are you satisfied with that state of affairs?'

People waiting for tables were queuing on the other side of the curtain and this gave her excuse to say: 'Don't you think we should go?'

'You've hardly eaten anything.'

'I'm not very hungry.'

Outside, in the bright, brief light of afternoon, with two hours of freedom before them, Charles asked: 'What would you like to do now?'

The question was a testing-point and, from his tone, she saw he expected her to refer the question back to him. She said casually: 'I've never been to the Lycabettos church. Let's go up there.'

'If you want to.'

He did not hide his resentment. Though he turned towards the hill, he made no pretence of interest in the excursion. She felt the distance between them and a bleak relief in not caring. The relationship would go no further.

She asked him about the possibility of a German attack. He gave an offhand answer: a German attack was 'on the cards'. It had been from the first.

She said: 'There is a rumour that the Germans are piling up armaments on the frontier.'

'That rumour's always going round.'

'If there is no attack, what do you think will happen? Can the Greeks win?'

'I don't know. I doubt it. Greek ammunition is running out. They say present supplies won't last two months.'

'But surely we can send them ammunition?'

'It would be no use. The Greek firearms were bought from Krupps. Our ammunition doesn't fit.'

'Can't we send both guns and ammunition?'

He answered with laconic grimaces, speaking, she knew, out of an inner grimness, conceding her nothing: 'We haven't the guns to send. In Cairo our own men are wandering about doing nothing because we have no arms to give them. But even if we had all the rifles in the world, there'd still be the problem of transport.'

'We can't spare the ships?'

'Our losses have been pretty heavy, you know!'

She gave him a sidelong glance and saw him sternly detached from her. She wondered if he were trying to frighten her and said appealingly: 'Things can't be as bad as that? Are you suggesting we might even lose the war?'

He gave his ironical laugh: 'Oh, I imagine we'll pull through somehow. We always do.'

The climb was a long one. The road ended at the terrace where the Patersons had their flat. Above that the path was rough. By the time they reached the church the sun was only just above the horizon and the whitewashed walls were tawny with the winter sunset. A chilly wind swept across the court-yard of the church. The place was deserted except for a boy who sold lemonade, and he was packing up his stall. Charles stood with an unforthcoming patience while Harriet leant against the wall and looked over the great sea of houses that ran into shadow against the new green of Hymettos. She turned and asked Charles if he had been before to the church.

He stared away from her. She thought he would not reply,

but after a moment he said he had been here at Easter when the Greeks made it a place of pilgrimage, carrying candles that could be seen from the distance like two lines of light, one passing up, the other down, the hill.

'I suppose you saw the processions? The burial of Christ and the great resurrection procession on Easter Sunday?'

'Of course.'

'Will they hold them this year, do you think?'

'They may, if things are going well.' He answered unwillingly as though she were forcing him to give her information but when her questions stopped, he said: 'The evzones are in Albania. The processions wouldn't be much without them. On Easter Sunday they wear their full regalia. You know – fustanella and tasselled caps and slippers with pompoms,' he suddenly laughed. 'The processions end up in the square . . . the girls on the hotel terrace had those sparkler things and they were shaking them down on the men's skirts, trying to set them on fire . . .'

She smiled and put out her hand to him: 'If they hold the processions this year, we might see them together.'

He took her hand but there was still something wrong. Staring down at the ground, he said: 'This is only a temporary posting. I probably won't be here at Easter. You do realize that, don't you?'

'No, I didn't realize . . .'

She moved away from the wall. The view had become meaningless. She noticed how cold the wind was; and the sun had almost set. They began walking down the steps.

While she had contemplated a long, developing relationship, he had, she now saw, been obsessed by the knowledge that their time was short. She had had an illusion of leisurely intimacy, imagining them trapped together here, likely to share the same fate. It had all been fantasy. Whatever their fate would be, he would not share it. Guy and she might not save themselves, but they were free to try.

He was a different order of being. His function was not to preserve his own life but protect the lives of others. In this present situation, he might run no greater risk than she herself; he was not more likely to lose his life – and yet, against reason, glancing sideways in the twilight, she saw him poetic, transfigured, like one of those sacrificial youths of the last war whose portraits had haunted her childhood. With his unmarred, ideal looks, he was not intended for life. It was not his part to survive. She was required to live but he was a romantic figure, marked down for death.

And the relationship was urgent.

It was not quite dark when they reached the bottom of the road. Lights were on in the shops but the black-out curtains had not been pulled across. They passed a small grocery-shop with empty shelves. From habit she looked in, just in case there was something for sale. She saw nothing but a jar of pickled cucumbers.

As they crossed the road to the Grande Bretagne, Charles said: 'Will you meet me again later? We could have supper at the Corinthian.'

The request was peremptory, almost a command, but she had to resist: 'I'm going to Guy's rehearsal.'

'Do you have to go?'

'I promised him.'

'I see.'

They had reached the main entrance of the hotel and he was about to enter without speaking again.

She said: 'Will you come to lunch on Sunday.'

'Where?'

'At our house. The villa beside the Ilissus.'

'I will if I can.' He turned to go then paused and added more graciously: 'I would like to come.'

'Yes. Do.' She spoke with enticing sweetness and he smiled and said: 'Then of course I will.'

17

Guy's position had not become wholly void. He had visited the Greek officials and persuaded them to return the keys of the School. As a result of his earnest and energetic appeal, they agreed that the library might remain open and the School premises be used as a club. He was now rehearsing the entertainment for the airmen at Tatoi and rehearsals were held in the Lecture Room.

Pinkrose did not object to this because he knew nothing about it. His appointment as Director of Propaganda had been confirmed. When Guy asked him to approve some action taken to restore the function of the School, Pinkrose said he was much too busy to be worried by matters of that sort. Guy could do what he liked.

Pinkrose came to the Information Office several days a week and shut himself into the room that had once been Alan's office.

'What does he do?' Harriet asked.

'He's writing a lecture,' Alan solemnly replied: 'His subject is "Byron: the Poet-Champion of Greece".'

'When will he deliver it?'

'That remains to be seen.'

The Tatoi entertainment was progressing. The theme song had been written by Guy himself and when he was home, which was not often, he sang it around the house until Harriet begged him to stop.

'Was I singing?' he would ask in apology. 'I didn't realize,' and in a moment would sing again:

'There's fun and frolic, jokes and sketches, too.
You'll find them all together in the R.A.F. revue.'

On the morning of Harriet's luncheon with Charles, Guy had mentioned that the chief item of the revue, a play called *Maria Marten*, would be given its first run through that evening.

'You can come and see it,' he said. 'You might even join the chorus.'

The invitation surprised her. In the past Guy had discouraged her from attending rehearsals. He had put her out of his production of *Troilus and Cressida* – a fact she had not forgiven – and when she protested, told her they could not work together. The trouble was, she did not take him seriously enough.

She said now: 'Do you really want me to come? Don't you find me a nonconforming reality in your world of make-believe?'

Untouched by mockery, he said: 'The revue's different. It's not like a serious production. In fact, it's just a joke. Why not come along this evening?'

'I might.' Remembering her past rejection, she would not commit herself, yet later in the day she said to Charles: 'I am going to Guy's rehearsal.'

There had, she decided, been a promise; and she set out, resolute, after supper, keeping her promise as a gesture of fidelity. When she reached the School, she could hear the rehearsal from the street. The chorus seemed to come from a hundred voices:

'There's fun and frolic, jokes and sketches, too.
You'll find them all together in the R.A.F. revue.'

Looking in through the glazed doors, she saw a hundred mouths opening and shutting. Or what seemed like a hundred.

She knew perhaps ten people in Athens. Guy knew more, of course. She could not keep up with his gregariousness. Though she took it for granted, she wondered: Where did he find all these people? Peering in cautiously, she realized that among them were almost all the women who had been at Mrs Brett's party. Confused by the number of Mrs Brett's guests, she had not tried to separate and identify them, but for Guy each had been an individual and, individually contacted, they had come here to help him; now they were singing, whether they could sing or not.

She saw Mrs Brett bawling away. And at the piano there was – of all people! – Miss Jay.

The chorus of pretty girls – students mostly, with one or two of the younger Legation typists – stood in line down the middle of the room. Behind stood an equal number of personable young males. They produced only a part of the uproar. Everyone was required to join in while Guy, acting as conductor, was inspiring, exhorting, giving himself and demanding that everyone else give, too.

'Come on: *give*!' he shouted, refusing any sort of compromise, requiring from them all the volume, vitality and abandon of which they were capable.

The only ones exempt from duty were the cast of *Maria Marten* – Yakimov, Alan Frewen and Benn Phipps who sat 'saving their voices' in a row along the wall.

Those who knew Harriet were too engrossed to notice her. Entering unseen, she sat beside Ben Phipps who, with hands in pockets and feet thrust out before him, watched the proceedings with a sardonic grin.

The song ended. Guy was far from satisfied. He scrubbed his handkerchief over his face and told the boys and girls of the chorus they would have to work. The others must work, too. They might be non-appearers, mere enhancers, but only their best was good enough. Now! He stuffed the handkerchief away, and signalled Miss Jay. The song broke out again.

Guy had thrown off his jacket. Singing at the top of his voice, he stripped off his tie and undid his collar button. He rolled up his sleeves but as he waved his arms in the air, his sleeves unrolled themselves and the cuffs flew around his head.

'Once more,' he demanded even before the chorus had panted to an end. 'What we want is spirit. Give it more spirit. This is for the chaps at Tatoi. Come on now, they don't get much fun out there. Put your heart and soul into it.'

Watching him urging the performers with the force of his personality, Harriet wondered: 'How did I come to marry someone so different from myself?'

But she had married him; and perhaps, unawares, it was his difference she had married.

Though she had no wish to know many people, could not endure for long the strain of company, she could take pride in his wide circle; even satisfaction, feeling that she lived, if only at second-hand. But to live at second-hand was to live at a distance. By withdrawing from Guy's exhausting enterprise, she withdrew from Guy. The activity was the man. If she were not willing to be dragged at his elbow then, she feared, she must watch him pass like a whirlwind and the day might come when she must wave good-bye.

The chorus sang the song again and again until at last, scarcely able to keep on their feet, the young people were dismissed and Guy, unwearied, called for the cast of *Maria Marten*. Looking round, he saw Harriet and waved, but he had no time to speak. Ben, Alan and Yakimov were already on their feet.

The rehearsal over, Guy walked in the midst of a noisy group to Omonia Square. The girls had to return home early and the male students were deputed to see them safely back. But that was not the end of the evening for Guy. He insisted that everyone else must come and have a drink.

Mrs Brett and her friends, intoxicated by all the commotion, let themselves be led to Aleko's, a café that at any other time they would fear to enter. When they were packed together in the plain little room behind the black-out curtains, Mrs Brett was as boisterous as she had been at her own party. Catching sight of Harriet for the first time, she gripped her wrist and shouted: 'You're a lucky girl!'

Harriet smiled: 'I suppose I am.'

'My, what a lucky girl you are.' She looked about her shouting above the noise. 'Isn't she a lucky girl!' confident she spoke for all present.

As no doubt she did. Harriet, becalmed against the wall,

saw Guy at the centre of the group shining and jubilant. She knew then the thing he loved most was the fatuous good-fellowship of crowds. Of course she had suspected it before. On the train to Bucharest, she had watched him surrounded by admiring Rumanian women, his face alight as though with wine, his arms extended to embrace them all. To someone so enamoured of the general, could the particular ever really mean anything?

Looking her way and meeting her speculative gaze, he thrust out his arm and drew her into the mêlée. 'What did you think of *Maria Marten*?' he asked.

'Very funny. The men will love it.'

'They will, won't they?' Had he been engineering some great work that would last for all time, he could not have been more gratified. He would not let her go. Holding her to him, his arm about her shoulder, he coaxed her into the talk as though she were a shy child.

But she was not a child, and she was only shy when forced, as she now was, into a confusion of people whom she scarcely knew. He was eager that she should share his joy in the company; while she, doing her best to smile, was eager only to escape it. Forcibly held in the centre of uproar, she bore the situation as long as she could, then managed to get away. He glanced after her, a little puzzled, a little grieved, wondering what more she could want. But the problem did not hang long on the air. Distracted by some question put to him about the production, he was caught again into a hurly-burly of suggestion and counter-suggestion, of public extrinsicality so pressing and time-absorbing that the problem of living had to be put on one side until tomorrow, or the day after or, indeed, until death should come and fetch him.

18

When Harriet mentioned to Guy that she had invited Charles Warden to luncheon, he said: 'Good! But I won't be around long.'

'I thought you would like to see him again.'

'I would, of course; but I'll be rehearsing all afternoon.'

Harriet also invited Alan Frewen. Hearing there were to be two guests, Anastea threw up her hands and asked what were they to eat? Her husband, who was a night-watchman, could sometimes, by joining a queue early in the morning, obtain food for the Pringles as well as for his family. But it was becoming more difficult; he might queue for three hours and at the end get nothing. Seeing the old woman distraught by the problem, Harriet promised to find something herself in Athens.

The villa, a flimsy summer structure, was very cold now. There was no oil for the heaters and on a fine day it was warmer outside than in. Sunday was bright and gusty. When Alan walked out to the villa with his dog, the Pringles took him up to the sheltered roof-terrace to drink ouzo. Harriet, looking towards the Piraeus road on which she expected the staff car to appear, said: 'Charles Warden is coming.'

'Is he?'

'You do like him, don't you? You must have known him before the war?'

'I did know him slightly. Rather a spoilt boy, don't you think?'

'I wouldn't say so.'

This reply daunted Alan who, made to feel that he had

shown discourtesy towards a fellow guest, bent down and spent some time adjusting Diocletian's collar.

A military car passed on the Piraeus road. Harriet watched it, unable to believe it had not gone by in error, but it did not come back. Guy looked at his watch and said his rehearsal was called for half past two. Harriet said: 'I think we had better eat.'

'What about young Warden?'

'We can't wait all day for him.'

Harriet had found nothing in Athens but potatoes which she told Anastea to bake. When they came to the table, they were mashed and served like an immense white pudding.

Alan laughed at Harriet's apologies: 'Potatoes in any form are a luxury to me. All we get at the Academy these days is salad made of marguerite leaves.'

'*Can* one eat marguerite leaves?'

'If they aren't marguerite leaves, I don't know what they are.'

When they had each taken a share of the potatoes, Harriet put the plate down for Diocletian. As the last vestige of potato was swept up by the dog's tongue, Anastea came from the kitchen and gave a cry. Usually so meek and accepting of her employers' peculiarities, she made a threatening movement at the dog, her face taut with anger. Alan paled and caught his breath.

Harriet had forgotten Anastea. She said: 'What can we give her?' but there was no answer to that question.

Guy put his hand in his pocket: 'I'll give her some money.'

'What good is money? She wants food.'

Anastea herself said nothing. Having made her gesture, she took the dishes and went.

This incident hastened Guy's departure; and Alan and Harriet went for a walk. They crossed the Ilissus and strolled through the sparse little pinewood where the trees had been dwarfed and distorted by the wind from the sea. Beneath the trees, the spikes of green were already shaping themselves into the foliage of future flowers. January was nearing its end and the light on the puddles on the glossy banks of wet clay had a new brilliance. Harriet said she could smell leaves in the wind. Alan said he could smell nothing but the brewery on the Piraeus road.

Harriet was contemplating a changed attitude to life. What she needed was independence of mind. She would turn her back on emotional involvements and seek, instead, the compensating interest of work and society. Charles was as good as forgotten; but when she returned to the villa, she asked Anastea if anyone had called in her absence.

'*Kaneis, kaneis,*' Anastea replied.

And that, Harriet decided, was that.

19

Sorry about yesterday. Lunch today?

Harriet answered: *No.*

The military messenger was back within ten minutes. The second message read: *Forgive and say yes!* Again Harriet replied: *No.* A third message came: *Dinner and explanations?* Harriet scribbled across it: *Impossible.*

Miss Gladys Twocurry said: 'We can't have this young man coming in and out of here with his noisy boots. He's upsetting my sister.'

'It's an essential part of my work,' Harriet replied.

'If it goes on,' Miss Gladys threatened, 'I'll complain to Lord Pinkrose,' but the messenger did not come back.

Miss Gladys also had a typewriter, a newer and finer machine than that provided for Miss Mabel. It stood on a billiard table and twice a week it was carried over to her desk by the Greek office boy. She used it to cut the stencil for the biweekly news-sheet, which Yakimov delivered on his bicycle. The stencil cutting, her chief employment, was treated as the most important activity in the office. The duplicator stood in a corner and when not in use was covered with a sheet. The Greek boy would uncover it and spread the ink from the tube. Then tutting, sighing, breathing loudly, Miss Gladys fitted on the stencil. This done at last, the office boy turned the handle and kept the copies neatly stacked. When twenty were ready, they were handed to Miss Mabel, who folded them and put them into envelopes. The envelopes then went to Miss Gladys, who addressed them from a list in a bold, schoolgirlish hand. When the addressed envelopes began to pile up, Yakimov would receive his call from the boy and appear ready-coated, bicycle-clips in place.

Everyone concerned treated the production and delivery of the News-Letter as a supremely exacting operation. If a query arose, it was discussed in whispers.

Yakimov, packing the letters into his satchel, would also speak in whispers; and setting out on his delivery round, he went with strained and serious face.

The last letter run off, folded, placed in an envelope, addressed and delivered, everyone was exhausted, but the most exhausted was Yakimov who, safely back in his office, would collapse into his chair and seem, like the runner Phidipides, about to die from his efforts.

Altogether some four or five hundred envelopes were sent out, some to Greeks but most to English residents in and about Athens. Harriet had been surprised to realize how many British subjects remained, and how much ground Yakimov had to cover on his bicycle. Letters, tied up in batches, were marked not only for the city centre, but for Kifissia, Phychiko, Patissia, Kalamaki, Phaleron and Piraeus.

The first time she had seen them prepared for delivery, she tried to break down Miss Gladys's hostility by saying: 'I never knew poor Yaki worked so hard.'

'Poor Yaki!' Miss Gladys caught her breath in horror. 'Are you referring to Prince Yakimov?'

Harriet did not improve matters by laughing. She might treat Yakimov as a joke, but he was no joke for the Twocurrys. Her casual manner towards a man of title marked her for them as one who had too high an opinion of herself. Several times in the office Miss Gladys often began remarks with 'I never presume' or 'I know my station', and she saw her station increased by the fact she worked with a lord and a prince.

The Twocurrys were not alone in respecting Yakimov's title. Several among the remaining English were delighted to have a prince drink himself senseless at their parties.

Alan told Harriet that soon after Yakimov arrived he was

seen standing on the balcony of a flat where a party was in progress. Singing mournfully to himself, he displayed the organ, the secondary function of which is the relief of the bladder, and sent a crystal trajectory through the moonlight down on to the heads of people drinking coffee at an outdoor café below.

Alan told the story with tolerant affection. In Rumania, where there were too many princes, most of them poor, it would have been told with venom and indignation. His situation there had become such he would, had Guy not given him refuge, have died, as the beggars died, of starvation and cold. In those days he used to speak contemptuously of Greek cooking, yet it was here in Greece that he had regained himself and found friendship.

Harriet, who saw him often, could not imagine why she had ever disliked him. He had become not only a friend, but an old friend. They shared memories that gave them the ease of near relationship.

When Alan and Yakimov went to Zonar's or Yannaki's, they would take Harriet with them. 'Do come, dear girl, we'd love to have you,' Yakimov would say as though it were he and not Alan who dispensed hospitality.

Yakimov did not buy drinks for his companions. The habit perhaps had been lost during his days of penury, but once in a while, when the glasses were empty, he would become restless as though, given time and money enough, it might return. It never did. Alan would say: 'How about another?' and Yakimov would remain poised for a second, then ask in hearty relief: 'Why not?'

Yakimov would contribute a joke, his own joke; but once conceived, it had to do long service. The joke of the moment, derived from his contact with the decoding office, was one that called for careful timing. He had to wait until a second order was given then, the waiter having come and gone, he would say with satisfaction: 'Three corrupt groups asking for a repeat.'

When at last Alan said, 'Need we repeat it again?' Yakimov

murmured sadly, "M growing old; losing m'*esprit*. Poor old Yaki,' and the joke went on as before.

Alan and Yakimov would discuss *Maria Marten* and the gossip of the rehearsals, and Harriet learnt more from them than she ever learnt from Guy.

It was Yakimov who mentioned that Dubedat and Toby Lush had approached Guy and asked if they might take part in the revue. Guy had made no promises and later the two found the rehearsals were proceeding without them.

'Bit of a jolt for them,' said Yakimov. 'Am told Dubedat was ruffled. Trifle put out, you know. Goes round telling people if it weren't for him that show we did in Bucharest – what *was* it called, dear girl? – would have been a fair foozle. Says that only his performance saved the day. Told the Major that. Bit unfair to the rest of us, don't you think? Or wouldn't you say so?' Yakimov gazed anxiously at Harriet, who, assuring him that in her opinion it was *his* performance that carried the production to the heights, said: 'You were Pandarus to the life.'

Much gratified, Yakimov said: 'Had to work very hard. Guy kept me at it.' He reflected for some minutes then a look of pique crumpled his face. 'But what came of it? Nothing. When it was all over, your Yak was forgotten.'

'Nonsense.'

'Yes, forgotten,' Yakimov insisted bleakly. 'Dear fellow, Guy. Best in the world. Salt of the earth, but a trifle careless. Doesn't understand how a poor Yak feels.'

Harriet was startled by this criticism – she had imagined she was the only one who criticized Guy – and the more startled that it should come from Yakimov. Yakimov, picked up when hungry and homeless, had been lodged by them for seven months and she felt angry that he should dare to criticize Guy, and criticize him in front of Alan.

Yet, startled and angry as she was, she realized he had spoken out of a genuine sense of injury. Guy had made much of him, then, the play over, had abandoned him. Guy imagined he was all things to all men, but did he really know anything about any man? Did he know anything about her? She doubted it. She, too, was beginning to accumulate a sense of injury.

Yakimov had suffered from coming too close to Guy. Guy was, she suspected, resentful of those near enough to hamper his freedom. It occurred to her that he might resent her. Why, for instance, had he not told her himself that Lush and Dubedat had asked for a part in the revue and been rejected? He may have forgotten to tell her, but more likely he had not chosen to tell her. He would not admit that he felt about them as she did. He would rather protect them against her judgement.

She felt his attitude betrayed the concept of mutual defence which existed in marriage.

But perhaps it existed only for her. It would be impossible to persuade Guy that he betrayed a concept that did not exist for him. He would condemn it as egoism. He might have his own ideas about marriage, but she doubted it. Having married her, he simply ceased to see her as another person. She had once accused him of considering her feelings less than those of anyone else with whom they came into contact. Surprised, he had said: 'But you are myself. I don't need to consider your feelings.'

In Bucharest, where he continued his classes for Jewish students in spite of Fascist demonstrations, he said: 'They need me. They have no one else. I must give them moral support,' yet he seemed unable to understand that, living as they did, she, too, needed 'moral support'. As she met every crisis alone, it seemed to her she had been transported to a hostile world, then left to fend for herself.

Here, if she had nothing else, she had her work and the friendship of Alan and Yakimov. Alan, seeing her daily, had become more easy company. He would talk freely enough, though he had areas of constraint. One of these was Pinkrose and everything to do with Pinkrose.

When Harriet asked, 'Does he object to my being in the office?' Alan shrugged and would not reply. Pinkrose had imposed himself on the office. Useless though he was, he had become Alan's superior and must not be discussed. Still, he could be mentioned in relation to the Twocurrys.

Alan said: 'Gladys appointed herself chief toady to Pinkrose the minute she set eyes on him. I suspect she's a bit infatuated with him.'

Harriet wanted to know how the Twocurrys ever achieved their position in the Information Office. Alan told her:

'We started the office on a shoestring. I had to take any help I could get. Later we got a grant and I could have had a real secretary: one of the delightful English-speaking Greek girls. Instead I kept on old Gladys and Mabel. They needed the money. I just hadn't the heart to chuck them out; and now I've got Gladys spying on everything I do and at the slightest upset rushing off to complain to Pinkrose. The moral of this story is: never let your heart get the better of your sense.'

'You could get rid of her now.'

'Oh, Pinkrose would never let her go. He described her the other day as "invaluable".'

'I suppose they aren't paid much?'

'Not much, no. They scarcely get a whole salary between them; but then, they scarcely do a whole job. Mabel, in my opinion, is more nuisance than she's worth.'

The letters sent in to be typed by Miss Mabel were written very carefully in letters an inch high. Her speech, which Harriet heard seldom and always found distressing, was understood only by Miss Gladys. She never moved unaided from her chair. If she had to visit the cloakroom, she put up a panic-stricken babble until Miss Gladys led her away. When the time came for their departure, Miss Gladys would first put on her own coat and hat then grip her sister by the upper arm and get her out of the chair. While Miss Mabel mumbled and moaned, demanded and protested, Miss Gladys fitted her into her outdoor clothing. Both wore hats of sunburnt straw. Miss Gladys's coat was bottle green and Miss Mabel's coat was of a plum colour reduced in its exposed places to shades of caustic pink. Miss Mabel, who was delicate, was not allowed out without a tippet of ginger-brown fur.

When they left the office, where did they go? How did they live? How did women like the Twocurrys come to be in Athens at all? Alan said they had been the daughters of an artist, a romantic widower, who had saved up to bring himself and his little girls to Greece. They had found two rooms in the Plaka and the father, while alive, made a living by drawing Athenian scenes which he sold to tourists. That had been way back in the '80s and the sisters still lived on in the Plaka rooms. Before the war Miss Gladys had worked at the Archaeological School piecing together broken pots. She had taken Miss Mabel with her every day and, said Alan, 'the Head, not knowing what on earth to do with her, shut Mabel up with a typewriter. Weeks later, mysterious sounds were heard through the door . . . thump-thump-thump. *She had taught herself to type.* When the war started, the Archaeological School closed down and the Twocurrys were thrown upon the world. I seized them as they fell. And now,' Alan gave his painful grin, 'you know their whole history.'

'So the office is all their life.'

'I doubt whether they have any other.'

Harriet doubted whether she herself had any other. But it was a life of sorts. Her position in the office, though minor, was recognized. She was even invited to a party by the Greek Minister of Information. Delighted by this courtesy, she wanted to share it and hurried to ask Alan if she might take Guy with her. Alan telephoned the Ministry and a new card was delivered addressed to Kyrios and Kyria Pringle, but Guy, when he saw it, said he could not accept. His revue was to be staged at Tatoi during the first week in February and rehearsals were now so intensive, he had no time for parties. In the end, it did not matter. Metaxas, whom the war had changed from a dictator to a hero, died at the end of January from diabetes, heart failure and overwork. The party had to be cancelled.

20

The revue, like the war, went on. Death was incidental to the times and the needs of the fighting men were deemed to be the major consideration. During the last week of rehearsals Guy disappeared from Harnet's view and the only daylight glimpse she had of him was at the funeral of an English pilot which they attended in the English church. He then had a look of frenzied incorporeity that came of not sleeping or eating or bating effort for three days at a time. In the few minutes that they spent together after the funeral ceremony, she protested that Guy was over-doing it. The revue, after all, was, as he had said, a joke. The audience of airmen would not be overcritical. But Guy could not do less than his utmost. He was just off to Tatoi for the dress rehearsal and would probably not manage to get home that night. Where would he sleep? Well, if he slept at all, he would probably doss down on the floor at the house of one of the Greek students who lived near the airfield. He had not returned to his adolescence; he had, she decided, never left it.

All evening she imagined him, exhorting the chorus and standing behind the stage, singing and shaking his hands in the air, possessed by a will to electrify the show and sweep it to the heights. When she went to bed in the silence of their empty suburb, she could imagine the day when Guy would be too busy ever to come home at all. They might meet occasionally for an instant or two, but he would disappear from her life. He would have no part in it. He would simply have no time for anything that was important to her.

Next evening, staff cars took the players and their friends

to Tatoi, where the main hangar had been rigged out as a theatre. The wind, sweeping over the dark reaches of the airfield, was wet with sleet. The women were not dressed against the dank and icy chill inside the hangar and the officer-in-charge, noticing that the visitors were shivering, sent to the store and fitted them all out with fur-lined flying jackets.

The curtain went up and the boys and girls, feverish from their all-night effort, burst into uproarious song:

> 'There's fun and frolic, jokes and sketches, too.
> You'll find them all together in the R.A.F. revue.'

Just as Harriet had imagined, Guy's hands could be seen waving wildly behind the two lines of the chorus.

The concert-party jokes were applauded with good-natured resignation. In spite of all the work, the first half of the show was neither better nor worse than most shows of its kind. It was *Maria Marten* that turned the entertainment into a triumph.

Maria, played by Yakimov, was met with unbelieving silence. Wearing false eyelashes, a blond wig, a print dress and sun-bonnet, he looked like a wolf disguised as Red Riding Hood's grandmother, but a wolf imitating outrageous, salacious girlhood. When he tripped to the footlights, put forefinger to chin and curtsied, a howl rose from the back of the hangar. The men, who had respectfully applauded the real women, were released into a furore of bawdry by the travesty of femininity. Yakimov acknowledged the shouts and whistles by fluttering his eyelashes. The howls were renewed. A full three minutes passed before anyone could speak.

Alan, a monstrous and sombre mother-figure, opened the play, saying: 'You have not been well of late, Maria dear! What ails thee, child?' to which Maria, in a light epicene voice, coyly replied: 'Something strange has happened to me, mother dear.' This produced a stampede over which could be heard cries of 'Watch it, girl', 'Up them stairs', and 'Meet me behind the hangar and I'll see what I can do'.

The text, concocted by the players themselves, had been bawdy enough in its original, but under the stimulus of rehearsals, much more had been added. While Yakimov held the stage, there was a cross-talk of ribaldry between actors and audience. Maria's violent death brought a sense of loss to both.

Her burial by William Corder, played by Ben Phipps, was followed in tense silence. Phipps made heavy weather of digging the grave but filling it in, he said: 'This is easier work than the other,' and the tension lifted. Someone shouted: 'Don't forget to camouflage it,' and uproar broke out again. The villain, peering villainously through his spectacles, found he had lost his pistol. Then a terrible realization came: he had buried it with the body. The audience groaned. Someone asked: 'Did you sign for it, chum?' Corder, lacking courage to reopen the grave, sloped off.

In the next act Corder, splendidly attired in a frock coat, his top-hat balanced on his arm, stood posed beside a potted palm. 'Well, here I am in London, and all is well,' he told the audience; but it was not well for long. Guy, stating that he was a Bow Street Runner, visited Corder and extended evidence of guilt: the pistol found in the grave. Corder repudiated it. In a rich voice of doom Guy declared: 'Here are your initials on the butt: W.C.' The rest was lost in catcalls. Corder, on the gallows, the rope about his neck, was permitted to make a last defiant speech. Not a sound came from the audience. Purged of pity and terror, it had shouted itself mute.

A party was given for the visitors in the officers' mess. Harriet had seen Charles Warden in one of the front seats. Not knowing whether he had joined the party or not, she kept her back to the room, feeling his presence behind her while she listened to Mrs Brett. Mrs Brett, having gathered Surprise and the other pilots about her, wished to make evident how much she knew of their flying conditions. 'It's disgraceful the way they won't let you have an airstrip near the frontier. That long haul – 200 miles, isn't it? – and all that snow and heavy cloud! No wonder the squadron's falling below strength.'

Surprise gave his carefree laugh: 'Is it falling below strength?'

'Oh, yes,' Mrs Brett assured him. 'And I'm told there's a shortage of spare parts. *Is* there a shortage of spare parts?'

'We manage.'

'Perhaps you do, but it's a serious situation.' Mrs Brett ducked her head in disgust but Surprise, an aristocrat of war from whom nothing could be demanded but his life, laughed again.

There was a touch on Harriet's arm. Prepared for it, she turned and faced Charles with a sociable smile. 'How did you enjoy *Maria Marten*?' she asked.

'Well . . . it was very funny. I've never seen anything quite like it before.'

'Not even at school?'

'Certainly not at school. I want to apologize – I could not come to luncheon that Sunday. Something kept me. I would have telephoned but the exchange could not find your number.'

'We have no number.'

'I had to stand by, I'm afraid. Someone flew in from Cairo H.Q.'

'Someone important?'

'Very important.'

'I suppose I mustn't ask who?'

'I'd better not say; though I imagine everyone'll know soon enough.'

'Is something happening?'

'It looks like it. Will you meet me tomorrow?'

'You mean you'll tell me then?'

'I can't.' He was annoyed by her flippancy and said: 'I may not be here much longer.'

'Where will you go? Back to Cairo?'

'No. Will you have lunch tomorrow?'

'I don't think I can.'

'The day after, then?'

'I would rather not.'

As he began to argue, she slipped past him and went to Guy who, relaxed and genial, was entertaining the senior officers with a description of the *Maria Marten* rehearsals. He put an arm round her shoulder and introduced her with pride: 'My wife.'

She looked back to where she had left Charles, but he was not there. She could not see him anywhere in the room. Her spirits dropped. The party had lost its buoyancy. She felt it was time to go home.

When Toby Lush entered the Billiard Room, Miss Gladys tittered flirtatiously: 'Why, Mr Lush, this is an honour! An honour indeed! We don't get you in often, do we?'

Toby spluttered and sniggered, doing his best to respond in kind, but the sight of Harriet quite unmanned him and Miss Gladys had to ask: 'Are you wanting his lordship?'

'Um, um, um.' Toby seemed not to know what he wanted. To gain time, he champed on his pipe, but the question had to be answered and he mumbled: 'Perhaps he'd give me a minute – if he's not too busy, that is.'

'Sit down, do. I'll see how things are in the inner office.'

Miss Gladys went off and Toby sat on the edge of Harriet's desk: 'Didn't know you worked here. Employed by old Pinkers, eh?'

'No. Alan Frewen.'

'Ah!'

Harriet had not spoken to Toby or Dubedat since the School closed, but had heard they were working for Cookson and had seen them driving round Athens in the Delahaye.

She asked if they had given up their flat.

'It gave us up. The old soul rented it from Archie Callard. Archie wanted it back, worse luck, but now he's got it, he doesn't live in it. He's always at Phaleron. But he's sick of Athens. He says he wants to do something big . . . go to Cairo, get into the war, join the Long Range Desert Group. The Major's working on it.'

'What can the Major do?'

'*The Major!* He can do anything.'

'But he can't produce transport where there isn't any.'

'Don't you be so sure. Planes come here from Cairo. If someone very important wanted to go back on one, he could wangle it.'

'Is Archie Callard as important as that?'

'No, but the Major is. And there's no knowing what Archie may do! He's talking of starting a private army.'

'Are there private armies these days?'

''Course there are. Plenty of them.'

'I hear you're employed by the Major?'

'We help a bit. There's not much staff at Phaleron. The chauffeur's gone, so I have taken over. The Major's very decent. He's given us the flat over the garage.'

'What does Dubedat do?'

'Helps around.' Toby lowered his voice as though disclosing something shameful: 'The old soul does a bit of gardening, cleans silver, makes the beds. The other day the butler told him to wash the hall tiles. Bit of a come-down, eh? Man like that washing tiles! If he'd had his rights, he'd have been Director. Can't get over it. Disgraceful, the way the old soul's been treated!'

Bleak and brooding, Toby stared at the floor until Miss Gladys reappeared. 'Come along,' she said, and rising and projecting himself in one movement, Toby nearly went down on his face.

Alan had always described the food at the Academy as 'execrable', but the Sunday on which he invited the Pringles to luncheon promised to be a special occasion. He would not explain further, having no wish to raise hopes that might not be fulfilled.

Walking between showers up the wide, grey, windy Vasilissis Sofias, Guy talked exuberantly about a new production of the revue that was to be bigger, funnier, and better dressed, and staged in Athens on behalf of the Greek war effort. The times were gloomy but once again Guy had escaped from them.

There were no victories now. The bells had ceased to ring. The Athenians, living under conditions that resembled those of a protracted siege, were bored with the present and saw little to cheer them in the future. The Greeks were bogged down in the mountains. They had come to a stop on the Albanian coast. Some said they had given up hope of taking Valona. The men were exhausted. There was no food. Ammunition was running out.

Turning off towards the Academy, Harriet looked into the forecourt of the military hospital and saw the wounded still dragging round the wet asphalt square.

Guy said: 'We'll have to improve our theme song. I don't think its bad, mind you, but we can't keep singing the same thing.'

'I suppose not.'

February, that in other years held intimations of spring, this year prolonged the bitter weather. Suffering to a point beyond endurance, the men in the mountain snows complained that supplies were not coming to the front. The Athenians, ill-fed, chilled to the bone, had no supplies to send.

Harriet said: 'They'll have to accept a truce.'

'What?'

'Look at those men. How can the Greeks go on like this?'

Guy looked, his face contracting, and after a long pause said: 'The British may be joining in.'

'Nobody seems to want them.'

The rumour that British troops were already on their way had caused as much alarm as rejoicing, for people feared they would do no more than expedite a German attack.

'Still,' said Guy, 'anything is better than this sort of stalemate.'

It was colder inside the Academy than out. A small wood fire had been lit in the common room but the damp hung like mist in the air. Most of the chairs were taken and the talk carried a surprising intonation of cheer. Alan had a bottle of ouzo on his table and he started filling the glasses as soon as he saw Guy and Harriet cross the room.

'So it *is* a special occasion!' Harriet said.

'It is,' Alan agreed; and when they were seated and warmed by the ouzo, he told them that one of the inmates, a man called Tennant, had been promised a piece of beef by an officer on a visiting cruiser. 'The promise,' said Alan, 'led to some slight disagreement. Miss Dunne, as usual, tried to boss the show. Before the beef had even arrived, she stuck a notice on the board saying that this Sunday guests would not be allowed. I appealed to Tennant who, after all, should be the one to decide. He said: "Ask whomsoever you like. The beef may not materialize. And if it does, it'll probably be bitched by that God-awful cook."'

Miss Dunne, defeated, sat beside the fire, her gaze on a book, apparently aloof from the famished anticipation that stirred the rest of the room.

Above the general animation Pinkrose's voice, precise and scholarly, carried clearly from some distant corner. He, also, had a visitor, to whom he was describing the intention and content of his lecture on Byron.

Wondering if the visitor could be Miss Gladys Twocurry, Harriet said: 'Do you think the younger Miss Twocurry has intentions towards Pinkrose?'

Alan nodded gravely: 'I'm sure of it. And, you must agree, she would make a very toothsome Lady Pinkrose.'

Listening for the luncheon bell, they listened perforce to the Pinkrose monologue which persisted until it had silenced all about it. At last the bell sounded and a sigh went over the room. The inmates did their best to leave in good order, letting the women go ahead. When Miss Dunne saw she was not the only one of her sex, she hastened to be the first from the room. Harriet now had a sight of Pinkrose's guest. It was Charles Warden.

The main meals at the Academy were taken round a table, as they had been when the diners were students with a common interest and lived as a family. Alan had said: 'I'm afraid our table talk wouldn't be out of place in a Trappist refectory. Sometimes someone makes a mention of work but not, of course, when visitors are present. You are liable to meet with complete silence.'

The meal was served. Everyone – Diocletian not forgotten – received a slice of beef, overcooked and dry, but still beef; and the diners gave a few appreciative 'hahs' and 'hums'. One man even went so far as to say: '*I say!*' Pinkrose, respecting the traditional taciturnity, talked below his breath. Charles, attentive, kept his eyes lowered.

A salad came with the meat. Harriet examined the coarse, dark leaves and said: 'They could be marguerite leaves.' Alan handed her oil and vinegar. 'Put on plenty,' he advised. 'It's only the olive oil that keeps us alive,' and Miss Dunne, sitting opposite, raised her brows.

Guy, not easily subdued, asked his neighbour if there were anything in the story that the British were about to intervene on the Greek front.

Stunned by the question, the man caught his breath and whispered: 'I shouldn't think so.'

'No? I've heard that British troops are already disembarking on Lemnos.'

Miss Dunne, usually pink, grew pinker; then, unable to restrain herself, burst out: 'If you've heard that, you've no right to repeat it.'

'It's being pretty widely repeated,' Alan said, and tried to divert Guy by suggesting to him that Naxos would be a more likely half-way house for troops bound for the Piraeus.

'But are they bound for the Piraeus?' Guy asked. 'They may go to Salonika.'

Miss Dunne, appalled by this discussion, gasped and goggled as though suffering strangulation; and Guy, observing her discomfort, leant towards her and asked with friendly interest: 'What is it you do at the Legation?'

Her answer was immediate: 'I'm not in the habit of discussing my work.'

Even for Guy, Harriet thought, that should be enough; but

far from it. Challenged by her awkwardness and vanity, he cajoled her as though she were a difficult student, telling her about the revue. There was to be a repeat performance and he suggested she might take part.

While he was talking, Miss Dunne wriggled so much her chair worked backwards until she was two foot or more from the table. When he paused for a reply, she gave her head a violent shake. Those nearby watched his tactics with apprehensive delight.

The revue dismissed, Guy said he was a tennis player himself. Would Miss Dunne be willing to give him a game?

At this, Miss Dunne's colour darkened and spread up among the roots of her red hair and down the front of her emerald green dress. At the same time a knowing smirk spread over her large carmine face. She said archly: 'I'll think about it.'

Harriet, turning a glance of appeal on Alan, caught Charles's eye. He gave her a sympathetic grin, and she grinned back. At this exchange, life lost its threatening desolation and the air grew bright.

Alan said he had arranged for their coffee to be sent to his room. Harriet, taken unwillingly upstairs, felt she was being taken from the one person she wished to see.

Alan's room, which had only one window, was smaller than that which had been occupied by Gracey. When the door shut, Harriet turned on Guy:

'That idiotic woman thought you were making advances to her.'

'Darling, really! You are being ridiculous.' He looked to Alan for support but Alan was inclined to side with Harriet.

'I admired your campaign,' he said. 'I really think you won Miss Dunne's heart. No small achievement. But, then, it would take a ruthless misanthrope to hold out against so simple and beneficent an approach to one's fellow men.'

Alan had recently collected some photographs, taken during his wanderings in Greece, which he had kept in store. Now, lifting the large prints one by one from the portfolios, he studied each tenderly and nostalgically before passing it to Harriet or Guy.

He was so pleased to have his friends share the sights he had seen, Harriet was touched and did her best to put Charles from her mind. Gazing into his pictures of rocky islands, olive trees, classical temples outlined against the sea, and chalk-white churches and houses taken at mid-day when the shadowed walls shimmered with reflected light, she said: 'We wanted to come here. This is the country where we most wanted to be, but we have seen nothing. We might as well be in prison.'

On an impulse, Alan said: 'I shall never leave Greece.'

'But if the Italians come, how can you stay?'

'I could hide out on the islands. I speak the language. I have friends everywhere. People would shelter me. Yes, I'm sure they would shelter me.'

Watching Alan as he spoke, Harriet saw him a ponderous man, quiet, sardonic yet gentle, patient and long-suffering. She had thought he loved only Greece and his dog, but now she saw that to him Greece was not only a love, it was sanctuary. But she could not suppose his plan to remain in hiding here was more than romantic fantasy. There had been English-women in Bucharest, ex-governesses, without friends or money outside Rumania, who were determined to stay but, in the end, they had left with the rest.

While Alan was talking, she heard Pinkrose's voice raised in the garden and, moving as though aimlessly, she went to the window. Pinkrose, muffled to the eyes, was standing on the carriage-way saying good-bye to Charles. She watched Charles as he saluted and turned and walked off towards the back garden gate. The lemon trees hid him from sight but she remained by the window, looking in the direction he had gone.

Guy and Alan were still intent on the photographs, with Alan giving a disquisition upon his photographic technique. Harriet knew Guy did not understand a word and it seemed to her that nothing Alan said had any relation to life. Nothing in the room had any relation to life. She could scarcely contain her impatience to follow Charles out of the garden and down to the town centre where at that moment he was probably wondering what had become of her.

Alan, transported by Guy's admiration for his work, dusted and opened more portfolios, and said with the emotion of a lonely man: 'You will stay to tea, won't you?'

Guy had had other plans for the afternoon, but the appeal was too much for him.

'We would like to stay,' he said.

21

Harriet was certain she would hear from Charles next morning. She suffered, as he had suffered, a feverish sense of urgency; but the messenger did not arrive. As the morning passed without a sign, her excitement died down. She had been mistaken. It had all been a mistake. There was nothing to hope for.

When she left the office at mid-day, Charles was passing the door. He gave her a sidelong smile but hurried on, too busy to stop. He did not look round. His long, quick strides took him down the square to the Corinthian. He disappeared inside.

Crestfallen, she, too, went down the square, but slowly, with no object in view. As she approached the Corinthian, Charles came out again. He stood at the top of the hotel steps, a cablegram in his hand. Seeing her, he came pelting down as though it were all some sort of game, and lightly asked: 'Where are you going to eat?'

'I haven't decided yet.'

She felt he expected something from her, but she did not know what. Irritated by the incident, she made to walk on and his face contracted with an odd, almost bitter, dismay: 'Don't go.'

'I thought you were busy.'

'Not now. I had to pick up this cable. It could have been important.'

'But it wasn't?'

'Not very. Anyway, not so important it can't wait.'

At a loss, she said: 'I expected to hear from you.'

'You turned me down at Tatoi. It rests with you now.'

'Does it?' she laughed and in her surprise examined him as though she had taken a step away from him. Behind his inculcated good manners, she had been aware of his demanding arrogance – the quality that had caused Alan to describe him as 'a spoilt little boy'. Now it was subdued. Perhaps he was being cautious, but he gave an impression of humility. His fixed, entreating gaze brought Sasha to her mind, and, stretching out her hand, she smiled and said: 'Then come and have lunch with me.'

In the second stage of their relationship, it seemed to Harriet she had no aim or purpose beyond seeing Charles; but she was not obsessed out of all reason. She knew the same compelling intention had once been directed on to Guy. Directed and deflected. Had Charles asked her, she would have said she had found her marriage hopelessly intractable. 'Don't blame me. It's all too difficult.' Charles asked her nothing. Apparently he had decided that explanations also rested with her. Unasked, she gave no answers. She had her own sort of loyalty.

The rain came and went. On wet afternoons they would take tea at the Corinthian. When it was fine, they walked about Athens, sensing the spring in the electric freshness of the air.

A haze of green was coming over the trees at the top of Constitution Square. During the weeks of winter Alan, unwilling to go far, had exercised his dog about the area of the Academy, and now that the weather was improving, he was aware of Harriet's withdrawal and would make no claim on her. If she cared to join him at his mid-day session with Yakimov, then she was welcome, but he did not ask her to come for walks in the gardens. Once or twice when he met Harriet with Charles in the street, he glanced away, preferring to remain unaware of her new relationship.

Unreasonably, she felt deprived by Alan's bashfulness. When she noticed the gardens coming to life again, she told Charles they must go in and visit the water-birds.

'Which water-birds?' he asked.

'Those on the pond in the middle of the gardens.'

'Oh!' He smiled, but made no other comment.

As they passed the palms that stood sentinel at the gate, she said: 'In this country even the trees are required to imitate columns.'

'Don't you think the first columns were meant to imitate trees?'

'I suppose they were. How clever you are! When you've taken your degree, will you become an archaeologist?'

'I don't think so.'

'What will you do?'

'I've really no idea.'

His vagueness perplexed her. Every other young man known to her had seen the future as a struggle for life, and had prepared his means of livelihood long before he reached the age of twenty. If Charles were unconcerned in this, then his background must be very different from hers. There was something unfamiliar in him – the unfamiliarity of the rich, the more than rich; but she would not question him. He did not ask her about her family and upbringing, and did not speak of his own.

Their sense of likeness astonished them. It resembled magic. They felt themselves held in a spellbound condition which they feared to injure. Although she could not pin down any overt point of resemblance, Harriet at times imagined he was the person most like her in the world, her mirror image.

Fearful that some revelation should break this enchantment, they instinctively suppressed their disparities. Their conversations were sporadic and strained; and often they would walk round the gardens without a word.

In spite of the war, the cold, the shortage of food and hope, the spring was beginning again with small red shoots on the wistaria and buds on the apricot trees. Threads of green, rising from seeds that had lain all the previous summer invisible, like dust among the dust, were already putting out minute leaves, each of its own pattern. Harriet listened for the noise

214

of children and birds, but there was no noise. As they advanced under the trees, the quiet grew more dense.

'Are you sure this is the place?' she asked.

He nodded and before she could speak again, they came out to the clearing. It was the same pond, filled by the winter rain. The sun broke through and dappled the water. On the sandy verge the iron chairs stood tilted to right and left. All the properties were there, but it was a stage without life. There were no children, no birds, no grown-ups, no old man to collect the small coins. The water was still. The air silent.

'Where are they all? What has happened to the birds?'

He gave his brief derisive laugh: 'What do you think?'

She wondered if her dismay had amused him, but he did not look amused. His smile was almost vindictive, as though she had hurt him and now was hurt in her turn. She said nothing. She shut herself off in silence, refusing to betray any emotion at all. They passed through the thicket to the formal gardens of the Zappion. The sunlight was cold; the low-cut shrubs offered no protection from the wind. Clouds, black with snow, were coming up out of the sea. At the end of the garden the monstrous columns of the temple of Olympian Zeus flashed against the heavy sky.

Harriet came to a stop and said: 'I won't go any further. I should get back. I have some work to do.'

Contrite, Charles said: 'Come and have tea with me first,' speaking as though this suggestion would put everything right.

'No. I'd better go to the office.' Harriet turned and walked back with her mind made up.

In sight of the Grande Bretagne, Charles said: 'Must you go in?'

'Yes.'

'Do come and have tea!'

She did not reply, but when they reached the office entrance, she walked on with him to his hotel.

The Corinthian was still new enough to look opulent. Its modernity had remained modern because no one had time these days to outdate it. The foyer, with its plum-red carpet and heavy, square-cut chairs, had strips of neon secreted behind the cornices. The main light came from the showcases, emptied now of everything except jewellery, which no one felt inclined to buy.

Though crowded with refugees and service-men, the hotel maintained such standards as it could, and was one of the few places where young Greek women might meet unchaperoned.

Several Greek girls sat at the walnut tables, some with fiancés on leave from the front. Harriet, following Charles through the plum-red gloom, noticed Archie Callard taking tea with Cookson. She caught Callard's glance, saw him look at Charles, then turn and murmur to Cookson who, staring pointedly in a different direction, grimaced with unreal amusement.

Seated beside Charles, she asked him: 'Do you see much of Cookson?'

'I see him occasionally. He sometimes gives me supper.'

'Has he ever invited you to one of his small and rather curious parties?'

'No. Does he give small curious parties? What happens at them? How are they curious?'

She was paused by the innocence of Charles's inquiry and, not attempting to answer, asked instead: 'How do you come to know Pinkrose?'

A slow and quizzical smile spread over Charles's face. 'He was my tutor. Surely you don't imagine I go to curious parties with Pinkrose!'

She blushed and did not reply, but after a moment said: 'If you dislike me so much, why do you want to see me?'

His smile went at once. A concerned and wondering expression took its place. He moved towards her and was about to speak when Guy's voice came in an anguished cry across the foyer: 'Darling!'

Charles started away. Guy, his glasses askew, his hair ruffled by the wind, his arms stretched round an untidy mass of papers, was hastening towards them, his whole natural disorder exaggerated by the heedlessness of misery. Something was wrong. Imagining he had sought her out to accuse her, Harriet sat motionless; but it was nothing like that. Reaching the table, he let the books and papers drop in a heap and said: 'What do you think has happened?'

She shook her head.

'Pinkrose has stopped the show.'

'What show?'

'Why, the revue, of course. The show we did at Tatoi. He forbids a second performance.'

'I don't understand . . .'

'He says it's indecent. We were rehearsing at the School when the boy from the Information Office brought a letter. He said he had received complaints about the revue and could not let the School be used for rehearsals. Also, he could not let Alan Frewen, Yakimov or me take any further part in it. As though it could go on without us!'

Harriet pulled herself out of her confusion and said: 'The trouble must be *Maria Marten*. Couldn't you leave it out?'

'But *Maria Marten*'s the chief attraction. Everyone's talking about it. Everyone wants to see it. Yakimov's performance was the success of the show. We've already sold most of the tickets.'

'I am sorry.' Harriet wished she could say more, but Guy had taken himself and his activities so far beyond her ambience, she could only wonder why he had brought his anxiety to her. She glanced up at Charles who had risen and now stood looking troubled, until Guy, as though seeing him for the first time, said: 'Hello.'

Charles said: 'Won't you have some tea?'

'Yes. I'd like some.'

Guy pulled up a chair and took over the conversation, unaware that they could have any topic of interest other than the revue and the calamitous ban Pinkrose had placed on it.

Harriet suggested that the Air Commodore at Tatoi be asked to reason with Pinkrose.

Charles said: 'The Blenheims have moved forward.'

Guy nodded: 'Ben says he'll try to contact the C.O., but that'll take time.'

Harriet said: 'We now know why Toby Lush came in to see Pinkrose.'

'*He* wouldn't complain, surely?'

'Someone complained. Yakimov says Dubedat was indignant at being left out of the revue. I bet he went snivelling to Cookson; then Toby Lush was sent in to complain to Pinkrose.'

'You think that?'

'Yes I do.'

'You could be right,' Guy said and looked dashed, as he usually did when Harriet revealed the prosaic wiring that lay behind the star-bursting excitements of life. Charles, too, looked dashed, but for another reason, and Harriet tried to distract him with an appeal:

'You saw *Maria Marten*. It is only a joke. You know Pinkrose. Can't you persuade him to be reasonable?'

As she spoke, she saw on Charles's face the resentment of a deprived child. He said: 'I don't think he'd be influenced by me,' and looked away. He would have to return to the office.

Harriet, though she was due back herself, let him go and delayed her own departure as a gesture of sympathy with Guy. 'How did you know where to find me?' she asked.

'Ben Phipps saw you come in here.'

Did he, indeed! She looked over to where Cookson and Callard had been sitting and was thankful to see they had gone. She suddenly felt impatient of Guy's quandary, knowing he was more than able to meet this situation without her aid.

She said she had to go to work. To her surprise he said he would meet her at seven o'clock. They could go home together. She had expected to see Charles, who had made a tentative suggestion, not confirmed, that they should hear the singer at the Pomegranate. If Guy wanted, for once, to go home, she could do nothing but agree.

The following morning carried an atmosphere of moment. Pinkrose and Alan Frewen, summoned to the Legation, went off in separate taxis. The News-Sheet, in preparation, carried

218

nothing more immediate than raids on Cologne and a 'brush' in Libya. No one knew what was happening, but Yakimov and Miss Gladys gumshoed about the Billiard Room, conversing in choked whispers as though they were being stifled beneath a blanket of secrecy.

At mid-day, when she found Charles waiting for her, Harriet gave him no opportunity to sulk. Seizing on him, she asked excitedly: 'What is going on?'

'Well . . . *something*.' He tried to maintain reserve but he, too, was stirred by events. 'It looks as though our chaps will be here in a day or two.'

'Does that mean you'll leave Athens?'

'I don't know. Not immediately, anyway. Come to the hotel for lunch. I'm supposed to remain on tap.'

When they reached the Corinthian, they were disconcerted to find Guy and Ben Phipps seated in the sunlight at one of the outdoor tables. Guy jumped up as if he had been waiting for them, and Ben Phipps, with unusual cordiality, pulled Harriet down to the seat beside him and asked her what she would drink.

The invitation did not include Charles who stood by the table, uncertain whether he had lost her or not. Ben Phipps grinned up at him. 'Well, you're a right lot of bastards! You've done for us this time.'

'Have we?'

'What do *you* think? Hitler's waiting to go into Bulgaria. We've only to move and he'll be on top of us in a brace of shakes.'

Trying to look knowledgeable but uncommunicative, Charles said, 'It's on the cards that they'll move first.'

'Maybe; and then what'll you do? The last offer was a force "not large but deadly". So bloody deadly, in fact, it couldn't frighten pussy. No wonder it was turned down. But how can you improve on it? What have you got?'

Charles maintained an impassive air, but he was too young and inexperienced to stand up to Phipps. He could not pretend to know anything Phipps did not know. Disconcerted, he said:

'There must be men available now Benghazi is in our hands.'

'A few units. What about supplies?'

Charles made an uneasy move away from the argument. 'The top brass know what they're doing.'

'If you think that, you're cuckoo.'

Charles gave Harriet a cold and angry smile, then ran up the steps into the hotel.

'Thank God we've got rid of that toffee-nosed bastard,' Ben Phipps grinned connivingly at Guy, but Guy did not look happy. He picked up one of Harriet's hands and caressed it with his thumb as though to erase memory of Phipps's brash and pointless attack on Charles. Harriet had lost weight and her hands, normally thin, now looked too delicate for use. 'Little monkey's paws,' he said.

Harriet watched the hotel door. The last time she had seen Charles disappear in that way, he had come out again almost immediately. This time he did not come out. Her impulse was to follow, to exonerate herself, but of course she could not do that.

Guy also knew she could not do that. He gave her hand a benedictory squeeze and dropped it. Charles had been routed and the two men were free to return to matters that interested them.

Harriet guessed that Phipps was behind all this. She had no doubt that it was he, with his sharp and suspicious awareness, who had seen her about with Charles and advised Guy to take action. It would be Guy's idea to recall her with a claim on her sympathy; Phipps had evidently enjoyed himself and yet – why was he concerning himself in Guy's affairs? Not out of love for Guy. There was something in his manner that caused her to relate his behaviour to himself. He had to have controlling power somewhere. Ousted from the Phaleron circle, he had taken over Guy and he wanted no distracting gesture from Harriet.

If he could not keep his friends away from their wives, he could at least control the wives and put a stop to what he called 'attention-getting ploys'. She was certain he had never considered her as a separate personality who might have just cause for revolt. She was a tiresome attachment that must be pushed into the background and kept there.

Catching her fractious eye, Guy said: 'I think we'd better find Harriet some food.'

Phipps rose, zealous on her behalf: 'Shall we try Zonar's?' He and Guy, unnaturally attentive as though she were near mental or physical collapse, walked her round to Zonar's where Ben Phipps had a talk in Greek with one of the waiters. The waiter went off to see what he could do and returned with the promise of an omelette. The men were delighted. Seeing her served with a small, lemon-coloured omelette, they seemed to think they had solved all Harriet's problems and removed her last cause for complaint. Ceasing to worry about her, they returned to a more crying need: the need to reform the world.

Although Guy had had to agree that Phipps was 'a bit of a crook', he respected him as one of the 'politically educated'. In a wider society Guy would have been entertained by him, but would not have chosen to associate with him. Here in Athens, each felt fortunate in finding anyone who shared his radical preoccupations. However much a crook Ben might be, Guy felt that he had more to offer the world than some fellow like Alan Frewen who merely wanted to lead a quiet life.

Ten years Guy's senior and an established left-wing figure, Phipps was adept at ferreting out the authors of misrule and was ready at any time to talk about the mysterious forces that had brought the world to its present pass. Some of these – such as the Zoippus Bank, the Bund and certain Wall Street Jews who had financed Hitler in the hope of forcing the whole Jewish race to move to Palestine – were new to Guy. Phipps sometimes said he had uncovered them by personal investigation. He could prove (Harriet had heard him do it more than once) that were it not for the machinations of bankers, big business, financiers, shareholders in steel and certain *intrigants* of the allied powers who were still, through the medium of the Vatican, in unnatural conclave with German cartels,

Hitler would never have come to power, there would have been no *casus belli* and no war. It seemed to Harriet that for Phipps this contention had become a gospel to which life itself was simply a contributing factor. Referred to, it answered all questions. It might have some sort of basis in truth, but a basis on which Phipps had built his own fantasy; and political fantasy bored her even more than politics.

When she had eaten the omelette, she became restless and thought of going for a walk. Guy put his hand over hers and held to her, saying: 'Listen to Ben.'

Ben, alerted by Guy, turned his gaze on her but could not keep it fixed anywhere for long. In ordinary exchanges he kept up an attitude of confident repose but when excited by his own disclosures, his pupils dodged about, black and small as currants behind his heavy lenses.

Harriet seized on a moment's silence to inquire about the revue. Guy said that Alan Frewen had undertaken to speak to Pinkrose. Harriet attempted another question but Guy motioned her not to interrupt Phipps. At last Phipps reached his usual conclusion and paused to let Guy expose his own belief that had the forces that brought about the war used their wealth and energy to further the concepts of Marx, the earthly paradise would be well established by now.

Both Guy and Ben Phipps were proud of their inflexible materialism yet, Harriet decided, Phipps had a mystic's insight into the workings of high finance, while Guy read *Das Kapital* as the padre might read his Bible. Seeing them hold to political mysteries as other men held to God, she told herself they were a pair of hopeless romantics. Their conversation did not relate to reality. She was bored. Ben Phipps bored her. Guy and Phipps together bored her. Would the day come when it was Guy who bored her?

She remembered when she had wanted him to take over her life. That phase did not last long. She had soon decided that Guy might be better read and better informed, but, so far as life was concerned, her own judgement served her better than his. Guy had a moral strength but it resembled one of those vast Victorian feats of engineering: impressive but out of place in the modern world. He had a will to believe in others but the belief survived only because he evaded fact. Life as he saw it could not support itself; it had to be subsidized by fantasy. He was a materialist without being a realist; and that, she thought, gave him the worst of both worlds.

Ben Phipps's talk came to a stop when he noticed the time. He had to return to write up events. Guy, speaking as one conscious of new responsibilities, offered to take Harriet that evening to the cellar café, Elatos, and asked: 'How about you, Ben?' Ben said: 'I'll join you but, things being as they are, I'll have to keep near to a telephone.'

It seemed that Guy did intend to take over her life. But too late. Much too late. And Phipps came with them wherever they went.

'Darling,' she said. 'I don't know how you can stand so much of him.'

Guy was astonished. 'He's a most lively, stimulating companion.'

'Well, I don't want to listen to him. Especially now, when things are happening here.'

'If more people had listened to him, none of this need have happened at all.'

'How can you be so ridiculous!' She was beginning to fear she had married a man whom she could not take seriously.

'Besides,' Guy added with reason: 'Ben knows what's going on here. He knows more than most people. He told me that British troops were disembarking on Lemnos, and he was right. Now he's found out they're moving to the mainland. I don't suppose even your friend Frewen could have told you that.'

'He could, I don't doubt; but he didn't. I imagine it's inside information.'

'Well, if you want inside information, you'd better stick to Ben.'

Important visitors arrived in Athens. The Parthenon was opened to them and Ben Phipps, intending to report the occasion, obtained tickets and took the Pringles with him. The British Foreign Secretary stood at the Beulé Gate and smiled at Harriet as she passed. Harriet, smiling back at the youthful, handsome, familiar face, was transported as though some part of England itself had come to be with them here in their isolation.

Ben Phipps kept silent till they were upon the plateau, then he grinned round to Guy, his eyes sparkling with ironical glee, his whole square, heavy body twitching in his eagerness to shatter the moment's awe. He began to say: 'I bet . . .' and Harriet said: 'Shut up.'

'Your wife's a bloody Conservative,' he complained.

'Oh no,' Guy put an arm round her shoulder, 'she's merely a romantic.'

'Same thing.'

'I wouldn't say so. Romantics are relatively harmless.'

Harriet moved from under Guy's restraining arm and made her way among the officers and officials who stood about on the hilltop in the last of the afternoon sunlight. Charles was not among them. She ran up the Parthenon steps and stood between the columns, watching Guy and Phipps crossing the rough ground; Phipps, in brown greatcoat, rocking heavy-footed on the stones, like a stout brown bear.

They decided to go to the Museum. As they walked inside the Parthenon, Charles, with two other officers, climbed the steps at the eastern end and came towards them. He saw Harriet. He looked at her companions and looked away. He smiled to himself. Neither Guy nor Ben Phipps noticed him. At the steps she managed to glance back, but he was already out of sight.

Not much was left in the Museum but enough to detain them. Harriet stood for a long time gazing at the archaic horses with their gentle curving necks, and thought: 'It doesn't matter. It was an impossible situation.' Now, thank goodness, it was over.

When they came out the sun was sinking and the important visitors had gone. The last of the officers were wandering, shadowy in the later light, towards the gate. Outside the gate Alan Frewen was making his way cautiously down the rocky slope to the road and Ben Phipps asked: 'What's the great man doing here?'

Alan laughed: 'I expect you know as well as I do.'

'Would he stand for an interview?'

'He might.'

'Where's he now?'

'Probably half-way to Cyprus.'

'Thanks for telling me. Come on, I'll give you a lift back.'

When Ben dropped Harriet and Alan at the office, Guy arranged to pick her up again at seven o'clock. He and Ben were taking her to supper at Babayannis'.

Even octopus was scarce now. At Babayannis' the menu offered lung stew and the laced up intestines that had given Harriet a chronic stomach disorder.

Guy said: 'What does it matter? There's plenty of wine!!'

Both men preferred drink to food; but Harriet would rather eat than drink. Made irritable by hunger, she felt she had been imprisoned long enough by Phipps and Guy; and she was further irritated by Guy's folly. Everything said seemed to confirm it. In the past she had complained because she did not have enough of Guy's company. Now she had too much.

Hacking away at the grey, slippery intestines, she heard Phipps repeat again Hemingway's reply to Fitzgerald's observation: 'The rich are different from us.'

'He said,' said Phipps gleefully, '"Yes, they have more money."'

She fixed Phipps in a rage and said: 'I suppose you agree with Hemingway?'

'Don't you?'

'I don't. I think his answer exposes both Hemingway and his limitations. He simply didn't know what Fitzgerald meant.'

'Indeed!' Ben Phipps smiled indulgently: 'And what did he mean?'

'He meant that the rich have an attitude of mind which only money can buy.'

'I can't say I've noticed it.'

225

'You should have noticed it. You hung around Cookson long enough.'

'Cookson amused me.'

'And you amused Cookson. I'm told you were the Phaleron court jester.'

'I certainly laughed at him and his money.'

'That was one way of defending yourself.'

'Defending myself?'

'Surely you know laughter is a defence? We laugh at the things we fear most.'

'She's joking,' Guy said, but Ben Phipps knew she was not joking. He lost his indulgent air. His expression hardened and she saw him control, but only just control, the impulse to insult her.

He disliked her as much as she disliked him, so why should she waste her life here, acting as audience to a man she despised? As for Guy, sitting there uneasily smiling, he seemed at that moment merely a gaoler who hemmed her in with people who did not interest her and talk that bored her. She had found no release in marriage. It had forced her further back into the prison of herself. Acutely conscious now of the passing of time, she felt she was not living but was being fobbed off with an imitation of life.

As the evening went on, Phipps returned, inevitably, to the sources of the world's mishap and Harriet, listening, reached a point of conscious revolt. At the mention of the mysterious Zoippus Bank, she broke in on him: 'There is no Zoippus Bank. There never was and never will be a Zoippus Bank. I'm quite sure no Jew ever financed Hitler. I know the Vatican was never involved with Krupps and Wall Street and Bethlehem Steel . . .'

'You know fuck all,' said Ben Phipps.

Harriet met the hatred of his small eyes, and said with hatred: 'You *ugly* little man!'

His mouth fell open. She could see that she had hurt him.

Guy was hurt, too. In shocked remonstrance he said: 'Darling!'

She jumped up, near tears, and hurried through the crowded restaurant. Guy caught her as she was leaving the front hall. He said: 'Come back.'

'No.' She turned on him, raging: 'Why do you drag me round to listen to Ben Phipps. You know I can't bear him.'

'But he's my friend.'

'Charles Warden was my friend.'

'That was different . . .'

'I don't think so. You want Phipps's company; I prefer Charles.'

'But you don't need Charles. You have me.'

Harriet did not reply to that.

Pained and puzzled, Guy reasoned with her: 'Why do you dislike Ben? He's much more amusing than the people you *do* like. I find Alan Frewen a dull dog; and as for Charles Warden! He's a pleasant enough fellow, but he takes himself too seriously. He's quite immature.' Guy looked to her for agreement and when she did not agree, said: 'But he's good-looking. I suppose that means something to you?'

'He is good-looking, it's true; but that has nothing to do with it. In fact, when I first saw him, I thought he had a vain, unpleasant face.'

'You don't think so now?'

'No.'

Guy lowered his head, frowning to hide his distress, and asked: 'Do you want to leave me?'

'Good heavens, no; there's no suggestion of such a thing.'

Guy's head dropped lower. Miserably embarrassed, he said: 'I suppose you want to have an affair with him?'

'Really!' Harriet was appalled at such a question. An unanswerable question at that! 'It's out of the question. As though one could, anyway – life being what it is! The impermanence of things; and the fact one has no time, no opportunity! But there never was any question . . . It was simply that I was lonely.'

'You're not lonely now. You're always out with Ben and me.'

'Ben bores me.'

'Darling, you know I don't want to deprive you of anything.'

'What is there to deprive me of? Charles isn't here for long. It's just that I would like to see him.'

'Very well. But come back to the table. Be nice to Ben. He knows he's ugly. No need to rub it in. Tell him you're sorry, there's a good girl?'

'I am sorry. I didn't want to hurt him.'

'Come along, then.' Guy took her hand and led her back into the restaurant.

22

The raids were more frequent now: a sign, Ben Phipps said, of impending events. Some mornings it was scarcely possible to get into Athens between the alerts. On one of these mornings, walking from the metro station at Monastiraki, Harriet came upon two British tanks. They had stopped just inside Hermes Street and the men were standing together in the road.

There had been snow during the night. The pavements were wet; the light, coming from the dark, wet sky had the blue fluorescence of snow-light, yet a tree overhanging a garden wall was in full blossom.

Harriet was not the only one who stopped to look at the tanks. Some of the people seemed mystified by their sand-coloured camouflage and the insignia of camels and palms. To Harriet they were familiar, but in a recondite, disturbing way as though they belonged to some life she had lived long ago. The young Englishmen also came out of the past. They all looked alike: not tall, as she remembered the English, but strongly built, with sun-reddened faces and hair bleached blond. When they became aware of her, they stopped talking. They looked at her, rapt, and she looked back, each remembering the world from which they had come, too shy to speak.

She made off suddenly. In the office the atmosphere was emotional and even Miss Gladys was moved to speech. To Harriet and to anyone who entered, she said: 'Our lads are arriving. Our lads are arriving. Isn't it great! I was in the know, of course. Oh yes, I've known all along. Lord Pinkrose let something drop, but not accidentally. Oh, no, not accidentally! He often says something to show that he trusts me.'

Ben Phipps, when he came in, did not wait to hear the whole of this speech but hurried through to the News Room, leaving all the doors open so, noisy and voluble, he could be heard shouting: 'We've had it now. We've issued a direct challenge to the Boche.'

He had just come from the Piraeus where he said troops were disembarking and supplies were being off-loaded on to the very steps of the German consulate.

'Does the Legation know this?' Alan asked.

'I telephoned them, but what can they do? The Greeks aren't at war with the Germans; at least, not yet. And there the stuff is, for all to see. The Italians are bombing it and the German Military Attaché is making notes. When I arrived, he was counting the guns. He gave me a nod and said: "*Wie gewöhnlich – zu wenig und zu spät!*"'

'Is this true?' Alan asked.

'It would be damned funny if it were.'

'I mean, is it true the Germans are watching the disembarkation?'

'It certainly is. Go and see for yourself.'

Alan put his hand to the telephone, paused and took it away again.

'Nothing to be done,' Phipps said. 'The usual army cock-up. But what does it matter? We don't stand a chance.'

'I'm not so sure,' Alan said. 'It's amazing what we can do in a tight corner. But whatever happens, it's better to suffer with the Greeks than leave them to struggle on alone.'

In the exhilaration of expectation and preparation for action that might, after all, succeed, Harriet felt justified in contacting Charles. She wrote: 'I want to see you. Meet me at one o'clock,' and gave the note to a military messenger in the hall.

Charles, waiting, unsmiling, at the side entrance, met her with a strained and guarded look of inquiry.

Fearing she had behaved unwisely, she said: 'I am going to the Plaka. Will you come with me?'

He did not reply but followed her through the crowds that

were out to see the British lorries and guns coming into the town. 'This is exciting, isn't it?' she said.

'I suppose it is exciting for you.'

'But not for you?'

'To me, it means I won't be here much longer.'

They came into the square where Byron had lived. Tables and chairs had been placed outside the little café but no one could sit in the bitter wind that cut the tender, drifting branches of the pepper trees. Having come so far, Charles suddenly asked: 'Where are you going?'

'To the dressmaker. I hoped you'd translate for me; my Greek isn't very good.'

He grew pale and stared at her in resentful accusation: 'Is that why you wanted to see me? You simply wanted to make use of me?'

'No.' She was wounded by his reaction. She had supposed he would see the request as a gesture of intimacy, would know at once that it was an excuse for summoning him: 'Don't you want to do something for me?'

His expression did not change. For some minutes he was silent as though he could not bring himself to speak, then burst out: 'Where is this dressmaker?'

'Here. But it doesn't matter. Let's go to Zonar's and see if we can get a sandwich.'

He neither agreed nor disagreed but turned when she turned and walked back with her towards University Street. Because she had been misunderstood, she did not try to speak but, glancing once or twice at his severe profile, she wondered what attached her to this cold, distant and angry stranger. This of course was the moment to break away, and yet the attraction remained. Even seeing him detached and unaccountable, she still had no real will to leave him.

Half a dozen Australian lorries had parked on Zonar's corner and the men had climbed down. Some were drinking with newly made Greek friends: others were lurching about between the outdoor tables, occasionally knocking down a chair, but still sober and reasonable enough. The Greeks seemed delighted with them but Charles came to a stop and, shaken out of his sulks, said: 'We'd better not go there.'

'Why ever not?'

'It's out of bounds to other ranks, which makes things awkward for me. But, worse than that, they're drinking, so there's likely to be trouble. I don't want you mixed up in it.'

'Really! How ridiculous!'

He caught her arm and led her away protesting. Laughing at him and refusing any longer to be restrained by his ill-humour, she said: 'If you won't go there, we'll go to the dress-maker!'

She walked him back to the Plaka where a young Greek woman was making her two summer dresses. Charles trans-lated her instructions with a poor grace, then said: 'I'll wait for you outside.' She half expected when she left to find he had gone, but he stood in the lane beside a flower-shop. He had been buying violets and, seeing her, he held the bunch out to her. She took it and put it to her mouth.

She spoke through the sweetness of the petals: 'We must-n't quarrel. There isn't time.'

'No, there certainly isn't.' Giving his ironical laugh, he asked: 'Now where do you want to go?'

'I don't mind where we go, but don't be cross.'

'We might get something to eat. It's too late for luncheon but, if we go to the Corinthian, I know one of the waiters. He'll find something for us.'

Racing back to the square, dodging the crowds on the pave-ments, Charles held to her, pulling her along, caught up in the inspirited air of the city centre where so much was happen-ing. They were both elated as the enchantment of their companionship renewed itself.

How much longer was he likely to stay in Athens? He did not know. The Mission was to be absorbed into the Expeditionary Force, but he still had his work at the Military Attaché's office and would remain until his detachment arrived. That could be within a few days, or not for two or three weeks. No one seemed to know when the different units would turn up. Hurriedly organized, its contingents mixed and withdrawn from different sectors, the campaign was in some confusion.

One thing only was certain – there was no certainty and very little time.

The lorries, crowding in now from the Piraeus, were trying to find their way to camps outside Athens. Several, having gone astray, had made their way into Stadium Street and one after another stopped to get directions from Charles. Each time, as the Englishmen talked, a little crowd gathered to watch. A girl threw a bunch of cyclamen up to the men who leant over the lorry side. At this the men began to call to the passers-by and more flowers were thrown, and a fête-day atmosphere came into the streets. Suddenly everyone was throwing flowers to the men and calling a welcome in Greek and English. All in a moment, it seemed, fear had broken down. British intervention might indeed mean that Greece was lost, but these men were guests in the country and must be treated as such. Then the men, who had been bewildered by the suspicion, the unexpected winter weather, the fact the girls would not look at them, were reassured and began good-naturedly to respond.

Amidst all the shouting and waving and throwing of flowers, Harriet held on to Charles and said: 'It's fun not to be alone.'

Charles smiled down on her, in quizzical disbelief: 'But are you ever alone?' he asked.

'Quite often. Guy is always busy on something. He's . . .' She was about to say 'He's too busy to live,' but checked herself. It was, after all, a question of what one meant by living. She said instead: 'He has his own interests.'

'Interests that you don't share?'

'Often they're interests I can't share. These productions, for instance: he enjoys putting them on but he prefers not to have me there. It's quite understandable, of course. The production is his world; he's the dominating influence – and he feels I don't take him seriously. When I'm there, I spoil it for him. And he does much too much. In Bucharest, when he staged *Troilus and Cressida*, he worked on it day and night. The Germans were advancing into Paris at the time. I never saw him. He simply disappeared.'

'What did you do? Were you alone?'

'Usually, yes.'

Charles watched her gravely, awaiting some conclusive revelation satisfactory to himself, but she said no more. After a moment he encouraged her: 'You must have been lonely, in a strange country at a time like that?'

'Yes.'

'You married a stranger, and went to live among strangers. What did you expect?'

'Nothing. We did not expect to survive. It's our survival that's thrown us out. However, as a potential, Guy seemed remarkable. Now I'm not so sure about him. As a potential, he probably is remarkable, but all he does is dissipate himself. And why? Do you think he's afraid to put himself to the test?'

Charles did not know the answer to this question, but said: 'He seems confident enough.'

'Guy's confidence really comes from a lack of contact with reality. He's stuck in unreality. He's afraid to come out.'

Trying himself to gain more contact with reality, Charles asked: 'What's he doing at the moment?'

'Rehearsing the revue again. They've all decided to defy Pinkrose, and the padre's letting them use the church hall. He's probably over there now.'

In this she was wrong, as she soon discovered. They passed a café. The day had brightened and sitting outside in the sun was Guy with a British army officer. 'See who's here,' he called out to her.

Harriet had already seen who was there. The officer was Clarence Lawson, one of their Bucharest friends, now dressed up as a lieutenant-colonel. Grinning, Clarence rose up, tall and thinner than ever, keeping his long, narrow head on one side as though seeking to efface himself. In fact, Harriet knew, he was not only aware but disapproving. He had given her a swift, appraising glance, and she saw him sum up the situation.

Clarence was not successful with women but he was a man whose life was lived in acute consciousness of the opposite sex, passing from love to love, preferring an unhappy passion to no passion at all.

She said: 'Why, hello!' hoping by her tone of hearty interest to distract him from the intimacy he observed between her and Charles. She held out her hand. He took it, but his eyes were on the hand that held the violets.

She rallied him on the rank he had reached since they last saw him. His grin became rueful and he mumbled:

'Doesn't mean much.'

Guy said gleefully: 'You could not have come past at a better time. Clarence is only here for a few hours. He's just arrived. I was on my way to the rehearsal when I bumped into him. Wasn't it an amazing bit of luck? Here.' Guy pulled up two chairs. 'Sit down, both of you. What will you have? Coffee?'

'We haven't eaten yet.'

'You won't get anything now, but they might make a sandwich.'

Harriet, glancing at Charles, saw his face shut against her. He did not meet her eyes but spoke to Guy as though she were not present.

'I'm afraid I can't stay. There's a lot going on at the moment. I ought to be at the office.' Giving no one a chance to detain him, he turned abruptly and crossed the road.

Watching him as he went, Harriet's sense of loss was so acute, she could not keep quiet: 'I must go after him. I can't let him go like that. I must explain . . .'

'Of course,' Guy said, voice and face expressionless: 'If you feel . . .'

'Yes. I do. I'll come back. I won't be long.' She sped off and managed to catch sight of Charles among the crowd on the opposite pavement. He went into a shop that sold newspapers and cigarettes. She slowed to regain her breath and reaching him, was able to speak calmly: 'Charles, I'm sorry.'

He swung round, startled to see her there beside him.

'Clarence is here for so short a time. I'll have to stay with them. I've no choice.'

'Part of your past, I presume?'

'No. At least, not as you mean it. Why do you say that?'

'He looked pretty sick when he saw I was with you.'

'He's only a friend; as much Guy's friend as mine.'

'You'll be saying that about me one day.'

She laughed and slid her fingers into his hand. He was still annoyed but let her hand rest with his. She said: 'I'll see you tomorrow?'

'Will you have luncheon with me?'

'Yes.'

She made to pull her fingers away; he held to them a moment, then let them go. The meeting arranged, they could part with composure. Harriet went back to join Guy and Clarence. Clarence was restrained, making his disapproval evident and she tried to rally him: 'I thought you were a conscientious objector?' she said.

'I still am a conscientious objector.'

'But you've joined the army.'

'Well . . . in a manner of speaking, yes.' Clarence, lolling as he used to loll, hiding his discomfort beneath an appearance of ease and indifference, would not respond to her raillery. Despite his disapproval, he was, as he always had been, on the defensive.

'Are you in the army or aren't you?'

Clarence shrugged, leaving it to Guy to explain that Clarence was not a real lieutenant-colonel. He merely belonged to a para-military organization intended to protect British business interests in the war zones. He was on his way to Salonika to keep an eye on the tobacco combines.

'Really! What a shocking come-down! Just an agent of the Bund, Wall Street and Zoippus Bank! He'd better not meet Ben Phipps.'

Clarence shrugged again, refusing to protect himself; and Harriet went on to ask what he had done since leaving

236

Bucharest in the company of Sophie, the half-Jewish Rumanian girl who had once hoped to marry Guy. He had been on his way to Ankara to take up a British Council appointment but Sophie had deflected him. She had decided that Ankara was not for her. When they left the express at Istanbul, she demanded that they take the boat to Haifa and from there make their way to Cairo.

'So that's where you ended up?'

'Yep.'

'What about the Council? Couldn't they hold you?'

'No. I was only on contract. They let me go.'

'And now you're a colonel! That's pretty quick promotion.'

'Yep. Lieutenant one day: major by the end of the week: lieutenant-colonel the week after. That's what it's like.' He snuffed down his nose in self-contempt. 'The office in Cairo is full of bogus half-colonels like me.'

'And what about Sophie?'

'She's all right.'

'Did you get married?'

'Yep.'

'Good for Sophie. And now she's the wife of a lieutenant-colonel! I bet she likes that?'

Clarence hung his head and did not reply.

Taking this for a happy conversation, Guy decided he could safely go. He handed Clarence over to Harriet, saying he had been due at his rehearsal at 2.30 and he could not keep the cast waiting any longer. 'I'll be back at seven,' he said. 'I'll meet you here. Think where you'd like to go for supper. Anyway we'll spend the evening together,' and, gathering together his papers and books, he was gone.

'Guy hasn't changed much,' Clarence said.

'Did you expect him to change?'

Harriet put the violets on the table in front of her and Clarence frowned on them. 'Guy's a great man,' he said.

'Well . . . yes.'

They had had this conversation before and Harriet could think of nothing new to say. She had seen a great deal of

Clarence, who in Bucharest had been her companion when, as usually happened, Guy was not to be found. She had accepted his generosity and given him nothing, but her chief emotion at the sight of him was irritation. Clarence, it seemed, was born to suffer. He wanted to suffer. If she had not ill-treated him, someone else would. But Clarence could take his revenge. He encouraged confidence and often gave sympathy, but was just as liable to snap back with: 'Don't complain to me. *You* married him,' or: 'If you didn't let him play on your weakness, he wouldn't impose these lame dogs on you.'

Now she was cautious. With the vindictiveness of the weak, he was likely to repay her behaviour with Charles; and given any opportunity, he would sink her with some appalling truth.

'A great man,' Clarence repeated firmly. 'He's not self-seeking. He's generous. He's a *big* person.'

'Yes,' said Harriet.

'You're jolly lucky to be married to him.'

'I suppose I am . . . in a way.'

'What do you mean: "in a way"? You're damned lucky!'

Harriet let it pass. The café produced a sandwich for her. As the sun passed off the outdoor tables, the cold returned. Though the damp breeze smelled of spring, and almonds and apricots were in bloom, an icy tang came into the air at twilight. The nights were cold enough for snow.

She left earlier than she need to go to the office. When she returned, Clarence had moved inside. He had been drinking cognac and his gloom had lifted. He now accorded her his old romantic admiration.

At eight o'clock Ben Phipps, on his way to the Stefani Agency, entered and came to the table, doing a favour but not willingly. He had a message from Guy and his delivery was off-hand: 'He says he'll have to rehearse the chorus again. But you're to go to the Pomegranate and he'll join you there.'

'Why the Pomegranate?'

'Don't ask me. That's what he said.'

'How long will he be, do you think?'

'God knows. You know what he's like.'

Clarence asked Phipps to join them for a drink, but Phipps, humorously patronizing, somehow implying that to him a lieutenant-colonel was a joke, said: 'Haven't time, old chap. *I* have to work for my living,' and went.

The Pomegranate was a night club and an odd choice for Guy. He may have thought that, as Clarence in his new glory could afford it, it would be an especial treat for Harriet.

She said: 'It's expensive, I'm afraid.'

'Oh well! If the food's good . . .'

'There's no such thing as good food these days.'

'You mean, not at any price?'

'Not at any price. But they have a singer who's very good; and it's run by a eunuch. A real one; one of the last of the old Ottoman empire.'

'Oh well! That's something.' Clarence got unsteadily to his feet.

The hallway of the Pomegranate was lit by an indefinite inkish glow from bulbs hidden inside paper pomegranates. The eunuch who sat there collecting the entrance fees was not fat as his kind are said to be, but marked by an appearance that resembled nothing but itself. His face was grey-white, matt, and very delicately lined, like crackle ware. It was fixed in an expression of profound melancholy. He appeared unapproachable. A walking-stick, resting between his legs, showed that he was a cripple. Harriet, who felt for him the same anguish that had been roused in her by the deliberately maimed beggar children of Rumania, had once seen him making his way like a wounded crab down University Street. People walked round him, avoiding him not because of his awkward movements but because he had been separated from human kind by an irreparable injury. He seemed to have retreated from society like someone who had been a centre of scandal and would not risk another brush with life. But he purveyed life of a sort. He had started the night club, the best in Athens, and, sitting in a basket chair at the door, watched all who came and went.

Those who entered found a vapid, colourless little hall with a dance floor. Most of the tables were taken. Any still unoccupied were marked 'reserved'. The 'reserved' ticket was taken off for Clarence and Harriet, and Clarence said: 'I hope this table wasn't intended for anyone else. I dislike being given special treatment because of my rank.'

His expression was smug and Harriet said: 'Don't worry. You are favoured not because you're an imitation colonel, but as a guest and an ally. The Greek army is professional: rank has nothing to do with class, only with proficiency. The Greek soldiers go wherever they can afford to go, so I hope the British command will stop all this nonsense about Other Ranks.'

'I'm pretty sure they won't.'

'Why not?'

'It's obvious.' Clarence spoke peevishly, disliking the discussion. The Athens streets had been noisy with the newly arrived troops who, coming in from camps, wandering about, lost in the darkness, blundered in between the black-out curtains of any door that seemed to offer a refuge. They had not managed to pass the eunuch at the Pomegranate. His fee was too high.

'You don't want them in here, do you?' Clarence asked. 'For one thing, there isn't room.'

There certainly wasn't much room. The people present resembled those who had been at Cookson's party. The dance floor was packed with couples clinched face to face and barely able to move. Among them Harriet saw Dobson with the widow of a shipping magnate, whom he was trying to marry.

'What shall we drink?' Clarence asked, insisting on happier things. He ordered retsina and when the third bottle was opened his smile had become mild, placatory and rather mawkish: 'Come on and dance,' he said, but Harriet was not dressed for dancing. When she refused, he said: 'If you won't, then I'll dance with that pretty girl over there.'

'She'll refuse you. Greek girls don't dance with foreigners.'

'Why ever not?'

'It's out of loyalty to their own men at the front.'

'Loyalty?' Clarence brooded on the word then added with feeling: 'Yes. Loyalty. That's the thing. That's what we need.'

An impassioned gloom came over him and Harriet knew he would now be willing to talk.

She asked gently: 'How is it between you and Sophie?'

'How do you think? The last time I saw her she was coming out of Sicorel's. She's just bought a thousand pounds' worth of evening dresses.'

'You're joking. Surely you're not as rich as that?'

'Rich? Me? You don't think *I* paid for them?'

'Who did, then?'

'A silly little Cherrypicker with a title and money in the bank. He paid for them and probably paid for a lot of other things as well.'

'You mean, she's left you?'

'Yep. Not surprising, is it? What had I to offer a girl like Sophie?'

'How long were you married?'

'Week. It took a week to get her passport, then she looked round, sighted something better and was off like a greyhound from a trap. I admit things were grim. I had no job – we had only one room, in a dreadful pension. She hated me.'

'Oh, come!'

'Hated me!' Clarence repeated with morose satisfaction: 'Anyway, off she went. In next to no time she'd got herself a poor devil of a major. Not that I pity him. A bloody ordnance officer, feathering his nest while better men rot in the desert. She didn't stick him for long. She went on to an Egyptian cotton king, but he was only an interlude. She didn't intend to lose a valuable passport just to go and live in the delta. I don't know who came next . . . I lost sight of her. Cairo is the happy hunting ground for girls like Sophie. They can pick and choose.'

'Are you divorcing her?'

'I suppose so. She said she might want to marry this last one. She does love dressing up. As she came out of Sicorel's, her face was glowing. It's the only time I ever saw her *really* happy.'

'But what can she do with so many evening dresses? Is Cairo like that?'

'O *Lord*, yes!' Clarence glanced critically at Harriet's plain suit, then stuck out his lower lip at the women with their faded dresses on the dance floor. His eyes ceased to focus. Lost in memory, he suddenly laughed: 'Sophie had something,' he said: according a benevolent admiration. 'She really was a little trollop.'

'You knew that when you married her.'

'Of course I did.' Clarence stretched back in his chair, relaxed and fired by wine, and smiled aloofly, having reached now the stage of philosophical titubancy which granted him insight into all things. 'You just don't understand. You simplify life too much. Things are subtle . . . complex . . . frightening . . . One does things because one does things. You're so clever, you don't know what I mean. But what a fate! Really, when you come to think of it. I don't envy her.'

'Who?'

'Sophie. He won't marry her. They never do. She'll be stuck there with her British passport. In a few years' time she'll be just like all those raddled Levantine wives who got left behind in Cairo after the last war. She'll keep a pension . . .'

'It's an old story.'

'Yep. Life's an old story. That's what's wrong with it. Still, it interests me. I interest myself.'

'I'd never have thought it.'

'Hah!' Clarence turned his moist reminiscent eye and now the admiration was for Harriet. 'You're a bitch. Sophie was only a trollop, but you're a bitch. A bitch is what I need.'

'I don't think so. You need someone who can share your illusions . . .'

'Go on talking. You do me good. You always despised me. Do you remember that night I came in drunk from the Polish party and David Boyd was there? You debagged me. The three of you. Guy and David held me down and you took my bags off.'

'Did we do that? What shocking behaviour. But we were young then.'

'Good heavens, it was only last winter. And before I left –

do you remember? – I asked for those shirts I'd lent Guy and you were furious. Quite rightly. I didn't really want them. I was just being bloody-minded. And you were *furious*! You took them out to the balcony and threw them down into the street.'

'What a stupid thing to do!'

'No, not a bit stupid. You were always doing extraordinary things – things no one else thought of doing. I loved it. I bet if I asked you, you'd get up on this table here and now, throw off your clothes, and dance the can-can.'

'I bet I wouldn't.'

Clarence sat up, urging her, 'Go on. Do it.'

'Don't be a fool.' She wondered if Clarence had always held such an absurd view of her, or had she, with the passage of time, become a myth for him?

Clarence was pained and disappointed by her refusal but the waiter arrived and he forgot the can-can. Their meal was served. Clarence took a mouthful and put down his fork.

'This is pretty terrible,' he said.

'It's better than you'll get anywhere else.'

'Then we'll need a great deal more to drink. Let's go on to champagne.'

The floor cleared and the singer came out: a stout woman, not young, not beautiful, but it was for her that people came to the Pomegranate. She sang 'Anathema' and Clarence asked: 'What is that song?'

'A curse on him who says that love is sweet.
I've tried it and found it poison.'

'God, yes!' Clarence sighed fervently and filled his glass. He gave up any further attempt to eat.

The singer sang: '"I've something secret to tell you: I love you, I love you, I love you."'

The pretty girl who had attracted Clarence closed her eyes, but a tear came from under one lid. Clarence gave her a long look and, dismally bereft, turned on Harriet:

'That chap you were with today: what's he doing here?'

'He has some sort of liaison job. He won't be here much longer.'

'No, he won't,' Clarence maliciously agreed. He sat up, preparing an attack, but at that moment Guy arrived.

'Ah!' said Clarence, his voice rich with interest, 'here he is at last.'

They watched Guy as he made his way round the room greeted by people Harriet did not know, talking to people she had never seen before. Dobson, dancing with the widow, flung out an arm as Guy passed and patted him on the shoulder.

'A great man! A remarkable man!' said Clarence, deeply moved.

Behind Guy came Yakimov, the hem of his greatcoat trailing on the floor.

Clarence said: 'Hell!' then added: 'Never mind, never mind,' and in a mood to accept anything, shouted: 'Good old Yakimov.' The reprimand intended for Harriet was delayed by the new arrivals and the need to order food and more of the gritty, sweet champagne. Eventually, when they had all settled down again, Clarence looked angrily at Harriet and said: 'You've the best husband in the world.'

'Yes,' Harriet agreed

'You're lucky – *damned* lucky – to be married to him.'

'So you keep telling me.'

'I'm telling you again. Apparently you need telling. What were you doing walking about holding on to that bloody little pongo?'

'I like that. You're a pongo yourself.'

Guy said: 'Hey. Shut up, you two.'

'I'm telling her,' Clarence explained to Guy, 'she's married to the finest man I've ever known . . . a great man, a saint. And she's not satisfied. She picked up with a kid one pip up . . .'

Guy said again: 'Shut up, Clarence,' but Clarence would not shut up. He continued to condemn Harriet and condemn Charles. He and Charles might have little enough in common,

244

but both had an instinct for intrigue. To each, the very sight of the other had roused suspicion, and Clarence took Harriet's guilt for granted.

She was angry but, more than that, she was shocked. She was particularly shocked that these accusations should be made in front of Guy who seemed to her, at that moment, like some one of an older generation, who must be protected against the atrocities of sex. When Clarence at last reached an end, she said to Guy: 'You know this isn't true.'

'Of course it isn't. Clarence is being silly.' Guy rose as he spoke, looking for a refuge, and seeing Dobson leave the floor, hurried over to his table.

'Now look what you've done!' Harriet said.

'What do I care!' mumbled Clarence. 'Someone had to say it,' and self-justified and self-righteous, he sank into a despondent half-sleep.

Yakimov, who had listened to none of this, was waiting for his food. When it came, the waiter was sent to summon Guy who looked round, waved, nodded and went on talking to Dobson.

Yakimov, smiling blandly, said: 'I think I'll begin,' and when his own plate was empty, peered at Guy's: 'Do you think the dear boy doesn't want it?'

The food, some sort of lung hash, had fixed itself, cold and grey, on Guy's plate. To Harriet with her disordered stomach it looked inedible, but nothing was inedible to Yakimov. She said: 'You might as well have it.'

When Guy eventually returned, she told him: 'I've given Yakimov your food.'

'It doesn't matter.'

Clarence began struggling up and calling the waiter. 'I've got to go,' he said frantically.

'Not yet,' Guy protested. 'I've only just got here.'

'You got here nearly an hour ago,' Harriet said crossly. 'You spent all the time at another table.'

'Why didn't you come over?'

'We weren't asked to come over.'

'Do you need to be asked?'

Clarence persisted that he must go. 'My berth's booked on the night train. I'll be in trouble if I miss it.'

'Oh, all right; but I've seen nothing of you.'

'Whose fault is that?'

'And I've had nothing to eat.'

Harriet said: 'You've only yourself to blame.'

'Really, darling, need you be so disgruntled? Clarence is only here for one night.'

'I must go,' Clarence moaned.

'All right. Don't worry. Harriet and I are coming with you.'

Yakimov was content to be left behind.

Outside in the passage, the eunuch had left his base. An Australian soldier was sitting in the basket chair weeping. Perhaps he had been excluded from the club, perhaps he could not afford to pay.

'What's the matter?' Harriet asked.

'Nobody loves poor Aussie,' he wept. 'Nobody loves poor Aussie.'

'He's drunk,' Clarence said in contempt. Stepping out to the street, he stopped a taxi in a businesslike way but, once inside it, fell across the back seat and lost consciousness.

The station was blacked out. The train, that used to be part of the Orient Express, stood darkly in the darkness. The station officials moved about carrying torches or oil lamps. One of the officials thought that Clarence must be the British officer who earlier in the day had left his suitcase in the cloak-room. Every man on the station joined in getting Clarence to his bunk. The two cases, whether they belonged to Clarence or not, were put up on the rack. Another British officer was leaning out of the window of the wagon-lit and it seemed that he and Clarence were the only passengers on the train.

Guy shook Clarence by the shoulder, trying to waken him: 'We're leaving,' he said: 'We want to say "good-bye".'

Clarence shrugged Guy off and turning his face to the wall, mumbled: 'What do I care?'

'Isn't there anything we can do for him?'

'Nothing,' said Harriet. 'It's another case of "Nobody loves poor Aussie".'

The station-master warned them that the train was about to leave and Guy, suddenly upset, said: 'We may not see him again.'

'Never mind. We must regard that relationship as closed.'

But Guy could not regard any relationship as closed. All the way back to Monistiraki he spoke regretfully of Clarence, upset that he had seen so little of an old friend who held him in such high esteem.

'I really liked Clarence,' he said as though Clarence had departed from the world.

And, indeed, it seemed to Harriet that Clarence was someone who had disappeared a long time ago and was lost somewhere in the past.

23

March, as it moved into spring, was a time of marvels. The British troops were coming in force now, filling the streets with new voices, and the splendour of the new season came with them. The men were wonderful in their variety. As the lorries drove in from the Piraeus, bringing Australians, New Zealanders and Englishmen of different sorts, the Greeks shouted from the pavement: 'The Wops are done for. When the snow melts, we'll drive them into the sea.'

At mid-day the air was warm as summer. Every waste place had become green and the budding shoots almost at once became flowers. There were flowers everywhere. The old olive groves up the Ilissus Kifissias Road, the grey banks of the Ilissus, the stark, wet clay about the Pringles' villa – all these places dazzled with the reds of anemones and poppies, with hyacinths and wild lupins, acanthus flowers and asphodels. The wastelands of Athens had become a garden.

The flower shops, packed to the doors with flowers, threw out such a scent the streets were filled with it. If there were nothing to eat, there were carnations. Wherever they went, the British soldiers were handed posies and in the bars they received gifts of wine.

People had feared the British expedition. Some had said the British would never fire a shot, that they had only to set foot on Greek soil and the wrath of Germany would descend; but here they were and nothing had been heard from Germany yet.

The snows were melting in Macedonia. The Greek forces, taking fresh heart, would advance again. Any day now there would be new gains and new victories. The fact the Germans had occupied Bulgaria meant nothing very much. At this festival of *philoxenia*, in the midst of spring, the old hopes had returned and people pointed out that Mussolini had made a fool of himself. 'Why should the Germans start another front simply to save the Duce's face?' More likely the Germans were enjoying the situation as much as the Greeks. In Athens the promise was: 'Victory by Easter; by summer, peace.'

The British troops went wherever they liked. The café-owners would not support regulations concerning officers and Other Ranks, and the military police could not keep the men within bounds.

The Greeks, for their part, made no complaints. They expected tumult and enjoyed it. As for the damage: that was also to be expected in a town crowded with foreign troops. They offered their losses up to the Greek cause. When the Australians were confined to barracks, the Greeks were indignant. And Mrs Brett was indignant. At the canteen she told Harriet how she had been stimulated by contact with men who were 'wild in such a natural way'.

They had come into the English tea-room while she was taking tea with the padre. There were three of them, each carrying a potted plant which he had lifted from someone's window-sill. The drinking must have started early for they were all unsteady on their feet and one of them, sighting Mrs Brett, invited her to dance with him. He swayed dangerously over the table and the padre, pointing out that there was no dance-floor and no music, suggested he should sit down. The Australian replied: 'Shut up, you pommie bastard.'

'Of course I know how to deal with men in that state,' Mrs Brett said. 'I've had experience of all sorts, and it pays to be agreeable. Talk to them, get them interested; so I said: "Sit down, there's a good fellow, and I'll you order you some tea."' The Australian had seated himself 'like a lamb' but unfortunately knocked over a chair. 'That's a crook chair,' he said in a threatening way and he began blaming the waiters for the chair's defect. Mrs Brett, afraid he might start trouble, tried to draw him into conversation: 'How are you enjoying Athens?' 'What's Athens?' he asked. 'Why this is Athens. Where you are now. Isn't it a beautiful city?' 'I wouldn't know, mem,' he said. 'I ain't never seed a city till they brought the draft through Sydney and we was all drunk when we got there.' 'What do you think of that! That shows judgment – *and* honesty! He didn't want any tea but I persuaded him to take a cup. "To oblige you, mem," he said, "I'll even drink the stuff." We had a nice long chat and he showed me all the photographs in his wallet – Mum and Dad and Sis and so on. D'you know, he became quite attached to me. It was my evening at the canteen – but *could* I get away! No, I could *not*. Every time I stood up, he pulled me down again. "Don't you go, mem," he said. "You stay here and talk to me." Really, you know, it was quite heart-warming, but the padre got restive. I said: "Don't be alarmed, padre. I understand men; this poor boy's missing his mother." "You're right, mem," said my Australian: "I never had a mom like the other fellas." "Now, now," I said: "What about that snapshot you just showed me?" "That's the old man's second wife," he said. "And a right cow she is!" *What* a fascinating language! At last I said, nicely but firmly: "I have to go now. You come tomorrow and have tea at my flat and you can tell me all your troubles." "Anything you say, mem," he said, and I wrote down the address. I can't tell you how much I'm looking forward to seeing him again.'

But the next day there were no Australians in Athens and Mrs Brett's new friend did not arrive for tea. When it was discovered later that the whole battalion had been condemned as a menace to the peace of Athens and hurried to camps up north, the Greeks protested: 'We liked them like that. They're human. They behaved as they wanted to behave. Not like you English.'

Still the fun went on. The English soldiers, their first awkwardness overcome, were found to be human enough. The homage due to the men-at-arms passed over on to the civilians, and in bars and restaurants the English, simply because they were English, received tribute of wine ceremonially laced with slices of apple or sections of orange. Harriet when out with Charles was accorded a special recognition for not only was she English but the companion of an English officer who, according to the Greeks, 'had the face of a young Byron'.

One day the Athenians were amazed to see Highlanders in the street: men skirted like evzones and carrying bagpipes like the shepherds of Epirus. At the cellar café of Elatos two of them took the floor, placed their knives on the ground and danced, grave-faced, without music, the rhythm marked by the pleats of their kilts that closed and opened about them like fans. As the Scotsmen toed and heeled and turned in unison, the Greeks, intent and silent, understood that this was a ritual dance against the common enemy.

Harriet asked Charles: 'Is there a Highland regiment here?'

'God knows,' he replied. 'Anyone or anything might turn up. The C.O. said: "Just for the record; don't call this a campaign. Put it down as a skimble-skamble."'

Harriet never saw the Highlanders again. No one knew where they came from, or where they went. Many of the men appeared in Athens one day and were gone the next. Others remained so long in the suburban camps that their faces became familiar in this bar or that as though they were on native ground; but everyone knew that sooner or later they would be gone. Expectations and preparations were in the air. The rumour that the Italians were asking for terms was not a popular rumour. No one these days wanted the Italians to ask for terms. Imagination was set on a great offensive that would finish the Italians for good and all.

Guy had postponed his production in aid of the Greek war effort. The demand was for entertainment in the camps, where entertainments were few. Immediately after the first landings, he offered the show to the tank corps at Clyfada. The offer was immediately accepted.

While Guy was absorbed into the business of entrepreneur, Charles had nothing to do at all. Like the other men, he awaited a summons, never knowing the day nor the hour when he must pack and go. He belonged to a Northumberland cavalry regiment that was sending units to Greece but had as yet heard nothing of where they would land or when.

'Do you come from Northumberland?' Harriet asked.

'Yes.'

'What a long way away!'

'Do you mean from Greece? Surely not much farther than London?'

'Oh, much. Much farther.'

They were walking by the sea at Phaleron, covering the same stretch of shore that Harriet and the others had covered on the Christmas walk. Now, in the light of spring air, it was a different shore. The sea was tender, the waves creeping in over sand that sparkled in the crystal light. Here, by the Mediterranean, looking across the blue of the water towards the blue-blacks and harebell colours of the Peloponnese, Northumberland seemed as remote as the Arctic.

'A distant country,' she sang. 'The edge of the world. Dark, silent, mysterious and far away.'

He laughed: 'You're thinking of Siberia.'

'Perhaps. Will it soon be warm enough to bathe?'

She had taken off her shoes and stockings but the water was glacial.

Charles had hoped they might find a restaurant open even though Harriet said on Christmas Day they had been all boarded up. Christmas was winter, he said. Now it was spring and the restaurants would be re-opening. He was wrong. They were still boarded up.

Barefoot in the white, powdery sand, feeling the edges of the shells, and the black, dry scratch of seaweed, Harriet was drawn on by a dream that the restaurant keeper who had fed them at Christmas might be there again; and she imagined Charles delighted as she had been delighted. When they came to the wooden hut on stilts, she ran up the steps and looked in through the window, but the place was deserted. She remained on the balcony with her hands on the boarding, feeling the warmth of the wood, while Charles watched her from the shore, puzzled by her behaviour.

She said: 'There's no one here.'

'I should have thought that was obvious. If we don't get back, we'll get nothing at all.'

Walking back she told him about the man who had fed them with fish bought for his own family. Charles said nothing, not wanting to hear of any part of her past in which he had no part.

Before they left the beach, she found a branch that had been washed a long time in the sea and now, thrown clear during the winter, was dried, bleached and so glossy it seemed to be some substance other than wood. She still had it in her hand when they came opposite the bus stop. The bus was coming. As he made towards the esplanade, saying: 'If we can't get anything else, we can get tea at the Corinthian,' she wandered down to the water's edge, unwilling to leave the dazzle of the shore.

Finding she had not followed him, he ran back to her.

'How fortunate we are! It will be wonderful here in the summer,' she said, as though their friendship would go on for ever.

'The bus is coming.' He took the branch from her hand and flung it a long way out to sea. His single, accomplished movement, like that of a cricketer pitching a ball into a field, startled her and she said: 'You're only a schoolboy. You remind me of Sasha,' suddenly seeing his contrarieties as no more than the defences of youth.

He appeared not to hear her. Telling her to put on her stockings and shoes, he went to the bus-stop and asked the driver to wait. On the journey back he seemed in an even humour but, while they sat talking happily at the Corinthian, he broke in on their contentment, accusing her: 'I suppose you've always had someone like me to trail round after you?'

'Why do you say that?'

'It is true, isn't it?'

'No, it's not. It's simply stupid.'

'Then who was Sasha?'

When she saw him again after the meeting with Clarence, Charles had asked: Who was Clarence? What was he doing there? Harriet said: 'He's gone to Salonika. He's in Greece to protect business interests.'

'Oh, that lot!' Charles's scorn had extingushed Clarence and she had heard no more about him. Sasha would be less easy to explain away. She had been unwise in mentioning him but, having mentioned him, she had to explain. 'He was a boy we knew in Rumania. His father was a banker. The father was arrested on a faked-up charge, and the son was forced into the army. He had a wretched time but, worse than that, he was in danger of being murdered because he was a Jew; so he deserted and came to Guy for help. He had been one of Guy's students. We hid him for a few months. That is all.'

But not enough for Charles. That she had related Sasha to him, that she had spoken Sasha's name in a special tone: these things roused Charles's suspicions and only the most complete vindication of them could satisfy him.

She said: 'If you like, I will tell you the whole story.'

His voice cold with mistrust, he said: 'All right. Go ahead.'

As she described Sasha's innocent gentleness, the affection he had roused in her and the plan to smuggle him from Rumania that was frustrated by his disappearance, Charles was reassured. How strange, she thought, that someone who had so many advantages in life needed to be reassured!

He said: 'You will never know what became of him?'

'I suppose not. The Legation was our last hope; but now we've broken off relations with Rumania. It's an enemy country.'

Sasha was finished and done with: and Charles, free to sympathize, touched her hand with a contrite movement and said: 'That day, when you ran after me into the shop, I knew . . .'

'What?'

'That you needed me.'

'But surely you must have known from the beginning . . .'

254

'Why? How could I know? Why should you need me? You're married. You seem quite happily married. You have a husband whom everyone likes and admires. There was no reason why you should need me.'

'What did you think, then?'

'I . . . well, I thought you were simply playing a game with me; amusing yourself while Guy was at work.'

She smiled and shook her head.

'There are girls who want to bowl over every man they meet, just to prove they can do it. You might have been like that.'

'But I'm not. You're important to me; you know that.'

'Yes; but why? I really don't know why.'

'You're a friend.'

'Is that all?'

'A particular friend. You are what I need most: a companion.'

'But only that? Nothing more?' He leant towards her and, moved by his looks, his ardent expectations, she felt the air charged between them. Her lips parted; she turned her head away and said: 'If it were possible . . .'

'You mean it is impossible?'

'You know it is. I have to think of Guy.'

He took that to be no more than conventional resistance. Catching her hand, he glanced towards the wide carpeted stair-way that led from the foyer to the upper floors, and said: 'We can't talk here. Come up to my room.'

The impulse to please him almost drew her from her seat, but as she turned towards the stairs she saw faces that were familiar to her: Dobson's woman friend was present; there were girls who went to the School or used the School library. Knowing how easily she could become a centre of gossip, she was chilled and drew her hand away. Laughing uneasily, she said: 'What would these people think if they saw me going upstairs with you?'

'Does it matter what they think?'

'That's a stupid question. I live here. Guy works here.'

While she spoke the waiter brought their tea-tray and she hid her confusion by pouring the tea. She imagined he would be sulking, probably blaming her for an ungenerous caution, but when she turned to hand him his cup, she found his gaze fixed on her with an expression of hurt entreaty that was more compelling than ardour. She was surprised and moved, but everything that came into her head seemed to her trite, heartless and flirtatious, so she said nothing. They took their tea in silence.

Several days passed before he made any reference to this incident. They were walking in the gardens and coming on the pergola where the wisteria was putting out a lace of leaves, he said:

'Tà kaïména tà neiáto
Ti grígorá pou pernoun . . .'

She looked inquiringly at him.

'You must have heard that song,' he said. '"Poor youth, how quickly it passes: like a love song, like a shooting-star, and when it is gone, it never comes again."'

Knowing he was blaming her for a waste of passion and misuse of time, she said: 'It would be better if we did not meet again.'

'Do you mean that?'

'I don't know.'

'You must know.'

'I only know this is an impossible situation.'

'If you want me to go, I won't trouble you again.'

'If you want to go, I can't stop you.'

'But I don't want to go.'

It was an argument carried on in the fatuity of emotional intoxication and they both knew that it would lead to nothing.

24

Guy had stopped singing the 'fun and frolic' chorus about the house. In the mornings, while bathing, shaving, dressing and preparing for the imponderables of the day, he sang in an energetic, swinging tune that stood up to his lack of tone:

> 'Oh, what a surprise for the Duce, the Duce!
> He can't put it over the Greeks.'

The words amused her at first but they soon reached a point of unendurable familiarity.

'Is that the *only* song in the revue now?' Harriet asked, speaking grudgingly, for she resented the revue and hardly ever mentioned it. Guy always had had, and always would have, some preoccupation or other, but she had persuaded herself that were it not for the revue she would not have turned to other company. Delighted by her interest, Guy did not give her the chance to add that if there were another song, she would prefer it, but rushed in to say how much the revue had improved since she had seen it in the Tatoi hangar. Then it had been no more than a parish hall show; but since the arrival of the troops the British residents, seeing the war in Greece as their own war, had taken up the revue in a remarkable way. The chorus was twice the size and made twice as much noise and the troops joining in singing the songs. Greek songs like 'Oh what a surprise for the Duce' had been translated into English, and special songs had been composed by an English businessman in honour of Greco-British unity. All the camps were clamouring for the revue. Everyone wanted to see it. It was a stupendous success.

'What about Pinkrose?'

'Not a squeak out of him. He knows he's defeated.'

'I can see you're having the time of your life.'

'You'd enjoy it. Come and see it tonight. We're going to Kifissia for a special show and the Naafi are supplying refreshments for the cast. Do come.'

Harriet had her own plans for that evening. 'I don't think I can,' she said, but Guy bent over her and, catching her by the shoulders, looked down on her with an urgent and questioning intentness, saying: 'I would like you to come.'

'Then of course I will.'

'Fine.' He was away at once, hurrying round, looking for this and that. The military lorries were picking up the cast and visitors in Kolonaki Square. 'I suppose you can get out of the office early?'

'I suppose so. I was seeing Charles. Do you mind if I bring him?'

'Bring anyone you like, but make sure you come yourself.'

He was gone. Harriet watched him through the large window as he slammed the front door behind him and sped up the lane past the villa, impelled by all the activities he had planned for the day.

Yakimov said of Guy: 'He's a dear, sweet fellow, but he doesn't understand how you feel.' She had thought Yakimov was right. Now she thought Guy saw more than he would admit to seeing, understood more than he appeared to understand; but he would not let observation or understanding impede him. He was a generous man, anyway in material matters. He loved her, but his love must be taken for granted. If she put it to the proof according to her needs, she found herself sacrificed to what he saw as a more important need: his need to be free to do what he wanted to do. Challenged, he never lacked justification. He did not recognize emotional responsibility and, unlike emotional people, he was not governed by it. She suffered compunction; he did not. It was compunction – a quite uncalled-for compunction – that caused her to disappoint Charles, who had booked a table at Babayannis', and demanded that he go to Kifissia instead. She knew that he enjoyed being fêted at Babayannis', but they could go there any night. She was surprised, shocked, even, when he refused to go to Kifissia.

The office had been stirred by the news that Yugoslavia had been presented with a German ultimatum. The fate of Yugoslavia presaged the fate of Greece; yet, in the face of this new crisis, Charles and Harriet could do no more than bicker over their evening's entertainment.

They went into the Zappion Gardens where everything was bright with spring, but nothing was bright for them. Each looked inward on a private injury, determined not to yield a point to the other.

Charles kept his face turned from her but he spoke in an agreeable tone that was as cruel as a threat: 'Don't worry about me. There are other things I can do. I've been neglecting my friends lately. I ought to write some letters. In fact, I shall be glad to have a free evening.'

'We have to think of Guy,' Harriet said. 'I promised him . . .'

'And you promised me; you promised me first. Still, it doesn't matter. Please don't worry. I shall be quite happy on my own.'

'Guy does not object to my seeing you. He's not mean or demanding; we owe him one evening. I think we ought to go . . .'

'*You* ought to go, certainly.'

'We will have other evenings . . .'

'Perhaps; and perhaps not.'

'What do you mean by that?'

Pale and inflexible, he stared down at the path and shrugged his shoulders. 'This Yugoslavia business. If they reject the ultimatum, every available man will be rushed to the frontier.'

The argument was not resolved but it came to a stop. They passed under the trees and came to the pond where children were playing in the water. Everything was in leaf and flower, but all without meaning. At the pond they turned and walked back to Constitution Square.

Though it was too early for the office, Harriet paused at the side entrance of the hotel and Charles walked on without a word. She called: 'Charles.' He looked round and she ran to him and took both his hands: '*Please* come to Kifissia,' she said.

He frowned and reflected, then said: 'Very well,' but he said it with a poor grace.

'Call for me here. Come early, won't you?'

'Yes.' He walked off, his face still sullen, but she did not doubt he would come as agreed. As she had expected, he was waiting outside when she left the office. He refused to speak as they went to Kolonaki where the lorries waited, surrounded by Guy's company, a few people known to her and a great many unknown.

Driving out of Athens, they passed the Yugoslav legation where the Greeks had gathered to sympathize with a country threatened like their own. So far as they knew, Yugoslavia was still considering the German ultimatum. Ben Phipps said he had faith in the ability of Prince Paul who would 'box clever', but Guy thought the Yugoslavs would fight.

He asked the driver to stop and jumped down from the lorry in order to add his condolence and encouragement to the demonstration. Whenever an official could be seen at one of the legation windows, the Greeks applauded but the Yugoslavs looked glum.

Ben, leaning over the lorry side, called to Guy: 'Come on. We're going to be late,' and, when Guy returned, said: 'Oh, dry the silent tear for *they* – are going to cave in.'

Guy nodded sadly and said: 'You may be right.'

Kifissia was fragrant with the spring. The houses and gardens that rose towards Pendeli were still caught in the honey gold of the evening sun while the shadowed area of the main road held a counter glow that was an intimation of summer. The lorry drew up beneath the pepper trees and as the passengers jumped down, the trees trembled in the first breeze of sunset.

The Naafi had hired a hall that had been unused since war began. Boxes of sandwiches and cakes, sent for the performers, were being carried into the back entrance. The lorry passengers followed, filing through a narrow, neglected orchard that was full of the scent of citrus blossom. The dark hall, when they reached it, smelt of nothing but dust. Charles touched Harriet's arm to detain her, saying: 'Need we go in?'

'I must see some of it.'

'Let's wait till it begins.'

Left behind by the others in the sweet outdoor air, Harriet smiled at Charles, coaxing him to smile back. From a camp somewhere in the distance came the Call which Harriet had heard in Bucharest coming from the palace yard. Feeling a nostalgia for lost time, she said: 'Do you know what that says? "Come, water your horses, all you that are able. Come, water your horses and give them some corn. And he that won't do it, the sergeant shall know it; he will be whipped and put in a dark hole."'

'Who told you that?' Charles jealously asked.

'I don't know. I think Guy told me. There's another Call that says: "Officers be damned; officers be damned."'

'The Officers' Call.' Charles still looked sullen.

They could hear Miss Jay striking chords on the piano and Harriet took his arm and led him inside. They sat in the back row beside Alan Frewen, Yakimov and Ben Phipps, who would not be required until after the interval.

Soldiers were filling the front rows. There were not many British troops left in Attika. There were New Zealanders, tall, sun-burnt men who seemed to maintain their seriousness like a reserve of power.

The airmen, Surprise and the others, had adapted themselves to their precarious, volatile life by treating it as a joke; the infantrymen, with feet on the ground, might find life funny but knew it was no joke.

Imagining their remote, peaceful islands, Harriet wondered

what had brought the New Zealanders to Europe? What quarrel had they here? They seemed to her the most inoffensive of men. Why had they come all this way to die? She felt, as a civilian, her own liability in the presence of the fighting men who were kept in camps, like hounds trained for the kill. However close one came to them, they must remain separate. Charles had warned her that, sooner or later, he would have to go. And soon they would all be gone.

When the soldiers had occupied the first dozen rows, the civilians waiting at the front entrance were admitted to any seats that remained. A great many people, Greek and English, had heard of the revue and had driven out to Kifissia in hope of seeing it. The hall was filled in a few minutes, then the curtain jerked open and the chorus, ordered to make immediate impact, rushed on, breathless before they had even begun to sing. Miss Jay struck a blow at the piano and the men in mess jackets, the women in blue and white ballet skirts began 'Koroido Mussolini', the song that described the Italians at war:

> 'They stay inside because it's raining
> And send communiqués to Rome,
> In which for ever they're complaining:
> "It's wet, so can we please go home?"'

The whole song sung, Guy, wearing a borrowed white mess jacket that would not button across his middle, came out as conductor of the revels. He demanded a repeat performance from the audience which, willing enough to participate and enjoy, sang louder and louder as Guy sang and waved his hands, exhorting those in front to give as much as he gave himself. He brought the hall to a state of uproar.

Ben Phipps, sitting hands in pockets, with chair tilted back and heels latched on to the seat before him, gave a guff of laughter and said: 'Look at him!' It was a jeer yet, unwillingly, as he repeated '*Look at him!*' admiration came into his voice:

'What can you do with a man like that? What's it all about, anyway? Where's it going to get him?'

Where indeed! Harriet, scarcely able to bear the sight of Guy cavorting on the stage, felt a contraction in her chest. She remembered how she had watched him haranguing the stage-hands in Bucharest, expending himself like radium in order to give two performances of an amateur production that would be forgotten in a week. She had thought then that if she could she would seize on Guy and canalize his zeal to make a mark on eternity. She felt now she had expected too much from him. He was a profligate of life. The physical energy and intelligence that had seemed to her a fortune to be conserved and invested, would be frittered away. And there was no restraining him. She might as well try to restrain a whirlwind. Watching him now, she felt despair.

The first half of the revue ended, the cast of *Maria Marten* went behind to dress.

Charles said: 'You don't want to see that play again, do you? Let's go for a walk.'

She had, in fact, been looking forward to the play, but she followed him out into the twilight of the orchard where moths moved through the damp, night-chilly air. The pepper trees were disappearing into a fog of turquoise and violet. A single light showed between the looped curtains of a taverna. Some men were gathered outside on the pavement, the only life in the suburban street.

It would soon be dark. Charles suggested they follow a lane that went uphill between the gardens in a scent of orange and lemon flower. Here there was no noise but the croak of frogs. Above the gardens, they came into an olive grove where the undergrowth, dotted over with a white confetti of flowers, reached higher than their knees. Walking through it, they trod out the sharp, bitter scent of daisies and startled the grasshoppers into a see-saw of sound.

Though he had managed to take her away from any company but his own, Charles was not prepared to talk. She commented on things and asked questions but could not get an answer from him. His unrelenting ill-humour filled her with a sense of failure. Why need time be wasted in this way? She felt him to be intolerably demanding and ungenerous, yet she was despondent because, in a few days, he would be gone and they might never meet again.

War meant a perpetual postponement of life, yet one did not cease to grow old. She had been twenty-one when it started. At the end, if there ever was an end, what age would she be? How could she blame Guy for dissipating his energies when all the resources of life were being dissipated? What else could he do? War was a time when mediocrities came to the top and better men must rot or die in the conflict.

As for Charles, whose prospects had been so much more promising than theirs, how must he feel at seeing his youth wasted on his present futile employment? He was uncomplaining, of course. His education and upbringing required him to be uncomplaining, but what secret misery did he express in his petulance and silences and sudden shows of temper?

She stopped speaking herself until Charles said: 'There's a walk along the top of Pendeli. It's rather fine. We might go up there one day.'

She looked up to the spine of the hill that showed black against the stars. 'Would we be allowed to go as far as that?'

'I think so. Anyway, I could get permits.'

'When could we go?'

'We'll have to wait until the weather is settled. It can be cold on the top, and there's no shelter if it rains.'

The quarrel, it seemed, was forgotten. Despite their uncertain future, they planned the walk as a possible, even probable, event in the time ahead. Harriet thought Guy would come and they wondered who else might join the excursion.

Talking, they made their way back between the gardens. By the time they reached the hall, they had decided to arrange the walk early in April.

Charles said: 'The first Sunday in April would be a good day.'

264

'Will you still be here?'

Charles walked up the length of the orchard path before he muttered: 'How do I know?'

Inside the hall the chorus, giving encore after encore, sang:

> 'Oh, what a surprise for the Duce, the Duce,
> He can't put it over the Greeks.'

Harriet and Charles went behind the stage where the refreshments would be served. The wooden trays covered with tissue paper were stacked one on top of the other. The cast of *Maria Marten*, back into everyday dress, were waiting for food and as the chorus waved the audience away and the hall emptied at last, Ben Phipps slapped his hands together and said: 'Now for the grub; and, *mein Gott, ich habe Hunger*.'

'Haven't we all, dear boy,' said Yakimov giving a whinny of gleeful anticipation. As he moved towards the trays, Mrs Brett pushed him aside and said: 'All right, Prince Yaki, I'm in charge of this department. I'll do the honours.' She lifted down the top tray and removed the paper. The tray was empty. The tray beneath it was empty. All the trays were empty. A crust or two, a single cherry, some fluted paper cups, proved that food had been there once.

Some local men, hired to put out the chairs and act as stagehands, were gathered with their women at the back door, watching, blank-faced and silent. Mrs Brett turned and raged at them in a mixture of Greek and English.

Smirking in embarrassment, they shook their heads and held out their hands, palms up; they had nothing, they knew nothing.

Guy said: 'They were hungry. Say nothing more about it.'

'We're all hungry. They'd've got their share,' Mrs Brett faced the employed men again, saying: 'If you didn't eat it all, where is it?' They looked at one another in wonder. Who could tell?

Their perplexity was so convincing, several people glanced suspiciously at Yakimov, but Yakimov's disappointment was plain. He picked up the crusts and ate them one by one, leaving the cherry for the last. Wetting a forefinger and pressing it down on the crumbs, he murmured: 'Sponge-cake.'

Mrs Brett said: 'We should have placed a guard on the food. But, there you are! One thinks of these things too late.'

The weary players went for their coats. Ben Phipps, seeing a telephone on a table, lifted it and, finding it connected, shouted to Guy: 'Half a mo': let's see if anything's happened.' He rang the Stefani Agency. The others stood around while Ben, his eyes shifting from side to side, shouted: 'They've signed, eh? They've signed . . .' He nodded knowingly to Guy: 'What did I say? While you were demonstrating your solidarity, it was all over. Paul's made a clever deal. The Germans will respect Yugoslav territory.'

They climbed into the lorry and sat close together in the cold night air while Guy affirmed his faith in the Yugoslavs: 'They'll never stand for an alliance with Hitler.'

'Be your age,' Ben said. 'If they can keep the Germans out, they'll save their bacon and probably save ours as well. If Hitler can't move through Yugoslavia, he'll be left sitting on the Bulgarian frontier. It's less than 300 kilometres, all mountain country. Olympus is our strong-point. We could trap the bastards behind the Aliakmon and keep them trapped for months.'

In spite of their hunger, in spite of the cold, in spite of themselves, the passengers in the lorry felt a lift of hope. Their new enemy might in the end be the saviour of them all.

PART FOUR

The Funeral

25

On the morning following the submission of Yugoslavia, the office boy, summoned by Lord Pinkrose, returned to the Billiard Room with a foolscap draft of material to be typed.

All such material went first to Miss Gladys who would look through it, then, with explanation and encouraging noises, set her sister to work. If anything of particular interest came to hand, she would keep it for herself.

The foolscap sheet caused her to squeak with excitement and she ordered the boy to bring her typewriter to her desk. Her preparations for work were always protracted. This morning there seemed no end to them. As she fidgeted with the typing paper, her grunts and gasps and heavy breathing told Harriet that the foolscap sheet contained matter of unusual import. She supposed it must relate to the Yugoslav situation. The Legation had telephoned Alan warning him that refugees from Belgrade were moving towards Greece, the direction left to them.

Harriet had been in the News Room that morning when the call came. While she waited to speak to Alan, Pinkrose entered and signalled that he had something to say more important than anything that might be said by the Legation. His chameleon face was grey with the sweat of panic. He drummed on the desk, too agitated to know or care that Harriet and Yakimov were watching him.

Imagining that Pinkrose's needs were more pressing than those of the refugees, Alan apologized to his caller, put down the receiver and turned his long-suffering gaze upon the Director of Propaganda.

Pinkrose shot a finger at the map on the News Room wall: 'You see what's happened, Frewen? You see . . . you see . . . !'

Alan moved round slowly in his chair. Harriet and Yakimov lifted their heads. They all looked up at the Greek peninsula that flew like a tattered banner towards Africa.

'They've got everything,' Pinkrose panted. 'The Italians are in Albania. The Germans have got Bulgaria and Yugoslavia. They've got the whole frontier.'

Yakimov murmured in admiring awe: 'So they have, dear boy!'

'What's going to happen here, I'd like to know? Something's got to be done. I was sent here in error. I came to the Balkans in all innocence. All innocence. Yes, all innocence. No one knew the dangers; they don't know now. If they did, they would order me back. But the Organization is bound to repatriate me; it is in my agreement. And now's the time. Yes, now's the time. I want it fixed up without delay.'

'I have nothing to do with the Organization,' Alan said with even patience. 'You are the Organization head. Surely it's up to you to fix your repatriation?'

'I *am* fixing it. I'm fixing it now. Here and now. Yes, yes, here and now, I'm putting it into your hands, Frewen. I look to you.'

'Oh? Well! I don't know what I can do, but I'll make inquiries. There's no regular transport; you know that. I've heard it suggested that a civilian – one of the top brass, of course – might, if the need arose, be given a lift to Egypt by the R.A.F.'

'I came on a service plane,' Pinkrose said eagerly. 'I travelled in a bomb bay.'

'Did you indeed! Well, I'll see what I can do.'

'Yes, yes, see what you can do. Give it top priority. Treat it as an emergency. Let me know within the next hour.'

'Good heavens, the next hour! I won't hear anything within the next week. There may be nothing for six weeks.'

'Six weeks? *Six weeks!* You speak in jest, Frewen.'

'I do not speak in jest. These things take time.'

Pinkrose's face quivered. Drawing in his breath, he cried in agony: 'Then I'm trapped?'

'We're all trapped, if it comes to that. But I see no immediate cause for alarm. The situation's no worse. If anything, it looks a bit brighter. The Germans have agreed to respect Yugoslav sovereignty; they say they won't send troops through Yugoslavia. I know you can't trust them, but they'll be tied up for a bit.'

Pinkrose stared at Alan, then asked in a small voice: 'Where did you get this?'

'It's official. And what about the lecture? Are we to call that off?'

Pinkrose swallowed in his throat and looked down at the floor. 'No,' he said after a long pause. 'I was precipitous, Frewen, I was precipitous. Hold your hand a while.'

'You don't want me to try to arrange a flight?'

'No. My duty is here. The lecture is of paramount importance. It must be given. Yes, it must be given. And there are other matters . . .' Turning abruptly, he hurried off to attend to them.

One of the other matters was no doubt now on Miss Gladys's desk. She had just begun to type it when Pinkrose flustered in with another foolscap sheet. 'Here's the rest,' he said and, speaking in a low, intimate and conspiratorial tone, he called Miss Gladys over to a table by the wall. Pushing the maps away and spreading the sheet out, he whispered: 'Read it through. Tell me if there's anything you don't understand.'

A long interval followed, during which Pinkrose, running his pencil along the lines, muttered under his breath and Miss Gladys whispered: 'I understand, Lord Pinkrose, I understand.'

Feeling that her presence was intrusive, Harriet decided to go to the News Room. As she rose, the others were alerted.

The muttering ceased. They turned to watch where she might go. She passed Miss Gladys's desk and stopped. Miss Gladys had typed: *REPORT ON GUY PRINGLE. In my opinion Guy Pringle is unsuited for Organization work* . . . Harriet picked up the draft.

In a stern tone, Miss Gladys said: 'How dare you touch that! That's a confidential report.'

Harriet read on. In the opinion of Pinkrose Guy had dangerous left-wing tendencies. He was a trouble-maker who mixed with notorious Greeks. He had become a centre of sedition and was disapproved by all responsible persons in Athens.

'What a pack of lies!' she said.

Further, he had staged an obscene production and complaints had been received from prominent members of the British colony. The Director had banned the production. In spite of that, Pringle was visiting army camps with a play liable to demoralize all who saw it . . .

'*Lord* Pinkrose!' Miss Gladys turned on her superior, indignant that he should give her no support, and Pinkrose began obediently to chatter:

'Put it down. Put it down, I tell you. Put it down.'

Harriet put it down and asked: 'What else have you written?'

'It's nothing to do with you.' As she approached, Pinkrose snatched up the paper: 'You have no right . . .' he shouted. The paper shook in his hand.

'Oh, yes, I have a right. The Organization does not permit confidential reports. If you write a report on Guy's work, you're required to show it to him. He's supposed to sign it.'

'Sauce!' said Miss Gladys.

'Required! Required, indeed! I'm the Director; I'm not *required* to do anything . . .' Beside himself with indignation, Pinkrose let his voice rise and at once Miss Mabel began to moan and give little cries of terror.

Miss Gladys spat at Harriet: 'Go away. You're upsetting my sister.'

'Yes, go away,' Pinkrose screamed. 'Leave this office. At once. You hear me, at once.'

Harriet went to her desk and gathered up her belongings. 'Before I go,' she said, grandiloquent with rage, 'I must say: I am surprised that at a time like this, anyone – even *you* Lord Pinkrose – could stoop to intrigue with Cookson, Dubedat and Lush in order to injure a man who is worth more than the whole lot of you put together.'

She went out. Alan and Yakimov were peacefully drinking the first ouzo of the day when she burst in on them to say:

'I'm going.'

'Where?' Alan asked.

'Pinkrose has sacked me; but if he hadn't, I'd go anyway.'

'Have a drink first.'

'No.'

Near hysteria, she ran to the church hall. It was shut. She took a taxi to the School. No one there had seen Guy since early morning. She went to Aleko's. The café was empty. She walked back down Stadium Street looking into every café and bar she passed, and came to Zonar's. Guy was not to be found.

Harriet was meeting Charles at the Corinthian. As she walked towards the hotel, Guy's voice, loud and cheerful, came to her from the distance.

She saw him helping the driver to take luggage from a taxi. The luggage was being heaped up beside a man who, impressive and large in a fur hat, fur-lined overcoat and fur-topped boots, had the familiarity of a figure in a fairy-tale. Harriet at that moment had no eyes for him but seized on Guy, furiously asking: 'Where have you been?'

'To the station, to meet the Belgrade Express.'

'Why?'

Guy stared at Harriet as though only she would not know why. 'I thought David Boyd would be on it.'

'Oh!' Harriet subsided. 'And was he?'

'No. He hasn't turned up yet. But . . .' Guy indicated that he had not returned empty-handed. Indeed, he seemed to think he had brought back a prize. Presenting the large, be-furred man: 'This is Roger Tandy,' he said.

Harriet had heard of Tandy. When he passed through Bucharest, he had been described in the papers as 'the famous traveller'. That had been before Harriet's time but Guy had met him briefly, and Tandy, famous traveller or not, had been grateful to see a familiar face when he turned up in Athens among the refugees from Belgrade. He and Guy had fallen on each other like old friends. Now Guy, playing the host, unloading and counting his luggage, wanted to know: 'How many cases should there be?'

Tandy replied: 'Only seven. I travel light.'

Other taxis were off-loading other refugees – political refugees, religious refugees, racial refugees, and English wives with small children. The hotel would be crowded, but Roger Tandy did not seem concerned. He seated himself beside an outdoor table and said pleasantly to Harriet: 'Come, my dear. Before we go in, we'll have a little snifter.'

'Hadn't you better make sure of your room?'

'No need. I booked well in advance. At my age one knows which way the wind is blowing.'

'Better make sure,' Guy said, and he sped into the hotel to confirm Tandy's booking.

Tandy patted the chair beside him.

Harriet, overwhelmed both by his looks and his foresight, sat down. His face was plum-red and his moustache was the colour of fire. The two reds were so remarkable, it was some minutes before she noticed that the little snub nose, the little pink mouth and the small, wet, yellow-brown eyes were altogether commonplace.

The midday sun was hot. Tandy's face broke out in globules of sweat. He threw open his greatcoat and unbuttoned the jacket of his cinnamon twill suit, and the sun gleamed on his waistcoat of emerald and gold brocade. His waistcoat buttons were balls of gold filigree. The eyes of passers-by, lighting first on Tandy's waistcoat, became fixed when they saw that his greatcoat was lined to the hem with resplendent honey-golden fur. One of the passers-by was Yakimov. He was on his bicycle, his own greatcoat, looped up for safety, also displaying a fur lining, but the fur had been old when Yakimov was young.

Yakimov wobbled into the pavement, put out a foot and somehow managed to get down. 'Dear girl,' he called to Harriet, 'is everything all right?'

She was reminded of her anxiety of the morning but felt this was no time to discuss it. In any case, she saw that Yakimov had stopped for one reason and one reason only. He meant to meet Tandy.

Introducing the two men, Harriet stressed Yakimov's title. Tandy's eyes grew sharp with interest.

'Sit down, *mon prince*,' he said, 'and join us in a snifter.'

Yakimov sat down at once. His own eyes, large and tender, examined, with no hint of envy, the immense, well-fed figure of Tandy who was dressed as, in better days, he would have dressed himself. The waiter was recalled and Yakimov asked for a brandy. It came at once and as he put it to his lips his excitement was evident. It seemed a destined meeting and saying: 'I must go and speak to Guy,' Harriet left them to find each other.

Guy was among the crowd at the desk. 'I want to tell you something,' she said.

Giving one ear to her and the other to the cross-currents about him, Guy said: 'Go ahead.'

'No. Come over here.' Exasperated by the fact he was worrying over Tandy's welfare as he would never worry over his own, she pulled him out of the press and said: 'I've something important to tell you.'

As Harriet told her story Guy's attention was on the bright out-of-doors and the enticing prospect of Tandy and Yakimov who at that moment were joined by Alan Frewen. She held on to him, and speaking quickly, gave the substance of Pinkrose's report.

Guy, frowning, said: 'It's not important, surely. No one's going to take any notice of Pinkrose.'

'Why not? He was appointed Director. They didn't appoint him in order to ignore him.'

'Perhaps not; but they must know the sort of man he is. I've seen reports that Inchcape sent on my work. They were excellent. First-class. If Pinkrose sends in this report – and, after what you said, he may realize he's doing the wrong thing – it will be compared with the others. They don't relate. Someone's talking nonsense and it isn't Inchcape.'

'How are they to know it isn't Inchcape?'

'He'll be called in. He'll be consulted.'

'He may be dead by then.'

'I don't think so. Inch always took good care of himself. He'll be flourishing; and I know he'll stand by me.'

'Will he? I wonder!'

'You're making too much out of this.' Impatient of her fears, he patted her shoulder and was ready to depart. 'Come and talk to Tandy. I've always wanted to meet him.'

'You go. I'll come in a minute.'

Without waiting to wonder what there could be to detain her inside the hotel, Guy sped off like a child allowed out to play. When he was through the door, Harriet took herself to the dining-room where she had arranged to meet Charles. She was very late.

Charles, at luncheon, got to his feet and waited for her to defend herself. She cut at once through any likely accusations by saying: 'I've lost my job.'

'I didn't know anyone could lose a job these days.'

'It wasn't incompetence. I had a row with Pinkrose.'

Charles, forced to laugh, motioned her to join him at the table.

She said: 'I can't stay. Guy is expecting me.'

'Oh!' His laughter came to a stop.

He sat blank-faced, while she told the story of the report and concluded: 'You know, this could wreck Guy's career with the Organization.'

'I'm sure it couldn't. There are more jobs than men . . .'

'I'm thinking of the future when there'll be more men than jobs.'

'The future?' Charles looked puzzled as though the future

274

were some unlikely concept he had not studied before, then he glanced aside: 'Yes, you must consider the future. You complain of Guy but you don't intend to leave him.'

'Do I complain of Guy?'

'If you don't, why are you wasting your time with me? You can't pretend to love me?'

'I don't pretend anything. But perhaps I do love you. I would like to feel we were friends for the rest of our lives.'

'Yes, indeed! You want me hanging around. You have a husband, but you must have some sort of *cavaliere servente* as well. There are a lot of women like that.' Throwing his napkin aside, he got to his feet. 'I can't stand any more of this. I'm going up to my room. If you want to see me, you'll find me there. If you don't come, I'll know you never want to see me again.'

'This is too silly—'

'If you don't come, you never *will* see me again.'

'An ultimatum?' Harriet said.

'Yes, an ultimatum.' He marched off, attracting attention as he passed through the room. He was watched, Harriet saw, not only with admiration, but something near tenderness. She could imagine that for these people he presented an ideal image of the ally who, with nothing to gain, had made this foolhardy venture to fight beside the Greeks. She herself had seen him a symbol touching and poetic of the sacrificial victims of war. Now she knew him better she scarcely knew how she saw him. He passed through the door, angered and injured, and made off to nurse his injury somewhere out of sight.

One thing was certain: she would not go after him. She would make sure of that by joining Guy and the other men outside, but not at once. Lingering in the dining-room, she saw again his swift, exact movement out of the room and felt drawn to follow him. Not knowing what to do, she sat on as though expecting something or someone to make the decision for her. Or perhaps Charles would come back, rather shamefaced, and treat his ultimatum as a joke.

Instead, Alan Frewen came to look for her. He said they

were all going round to Zonar's. He did not ask what she was doing there, alone in the dining-room, sitting opposite someone's uneaten meal, and she realized he did not need to be told. He asked nothing, and said nothing. He did not criticize his fellow men; nor did he wish to become involved in their problems.

'Guy thought you would like to come with us?'

'Yes. I'll come with you.'

As they passed through the foyer, she glanced up the staircase with a vision in mind of Charles hurrying down to her. But there was no one on the stair and no sign of Charles.

Alan said: 'Surely you haven't left the office for good? I need someone to edit my notes on the German broadcasts to Greece.'

Harriet was beginning to regret her lost employment, but said: 'I can't work in the Billiard Room with the Twocurrys.'

'I thought you'd have more space there; but if you like, you can join Yaki and me in the News Room.'

'I'd like that,' she said.

26

Prince Paul claimed that he and his faction had saved Yugoslavia. Perhaps they had unintentionally saved Greece. No one had time to find out. The Regent was gone in a night and next morning all the talk was about revolution. The Regency was terminated. Peter had displaced Paul. The quisling ministers had been arrested. The English, Americans and Russians were being cheered in the streets of Belgrade, and the whole of Yugoslavia was a ferment of rejoicings and anti-Axis demonstrations.

'Magnificent,' said Ben Phipps. 'But what happens next?'

'It's magnificent,' Guy said, 'chiefly because they didn't stop to ask what happens next. They could not accept German domination. They revolted against it without counting the cost. That was certainly magnificent. And what would have happened in any case? Would the Germans have kept the terms of the agreement?'

Called to order, Ben murmured: 'Not very likely,' and Harriet noted that these days Guy was more inclined to call Ben Phipps to order and Ben Phipps more ready to agree with him. As a result, although she still disliked Phipps, she was less resentful of his influence over Guy.

'Still,' he said. 'What *will* happen next?'

Tandy grunted once or twice and Guy and Ben looked at him. He spoke seldom. When he did speak, it was slowly, with pauses and grunts that promised some deep-set thought, not easily brought to birth. Now, at last reaching the point of speech, he said: 'We must wait and see.'

Waiting to see, they waited in the ambience of Tandy who

spent most of his day at Zonar's, usually at an outdoor table he had adopted as his own. He could always be found by anyone in need of companionship. Although he had only just arrived and might soon be returning whence he had come, he was already an established figure in Athens. Large and splendid, he seemed, in a changing world, permanent and unchanging. People gathered about him as about a village oak.

Tandy came like a gift, a distraction heaven-sent, just when the fine hopes of March were changing to doubts again. Guy had discovered him but Phipps took him up with enthusiasm, and Yakimov clung to him like a lover. In spite of his fame, no one knew much about him. From occasional remarks, they gathered he had begun the war very comfortably in Trieste but, fearing to be trapped there, had moved to Belgrade shortly before the Italians entered against the Allies.

'Doesn't do to stay anywhere too long,' he said.

Ben Phipps said: 'You certainly left Belgrade in good time.'

Tandy gave him a reproving look. He said nothing then but later conveyed, almost without words, the fact that his flight from Belgrade had not been impetuous; nor, as it might seem, premature.

'Not a private person,' he mumbled. 'Under orders.'

'Really?' said Harriet. 'Whose orders?'

Tandy silenced her with the same reproving look and Guy and Ben Phipps, when they later had her alone, told her one did not ask questions like that. The two men, conferring together, decided that Tandy must be an exile who had been placed in jeopardy by his extreme left-wing activities and would, when he received the word, rejoin the Yugoslav revolutionaries as a sort of classical demagogue.

They were displeased when Harriet said: 'He seems just another Yakimov to me.'

'That's only the get-up,' Ben Phipps said.

Yakimov was a joke: Tandy was not. He certainly managed, while speaking seldom, to extrude a sense of gravity and intellectual weight beside which Yakimov seemed a shadow. When anyone expressed an opinion or expounded a theory, he gave

278

the impression that he knew what was about to be said but wouldn't spoil the fun by saying it first. He could also disconcert the speaker by dropping his eyelids so there was no knowing whether he agreed or disagreed.

When news of the Yugoslav revolution went round, he had seemed to share Guy's enthusiasm while, at the same time, reflecting Ben Phipps's qualms. They waited to see what he would do now. Forty-eight hours later he was still in Athens, still sitting at his table outside Zonar's, and Harriet said: 'Doesn't look as though he's going back, does it?'

Ben Phipps snorted: 'I don't know what he's up to, but I'm beginning to think it's nothing very much.'

Guy laughed, agreed and said: 'Never mind. I like the old buffer. He may be another Yakimov, but he pays his round.'

Finding he said little when drunk and nothing much when sober, Guy and Ben ceased to consult Tandy on political matters and, talking across him, did not even look to see whether he dropped his eyelids or not. Even though curiosity about him had gone down in disappointment and boredom, they liked him to be there. He was a centre of companionship, and was, as Guy said, scrupulous in paying his round. He was equally scrupulous in seeing himself repaid. He was the only person with whom Yakimov drank on equal terms. Though he paid from a bulky crocodile wallet with gold clasps and Yakimov, when his turn came, had to search his torn pockets for a coin, Tandy, compassionless, let Yakimov search. He was tolerant of Yakimov, no more. He made no concessions and this fact seemed to heighten Yakimov's regard for his new friend. Charmed and challenged by the first sight of Tandy, Yakimov, in the News Room, would murmur to himself: 'Remarkable chap!' and bring Tandy's name into conversation as though he had him constantly in mind.

'We're fortunate in having him here,' Yakimov said.

'Why?' Harriet asked.

Yakimov shook his head slowly and drew in an appreciative breath, marvelling at Tandy's quality. 'He's travelled, dear girl. Your own Yak got around in his day but that one – *That One* has trotted the globe.'

'But would you say that travel, in itself, is an achievement. It only calls for money and energy. Has he travelled to any purpose? Has he, for instance, written anything about his travels? I don't think so.'

'Scarcely surprising,' Yakimov smiled at her ingenuousness. 'The dear boy's tied down by the Official Secrets Act.'

'You mean he was sent abroad? He's a secret agent?'

'Indubitably, dear girl.'

'I can't believe it. No secret agent would dress like that.'

'I think I ought to know, dear girl.'

'How did you know?'

Yakimov shook his head again, wordless with admiration of the man. He had told Ben Phipps: 'At first sighting, I recognized Roger as a Master Spy.'

'How did you do that?' Phipps asked.

'There are signs. That wallet stuffed with the Ready – the money comes from *somewhere*. But there's more to it than that. He recognized your Yak. Nothing said, of course; but we made contact.'

'You tipped each other the wink, eh? How'd you do it? Tell me. A handshake, like the Freemasons?'

'Not at liberty to say, dear boy.'

Guy and Phipps were now inclined to laugh at Tandy, but Yakimov refused to join in.

'Remarkable man,' he insisted. 'Most remarkable man! In disguise of course.'

'Odd sort of disguise,' Phipps said.

'All disguises are odd,' Yakimov said in a tone of reprimand, gentle but dignified.

Harriet, who had not expected much of Tandy, did not share Guy's disappointment. She had liked him well enough at first and still liked him after the brief myth died. He made no demands, but he was there: his table was a meeting place, a lodgement during stress and a centre for the exchange of news.

Charles intended, apparently, to keep his word. She had rejected his ultimatum and would not see him again; and so was drawn like an orphan to Tandy's large, comfortable, undemanding presence.

'May I adopt you as a father figure?' she said, approaching his table. For answer, he rose and bowed.

His size helped him to an appearance of good nature. But would his good nature stand up to the test? It might be nothing more than the *bonhomie* of an experienced man who knew what would serve him best. She did not hope to uncover the truth about Tandy. Time was too short. He had arrived in a hurry, was hurriedly adopted as a prodigy and as hurriedly dropped. Whatever the truth might be, she suspected he had adapted himself so often to so many different situations, he had lost touch with his real self. But what did it matter? With Tandy as her chaperon, she could sit and watch the world go by.

As she expected, Charles walked past. He had said she would never see him again, but while they remained in one community, they must meet; and, meeting, she knew they would be drawn together.

He noticed Tandy first, then saw that Harriet was with Tandy. He looked away and did not look back.

Next day, he reappeared. This time, he eyed her obliquely and smiled to himself, amused at the company she was keeping.

The third time she saw him, Yakimov and Alan were present.

Alan called: 'Hey!' and held out his stick. Charles stopped, growing slightly pink, and talked to Alan while Harriet devoted herself to Tandy and Yakimov. The discussion at an end, Charles went off without giving her a glance.

'I was having a word about the Pendeli walk,' said Alan.

'The Pendeli walk?' Harriet asked in a light, high voice.

'You are coming, aren't you?'

'Of course. But is Charles coming?'

'He'll come if he can.'

The rest of the party would be Alan, Ben Phipps and the

Pringles. Alan now suggested that Yakimov and Tandy should join them. Yakimov looked at Tandy, the globe-trotter, and Tandy shook his head. Yakimov echoed this refusal: 'Your old Yak's not up to it.'

As the sun grew warmer, Tandy threw off his coat, but kept it safely anchored by the weight on his backside. With an identical gesture, Yakimov threw off his own coat, saying to Tandy: 'Did I ever tell you, dear boy, the Czar gave this greatcoat to m'poor old dad?'

'You've mentioned it . . .' Tandy paused, grunted and added: '. . . repeatedly. Um, um. Right royal wrap-rascal, eh?'

Yakimov smiled.

His coat-lining, moulting, brittle and parting at the seams, had been described by Ben Phipps as: 'Less like sable than a lot of down-at-heel dock rats wiped out by cholera,' but Yakimov saw no fault in it. He had a coat like Tandy's coat. Tandy, globe-trotter and secret agent, owning a crocodile wallet stuffed with 100-drachma notes, was Yakimov's secret Yakimov. Tandy, too, had a coat lined with – whatever was it?

'Wanted to ask you, dear boy,' Yakimov asked: 'What kind of fur is that you've got inside?'

'Pine marten.'

Yakimov nodded his approval. 'Very nice.'

He would have spent the day at Tandy's elbow had he not had to earn a living elsewhere. Gathering himself together, he would say: 'Have to go, dear boy. Must tear myself away. Must do m'bit.' Departing, he would sigh, but he was proud of his employment. He liked Tandy to know that he was in demand.

As the British troops went, sent away with flowers and cheers, the camps closed down and Yakimov was no longer neded to play Maria. There was still talk of a 'Gala Performance' to aid the Greek fighting men, but Pinkrose had complained to the Legation. Dobson telephoned Guy with the advice: 'Better let the show rest for a bit.' Yakimov, resting, still talked of his Maria that had been *un succès fou* and his

Pandarus which he had played to 'all the quality and gentry of Bucharest'.

But these triumphs were in the past; his job at the Information Office lived on. 'Lord Pinkrose needs me,' he would say. 'Feel I should give the dear boy a helping hand.'

When he saw Harriet installed in the News Room, Pinkrose said 'Monstrous!' but he said it under his breath. After that he always seemed too busy to notice she was there.

He had said no more about leaving Greece. He had accepted Alan's reassurances and was apparently unaware that the revolution had cancelled them out. He may not have known there had been a revolution. The news did not interest him. He had time now for nothing but his lecture that would, he told Alan, be given early in April. The exact date could not be announced until a suitable hall was found. Alan was required to find a hall and Pinkrose came hourly into the News Room to ask: 'Well, Frewen, what luck?'

Alan's task was not an easy one. Most of the halls in Athens had been requisitioned by the services. The hall attached to the English church was much too small. Alan recommended the University but Pinkrose said he wanted the lecture to be a social rather than a pedagogical occasion.

He said: 'I cannot see the beautiful ladies of Athens turning up in the company of students. It would be too . . . too "unsmart".'

'If you want that sort of occasion,' Alan said, 'I'm afraid I can't help you. I haven't the right connections. You'd do better on your own.'

'Now, now, no heel-taps, Frewen! Soldier on. Myself, as you well know, have other things to do.'

When Pinkrose came in again, he found Alan had no more suggestions to make. He said crossly: 'You're being unhelpful, Frewen. Yes, yes, unhelpful. I'll go to Phaleron. I'll appeal to the Major.'

'An excellent idea!'

Pinkrose stared at Alan's large, sunken, expressionless face, then went angrily to the Billiard Room. A little later a taxi called for him. He set out, fully wrapped, for Phaleron.

All the Major could offer was his own garden, but it was, Pinkrose said, 'glorious with spring', and in the end he accepted it. He announced the arrangements to Alan, saying: 'The lecture will be combined with a garden party. There will be a buffet luncheon for the guests. I think I can safely say, knowing the Major, that it will be a sumptuous affair. Yes, yes, a sumptuous affair. I am an experienced speaker, not daunted by the open air; and it's in the Greek tradition, Frewen; the tradition of the Areopagus and the Pnyx. Oh yes! the Major has been very kind. As I expected, of course. As I expected.' Pinkrose sped away, to return fifteen minutes later, his voice hoarse with excitement: 'I have decided, Frewen; yes, I have decided. I will give my lecture on the first Sunday in April.'

Alan gave a sombre nod. When Pinkrose went, he returned to his work, not meeting the eyes of Harriet or Yakimov. In a minute Pinkrose was back again. 'I think the list should be left to the Major. The Major must compile it with my help, needless to say.'

The list took so long to compile there was no time to have the invitation cards engraved and Pinkrose refused to have them printed. They had to be written out. Pinkrose suggested that those for persons of importance should be written by Alan. The cards were placed on Alan's desk but remained untouched until Pinkrose took them away and wrote them himself. Invitations for persons of less importance were written by Miss Gladys. The rest were typed by Miss Mabel after attempts proved that neither Yakimov nor Miss Mabel could write a legible hand.

'Frewen,' said Pinkrose, when at last the piles of envelopes were complete, 'I want them delivered on the bicycle. One can't trust these Athens post-boxes. Anyway, hand delivery is more fitting. It gives a better impression; and they will arrive in time.'

'How many are there?'

'About two hundred. Not more. Well, not *many* more.'

'They could go with a News Sheet.'

'Oh, no. No, Frewen, *no*. A letter handed in with a News Sheet could be overlooked. Besides, it is quite a different list. There will be English guests, but it is essentially a Greek occasion. Some of the names are very distinguished indeed. It calls for a special delivery.'

'Very well.'

Yakimov, half asleep during this conversation, did not grasp its import until the office boy handed him the envelopes and the list. He accepted the task without complaint but looking through the list, cried in dismay: 'He hasn't invited me.'

Yakimov had always treated Pinkrose with deference. When a detractor mentioned him derisively, Yakimov might smile but it was an uneasy smile and if there was laughter he would glance round fearful that Pinkrose might be in their midst. 'Distinguished man, though,' he would say. 'Must admit it. Scholar and gent, y'know. Aren't many of them.' He went through the list again, finding the names of Alan Frewen and both Twocurrys, but still no mention of his own. So there was no reward for deference and defence! He brooded over his omission until Alan looked at the clock and said: 'You'd better get under way.'

Yakimov pulled himself together. He began sorting the cards into batches, then suddenly wailed: 'There's one for Roger Tandy! Suppose he sees me delivering it! What will he think?'

'I'm going to the Corinthian,' Alan said. 'I'll leave it in.'

'And . . . Oh dear, it isn't fair! I've got to go all the way to Phaleron to leave cards on Lush and Dubedat.'

'Get on with it. There's a rumour that Dubedat's appearing as Lord Byron. You might get a look in at the dress rehearsal.'

But Yakimov was not to be amused. He put the batches for delivery into his satchel and went without a word.

The Sunday of the lecture was the day of the Pendeli walk. Harriet said to Alan: 'So you won't be coming?'

'Oh yes, I will. We're going to Pendeli to welcome the spring. I'd rather take Diocletian for a walk than listen to Pinkrose.'

Charles was also invited to the lecture. Harriet hoped he, too, would choose to come to Pendeli – if he were still in Athens to make the choice.

Yakimov, on his old upright bicycle, laboured three days to deliver the invitations. He could not avoid being seen as he went round the town with his brim-broken panama pulled down like a disguise about his eyes. Tandy watched him unmoved. When Yakimov returned to the office, tear-stained from grief and exhaustion, he threw the list on to Alan's desk. 'What a way to treat poor Yaki!' he said.

27

Sunday was fine. Stepping out into early morning, the Pringles heard the sirens. They stood on the doorstep, listening for the raid. The sky was clear. The sun warm. A bee came down the lane, blundering from side to side as though making the first excursion of its life. Its little burr filled the Sunday quiet a while, then faded into the distance. There was no other noise. The silence held for a couple of minutes, then the all-clear rose.

It was not until they reached the centre of Athens that they realized there was something wrong. It was a brilliant day, a feast day of the church, yet people, standing about in their Sunday clothes, had mourning faces or made gestures of anger or agitated inquiry. They were gathered outside the Kapnikarea, the men in dark suits, the women with black veils over their hair, as though distracted from worship by news of some cataclysmic act of nature.

The Pendeli party was meeting outside the Corinthian where Roger Tandy sat eating his breakfast in the morning sunlight. Yakimov had already joined him. Ben Phipps and Alan, standing by, moved to meet the new arrivals as though they could not wait to deliver their dire news.

Germany had declared war on Greece. The night before, a German broadcast in Greek had spoken of a raid, the like of which the world had never seen before: a gigantic, decisive raid that would wipe out the central authority of the victim country and permit the invading army to advance unhindered through confusion. They had not mentioned the name of the threatened city. Everyone believed it would be Athens, yet the blue, empty sky remained empty. The sirens had announced not a raid but the fact that Greece was at war with Germany.

The Pendeli party joined Roger Tandy and watched him as he spread quince jelly on a little, hard, grey piece of bread.

What should they do? Could they go to Pendeli at such a time? It might look as though they were fleeing Athens in alarm. Yet, if they remained, what was there for them? There was no point in sitting about all day waiting for destruction. They decided to delay their decision until Charles Warden turned up.

In a quavering, suffering voice, Yakimov asked: 'Do you think they'll hold that garden party at Phaleron?'

'Why not?' said Phipps. 'The world hasn't come to an end.'

No one agreed with him. They sat waiting round the table in the delicate spring sunlight, in the midst of a city that seemed to be holding its breath, poised for the end.

Yakimov, looking thoughtful and melancholy, said nothing more until, suddenly, he leant towards Harriet and said: 'Dear girl! Saw rather a remarkable sight. Quite remarkable, in fact. Haven't seen anything like it for years.'

'Oh, what?'

'Just round the corner. Come and see. I'd like to take another look.'

Though her curiosity was roused by his unusual fervour, Harriet did not move until Guy said: 'Go and see. You can tell us about it when you get back.'

Yakimov led her into Stadium Street and came to a stop at Kolokotroni where a man sat on his heels in the gutter with some objects arranged on the kerb before him.

'What are they? Beans?'

'Bananas,' Yakimov said eagerly.

The bananas, very green and marked with black, were about two inches in length – but they were bananas. Harriet wondered how the vendor came to have a banana palm and how far he had walked to bring his rare and valuable fruit into Athens for the feast-day. Seeing the two foreigners, he shifted on his hunkers and prepared to speak, but was afraid of speaking too soon.

'Haven't tasted one for years,' Yakimov said. 'Never seemed to see them in the Balkans. They're a luxury here. Was wondering if you'd care to possess yourself of them.'

When living with the Pringles in Bucharest, Yakimov often suggested that Harriet should buy something he had seen and envied in the shops. His penury there had been an established fact, but now she said: 'Why don't you buy them yourself?'

Nonplussed, Yakimov murmured: 'I suppose I *could*. Don't think I want to.' He bent closer and peered at the bananas in an agony of greed and caution, then came to a decision. 'Rather have an ouzo.' He turned away.

The vendor sighed and sank back on his heels and Harriet, pitying him, offered him a small coin. The man, surprised, jerked up his chin in refusal. He was not a beggar.

When they returned to the square, Charles had joined the group. He swung round as he heard Harriet's voice, and seeing him, she joyfully asked: 'Well, are you coming with us?'

'I'm afraid not. I'll have to stand by.'

'Let's get going, then,' Ben Phipps jumped up cheerfully, saying: 'We've wasted enough time.' When the others made no move, he began urging them to their feet.

Charles watched disconsolately. He had been up to the Military Attaché's office and Alan, tugging Diocletian out from under the table, asked: 'What do they think? Have we a chance?'

'Of course.' Charles assumed his air of professional optimism. 'The Greeks are determined to fight it out. This isn't easy country for armour. It defeated the Italians; it may defeat the Germans.'

'It may; but the Greeks have had a hard winter.'

'They survived it. That counts for a lot.'

'I agree.'

Guy and Ben strolled on. Harriet, waiting while Alan put the dog on to a lead, glanced at Charles and found his gaze fixed on her; he raised his brows as though to ask: 'Must you go?' What else could she do?

'Come on, then,' Alan said, moving off.

Charles made a gesture of appeal and when Harriet lingered, whispered: 'Tomorrow. Tea-time.'

She nodded and went. Following Alan into the null and pointless day ahead, she felt she was leaving her consciousness behind her.

At Kolonaki, she was jolted out of her dejection by the sound of spoliation ahead. Diocletian growled. Alan gripped him by the collar. They turned a corner and found the enraged Greeks breaking up the German Propaganda Bureau. The bureau was a small shop and already almost wrecked. A young man dangling a portrait of Hitler from an upper window had roused an uproar and as the portrait crashed down, the Greek rushed forward to dig their heels into the hated face. The road and pavements were a litter of broken glass and woodwork. Books had been ripped up and heaped for a bonfire. 'A bonfire of anti-culture,' said Ben Phipps. Almost the only spectators were some New Zealanders who watched with unsmiling detachment.

One of the books, its covers gone, fell at Harriet's feet. She picked it up and at once a young Greek, afire and abristle like a battling dog, held her as though he had the enemy in his hands. She appealed to the New Zealanders who said: 'Let her go. She's English.' 'English?' the Greek shouted in disgust, but he let her go and Harriet was left with a book she could not read and did not want.

'Let me see!' Alan looked at it and laughed: '"*Herrenmoral und Sklavenmoral.*" Poor old Nietzsche! I wonder if he knew which was which?' He put the book into his hip pocket: 'A souvenir,' he said.

'Of what?'

'Man's hatred of himself.'

The bus took them to the lower slopes of Pendeli and they climbed up among the umbrella pines, following a path fringed with wild cyclamen. Guy and Ben Phipps, stimulated by some lately uncovered piece of political chicanery, kept well ahead of the other two.

Alan began to limp on the rough ground but would not

slacken his pace. Here, in the bright mountain air, away from other claims on her attention, Harriet could see how greatly he had changed. He had been a heavy man. The hungry months of winter had caused his muscles to shrink. He had belted in the waist of his trousers but the slack hung ludi-crously over his hind-quarters and his coat slipped from his shoulders. His shoes had become too big for him but by balancing on his better foot and persuading the other after it, he kept going as though the walk were a challenge he felt bound to meet.

Diocletian, darting about under the pines, was a phantom dog. He was worried by the tortoises that crawled in hundreds over the dry, stony, sun-freckled earth. Tortoises were the only creatures that thrived these days and Harriet wondered if anyone had ever tried to eat them. Diocletian, sniffing, wagging his tail, was turning to Alan in inquiry, seemed to have the same idea. It was painful to watch his bones slide against his skin as he trotted to and fro, possessed by his inquisitive energy, and hungry, too. He kept coming back to the path with a tortoise in his mouth – but what could he do but drop it? When it felt safe, it crawled away, unharmed and unconcerned.

Diocletian, perplexed, looked at Alan, then looked down at the tortoise. What had they here? A moving stone?

Alan, his face crumpled with love, waved his stick at the dog. 'Beaten by a tortoise! Go on, you ridiculous dog!'

They paused to rest at a hut that sold retsina. Sitting on the outdoor bench, they saw the whole of Athens at their feet, with the Parthenon set against the distant rust-pink haze like a little cage of pearly bone. There had been no raid. Ben Phipps, expecting a spectacle of fire and devastation, had brought a pair of field-glasses which he offered to Guy, and the two short-sighted men passed the binoculars back and forth until the retsina came.

Diocletian lay belly up, the pennant of his tongue lolling red between his teeth. Alan asked the proprietor for a pan and filled it with retsina.

'Good heavens, will he drink that?' the others asked.

'You wait and see.'

They watched, delighted, as Diocletian emptied the pan.

Ben Phipps, the binoculars up, shouted excitedly: 'Look, look!' Half a dozen aircraft were coming in from the south, but there was no warning, no gunfire, no bombs, and the aircraft, turning over the city, began to play like dolphins in the sea of air.

They were unlike anything Alan or Phipps had seen before. Drowsy with wine, the four sat for a long time, backs to the warm wall of the hut, breathing the scent of pines, hearing a twittering of cicadas so constant it was like silence, and watching the planes dip and circle and loop in the hyacinth sky. At this distance, the display was silent; if the aircraft were a part of conflict, it seemed a conflict too distant to have meaning.

Harriet said: 'Perhaps they belong to the future. Without knowing it, we may have been here a hundred years and the war is over and forgotten.'

Alan grunted and sat up. Diocletian, who had his eye on his master, was on his feet at once. The walk now took them above the pines where the shale began and the going was difficult. Guy offered Alan an arm but he insisted on making his way alone, balancing and sliding on the grey, sharp, treacherous stone until they reached the top where the wind struck them violently and they knew it was time to go home.

Athens, in the light of evening had passed out of shock. It had been a resplendent day. There was no doubt now that the winter was over and the freedom of summer was at hand. Everyone was out in the rose-violet glow, crowding the pavements, their faces washed over with the sunset, carrying flowers and flags; Greek flags and English flags.

The four from Pendeli, as though they had been in some elysium outside the range of war, wandered about together, seeing the city anew. The Athenians had taken heart again. When Alan stopped a friend and asked about the strange aircraft, he was told they were British fighter planes flown from Egypt for the protection of Athens. There had been no raid but now, if the Luftwaffe came, it would not get far. The people seemed almost to be rejoicing that the worst had happened. They had a new and stronger enemy, but he would be vanquished like the other.

In University Street, where people swept to and fro across the road, an English sailor was hoisted up and with his cap on the back of his head, a carnation behind his ear, he sat on the shoulders of two men and waved happily to everyone around him. He was handed a bottle. As he tilted back his head to drink, his cap fell off and the audience applauded and shouted with joy.

Guy said: 'Where has Surprise gone?' but no one knew. Surprise had gone without a word to anyone. Now another man, bearded like Ajax or Achilles, was being held aloft and, swinging the bottle round his head, he was swept away just as Surprise had been swept away. Heroes came and went these days. When they were gone, it seemed they were gone for ever.

Ben Phipps went off to his office and the others decided that Babayannis' would be the place that night; all the fun would be there. But there was no fun. A terrible sobriety had come down with the rumour that there had been a raid, just such a raid as the German radio had described. It was Belgrade that had suffered. Now the word was: 'Belgrade today; Athens tomorrow.' At Babayannis' there was no dancing; the songs again were sad. When Ben Phipps arrived, he said: 'Those were Spitfires we saw today; a new kind of fighter aircraft. They only came to cheer us up. When it was dark, they flew back home again.'

The sirens sounded. People said from table to table: 'Here it comes!' but the raid was the usual raid on the Piraeus. It lasted a long time. When Guy and Harriet reached home, a rosy smoke was welling up out of the harbour. A little crowd of local people were gathered, dark and coagulate, on the hill behind the villa. Dazed after the long day of sun and air, too tired to feel curiosity about anything, the Pringles went unsuspecting to bed. In the small hours, an explosion flung them out of bed.

Guy felt his way up from the floor but Harriet lay under the repeated roaring reverberations, imagining herself flattened beneath the water of a broken dam. Guy tried to pull her up but she clung to the floor, the only security in a disintegrating world. The house quivered. A second explosion overlay the echoes of the first and, as the stupendous clamour rose to a climax, there came from some other dimensions of time the clear, fine tinkle of breaking glass.

Guy managed to lift Harriet and seat her on the edge of the bed. Her chief emotion was indignation. 'This really is too much,' she said and Guy laughed helplessly. She dropped back on the bed, hearing above the final sibilations of sound, the howls of dogs; and then, when quiet eventually came, a scandalized chattering.

There were still people watching on the hill. Guy said he would go out and see what had happened. 'Do you want to come?' he asked.

'Too tired,' she whispered and, putting her face into a pillow, went at once to sleep.

Anastea arrived at breakfast-time garrulous with the horrors she had seen. Guy had been told that a ship, set on fire during the raid, had exploded. Anastea said the explosion had wiped out the Piraeus. The harbour was in ruins. Everyone was dead. Yes, everyone; everyone. Not a soul moved in the town. If she and her husband had not gone last year to Tavros, they would be dead, too. But they had gone. They had had to go because their house was pulled down over their heads They had been martyred by the authorities, but now they knew that God was planning to preserve them. It was a great miracle and Anastea, crossing herself, declared that her faith had been renewed. Then she went all over the story again.

Guy could make nothing of it. What sort of ship was it that, exploding, convulsed the city like the explosion of a planet?

Harriet shook her head, feeling detached from the problem. She said: 'I think the blast blew me out of my body; I haven't come back yet.'

On the Piraeus road the homeless were wandering along,

carrying bundles or pushing anything that could be pushed. Those that had given up were seated round the bus stop and Guy tried to question them but, too dazed to answer, they merely shook their heads. The Pringles joined the refugees walking through the glass from street lights, windows and motor cars. It was an opalescent day that seemed, like the people about them, tremulous with shock.

At Monastiraki, they parted. Harriet went on to the office while Guy turned off to the School. Each learnt something about the events of the night.

The exploded ship had been carrying a cargo of TNT. It was to be unloaded on Sunday but, for no known reason, the unloading had been delayed. Left by the dockside, it had been set on fire during the raid and a British destroyer tried to tow it out to sea. The tow rope broke.

The two ships were still in the harbour when the explosions came. The destroyer and all aboard her had been annihilated.

'It was sabotage,' shouted Ben Phipps when he came into the News Room.

Alan shook his head unhappily but did not deny it.

Harriet thought of the sailor they had seen seated on high with a bottle in his hand and a carnation behind his ear. Likely enough, he had been one of the crew of the lost destroyer. 'A doomed man,' she thought, a man upon the brink of death. And Surprise, too. She remembered them as valiant but insubstantial, as though already retreated a degree or two from life. But they were all upon the brink of death. In her shocked state, she felt she had gone too far and might never return to reality.

'The rope broke three times,' said Phipps. 'Three times! Think of it. A rope intended for just such an emergency. It broke three times.'

Yakimov, exhausted by fear and lack of sleep, asked in a faint voice: 'But who would do it, dear boy?'

'Who do you think? Pro-Germans, of course. Fifth columnists. The town's full of them. Just now they're ringing round all the offices to say more explosions are coming.

Worse explosions. They say: "You wait until tonight." People are so unnerved they'll believe anything. Work's at a standstill. There's a real danger of panic.'

Yakimov was amazed at what he heard. 'But where do they come from, these pro-Germans?'

'They've been here all the time.'

'All the time,' murmured Yakimov and the others, abashed, felt that Greece was a stranger country than they knew. Living here among allies, smiled on, they had imagined themselves loved. But not all the friends were friends; nor the allies, allies. Some who had smiled just as warmly as the rest had been following a different banner and applauding, in secret, the exploits of the other side.

'How about the Phaleron do?' Ben asked. 'Was it cancelled?'

'On the contrary,' Alan told him. 'It was a great success. And why not? I imagine quite a few of the Major's guests are hoping to shake Hitler by the hand.'

'And how did the lecture go?'

'I only know that Miss Gladys looks as though she's passed through a mystical experience. She did not mention the explosion. It was nothing compared with Pinkrose's performance. I said: "What was the lecture like?" She replied in a muted voice: "Awe-inspiring." Anyway, it's flattened Pinkrose. She came in to tell me that he'd be staying for a few days at Phaleron to recoup.'

Harriet was to meet Charles at tea-time. During the morning she held to this fact as a sleep-walker might hold to a banister. She would not go out into the troubled streets. She sent the boy to buy her a sandwich and remained in the News Room until four o'clock. She arrived early at the Corinthian, not expecting to find Charles. He was already there.

She said: 'I'm early.'

'I thought you might come early.'

She sat down and asked: 'What is the news?'

'I don't need to tell you about the explosion.'

'I've heard the whole story. What else? Any rumours?'

'Nothing good.'

296

He was holding a book. She put out her hand to take it from him, but he shut it and placed it on the sofa out of her reach. He was frowning slightly as though trying to recall something, examining her face as though whatever it was, was there.

Gazing at each other, they seemed on the brink of revelation but there was nothing to be said. If they began to converse now, it would take a life-time, and they had no time in which to begin.

Suddenly, like someone forced to confess under duress, he said: 'I love you.'

When she did not reply, he said: 'I suppose you knew that?' He insisted against her silence: 'Didn't you? . . . Didn't you?'

Unable to speak, she nodded and his face cleared. Now, his expression implied, he had given her everything; there were no grounds for any sort of excuses or delays.

He took her hand and, gently pulling her, brought her to her feet and led her towards the stair.

There may have been people watching them, but she had no consciousness of other people in the foyer and later, when she tried to remember how they had reached the floor above, it seemed to her she had been levitated, as though in a dream. They went down a passage with numbered doors. There was no noise. She thought there was no one else in the hotel – at least, no one who mattered: yet when a door opened in the passage, she had an immediate prevision of encounter. She stopped, alarmed. Charles, with no such feelings, tried to pull her on.

The door, opening at the end of the passage, showed a lighted window. When, for a moment, a tall young man was outlined against it, Harriet recognized him at once. She jerked her hand from Charles's hold. The young man, closing the door behind him, moved towards them with an apologetic smile and, reaching them, stood aside.

Harriet said: 'Sasha.'

The young man, slight, with drooping shoulders, his smile unchanged, lowered his head and tried to sidle past her.

'It's Harriet,' she said.

He said: 'I know.'

'You seem to have forgotten me.'

'No.'

'Then what's the matter?'

Still smiling, he shook his head. Nothing; nothing was the matter. He only wanted to pass and get away. Puzzled and hurt, she said: 'They must have done something to you.'

'No. They didn't do anything. I'm all right.'

He certainly looked well enough. He was wearing a suit of fine English cloth – an expensive suit in this part of the world. His face, with its prominent nose and dark, close-set eyes, showed no sign of ill-treatment or spiritual damage, yet it had changed. It was no longer the face of a gentle domestic animal, unconscious of its enemies, but an aware face, cautious and evasive. The meeting, that should have been a delight for both of them, had merely embarrassed him.

At a loss, she looked at Charles and said: 'This is Sasha.'

'Is it?' Charles smiled, a slight, sardonic smile. At one time she might have thought he was amused by the incident; now she knew better. He could hide his anger, but not his pallor. Cheated and humiliated, or so he imagined, his desire had changed to rage. He was, she realized, transported by rage and she thought how quickly she had come to know him. If she had lived with him half a century, she could not know him better.

She did not try to speak to him but turned to Sasha and asked where he was going. Sheepish and miserable, the boy replied: 'Just downstairs. I'm here with my uncle. He'll be back soon.'

'Let's all go and have tea.' She gave Charles an appealing look that said: Let me solve this mystery, then we can talk.

He laughed and moved down the passage. 'Not me, I'm afraid. I have too much to do.' He entered his room and shut the door sharply and firmly. And that, she was made to understand, was that. She went downstairs and Sasha followed, meekly enough. She talked about the explosion. He said it had broken windows at the top of the hotel but he spoke as though it meant nothing. It was not his concern.

She led him to the sofa where Charles's book still lay. As soon as they sat down, she began to interrogate him with a vigour that resulted from her own painful confusion.

He said he had come from Belgrade with an uncle, his mother's brother. How did he get to Belgrade? The Rumanian authorities had given him a ticket and put him on to the train. He was more interested in the future than in the past and, as soon as he could break in on her questions, he told her that his uncle was trying to arrange their departure from Greece. They did not care how they got away: all they wanted was to leave Europe and as soon as possible. His uncle kept going to the Yugoslav legation. He had been there that afternoon. The official said the British would arrange for the evacuation of the Yugoslavs who were either here or on their way here. He supposed they would be sent to Egypt, but his uncle was in touch with Sasha's sisters and aunts who were now in South Africa. His uncle had said: 'It'll be a long time before the Germans get to Cape Town,' so that was where they would go. They intended to fly there at the first opportunity.

This finished, Harriet said: 'Guy went once or twice to meet the Belgrade train. I suppose you didn't see him?'

'Yes, I did. He didn't see me. He was talking to a man.'

'And you made no attempt to speak to him?'

Sasha did not reply.

'Why? I don't understand, really I don't. What is it all about? Why didn't you speak to Guy?'

He looked blank, having, apparently, no explanation to offer. When their tea had been set out, she pinned him down in a more decided manner. 'Now! That night our flat was raided – the night you disappeared – what happened? The men who came in were Guardists, weren't they?'

'Yes.'

'Did they do anything to you? Were they brutal? Did they try to bully you?'

'No. They knew who I was. They had my picture at head-quarters: they said they'd been looking for me. They made me sign a paper . . . It was for the Swiss Bank. They said if I signed, they'd let me go.'

'So you signed your money away?'

He gave a shrug, slight, expressive, his head hanging down in a shamefaced way. Something about his manner suggested that he was reassuring her. He had not been physically ill-treated, so she need not reproach herself.

'And did they let you go?'

'Not then. When I'd signed the paper they locked me up. I said: "When can I go?" and they said: "This has to be arranged." They kept me so long I thought they wouldn't let me go. I thought, "Now, they'll put me in prison, like my father", but one night they took me in a car to Jimbolia. My uncle was wait-ing on the other side. One of the men had a permit to cross and my uncle gave him a lot of money – three million *lei*, I think it was: so I was allowed to go. They gave me papers. Everything was in order and I was able to walk across the frontier. It was terribly exciting. And the Guardists were quite decent, really. As soon as the man came back with the money, they were all jolly and laughing and we all shook hands. Then I found my uncle at the Rakek Customs and he took me to Belgrade.'

'I didn't know you had an uncle in Belgrade.'

'I didn't know where he was, but they knew. They knew where all my relatives were.'

'So they held you to ransom! I never thought of that. And what of your father? Did you learn anything about him?'

Sasha, his voice more defined, said: 'They said he was dead.'

'I'm afraid that could be true.'

'I hope it's true.'

She paused in her interrogation while she poured the tea. After she had handed him a cup, she asked: 'When the Guardists took you to headquarters, what did they tell you?'

He gave her a sudden side glance but did not reply.

'Did they say anything about Guy and me?'

He shrugged, head hanging again.

'You didn't think it was our fault that they came to the flat and found you?'

'How could I tell?'

'You thought we'd informed on you?'

His head jerked up and he gave her a swift smile, placatory, suspicious and wretched.

'What did they tell you?'

'They said: "See what your English friends have done to you."'

'Meaning, we'd given you away?'

'Yes, they did mean that.'

'But you didn't believe them?'

'I didn't know. How could I know.'

She saw he had not only believed them: it had never entered his head not to believe them. She was shocked into silence. In any case, there was nothing to be said.

When he had lived with them, a sort of domestic pet, he had seemed too innocent and unsuspecting to be allowed out into the world alone. He had been brought up in the shelter of a wealthy and powerful family, and though he must have heard the family stories of persecution, he had been insulated against mistrust by his own artlessness. Yet one lie – less than a lie, a hint that he had been betrayed by friends – had precipitated the settled doubts of his race. She was certain that however she argued, she would never convince him that they had had no hand in his arrest. One lesson had been enough. He now accepted the perfidy of the world and acceptance was born in him, an inheritance not to be changed.

She said: 'If you thought we informed on you, weren't you surprised when they broke up our flat?'

'Did they break up your flat?'

'Surely you saw it happen?'

'No. Despina opened the door. They came straight in and put on all the lights. I was in bed and they said: "Get up and get dressed", and they took me away.'

'So you didn't see them turning out the drawers and pulling down the books?'

'No, I didn't. They did nothing like that while I was there.'

'They did it after you went. When we came back, the flat was in chaos. We didn't sleep there. We went to the Athenée Palace.'

He gave an 'Oh!' of polite concern, and she knew he would never be convinced. Although his manner was still gentle, his attitude still meek, he saw the truth as he saw it, and no one would change him now.

Looking at his face, the same face she had known in Bucharest and yet a different face, she could see him turning into a wily young financier like the Jewish financiers of Chernowitz who still proudly wore on their hats the red fox fur that had been imposed on them long ago, as a symbol of cunning. No doubt he would remake the fortune that he had signed away. That would be his answer to life. She did not blame herself, but she felt someone was to blame.

She had mourned Sasha – and with reason. She had lost him indeed and the person she had now found was not only a stranger, but a stranger whom she could not like.

She said: 'Guy will want to see you.'

When he did not reply, she asked: 'You do want to see him? Don't you?'

'We're leaving here.'

'Yes, but not at once. There are no regular services . . .'

'I mean, we're leaving the hotel.' There was an anxious impatience in his interruption: 'We're going to stay with some people . . . friends of my uncle.'

'I suppose Guy could visit you there?'

'I don't know where they live.'

'If I gave you our address, you could get into touch with Guy yourself?'

He answered: 'Yes,' dutifully, and took the address which she wrote down for him. She watched him put it into his breast pocket and thought: now it rests with him.

People were coming and going through the hotel door and Sasha was watching for his uncle's return. She felt his eagerness to be gone and she knew he did not want to see Guy.

Even if she could convince him that they were guiltless, he had left them and did not want to be drawn back to them. And she had no wish to draw him back. Why, after all, should they draw him back? He was not the person they had known.

A man entered the hotel.

'There's my uncle,' Sasha said, his voice rising in relief. 'I must go.'

'Of course.'

He leapt away, forgetting to say good-bye. She watched the men meet. The uncle, his shoulders hunched, his head shrunken into the astrakhan collar of his coat, was half a century older than the nephew, yet, seen together, the two looked alike. Their likeness was increased by the sense of understanding that united them. They belonged not to a country but to an international sodality, the members of which had more in common with each other than they had with the inhabitants of any country in which they chanced to be born.

'Jews are always strangers,' Harriet thought, yet when Sasha followed his uncle upstairs, she felt a sense of loss.

While taking tea, she had seen Charles leave the hotel. He had run down the stairs, not looking to right or left. He was still pale, still angry. She knew the situation might never be redeemed – and it had all been for nothing. Sasha, knowing she and Guy were in Athens, had made no attempt to contact them. He could have come and gone without their knowing he had even been here. Yet, out of all the seconds in a day, he had chosen that second to appear and estrange her from her friend.

She picked up the book which Charles had left on the sofa and saw it was in Greek. The fact he read this language not as an exercise but as a pleasure seemed to emphasize their division.

An acute sadness of parting and finality came down on her. Her friends were dispersing and she felt that life was reaching towards an end. She thought of Guy and knew that whatever his faults, he possessed the virtue of permanence.

She decided she would not tell him about her meeting with

Sasha. She could imagine him trying to override Sasha's recoil and forcing an understanding; or an appearance of understanding, a pretence that all was well. She could not bear that. Now it would rest with Sasha and if he made no effort to see them, Guy, knowing nothing, would not be hurt.

But, the days passing, she found it impossible to keep from Guy the fact the Sasha was alive.

She said suddenly: 'Who do you think I've seen?'

Guy replied at once: 'Sasha Drucker.'

'*You've* seen him? Where?'

'In the street.'

'You didn't tell me.'

'He told me he was just leaving. His uncle had managed to charter a private plane that would take them to Lydda. I meant to tell you. I forgot.'

'Did you find him changed?'

'Yes. Of course, he's been through the sort of experience that would change anyone. I was glad to know he was safe and well.'

'Yes. Yes, so was I.'

And by an unspoken consent neither mentioned Sasha again.

It took the Germans forty-eight hours to break through the Greek defences and occupy Salonika.

Vourakis, a journalist who sometimes came to see Alan, told them in the News Room that the Yugoslav southern army had withdrawn, leaving the Greek flank exposed.

'But the advance was halted. It was halted by Greek cavalry. Real cavalry, you understand! Men on horseback.'

'For how long?' Alan asked.

Vourakis shook his head sadly. 'Why ask for how long? It would be like blocking a howitzer with a naked hand. And there were two forts that held the pass till the area could be evacuated. A hundred men stayed in the forts. They knew no one could rescue them, no help could come to them: they knew they must die. And they died. The forts were destroyed and the men died. It was a Thermopylae. Another Thermopylae.'

Everyone was moved by the sacrifice of the men in the Rupel Pass forts, but the Germans had no time for Greek heroics. Riding over the defenders who had become the wonder of the war, they came with an armoured force which was described by refugees as 'more powerful than anything the world has ever seen'.

Nothing was known for sure. The news was blocked. As a precaution against panic, the authorities had decided that no one should know anything. The fall of Salonika had been expected, they said. It was inevitable from the first. They might even have planned it themselves. Whether expected or not, no one had been warned and the English who managed to get away left the town as the German tanks came in.

Harriet said to Alan: 'A friend of ours went up to Salonika. An army officer. What do you think would happen to him?'

'Oh, he'd have his wits about him: he'd get away.'

Which was exactly what Harriet did not think. She could imagine Clarence, with his self-punishing indifference, remaining till it was too late. But there may have been someone to harry him into a car and drive him to the Olympus line. An imitation officer, he would then be returned to Athens, so they perhaps would see him again one day – a man saved in spite of himself.

The refugees brought all sorts of stories. Now that everyone was dependent upon rumour, there was no telling truth from lies. Some people said the German tanks would reach Athens in a week and some said in a couple of days. They all said that Yugoslavia would not last the night.

Guy, meeting train after train, all packed with refugees, saw the Yugoslav officers arrive, brilliant in their gold braid. He was always picking up someone whom he had seen somewhere before, but he could get no news of his friend David Boyd.

Pinkrose returned to the office in high spirits. He came into the News Room smiling and his parted lips revealed what few had seen before – his small, neat, grey-brown teeth. No one smiled back. It was not much of a day for high spirits.

Beaming, excited, he said to Alan: 'I was surprised, most surprised . . . Yes, I was *most* surprised not to see you at the lecture.' When Alan neither explained nor excused his absence, Pinkrose went on: 'Ah, well! You were the loser, Frewen. You were the loser. You missed an excellent party. Yes, yes, an excellent party. The buffet was a splendid sight. The Major certainly lays things on. And it was a glittering party. I must say it was, indeed, glittering. The Major said to me: 'Congratulations, my dear Pinkrose, you've collected the cream." Dear me, yes! Indeed I had. I can't pretend I knew everyone, but my eye lit on some very handsome ladies, and their praises were such that I blushed; I positively blushed. Even if my little talk did not interest you, Frewen, you would have enjoyed the food. It was delicious. I haven't eaten such food for many a long day.'

Yakimov gave a sigh, his expression almost vindictive with hunger.

Pinkrose, tittering and wriggling gratified shoulders, said: 'I think I gave a fillip – yes, definitely a fillip – to Greek morale.'

'Badly needed,' Alan said.

'No doubt.'

'Last night the Germans occupied Salonika.'

'Surely not? Is this official?'

'Not yet, but . . .'

'Ah, a *canard* merely.'

'I think not. The Legation said someone rang at day-break and told them German tanks were coming down the street. After that, the line went dead.'

'Dear me!' Pinkrose lost his smile. 'Grave news, indeed!'

Yakimov, glooming over the Major's hospitality, noticed nothing, but Harriet and Alan observed that Pinkrose was taking the news extraordinarily well. They waited for him to absorb it, then clamour, as he had done in the past, for immediate repatriation. Instead, he said firmly: 'We can do nothing, so we must keep calm. Yes, yes, it behoves us to keep calm. Our Australian friends are holding the coast road and, by all accounts, they're the fellows for the job. The Germans won't get past *them* in a hurry.' He smiled again but, noting the bleak faces of Alan, Yakimov and Harriet, lost patience with them all: 'I've made my contribution,' he said: 'Now I must leave it to others. Several ladies said my lecture was an inspiration. They said it would spur the men to greater efforts. I must say, I don't see what else I can do.'

'Why not go to Missolonghi and die, dear boy!'

Pinkrose had moved off before the words were spoken, yet they reached him. He stopped, looked round and fixed Yakimov in amazement.

Immediately Yakimov's spirit fell. He said in terror: 'Only a little joke,' he pleaded.

Pinkrose went without a word.

Eyes moist, lips trembling, Yakimov said: 'D'you think the dear boy's piqued?'

'He didn't look too pleased, did he?' said Alan.

'It was only a little joke.'

'I know.'

'What d'you think he'll do?'

'Nothing. What can he do? Don't worry.'

But Yakimov did worry. Throughout the morning, pondering his folly, he repeated: 'Didn't mean any harm. Little joke. Look how he treated your poor old Yak! Telling me about food when I haven't had a meal for months!'

'Don't take it to heart. Worse things are happening at the front. I keep thinking of that proverb: "Better a ship at sea or an Irish wife than a house in Macedonia."'

Yakimov looked pained. 'Not a nice thing to say, dear boy. M'old mum was Irish.'

'You're right. It wasn't "Irish". I've forgotten what it was. Probably "Albanian".'

Nothing would amuse Yakimov. He refused to be comforted. Something in Pinkrose's face had aroused his apprehensions and, it proved, with reason. At mid-day the office boy entered and said that Lord Pinkrose wished to see Mr Frewen in his office. Surprised by this summons, Alan pulled himself out of his chair and went without a word. Yakimov gazed after him in fear. When he returned, his sombre face was more sombre, but he did not look towards Yakimov and he seemed to have nothing to say. After a while, when marking on a hand map the disposition of the British troops in Greece. he said casually: 'Yaki, I have to tell you: the job's at an end. Pinkrose wants you to leave at once.'

'But he can't do it,' Yakimov wailed, his tears brimming over.

'I'm afraid he's done it. He telephoned the Legation and told them that there was nothing for you to do. We have to stop the News Sheet, so there'll be nothing to deliver. And . . .' Alan lifted his head and looked at Harriet: 'I'm afraid he also said that you must go. The work is minimal now. That's a fact. There wasn't much I could say to the contrary.'

Yakimov sobbed aloud: 'Yaki will starve.'

'Come on,' Alan said. 'Pull yourself together. You know we won't let you starve.'

'And what about Tandy? I've told him I'm indispensable. What will he think?'

Alan took out a five-drachma piece. 'Go and buy a drink,' he said.

Harriet and Yakimov left together. Harriet had seen her work coming to an end and accepted dismissal with the indifference of one who has worse to worry about, but Yakimov bewailed his lot so loudly people turned and looked after them in the street.

'It's too bad, dear girl; it really is. Thrown out on m'ear just as I was making such a success of things. How could anyone do it, dear girl? How *could* they?'

This went on till Zonar's came in sight, then, glimpsing Tandy in his usual seat, Yakimov's complaints tailed away. His resilience, that had carried him through the shifts and disappointments of the last ten years, reasserted itself and he began to replan his life. 'Have a friend in India; dear old friend, 'n fact. A Maharajah. Very tender to your Yak. Always was. When the war started he wrote and invited me to his palace. Said: "If there's a spot of bother in your part of the world, you'll always be welcome at Mukibalore." Charming fellow. Fond of me. Suggested I go and look after his elephants.'

'Would you like that?'

'It's a career. Interesting animals, I'm told. Got to think of the future. Your Yak's becoming too old to rough it. But I don't know,' he sighed. 'They're large, you know, elephants. Lot of work, washing'm down.'

'You'd have boys to do that.'

'Think so? You may be right. I would, as it were, administrate. I'd do *that* well enough. Got to get there, of course. D'you think they'd fly me as a V.I.P.? No, probably not. Must have a word with Tandy. Now, there's one that knows his way around!' They had stopped on the corner and in his enthusiasm Yakimov become hospitable. 'Come and have a snifter, dear girl.'

'Not just now.' Leaving Yakimov in jaunty mood, she wandered on with nothing to do and nowhere to go, but restless with the anxious susceptiveness of someone who has lost something and still hopes to find it. She had heard nothing from Charles and this time she had no hope that, meeting, they would be drawn together again. He would not forgive her. She had nothing to gain by meeting him. Their relationship, without reason, had destroyed itself, yet she longed to come face to face with him. Although she looked for him among the mid-day crowds she was startled, when she saw him, into a state of nausea.

He was standing beside a military lorry in Stadium Street. The lorry was one of a convoy preparing to move off. Harriet, on the opposite pavement, watching him examining a map of some sort, expected him to feel her presence and cross over to her, but she soon saw there was no time for subtleties of that sort. One of the drivers spoke to him. There was a movement among the men. In a moment he would be gone. She ran across the road. Perturbed and breathless, she managed to call his name. He swung round.

'You're going?' she asked.

'Yes. We're off, any minute now.'

'Where will you go? Have you been told? Alan says the English forces are at Monastir.'

'They were, but things are happening up there. We won't know anything till we get to Yannina.' Speaking with even detachment, he smiled formally, a guarded, defensive smile, and moved a little away as though on the very point of taking his departure; but she knew he would not go. This was the last moment they would have here, perhaps the last they would ever have. He could not leave until something conclusive had been said.

'Is there any chance of your coming back to Athens?'

'Who knows?' He gave his brief ironical laugh. 'If things go well, we'll drive right through to Berlin.' He moved towards her, then edged away, suspicious of the attraction that even here gilded the air about them. He wanted to turn his back upon the deceptive magic.

'I may not see you again, then?' she said.

'Do you care? You have so many friends.'

'They aren't important.'

'They only seem to be?'

The argument was ridiculous. She could not carry it on, but said: 'It was difficult. Among all these alarms and threats, coming and goings, no one has a private existence. When it is all over . . .' She stopped, having no idea when it would be over and knowing time was against her. To interrupt a spell was to break it. Whether they met again or not, they had probably come to an end.

The convoy was ready to start. The driver of the first lorry climbed to his seat and slammed his door shut. The noise was a hint to Charles: he must get his farewells over and return to duty.

'Good-bye, and good luck,' Harriet said. She put her hand on his arm and for a second his composure failed. He stared into her face, anguished, and she was appalled to realize he was so vulnerable.

There was no time to waste now. He said: 'Good-bye' and, crossing the pavement, swung up beside the driver and shut himself in. He could now look down on her from a safe distance, apparently unmoved, smiling again.

Some Greeks had gathered on the pavement to watch the convoy set out. As the first lorry started up, a woman threw a flower into the cabin, the valediction to valour. Charles caught it as it came to him and held it up like a trophy. The lorry moved. The last thing Harriet saw was his hand holding the flower. The second lorry obscured the first. The other lorries followed, driving eastwards, making for the main road to the north.

She went after them, returning the way she had come, and watched them as they went into the distance. With the last of them out of sight, she no longer had any reason for going in that direction, but she had no reason for going in any other. She had been left alone with nothing to do and no reason for doing anything.

Her sense of vacancy extended itself to the streets about her. It was a grey, amorphous day in which people and buildings had lost identity, dissolving with every other circumstance, into insipidity. The town had the wan air of a place in which human life had become extinct. The streets seemed empty: left there without object or purpose, she felt as empty as the streets.

When she found herself back at Constitution Square, she stopped out of a sense of futility. Why go anywhere? She simply stood until she saw Guy coming towards her. Her impulse was to avoid him, but he had already seen her and as he came towards her, he asked: 'What's the matter?'

'Charles has gone.'

'I'm sorry.' He took her fingers and squeezed them, looking at her with a quizzical sympathy as though her unhappiness were something in which he had no part. He was sorry for her. Feeling she did not want this sort of commiseration, she detached her fingers from his hold.

He asked where she was going? She did not know but said: 'We could see if the Judas trees are coming out.'

Guy considered this, but of course it was not possible: 'I've a date with Ben,' he said. 'He's trying to get a call through to Belgrade. If he can't reach Belgrade, he'll try Zagreb. He may be able to find what's happened to the Legation people.'

'No sign of David yet?'

'None; no news of any sort. I've met most of the trains. The road beside the School runs straight through to the station, so I can get there quickly. The trains are packed to the doors. I've spoken to a lot of people, but there's such a flap, it's hard to discover what's happening inside Yugoslavia. I suppose the Legation will see it out to the end.'

'But David has no diplomatic protection?'

'No. Well, I must get on.' Before leaving, Guy wanted to see her comfortably disposed and said: 'Tandy and Yakimov are at Zonar's. Why don't you go and have tea with them?'

'No. I won't be in the office this evening. In fact, I won't be going back there. My job's packed up. I think I'll take the metro home.'

'Yes, do that. I can't get back for supper, but I won't be late.'

Guy sped happily on his way, seeing her problems as settled.

The climbing plant on the villa roof had come into leaf and, spreading over the pergola, was forming a thatch against the sun. It had budded and now the buds were starting to open. The little white waxen flowers had a scent like perfumed chocolate. Anastea had told Harriet that in summer the Kyrios and Kyria would take their breakfast and supper under the pergola at the marble table, and soon the Pringles would be able to do the same thing.

Since the district had taken on the verdancy of spring, its atmosphere had changed. Harriet sometimes walked beside the little trickle that was the Ilissus, or up among the pines that overhung the river-bed. The villa was at last beginning to seem a home, but a disturbed, precarious home. Though it was not within the target area, it was near enough to the harbour to be shaken by gun-fire, and when there were night raids, the Pringles would sit up reading, having no hope of sleep till the 'all clear' sounded.

Up among the pine trees she had met a cat which followed her to the edge of the wood but would not come into the open. It was a thin, little, black female, its dugs swelling out pink from the sparse black fur, so she knew it had kittens somewhere. She thought it must have a home in one of the shacks beyond the trees. It was obviously a home where there was not much to eat, but there was not much to eat anywhere these days. Harriet knew the cat's eager attentiveness was an appeal for food. There was nothing at the villa except the grey, dry tasteless bread they had for breakfast. She took some to the wood and the cat devoured it with savage exultation.

She asked Anastea to whom the cat might belong, but Anastea treated the question with contempt. Seeing Harriet put the bread into her pocket, she grumbled to herself. Harriet did not understand what she said but could guess: if there was bread to spare, there were human beings in need of it.

One day Harriet saw the kittens. She had crossed the wasteland as far as the first of the shacks and when she reached it, she found it derelict. The cat was a wild cat. The kittens were plain, starved creatures, tabby and white, and Harriet wondered how the mother had managed to bring them up; but they played happily in the sunlight, not knowing they were among the underprivileged of the world. One day when Harriet went to feed them, they had gone. The cat was there, perplexed and anxious, but the kittens had disappeared.

When she returned home on the afternoon of Charles's departure, Harriet had the cat in mind. It gave her some sort of attachment to life. She had fed it before out of a sense of duty to a creature in need; now, suddenly, she felt love for it, and began to fear that in her absence some harm could have come to it. She went first to the large grocery shop in University Street and queued for bread. It was a shop that in peace-time sold only the finest European foods. Now the shelves were empty. Behind the counter there were some boxes of dried figs and a sack of butter-beans. Harriet was allowed a few grammes of each, and because she was English the assistant opened a drawer and took out a strip of salted cod. He cut off a small piece and she accepted it as a sign of favour, although she felt she had no right to it.

Back at the villa, she found Anastea in the kitchen. A little skeleton of a woman in a black cotton dress and head-scarf, she was sitting on a stool, her hands lying in her lap, upwards, so Harriet could see the hard, pinkish skin of the palms scored over with lines, like the top of an old school desk. Her work was finished; she was free to go home, but she preferred to remain amid the splendours of the rich people's home.

Harriet kept the food in her bag and took it to the bathroom where she cut the fish with scissors and soaked it in the wash-hand basin. When she had got some of the salt from it, she took it to the wood and fed the cat.

28

Some time during the night an anti-aircraft gun was placed on the hill behind the villa.

Guy had almost reached the bus-stop next morning when the sirens sounded. At once the new gun opened up, so close that the noise was shattering. He hurried to the villa where he found Harriet, who had been in the bath, crouching naked under the stairs while Anastea, on her knees near by, was swinging backwards and forwards, hitting the floor with her brow and crossing herself, while she muttered prayers in an ecstasy of terror. The two women were completely unhinged by the uproar overhead.

As Guy stared at them in wonder and compassion, Harriet flung herself upon him crying: 'What is it? What is it?'

'Good heavens, it's only an anti-aircraft gun.' His own nerves were untouched by the racket but after two hours of it – the raid was the longest of the war – Harriet had become used to it while he, trapped inactive in the villa, felt he could bear no more.

'We can't live here with this banging away at all hours. The house has become unlivable-in,' he said. 'We'll have to find somewhere else.'

Harriet, who could scarcely face another move, felt the responsiblity of the cat and said: 'It's scarcely worth leaving now. We've stuck it so long, we might just as well stick it to the end. Besides, where can we go?' Many hotels had been requisitioned by the British military and those that remained had been packed by repeated waves of refugees. She said: 'We can't afford the Corinthian or the King George; even if we

315

got into a small hotel, heaven knows what we'd have to pay now.'

The raid over, they went up to the roof and watched smoke rising in black, slow, greasy clouds from somewhere along the coast. Anastea, who had followed them, said the smoke came from Eleusis where there was a munitions factory. The sight seemed to inspire her and she began to talk very quickly, making gestures of appeal at Guy. Apparently she was urging him to do something, but it was some time before he understood that men of the district were cutting an air-raid shelter in the rock by the Ilissus. The shelter was to contain seats which would be reserved for those who could pay for them. Anastea had learnt this from the men that morning. When she said she could not afford a seat, they told her to ask Guy to buy her one. How much were the seats? Guy asked and she replied, 'Thirty thousand drachma.' Guy and Harriet looked at one another and laughed. The sum seemed fantastic to them, but it had no reality for Anastea. Foreigners who could afford a villa with bathroom and kitchen could afford anything.

'Do you think the men were pulling her leg?' Harriet asked. 'It's probably thirty drachma.'

But Anastea insisted that the sum needed was thirty thousand. When Guy explained that it was far beyond anything he could afford, Anastea's face fell dolefully.

'How old do you think she is?' Guy asked when she had gone downstairs.

'She looks eighty but perhaps she's not much more than seventy.' Whatever she was, she had been aged out of calculable time by work, hardship and near-starvation. Harriet wondered would she herself, when half a century or more had passed, be so eager to preserve her life. Not long ago, she had spoken of life as a fortune that must be preserved, yet already its riches seemed lost – not squandered or misapplied, but somehow forfeit as a result of misunderstanding. She did not think that any explanation could bring them back and did not, in fact, know what explanation to give.

When Guy set out again, he asked her if she were coming into Athens, too. She could think of no reason for going: she had no job, nothing to do and would have to spend her time walking about in streets that could hold nothing for her. At least, if she remained, she had the cat.

Guy said, as he had said often before: 'I'll get back early.'

She laughed unbelievingly, having no faith in these promises, and found him watching her with the same quizzical but detached concern that he had accorded her when she told him Charles had gone.

'Of course I will,' he assured her. 'Tell Anastea to try and find something for supper. We'll eat at home, shall we?'

'All right.' She was pleased, but his insistence that he would indeed return disconcerted her like a solution of a problem that had come too late. The problem did not affect her any longer: it had not been solved but it had, she felt, been bypassed. Much more to the point these days was the question of what to give the cat. She sent Anastea to the shops and when the old woman was safely out of the way, she went to the kitchen and collected some scraps of food, but the cat was not in the wood. She walked to the hut where the kittens had lived. The cat was not there. She stood for a long time calling it, but in the end gave up the search, supposing it had gone off on a food-hunt of its own.

The evening was one of the few that they had spent in their living-room with its comfortless, functional furniture. The electric light was dim. Shut inside by the black-out curtains, Harriet mended clothes while Guy sat over his books, contemplating a lecture on the thesis: 'A work of art must contain in itself the reason why it is so, and not otherwise.'

'Who said that?' Harriet asked.

'Coleridge.'

'Does life contain in itself the reason why it is so, and not otherwise?'

'If it doesn't, nothing does.'

'But you think it does?'

'It must do.'

'You're becoming a mystic,' she said and after a long pause, added: 'There are so many dead bodies in the ruins of Belgrade, people have stopped trying to bury them. They just cover them with flowers.'

'Where did you hear that?'

'I heard it before I left the office. It was the last piece of news to come out of Yugoslavia.'

Guy shook his head, but did not try to comment. There was a period of quiet, then a sound of rough and tuneless singing came from the top of the lane where some men had gathered in one of the half-built houses to raise their voices against the darkness.

As the singing went on and on, Harriet began to feel it unbearable and suddenly cried out: 'Make them stop.' Before Guy could say anything, she ran to the kitchen and told Anastea to go out and deal with the singers. Anastea shouted a command up the lane and the song came abruptly to a stop.

Shocked, Guy asked: 'How could you do that?'

Harriet did not look at him: she was nearly weeping.

'They may be men on leave, or invalided from the front. Really, how *could* you?'

He was so seldom angry that she felt stunned by his reprimand. She shook her head. She did not know, she really did not know how she could do it, or even why she did do it. She wanted Guy to forget the incident but as he returned to his books, his face was creased with concern for the men slighted in that way. It did not relax, and suddenly she collapsed and began to cry helplessly, unable to swallow back her own guilt and remorse and the personal grief shut up inside her.

Guy watched her for a while, too upset to try to comfort her, then said as though it were only now he could bring himself to say what he had to say: 'We're leaving here. Alan Frewen thinks he can arrange for us to have a room at the Academy.'

'But I can't go. I can't leave the cat.'

'We have to go. It's not just the raids and the lack of sleep.

318

He says we must be somewhere where we can be reached by telephone.'

She sat up, jolted by the alarm that in Rumania had become a chronic condition. 'Are things worse? What is happening?'

'I don't know. Nobody knows. There's a complete ban on news.'

'But surely there are rumours?'

'Yes, but you can't rely on rumours. The thing is: we have to move from here, simply as a precaution. Nothing more than that. Alan will let me know tomorrow.'

They had only clothing and books, yet in her exhausted state it seemed almost beyond her power to cope with them. She begged him: 'Couldn't you help me move?'

'But, of course,' he said, surprised by her tone. 'Why not?'

'You're usually too busy.'

'Well, I'm not busy now. The revue's at an end and there's hardly anyone at the School.' He sounded exhausted, too, and spoke as though he had been defeated at last. She was about to ask him what he did with himself in Athens now but at that moment Anastea came in to take her leave and Harriet said instead: 'I think I'll go to bed.'

The raid went on all night. There was no respite for the men at the guns, and no rest for anyone withing hearing. By morning Harriet was quite ready to move anywhere, it did not matter where, so long as she could sleep.

Guy was seeing Alan at luncheon and said he would be back as soon as he knew what arrangement had been made for them. He got out his rucksack and began taking his books from the shelves. Anastea, who had been expecting something like this, noted what he was doing, went to the kitchen and returned with a tea-pot which Harriet had bought a couple of months before. The villa did not contain much kitchen equipment, and this was the only piece that belonged to the Pringles. Nursing it in the crook of her arm, smoothing the china with her ancient, wrinkled hand, Anastea pointed out that there had been no tea in the shops for weeks. Harriet nodded and told her to leave the pot on the table, but Anastea clung to it, stroking it and patting it as though it were something of unusual value and beauty. She began to beg for it, pointing to the pot and pointing to her own bosom, and Harriet, surprised, said: 'She doesn't drink tea. She doesn't even know how to make it. We ought to give it to someone who'll have a use for it.'

Guy said: 'There won't be any more tea, so let her have it.'

Harriet waved her away with the pot and she was so eager to take it home, she forgot the money owing to her and had to be called back.

It was late afternoon when Guy returned. By that time Harriet had completed the packing and had made repeated journeys across the river-bed to try to find the cat. It had been a rather dirty little cat with scurfy patches in its fur, but its response to her had touched her out of all reason. A sort of obsessional frenzy kept her searching for it. She told herself that animals were the only creatures that could be loved without any reservations at all, and this was the only creature she wanted to love. She knew it would not be welcome at the Academy but she would take it with her. She was determined to find it.

She kept going back to the wood, expecting to find the cat at her heels, but each time met with nothing but silence. She was in the wood when Guy came back. He found her walking frantically backwards and forwards over the same ground, calling to the cat and pleading with it to appear. He did not like the gloom under the trees and, unwilling to enter, shouted to her from the river-bank. He had brought a taxi which was waiting for them.

She came to the edge of the wood and said: 'I can't go without the cat,' then walked back into the shadows, feeling he was a hindrance to her purpose which was more important than anything he could offer. He climbed up the bank and stood watching her, baffled. He wondered if she were becoming unbalanced. As for the cat, he decided someone had probably killed it for food, but said: 'The gun-fire's frightened it. It's gone to a safer place.'

'Quite likely,' she agreed, still wandering round.

He said firmly: 'Come on, now. The taxi's waiting and it's getting dark. You've got to give up.'

'I can't,' she said. 'You see, this cat is all I have.'

'*Darling!*'

His cry of hurt surprise stopped her in her tracks. She saw no justification for his protest. He had chosen to put other people before her and this was the result. Each time he had overridden her feelings to indulge some sense of liability towards strangers, a thread had broken between them. She did not feel there was anything left that might hold them together.

He called her again, but she did not move. He stood there obstinately, a shadow on the edge of the wood, and she resented his interference. She had supposed this large, comfortable man would defend her against the world, and had found that he was on the other side. He made no concessions to her. The responsibilities of marriage, if he admitted they existed at all, were for him indistinguishable from all the other responsibilities to which he dedicated his time. Real or imaginary, he treated them much alike, but she suspected the imaginary responsibilities had the more dramatic appeal.

'Darling, come here!'

Reluctantly she moved over to him. During the last weeks she had almost forgotten his appearance: his image had been overlaid by another image. Now, seeing him afresh, she could see he was suffering as they all suffered. He had become thin and the skin of his face, taut over his skull, looked grey. He had at last come to a predicament he could not escape. He would have to share the stress of existence with her, but it did not matter now. She had learnt to face it alone. Still, she pitied him. He had nothing to do. His last activity had deserted him: but no activity, however feverishly pursued, could hide reality from him. They were caught here together.

His troubled face pained her. She put her hands on to his hands and he held her in his warm, familiar grasp.

She said: 'I'm sorry. I did not mean to desert you.'

'I did not think you did.'

'You see, Charles loved me.'

'Do you think I don't love you?'

'You love everyone.'

'That doesn't make me love you less.'

'I think it does.'

It was not his nature to argue. He always expected understanding, and perhaps expected too much. He said simply: 'We must go. They're expecting us for supper at the Academy. If there's a raid, we could get caught here again for a couple of hours.'

She went back with him to collect their possessions and lock up the villa. She had lost hope of finding the cat, but she did not feel that their talk had changed anything.

29

The Pringles were given the room which had belonged to Gracey. There was no sign that anyone else had lived in it since he left.

Harriet looked out on the twilit garden where, from the dead tangle of old leaves, the new acanthus was rising and uncurling, and the lucca throwing up a spike of buds. The garden smell, dry and resinous, that she had described as the smell of Greece, was overhung with the fresh, sweet scent of the lemon trees.

The room was bare but here, in touch with their protectors, the Pringles felt they were safe. Her despondency lifting, Harriet said: 'I like this, don't you?'

'I certainly do.' Guy began to unpack and arrange his books on top of the chest-of-drawers, taking trouble as though they might be here for a long time.

The house, secluded in its garden, seemed a place safe from the racket of war, but this impression was dispelled when they reached the dining-room. Alan had not come in to supper. Pinkrose, though he had kept on his room at the Academy, spent most of his time at Phaleron. The other inmates were talking in a subdued way but came to a stop at the entry of the outsiders. Harriet felt their retreat into discretion, but the atmosphere carried an imprint of consternation.

Guy, who wanted to associate himself with the life of the place, reminded Miss Dunne that he would like to join her at tennis.

She said: 'I'll give it thought,' making it evident that she had more important things on her mind.

When Guy began suggesting days and times, she twitched her shoulders impatiently but could not keep from blushing.

They were served with goat's cheese and a salad of some sort of green-stuff that roused a mild interest. Tennant went so far as to say: 'This is a new one on me!'

Guy suggested that it might be samphire and quoted: 'Halfe way down Hangs one that gathers Samphire; dreadful Trade.' Tennant smiled, but it was clear to Guy that this was no place for badinage.

Supper over, he was eager to get down to the centre of the town and find his companions. In the Academy garden the evening was milky with the rising moon. Harriet wanted to stay out of doors and Guy followed her reluctantly into the Plaka where she walked quickly, driven still by a sense of search and conscious of having nothing she might find. She led the way towards the Acropolis.

The sky was brilliantly clear. As they climbed upwards, the Parthenon became visible, one side still caught in the pink of sunset, the other silvered by the full moon. As the sunset faded, the marble became luminous like alabaster lit from within and the Plaka shone with a supernatural pallor.

The Athenians remembered the threatened raid, knowing that some such shimmering, verdant night as this would be the night for destruction. Moving darkly in dark doorways, watching out at the passing strangers, people seemed expectant and distrustful.

Guy, who did not know the area, was afraid they would get lost in the dark. Harriet, beginning to tire, was willing to go back.

Tandy had left Zonar's. It was warm enough to sit out after dark and they found him with the others on the upper terrace of the Corinthian. They were seated round a table by the balustrade, uneasy like everyone else in a city that, salt-white and ebony, was defined for slaughter. And they were uneasy for another reason.

Ben Phipps, who had his own sources, said the British troops were already in retreat.

'If the Florina Gap's evacuated, then Greece is wide open.'

'You think the Germans are on their way down here?' asked Tandy.

'It's likely. Almost certain, though there's nothing definite. I'm inclined to blame the Greek command. Papagos agreed to bring the Greek troops out of Albania and reinforce the frontier. He didn't do it. He said if they had to renounce their gains, the morale of the men would collapse. I don't believe that. I know the Greeks. Whatever happened, they would defend their own country. And now what's the result? The Greek army's probably done for. One half's cut off in Albania, and the other half's lost in Thrace.'

They sat for a long time in silence, contemplating the possibility of defeat.

'Still,' said Guy, trying to dispel the gloom, 'we're not beaten yet.'

Phipps gave a snort of derisive laughter, but after a pause said: 'Well, perhaps not. The British aren't easily beaten, after all. And we're bound to hold on to Greece. It gives us a foothold in Europe. We just can't afford to lose it. We're an incompetent lot, but if we have to do a thing, we usually do it.'

'If we hold,' Alan said, 'we could regain everything.'

Ben agreed: 'There have been miracles before.'

Miracles offered more hope than reason and Yakimov, his eyes wide and lustrous in the moonlight, nodded earnestly. 'We must have faith,' he said.

'Good God!' Tandy stirred with disgust. 'Surely things aren't as bad as that!'

'Of course not,' Alan Frewen said.

There was silence, then Guy asked: 'What news of Belgrade?'

'It's off the air,' Ben told him. 'Not a good sign. Rumour says the Germans reached the suburbs two days ago.'

'Is that fact?'

'It's rumour, and rumours these days have a nasty habit of becoming fact.'

'Then David Boyd must have left. He's sure to come tonight. The train's almost due.' Guy looked at his watch, preparing to start for the station, and Ben Phipps held his arm.

'You don't imagine there'll be another train, do you? The Germans will have cut the line south of Belgrade. If your friend's stuck, he'll make for the coast. He might get a boat down from Split or Dubrovnik.'

'Is it likely?'

'It's possible.'

Ben Phipps, bored with Guy's anxiety for his missing friend, threw his head back and stared at the moon. His face blank, his glasses white in the moonlight, he said mockingly: 'Don't worry. Even if Boyd isn't a diplomat, he'll be covered with angels' wings. If he's caught, the F.O.'ll bail him out. There's always something prepared for those chaps. Here they've got a yacht standing by. That'll take everyone of importance.'

'And the rest of us?' Tandy asked.

Ben Phipps looked him up and down with a critical and caustic smile. 'What have you got to worry about? You can walk on the water, can't you?'

Tandy though he laughed with the others, had a remote and calculating expression in his little eyes. He had declared his policy for survival. He did not stay anywhere too long, but here he was in a cul-de-sac. What would he do now?

As no one could answer this question, they turned their backs on a situation that was likely to defeat even Tandy, and began to talk of other things. Ben Phipps said Dubedat and Toby Lush spent their time standing in food queues. He had seen them in different shopping districts, buying up tinned foods that were too expensive for most people.

'They'll pay anything for anything,' he said. 'A bad sign if the Major's running short. How about Pinkers? How's he facing up to the emergency?'

'Splendidly,' said Alan. 'He's got only one worry: who should he get to translate his lecture into Greek? He wants it published in both languages. He keeps saying: "I must have a scholar. Only a scholar will do," and every day he trots in with a new suggestion. When this problem is settled (if it ever is!) we will have to decide who should print the work, then a distributor must be found . . .'

'Are you serious?'

'My dear Ben, you think the question of the moment is: Will the Germans get here? If you worked in the News Room you would be required to ponder a question of infinitely greater import: how soon can we get Pinkrose's lecture into the bookshops?'

'So he's no longer concerned about his safety?'

'Never speaks of it.'

'Think he's got an escape route up his sleeve?'

'If he has, I'd like to know what it is. A lot of people have to be got out of Greece: British subjects, committed Greeks, refugee Jews; four or five hundred, and quite a few children.'

'I thought the children went on the evacuation boat?'

'Not all. Several women wouldn't leave their husbands. And life goes on. English babies have been born since the boat went.'

'What has the Legation got in mind?'

'We must wait and see.'

There were two narrow beds in the Pringles' room. Guy and Harriet had not slept apart since their marriage but now they would have the width of the room between them. Each felt cold alone, the covers were thin; and sandflies came in through the broken mesh of the window screens.

In the middle of the night Harriet woke and heard Guy moaning. He had been reading, propped up with a pillow, and had fallen asleep with the light on. She could see him struggling in sleep as against a tormentor. She crossed the room to where his bed stood under one of the windows and saw the sandflies shifting, as he struck out at them, in a flight leisurely but elusive. A moment later they attacked him again. He did not wake up but was conscious of her, and whimpered: 'Make them go away.'

She had bought a new box of pastilles and, after placing

them on the table, the bed-head and the window-sill, lit them so the smoke encircled him like a *cheval-de-frise*. The pillow had dropped to the floor. She put it under his head, then stood at the end of the bed and watched while the flies dispersed. He sank back into sleep, murmuring: 'David has not come.'

She said: 'He may come tomorrow.'

From some outpost of sleep, so distant it was beyond the restrictions of time, he answered with extreme sadness: 'He won't come now. He's lost.'

'Aren't we all lost?' she asked, but he had gone too far to hear her.

Back in bed, she thought of the early days of their marriage when she had believed she knew him completely. She still believed she knew him completely, but the person she knew now was not the person she had married. She saw that in the beginning she had engaged herself to someone she did not know. There were times when he seemed to her so changed, she could not suppose he had any hold on her. Imagining all the threads broken between them, she thought she had only to walk away. Now she was not sure. At the idea of flight, she felt the tug of loyalties, emotions and dependencies. For each thread broken, another had been thrown out to claim her. If she tried to escape, she might find herself held by a complex, an imprisoning web, she did not even know was there.

Rumours, that the authorities did not deny, grew more coherent. By Sunday they had taken on the substance of truth. It was Palm Sunday and the beginning of Easter week, but no one gave much thought to Easter this year. It was a dull, chilly day with a gritty wind that seemed to carry anxiety like an infection. Everyone was out of doors, moving about the main streets, restless, aimless and asking what was happening.

Alan Frewen, walking from the Academy with the Pringles, was several times stopped by English people who lived at Psychico or Kifissia and usually spent their Sundays at home. This Sunday, like everyone else, they had caught suddenly and for no reason they could name, the *frisson* of alarm. They had felt themselves drawn to the city's centre, imagining that someone there might tell them something. Alan, as Information Officer, would know what was going on. Again and again he was asked to deny the rumour that German mechanized forces were driving almost unopposed through the centre of Greece. It could not be true. Everyone knew the fall of Salonika had been inevitable. The northern port was too near the frontier. It could not be held. But this talk of the British being in retreat! British resistance was not so easily broken. The stories must be the work of fifth columnists?

Alan, listening with sombre sympathy, agreed that the fifth columnists were doing their worst. It was true the British had withdrawn from the Florina Gap, but that, likely enough, was part of a plan. He did not think anyone need feel unduly anxious. The British were not beaten yet.

People accepted his comfort, realizing that he was doing his best but knew no more than they did themselves. They thanked him, looked cheerful, and went off in search of other informants.

One man, Plugget, with a mottled face, wiry moustache and the brisk yap of a terrier dog, did not play his part so well. The Pringles had never seen him before. He worked for an English firm but had married a Greek and associated chiefly with Greeks, but now, like everyone else, had come out in search of news. He rejected Alan's consolation out of hand.

'Don't believe it,' he said. 'Things look bad, and I think they're worse than bad. I don't like it at all. What's going to happen to us? And what did our chaps come here for? Retreating without a shot fired! What's the idea? They just caused trouble, and now they'll be getting out and leaving us to face the music. Not a shot fired! It's the talk of the town,' he insisted, while his wife stood on one side looking ashamed for him.

'If that's the talk of the town, it's being put round by fifth columnists,' said Alan.

'You're deceiving yourself, Frewen. There aren't all that

329

number of fifth columnists. It's a terrible business. We went to see a lad in hospital, relation of the wife. He'd just been sent down from a field depot. He said it's chaos up there.'

At last, in need of comfort themselves, Alan and the Pringles were able to move on to Zonar's. Tandy, who had gone inside out of the wind, was seated with Yakimov and Ben Phipps at a short distance from a party of English women which included Mrs Brett and Miss Jay. At the sight of Alan, Mrs Brett jumped to her feet and hurried to him, calling out: 'What's the news? They say our lads are on the run. You can tell me the truth. I'm English. I shall keep my head.'

Standing over her with his mountainous air of pity, Alan let her repeat over and over again: 'I'm not alarmed. No, I'm not alarmed. If we're in a fix, don't hesitate to let me know.'

When his chance came, Alan said slowly and firmly: 'It's a perfectly orderly withdrawal: a piece of strategy. They've decided to reinforce the Olympus Line.'

Mrs Brett gave a cry of rapture: 'I knew it was something like that. I've been telling everyone it was something like that. And we can rely on the Olympus Line, can't we? That's where the Australians are.' She returned to her friends shouting: 'I told you so . . . nothing to worry about . . .' but her manner was too confident, too much what might be expected from an Englishwoman who sees calamity ahead.

Ben Phipps watched her with a sour approval and when Alan sat down, asked: 'Have you any reason for making that statement?'

'We must hope while we can.'

'Nothing definite, then?'

'Nothing. And you?'

'Nothing at all. And probably won't be. They could keep us in the dark till the Jerries walk in. That's what happened in Salonika. There was a camp full of Poles: no one told them, no one did anything about them. Some of the English did a last-minute bolt, but they got no warning. It could happen here.'

'I doubt it,' Alan said, but there was over all of them the fear of being overtaken unawares. Their instinct was to keep together. If one knew something, then the rest would know. If they were overtaken, they would not be alone. Even Guy was distracted from the urge to find distraction and stayed with the others, knowing there was nothing to be done but wait.

Though nobody except Yakimov preserved any extravagant ideas about Tandy, he acted as a nucleus for the group. He was, if nothing else, experienced in flight. Even Phipps agreed that Tandy knew his way around. If anyone escaped, he would escape; and the rest of them might escape with him.

Less than a week after Charles left, Harriet saw the first English soldiers returning to Athens. There were two lorry-loads. The lorries stopped outside a requisitioned hotel but the men made no attempt to move.

She went over to them thinking if there was news, they would have it. The tail-board of the first lorry was down and she could see the men lying, some on the floor, some propped against baggage, one with his head drooping forward, his hands dangling between his knees. They seemed dazed. When she asked: 'Where do you come from? Is there any news?' no one answered her.

Two of the men wore muddy bandages on their heads. Several moments after she had spoken, one of them lifted his eyes and looked through her, and she took a step back, feeling rebuffed. They were exhausted, but it was not only that. A smell of defeat came from them like a smell of gangrene. Their hopelessness brought her to the point of tears.

People on the pavement stopped and stared in dismay. It had been no time at all since the British troops drove out of Athens singing and laughing and catching flowers thrown by the girls. Now here they were, back, so chilled by despair that a sense of death was about them like frozen mist about an iceberg.

It had been raining and the sky, bagged with wet, hung in dark boas of cloud over the hills. The wind was tearing up the blossom and the pink and white petals circled on the ground among the dust and paper scraps.

An officer came out of the hotel and an elderly business-man on the pavement said in English: 'We've been told nothing. We want to know what's happening.'

'You're not the only one,' the officer said, and, going to the lorry, he shouted at the men: 'Get a move on there.'

Somehow the men roused themselves and slid down from the lorry like old men. As they crossed the pavement, someone put a hand on the arm of one of the wounded. He shook it off, not impatiently, but as though the weight of a hand were more than he could bear.

When they had all gone inside, Harriet remained standing, uncertain which way she had been going. She had left Guy in the bookshop in Constitution Square to go round the chemist shops in search of aspirin, but the aspirin was forgotten and she hurried back to the square. She had had proof of disaster. Guy, seeing her, was startled. At first she could not speak, then she tried to describe what she had seen but, strangled by her own description, sobbed instead. He opened his arms and caught her into them. His physical warmth, the memory of his courage when the villa was shaken by gun-fire, her own need and the knowledge he needed her: all those things overwhelmed her and she held to him, saying: 'I love you.'

'I know,' he answered as lightly as he had answered when she first said the same thing on the train to Bucharest. Suddenly angry, she broke away from him, saying: 'No, you don't. You don't know; you don't know anything.'

He had hold of her hand and now shook it in reproof. 'I know more than you think,' he said.

'Well, perhaps.' She wiped her eyes like a child that is promised another doll for the doll that is broken, and scarcely knew which meant more, her loss, or her hope of recompense.

'Come on, you need a drink,' Guy said and, pulling her hand through his arm, led her from the shop.

During the day more lorries arrived, small convoys bringing in soldiers stupid with fatigue. At first people stood amazed in the streets, then they knew the rumours were right. These stricken men meant only one thing. The battle was lost. The

English were in retreat. Yet people remained standing about, expecting some sort of explanation. There would surely be an announcement. Their fears would be denied. The day passed, and no announcement was made. The Athenians could be kept in ignorance no longer. Disaster was upon them. They had seen it for themselves.

In the early evening, impelled to get away from a town benumbed by reality, Alan Frewen said he must give his dog a run. He suggested that they all take the bus down to the sea front and walk to Tourkolimano.

Unlike the rest of them, Ben Phipps was in an excited state for he had narrowly escaped death. While driving in from Psychico, he had been caught in a raid and had joined some men sheltering in a doorway. Two Heinkels had swooped down like bats, one behind the other, and opened fire, pitting the road with bullets. No one had been hurt and when the aircraft were gone, Ben had run out and picked up in his handkerchief a bullet too hot to hold. He could talk of nothing but his adventure and on the esplanade he brought on the bruised bullet and threw it into the air, saying: 'I've been personally machine-gunned.'

His delight amused Alan, who watched him much as he watched the gambols of Diocletian. 'You have not gone to the war,' Alan said. 'But the war has come to you. Could any journalist ask for more?'

The clouds had broken with evening, revealing the vast red and purple panorama of sunset. When the colours had faded, a mist rose over the sea, jade-grey yet luminous, reminding them of the long twilights of summer. Alan began to talk of the islands and the seaside days that lay ahead.

Melancholy and nostalgic, they reached the little harbour of Tourkolimano as darkness fell. 'We have been deprived of heaven,' Harriet said.

'It will come again,' said Alan. 'Even the war can't last for ever.'

They made their way through streets devastated by the explosion, climbing among broken bricks and wood, intending to catch a bus on the Piraeus road. When they saw a thread of light between black-out curtains, they stopped, glad to get under cover. They crowded into the narrow café where there were a few rough tables lit by candle-ends. The proprietor, who sat alone at the back of the room, welcomed them with a mournful courtesy so it seemed, in the silence and solitude, that they had come to a region of the dead.

During the last few days the men had taken to telling limericks and stories and talking about life in a large general way while they all drank themselves into a state of genial intoxication. In such close companionship, the sense of danger receded and was sometimes forgotten. Sitting knee to knee in the little café served with glasses of Greek brandy, they tried to remember some comic verse or anecdote that had not yet been told. Harriet said to Yakimov: 'Tell us that story you told the first time we met you. The story about a croquet match.'

Yakimov smiled to himself, gratified by the request, but not quick to comply. He was penniless again and dependent for his drinks on anyone who would buy them, but had no wish to return to his old arduous profession of raconteur. His pale, heavy eyelids drooped and he gazed into his glass. Finding it empty, he slid it on to the table and said: 'How about a drop more brandy?'

Guy called to the proprietor and the brandy bottle was placed beside Yakimov, who sighed his content and said: 'Dear me, yes; the croquet match!'

The story that had been funny in Bucharest was here, at the dark end of the lost world, almost too funny to bear. Every time Yakimov, in his small, epicene voice, said the word 'balls', his listeners became more helplessly convulsed until at last they were lying about in their chairs, sobbing with laughter. The proprietor watched them in astonishment, never having seen the English behave in this way before.

When no one could think of a story that had not been told, they sat abstracted, conscious of the quiet of the ruined seafront and the streets about them.

After long silence, Alan said: 'When I camped out on the

battlefield of Marathon, I was awakened by the sound of swords striking against shields.' He seemed to be confessing to an experience which in normal times he would not care to mention, and the others, impressed against reason, knew he spoke the truth. Ben Phipps said that he came from Kineton and had often been told that local farmers would not cross Edgehill at night.

Roger Tandy grunted several times and at last brought out: 'Everyone's heard something like that. In Ireland there's a field where a battle was fought in the fourth century of the world – and the peasants say they can still hear them banging away.'

The others laughed but even Guy, the unpersuadable materialist, was caught into the credulous atmosphere and discussed with the others the theory that anguish, anger, terror and similar violent emotions impressed themselves upon the ether so that for centuries after they could be perceived by others.

Harriet imagined their own emotions impinging upon the atmosphere of earth and wondered how long her own shade would walk through the Zappion Gardens, not alone.

Ben took his bullet out of his pocket and rolled it across the table. Did they suppose, he asked, that his emotions had become fixed in the doorway where he had been a target for the German air-gunners?

Yakimov tittered and said: 'Must have been harrowing, dear boy. Did you change colour?'

'Change colour? I bloody near changed sex.'

Alan gave a howl of glee and, leaning back against the wall, wiped his large hands over his face and gasped: 'Oh dear!' In this exigency, fear was the final absurdity. They could do nothing but laugh. They were still laughing when the proprietor told them apologetically that he had to close the café. In happier days he would be glad to have them drink all night; but now – he made a gesture – the explosion had destroyed his living quarters and he had to walk to his brother's room at Amfiali.

No one had come into the café except the English party and Alan asked the proprietor why he troubled to stay open.

He replied that during the day the café was used by long-shoremen and dock workers, and sometimes a few came in after dark. Apart from them, the district was deserted.

'Where has everyone gone?'

The man made an expressive gesture. Many were dead, that went without saying; so many that no one yet knew the number. Others were camping in the woods round Athens.

'God save us,' muttered Tandy. 'We've had war and famine; the next thing'll be plague. We've all got dysentery, and if we don't get typhoid, it'll be a miracle.'

Sobered, they went out in the cold night air and made their way to the bus stop by the light of the waning moon.

There were English soldiers again in the cafés but they had lost their old sociability. They knew they would not be in Greece much longer and, conscious of the havoc they had brought, were inclined to avoid those who had most to lose by it.

One of Guy's students shouted at him in the street: 'Why did they come here? We didn't want them,' but there were few complaints. The men were also victims of defeat. Seeing them arriving back in torn and dirty battle-dress, jaded by the long retreat under fire, the girls again threw them flowers; the flowers of consolation.

On Wednesday evening Guy went to the School and found it deserted. Harriet had walked there with him and on the way back they looked into several bars, hoping to see someone who could give them news. In one they saw a British corporal sprawled alone against the counter and singing to a dismal hymn tune:

> 'When this flippin' war is over,
>   Oh, how happy I shall be!
> Once I get m'civvy clothes on
>   No more soldiering for me.
> No more asking for a favour;
>   No more pleading for a pass . . .'

He broke off at the sight of the Pringles and when Guy invited him to a drink he straightened himself up, and assumed the manners of normal life.

'English are you?' he said and, too polite to express his bewilderment at their presence in this beleaguered place, eyed them cautiously from head to foot.

They began at once to ask him about events. He shook his head and said: 'Funny do. They say there were millions of them.'

'Really? Millions of what?'

'Jerries on flippin' motor-bikes. The Aussies picked them off so fast, there was this pile-up and they had to dynamite a road through them. And all the time Stukas and things buzzing round like flippin' hornets. Never saw anything like it. Didn't stand a chance. Right from the start; not a chance.'

'Where are the Germans now?' Harriet asked.

'Up the road somewhere.'

'Not far, you think?'

'Not unless someone's stopped them.'

Guy said: 'They say the New Zealanders are still holding at the Aliakmon.'

'When did y'hear that, then?'

'Yesterday.'

'Ho, yesterday!' the Corporal grunted: yesterday was not today. When Guy ordered him another drink, he looked the Pringles over again and felt forced to speak: 'What are you two doing here, then? You're not hanging on, are you?'

'We're hoping something will happen. The situation could be reversed?'

'Don't know about that. Can't say.'

'And you? What are going to do?'

'We're told to make for the bridge.'

'Which bridge?'

'Souf,' said the Corporal. 'Our lot's going souf,' then as it occurred to him that he was saying too much, he downed his drink at a gulp, picked up his cap and said: 'Be seeing you,' and went.

From this information, such as it was, the Pringles surmised that the British forces intended to hold the Morea. They set off to take their news to Tandy's table; but Ben Phipps was there before them and his agitated indignation put the Corporal right out of mind.

'What do you think?' Phipps demanded of them. 'You'd never believe it. I've just come from the Legation. There's nothing laid on. Not a thing. Not a ghost of a plan. Not a smell of a boat. We're done for. Do you realize it? We're done for.'

'Who told you this?' Tandy asked.

'They told me themselves. I said: "What are the arrangements for evacuating the English refugees?" and they just said, they just *calmly* said: "There aren't any arrangements." The excuse is they didn't know what was going to happen. "Well, you know now," I said. "And people are getting anxious. No one's making a fuss, but they want to know what's being done for them. They can't just sit here waiting for the Germans to come. What's laid on?" I asked. Nothing they said: just nothing. There aren't any ships.'

Yakimov said, shocked: 'Dear boy, there must be ships.'

'No,' Ben Phipps shook his head in violent denial. 'There are no ships.'

'The Yugoslavs say they're going,' Tandy said.

'Oh, yes. The Yugoslavs are being looked after. The Poles, too. Someone's fixed them up – don't ask me who – but there's nothing for the poor bloody British. I said: "Can't you pack us in with the Jugs and Poles?" And they said: "Their boats are already overcrowded".'

Tandy stared at the street with a reflective blankness. Only Ben Phipps had anything to say: 'The usual good old British cock-up, eh? Isn't it? I said: "Don't you realize the Germans could be here in twenty-four hours?" and what d'you think they said? They said: "It all happened so suddenly." *Suddenly!* Yes, it did happen suddenly, but that doesn't mean it wasn't obvious from the start. We ought to have kept out of this shindig. It's not only that we've done no good. If we hadn't stuck in our two-pennyworth, they might have got away with it. We send a handful of men up with a few worn-out tanks, then say: "We didn't know." I ask you! What did they think?'

'They thought we'd get through to Berlin,' Harriet said.

Phipps gave a snort of bitter laughter: 'No foresight. No preparations. No plans. And now no ships.' Biting his thumb, he muttered through his teeth with the morose rage of one who realizes that his blackest criticism of authority was never black enough.

There was a long silence at the end of which Guy mildly asked: 'Meanwhile, what news, if any?'

'We've admitted a strategic withdrawal along the Aliakmon Line.'

'What do you think that means?'

'Only that the Jerries are coming hell for leather down the coast road.'

Tandy grunted and pulled out his splendid wallet. He put a note on the table to pay his share of the drinks and said: 'Not much point in saving drachma now. If things fold up here, it won't be much use anywhere else. How about coming to my hotel for a valedictory dinner?'

'How about it, dear boy!' said Yakimov, joyfully taking up the invitation. He and Tandy began at once to rise, but Alan Frewen had not arrived and the others were unwilling to go without him.

Eager to be off, Yakimov persuaded them: 'He'll be at the office. We'll pick him up on the way.' They went to the side entrance of the Grande Bretagne and, finding it shut, walked on to the Corinthian, where the refugees were ordering their departure. Although the passengers for the Polish and Yugoslav ships – among them the gold-braided Yugoslav officers – were not due to embark until next morning, they were having their heavy luggage brought down and heaped ready at the hotel entrance. The English party, making a way through the hubbub, saw Alan Frewen sitting in a corner, alone except for the dog at his feet.

Ben Phipps, carrying his anger over on to Alan, said: 'Look at him, the bastard! He's avoiding us.' He caught hold of Guy to prevent him from approaching the lonely man, but Guy was already away, dodging between chairs and tables in his eagerness to rescue Alan from solitude.

Alan looked discomforted when he saw the friends to whom he could offer so little hope, but assumed a confident attitude when Ben Phipps at once accused him: 'Don't you realize we're stranded? Don't you realize that nothing's been done?'

Alan said soothingly: 'There'll be something tomorrow.'

'Nothing today, but something tomorrow! What, for instance? Where are they going to find it?'

Alan checked him, speaking with the quiet of reason: 'You know the problem as well as I do. The explosions wrecked everything in the harbour. Thousands of tons of shipping went to the bottom, so there's a shortage of ships. You can't blame the Legation for that. The water-front was wiped out. Dobson tells me it's absolute desolation down there.'

'Is Dobson in charge of the evacuation, supposing there is evacuation?'

'No, but he's been down to the Piraeus to look around. He's doing his best for you all.'

'A last-minute effort, I must say. This situation should have been foreseen weeks ago.'

'If it had been, we'd have chartered ships; and they'd've gone to the bottom with the rest.'

'So nothing has been done, and nothing will be done? Is that it?'

'Plenty's being done.' Glancing at Harriet's pale face, then back to Phipps, Alan said: 'For God's sake, have some sense!'

Tandy had not stopped to listen to this discussion. As though unconcerned in it, he strolled on to the dining-room and Yakimov, who could not bear to let him out of sight, said to Alan: 'Do come, dear boy. We're all invited. Friend Tandy is standing treat.'

Alan nodded and Yakimov hurried ahead. Though not the bravest of men, he still had more appetite than the rest of them, and apparently felt that while he remained in the lee of Tandy's large, sumptuous figure, he had nothing to fear.

They were served with some sort of stewed offal which tasted of nothing at all. Alan gazed at his plate, then put it down in front of the dog.

'Dear boy!' Yakimov murmured in protest, but the plate had already been licked clean.

The second course comprised a few squares of cheese and dry bread and Alan left his share for Yakimov.

Jovially chewing cheese, Yakimov added: 'How is the noble lord these days?'

'No idea,' Alan said. 'He hasn't been in for a week. The office is empty except for the Twocurrys. Mabel of course, doesn't know what's going on, and Gladys isn't telling her.'

'So you're in charge? Then how about getting your Yak back on the payroll?'

Alan's face collapsed in its odd, pained smile: 'I'll see what can be done,' he promised.

The air-raid sirens sounded and the dining-room became silent as the diners sat tense, awaiting the raid that would reduce Athens to dust. The minutes passed and all that could be heard was the distant thud of the Piraeus guns.

Alan sighed and said: 'Just a reconnaissance buzzing around.'

'What do they hope to find?' Tandy asked.

'They think we might send reinforcements. They don't know how little we've got.'

'Perhaps we will send something.'

'We've nothing to send.'

They went up to the terrace and waited for the All Clear. A waning moon edged above the house tops, casting an uneasy, shaded light that accentuated the clotted darkness of the gardens. The raid had brought the city to a standstill. No one moved in the square and there was nothing to be seen but a group of civic police standing, shadowy, among the shadows.

Tandy was exercising himself. Marching with a military strut, he went from one end of the terrace to the other, and Yakimov trotted at his side. Tandy lit one of his Turkish cigarettes. Yakimov, though he hated Turkish cigarettes, felt bound to imitate his companion. So they walked backwards and forwards, filling the air with a rich Turkish aroma.

Harriet, seated by the rail, watching them as they reached the end of the terrace, turned in unison and came towards her with their long coats sweeping out behind them, was reminded of other wars, remote if not distant, when aristocratic generals conferred on fronts that were not demolished in a day.

Both men were tall but Tandy, topped by the big fur hat that in battle would be an object of terror, looked too large for life. Harriet felt sorry for Yakimov, the fragile ghost, bowed with the effort of keeping up with his monstrous companion. When they came near her, she called him to her. He paused. She lifted the edge of his coat, admiring the lining: 'A wonderful coat,' she said. 'It will last a lifetime.'

'Two lifetimes, dear girl, if not three. M'poor old dad wore it, you know, and the Czar gave it a bit of wear before it was passed on. I wonder, *did* I tell you the Czar gave it to m'poor old dad?'

'I think you did.'

'Magnificent coat.' Yakimov stroked the fur then turned to Tandy, who was stopped beside him, and happy to share this admiration, said: 'Yours is a fine coat, too, dear boy. Where did y'get it? Budapest?'

'Azerbaijan,' said Tandy.

'Azerbaijan,' breathed Yakimov and, putting his cigarette to his lips, he caught his breath in awe.

Their voices had carried on the noiseless air and the police were looking up. As Yakimov drew on his cigarette, they shouted a command which no one but Alan Frewen understood. Yakimov drew again and the command was repeated.

Alan raised himself in his chair, saying urgently: 'They're telling you to put out that cigarette,' but he spoke too late.

The police were armed. One drew his revolver and fired. Tandy ducked and Yakimov folded slowly. He said in a whisper of puzzled protest: 'Dear boy!' and collapsed to the ground. His face retained the expression of his words. He seemed about to speak again but, when Harriet knelt beside him, his breathing had stopped. She pulled his coat open and put her hand on his heart: 'I think he's dead,' she said.

As she spoke, Guy, who had been watching, dazed by what had happened, was suddenly possessed by rage and went to the rail and shouted down: 'You murderous swine! Do you know what you've done? Do you care? You bloody-minded maniacs!'

The police stared up, blank-faced, understanding him no more than Yakimov had understood them.

The shot had brought people to the terrace, among them the hotel manager. Harassed by all the bustle inside the hotel, he had neither time nor sympathy for what had happened outside. He looked at the body and ordered those around it: 'Take him away,' but as no one could leave during a raid, he turned in exasperation and went in again.

Harriet pulled Yakimov's coat about his body and a waiter covered his face with a napkin. When she stood up, she felt dizzy. Spent by the accumulation of events, she collapsed into a chair. Midnight chimed on some distant clock.

Ben Phipps asked Alan where Yakimov lived. No one knew, but Alan thought it was one of the small hotels in Omonia Square. He said with the practicality of shock: 'No point in taking him there; no point in taking him anywhere. If they'll let us, the thing would be to leave him here. He'll have to be buried first thing tomorrow. We may all be gone in twenty-four hours. Where's Tandy? Tandy lives in the hotel: he's the one to talk to the manager.'

But Tandy, unnoticed by any of them, had gone to bed.

'Trust him,' Ben said bitterly. 'Not much bed for the rest of us. It'll take all night to sort things out. When's this damned raid going to end?'

The manager, his fury forgotten, returned with the police. They talked to Alan, making gestures of compunction and inculpability, and explained that the man who fired had intended only to frighten his victim. Yakimov's death had been an error. The fact that he was an Englishman made the incident particularly regrettable, but he had disobeyed an order twice repeated; and in these times there were so many deaths!

They looked at the body. They wanted to see Yakimov's *carte d'identité*, his *permis de séjour*, his *permis de travailler*, and his passport. When all the papers had been found in different pockets of Yakimov's clothing, his long, narrow corpse was rewrapped in its greatcoat as in a shroud, and the napkin rearranged over his face.

One of the police handed back Yakimov's passport and gave a salute and a little bow. The English would be troubled no further. The victim was free to go to his grave.

The manager agreed to let the body rest for the night in one of the hotel bathrooms. The four friends followed as it was carried away from the terrace and placed on a bathroom floor. As the door was locked upon it, the all clear sounded. The manager, offering his commiserations, shook hands all round and the English party left the hotel. Alan, hourly expecting an evacuation order, had decided to spend the night in his office. Ben Phipps, on his way to Psychico, dropped the Pringles off at the Academy.

A message was waiting for Guy on the pad in the hall. He was to ring Lord Pinkrose at Phaleron no matter how late his return. Harriet stood beside him as he dialled the number. The Phaleron receiver was removed at once and Pinkrose asked in an agitated scream: 'Is that you, Pringle? The Germans are less than six hours from Athens. They'll be here by morning. If you're wise, you'll go at once.'

'But how can we go?' Guy asked. 'There are no ships.'

'Get down to the Piraeus. Board anything you can see. *Make* them take you.'

'We've been ordered to stand by . . .' Guy protested, but Pinkrose was not listening. His receiver was replaced.

'Is that what he intends doing himself?' Harriet asked. 'Do you think he's going to the Piraeus to get on to any ship he can see?'

'God knows. Let's pack our things and think about it.'

The upper corridor was in darkness. No light was showing

344

under any of the bedroom doors. They met no one whom they could ask for guidance. The silence was such, the building might, for all they knew, have emptied in their absence.

As they got their belongings together, Harriet asked: 'Why do you think he warned us like that?'

'I suppose he feels some responsibility for us. He's still my boss, you know.'

'I wish he hadn't bothered.'

Their indecision was painful. Guy hung over his books, sorting out those that could be left behind and collected one day, when the war was over. Harriet threw her things pell-mell into a suitcase, then fell on to her bed and, lying there, eyes closed, felt herself sinking down into the darkness of the earth.

'Well, what do we do now?' Guy asked.

Rousing herself, she saw him standing in the middle of the wide, bare floor, his shirt-collar open, his shirt-sleeves rolled up. He was holding a book she knew well; the book that six months before he had picked out of the wreckage of their Bucharest flat. He was trying to look undaunted by events, but the droop of his face told her that he was as tired as she was and had no more answer than she to the problems that beset them. He presented an unruffled front to life, but she saw he was as much at sea as she was.

They had learnt each others' faults and weaknesses: they had passed both illusion and disillusion. It was no use asking for more than anyone could give.

War had forced their understanding. Though it was, as Guy said, a pre-war marriage, it had been a marriage in war, and the war had not ended yet. For all they knew it would not end in their lifetime. Meanwhile, they were still alive and still together; and they must face their commitments. She had chosen to make her life with Guy and would stand by her choice. The important thing, she thought, was that in a final contingency, they should not fail each other.

She asked: 'What do you want to do?' He sighed. She held out her arms to him and he crossed the room and sat on the edge of the bed, saying: 'Do you want to go down to the Piraeus now? Do you want to force your way on to some boat that is not meant for us? There are hundreds of English people here, some with children – they have as much right to go as we have. If everyone scrambled down to the docks and fought their way on to boats reserved for Yugoslavs and Poles, there'd be chaos. We don't want to make things worse for others. I feel we should take our chance with the rest. I don't believe they'll abandon us.'

'Neither do I.'

She put her arms round him and he lay down beside her. Too tired to undress, they slept, each holding the other secure upon the narrow bed.

Next morning, all the inmates of the hotel were sitting round the breakfast table, subdued, but scarcely more subdued than usual. Guy said: 'Someone told us last night that the Germans were only six hours from Athens. He seemed to think they'd be here by morning.'

'They're not here yet,' Tennant said. He smiled and, knowing things were too far gone for rebuttal, said slowly: 'But your informant was partly right. We heard that German parachute troops had dropped on Larissa, but that didn't mean they were coming straight here. They've still got to negotiate the pass at Thermopylae, the old invaders' bottleneck. Of course, it's not as narrow as it was. When the Spartans held it against Xerxes it was only twenty-five feet at the narrowest point. Now . . . how wide is it, would you say?' Tennant turned to consult his colleagues.

'Still, they are at Larissa?' Harriet asked.

'They may well be.' Tennant bent towards Harriet, giving her a smile of surprising sweetness: 'Please do not think I am withholding the truth from you. No one really knows anything. The train lines are cut in Macedonia. Telephone communication with the front has broken down. We are as much in the dark as you are.'

The mourners had arranged to meet in Alan's office. At the bottom of Vasilissis Sofias the Pringles were passed by Toby

Lush and Dubedat in the Major's Delahaye. Toby gave them a cheerful wave and Harriet said: 'Don't you think that those two are putting a surprisingly brave face on things?'

'What else can they do?' Guy said.

'Well, Pinkrose wanted us to bolt last night. Why didn't they bolt?'

'I don't know, but they evidently didn't. Perhaps they felt as we did about it.'

'Perhaps.'

'They aren't such bad fellows, really.'

Harriet did not argue. She saw that having grown up without faith, in an inauspicious era, Guy had to believe in something and so, against all reason, maintained a faith in friendship. If he chose to forget his betrayal, then let him forget it.

Ben Phipps was already in the News Room. He sat in Yakimov's old corner while Alan, behind his desk, talked into the telephone. He was saying as though he had said it a hundred times before: 'Don't worry. You'll be rung up just as soon as transport is available. Yes, yes, something is being done all right,' and putting down the receiver, said: 'Can they take horses, dogs, cats, fishes? I don't know! What does one do when one has to give up one's home and all the dependent creatures in it?' He rubbed his hands over his face and, eyes watering from lack of sleep, looked about him as though he scarcely knew where he was.

'So nothing's been arranged yet?' Guy said.

'No. Not yet.'

Ben got to his feet: 'What about the poor old bastard in the bathroom.'

'Yes, let's get that over,' Alan agreed. He edged himself out of his chair and waited while Diocletian came from under the desk with a scratch and a snuffle. As they left the office, the Pringles told the story of Pinkrose's panic order the previous night. Had Pinkrose gone himself?

Alan said: 'No, he rang this morning. He didn't seem unduly alarmed.'

347

'It's odd,' said Harriet, 'that he's not more alarmed. And it's even more odd that Lush and Dubedat are taking things so calmly.'

Guy and Alan said nothing, but Ben Phipps stopped on the pavement, screwing up his face against the sunlight, and stared at his car, then swung round and blinked at Harriet: 'It *is* odd,' he said. 'If you ask me, it's damned odd,' and, crossing to the car, he got in and drove away.

Alan looked after him in astonishment. 'Where's he off to?'

Guy said: 'To his office, most likely. He'll be back.'

'He'll have to hurry. Dobson has ordered the hearse for ten o'clock.'

They strolled to the Corinthian that was in ferment with the departing Poles and Yugoslavs. Though the ships were not due to sail before noon, the voyagers were shouting at porters, harrying taxi-drivers and generally urging their own deliverance with a great deal more flurry than was shown by the English who might not be delivered at all.

Six Yugoslav officers, their gold aflash, came at a run down the front steps, threw their greatcoats into a taxi and crying: 'Hurry, hurry,' threw themselves in after and were gone.

Some Greeks stood on the pavement, watching, silent, their black eyes fixed in an intent dejection.

Tandy, who usually took his breakfast out of doors, was not among those sitting round the café tables. Guy offered to find him, and Alan said: 'Tell him to hurry. It's nearly ten o'clock.'

Alan and Harriet felt it was scarcely worth sitting down and were still standing among the café tables when Guy returned. He was alone.

'Well, is he coming?' Alan asked.

Guy motioned to the nearest table. Harriet and Alan sat down, puzzled by Guy's expression. It was some moments before he could bring himself to tell them what he knew. He said at last: 'Tandy's gone.'

'Gone where?'

'To the Piraeus. He left early. Apparently he came down

about seven a.m., asked for his bill and told them to fetch down his luggage and call a taxi. He mentioned to one of the porters that he was going on the *Varsavia*.'

Harriet looked at Alan: 'Would he be allowed on?'

'He might: one man alone. And he took the precaution of going early, did he?' Alan laughed: 'Didn't want to be saddled with the rest of us.'

'He forgot this.' Guy opened his hand and showing the bill for Tandy's valedictory dinner, said apologetically: 'I'm afraid I hadn't enough to settle it all, so I gave them half and thought . . .'

Alan nodded and took the bill: 'I'll pay the rest.'

Tandy's flight silenced them. They not only missed his company, but were absurdly downcast by a superstitious fear that without him they were lost. They waited without speaking for the hearse to arrive and Ben Phipps to return.

An hour passed without a sign from either and Harriet said: 'Perhaps Ben Phipps has got on the *Varsavia*.'

Guy and Alan were shocked by her distrust of a friend. When Guy said: 'I'm perfectly sure he hasn't,' Alan grunted agreement and Harriet kept quiet for a long time afterwards.

They were joined by persons known to them who, stopping as they passed, gave different opinions: one that the Germans would be held at Thermopylae; another that they could not be held, but would drive straight through to Athens. As usual, no one knew anything.

Vourakis, with a shopping basket in his hand, stopped and said: 'Of allied resistance there is nothing but a little line from Thermopylae to Amphissia.'

'An important line, nevertheless,' Alan said. 'We could hold on there for weeks.'

'You could, but you will not. They will say to you: "Withdraw. Save yourselves, if you can. We want you here no more." That is all we can say to our allies now.' Vourakis spread his hands and contracted his shoulders in a gesture of despair. 'This is the end,' he said.

The others kept silent, not knowing what to reply.

349

'I have heard – I do not know how true – that some members of the Government want an immediate capitulation. Only that, they say, can save our city from the fate of Belgrade.'

'Royalists, I suppose?' said Guy.

'No. Not at all. The King himself is against capitulation and he has refused to leave Athens, though many say to him: "Fly, fly." Believe me, Kyrios Pringle, there are brave men in all parties.'

Guy was quick to agree, and Vourakis stood up, saying his wife had sent him out to buy anything he could find. The Germans, people knew, would take not only the food but medicines, clothing, household goods, anything and everything. So they were all out buying what they could find.

He passed on. It was now midday and still no hearse and no Ben Phipps.

Alan went to telephone the undertaker's office. He was told the hearse had gone to the funeral of an air-raid victim. The need these days was great, the servitors few. He returned to say: 'The hearse, like death, will come when it will come.'

'An apt simile,' said Guy, and Harriet, growing restless, decided to go and buy some flowers.

In case they came to look for her, she said she would go to the flower shop beside the Old Palace, but when she reached the corner she hurried into the gardens through the side entrance and went to the Judas grove. As Alan had promised, the trees had blossomed for Easter. She stood for a full minute taking in the rosettes of wine-mauve flowers that covered the leafless wood, devouring them in mind like someone who gazes into a lighted window at a feast, then she hurried to the shop and bought carnations for Yakimov.

With nothing else to do in a city where life was ebbing to a stop, the three sat on and watched the sun move off the square. It was late in the afternoon when the hearse and carriage drew up before the hotel.

'They've done him proud,' Guy said.

Four black horses, with silver trappings and tails to the ground, drew a black hearse of ornamental wood and engraved glass, surmounted by woeful black cherubs who held aloft black candles and black ostrich plumes. These splendours pleased the mourners but they did not please the hotel management. As soon as sighted, a porter came pelting down the steps to order them round to the back entrance.

While Alan and the Pringles stood in the kitchen doorway Dobson arrived in a taxi and joined them. The undertakers had taken the flimsy coffin up to the bathroom and the living listened to the arguments and the scraping of wood as it was manoeuvred down the grey and grimy cement stairway.

Dobson, sniffing the smell of cooking-fat, rubbed his head-fluff ruefully and said: 'This is really too bad!'

'It could be worse,' Guy said. 'Chekov died in an hotel and they smuggled him out in a laundry basket.'

The coffin edged round into view and reached the hall where the bearers, placing it on the ground, lifted the lid so all might see that Yakimov and his possessions were intact.

'We forgot to close his eyes,' Harriet said in distress and, looking into them for the last time, saw they had lost their lustre. Despite his greed, his ingratitude, his long history of unpaid debts, he had a blameless look and she found herself moved by his corpse, wrapped there in the Czar's old coat, as she had never been moved by him in life. He had died demurring, but it had been a gentle demur and the gaze that met hers was mild, a little bewildered but resigned to the mischance that had finished him off. Her own eyes filled with tears. She turned away to hide them; the coffin lid was replaced, the carnations placed upon it, and the cortège set out.

Dobson had asked the English *popa* Father Harvey to conduct the service: 'After all,' he said, 'Yaki must have been Orthodox.'

'But Russian Orthodox, surely?' said Alan.

'His mother was Irish,' Harriet said. 'So he may have been a Catholic.'

'Oh, well,' said Dobson. 'Harvey's a dear fellow and won't hold it against him.'

They drove at a solemn pace past the Zappion and the Temple of Zeus and came to a district that no one except Alan had visited before. Above the cemetery wall, tall cypresses rose into the evening blue of the sky. Father Harvey had already arrived. In his *popa*'s robes, with his blond beard, his blond hair knotted behind the veil that fell from his *popa*'s hat, he led the funeral procession through the gate into the graveyard quiet.

There had been no one to buy a plot for Yakimov. The Legation was paying for the funeral, but the coffin would have only temporary lodging in the ground. Alan mentioned that he had had to identify the remains of a friend who had died while on holiday in Athens.

'What was there to identify?' Dobson asked.

'Precious little. Bodies disintegrate quickly in the dry summer heat; soon there's nothing but dust and a few powdery bones and bits of cloth. They put it all into a box and place it in the ossuary. I prefer that. I don't want to lie mouldering for years. And think of the saving of space!'

'There'll be no one to identify Yakimov,' Harriet said.

Alan sadly agreed.

There would be no one left who had known him in life or remembered that the scraps of cloth lying among his long, fragile bones, had been a sable-lined greatcoat, once worn by the doomed, unhappy Czar of all the Russias.

Passing among the trees and shrubs, they came on small communities of graves that seemed like gatherings of friends, silent a moment till the intruders went by. When the ceremony was over, Harriet fell behind the party of mourners and, walking soundlessly on the grass verges, lingered to look at the statues and photographs of the dead. She did not want to leave this sequestered safety, where the ochre-golden light of the late sun rayed through the cypresses and gilded the leaves.

The richness of the enclosing greenery secluded her and gave her a sense of safety. When the men's voices passed out of hearing, a velvet quiet came down so she could imagine herself dead and immaterial in a region where the alarms of the present could affect her no more than those of the past. She wandered away from the direction of the gate, unwilling to leave.

Guy called her. She came to a stop beside a stone boy seated on a chair. Guy called again, breaking the air's intimate peace, and she felt her awareness contract and concentrate upon the destructive and futile hazards outside.

Guy came through the trees, reproving her: 'Darling, do come along. Dobson has to get back to the Legation. There's a lot to be done there.'

On the return journey, Harriet asked what they were doing up at the Legation.

'Oh!' Dobson gave a gasp of amusement at the ridiculous ploys of life. 'We're burning papers. We're sorting out the accumulation of centuries. All the important, top-secret documents written by all the important top-secret characters in history are being dumped on a bonfire in the Legation garden.'

Alan was returning with him to help in this task so the Pringles, dropped in the centre of Athens, found themselves alone.

Guy was certain that Ben Phipps would be waiting for them at the Corinthian, but there was no sign of him.

'Let's try Zonar's.'

They walked quickly in the outlandish hope that Tandy might, after all, be there. But he was not there. And Ben Phipps was not there. The table was unoccupied. Disconcerted, disconsolate, they stood and looked at it. What they missed most was Tandy's welcome. He had liked them; but he had liked everyone, in a general way, as some people like dogs, and might have excused himself by saying: 'They are company.' He had been in Athens only ten days and in that time had become a habit. Now he had gone, it was as though a familiar tree had been cut down, a landmark lost.

They felt no impulse to sit down without him. While they stood on the corner of University Street, some English soldiers came and began to set up a machine-gun.

'What on earth's happening?' Guy asked.

'Martial law,' said the sergeant. 'I'd go in if I were you. There's a report that the fifth column mean to bump off all the British.'

'I don't believe it.'

The sergeant laughed: 'Tell you the truth, I don't, neither.'

The Greeks seated in the café chairs watched apathetic, as the gun was placed in position, resigned to anything that might happen in a city passing out of control.

Standing there with nothing to do, nowhere to go, Harriet could see from his ruminative expression that Guy was trying to think of some duty or obligation that might protect him from the desolation in the air. Fearful of being left alone, she caught his arm and said: 'Please don't leave me.'

'I ought to go to the School,' he said. 'I've left some books there; and the students might come to say good-bye.'

'All right. We'll go together.'

The sun had dropped behind the houses and long, azure shadows lay over the roads. With time to waste, the Pringles strolled back to Stadium Street where other machine-guns stood on corners. Soldiers were patrolling the pavements with rifles at the ready. Most of the shops had shut and some were boarded and battened as a precaution against riots or street-fighting. Yet, apart from the guns, the soldiers and the boarded shops, there was no visible derangement of life. There was no violence; there were no demonstrations; simply, the everyday world was running down.

A sense of dream pervaded the town. Even at this time, human beings were entering the world, or leaving it. Yakimov had died and had to be buried, but his death had been an event in another dimension of time. Now, it was amazing to see the tram-cars running. When one of them clanked past, people stared, bewildered by men who had still the heart to go on working. The rest of them seemed to be without occupation, employment or interest. They had nothing to do. There was nothing to be done. They had wandered out of doors and now stood about, blank and silent in the nullity of grief.

354

Before they reached Omonia Square, Harriet was stopped by the sight of a shoe standing in an empty window: a single shoe of emerald silk with a high, brilliant-studded heel. Peering into the gloom of the shop, she saw there was nothing else. Cupboards stood open; drawers had been pulled out; paper and cardboard boxes had been kicked into corners. The only thing that remained was the shoe with its glittering heel.

In the square they saw Vourakis again, still carrying his shopping-basket, though there was nothing left to buy. A few shops had remained open but the owners gazed out vacantly, knowing the routine of buying and selling had come to an end like everything else.

Vourakis was tired. His eyelids were red and his dark, narrow face had sunk in as though in the last few hours old age had overtaken him. He had spoken to Guy only once or twice but caught his arm and held to him, saying: 'You should go, you know. You should save yourselves while there is time.'

'They can't find a ship for us,' Guy said.

Vourakis shook his head in compassion. 'Let us sit down a while,' he said, and led them to a café that smelt strongly of aniseed. The only thing kept there was ouzo and while they drank a couple of glasses, Vourakis told them stories of heroism and defiance that he had heard from the wounded who were now coming in in thousands from the field hospitals. Even now, he said, when all was lost, there were Greeks resisting and determined to resist to the death.

These stories of gallantry in the midst of defeat filled Guy and Harriet with profound sadness; and they felt the same sadness about them everywhere in the hushed city.

Vourakis suddenly remembered that his wife was waiting for him: 'If you cannot escape,' he said, 'come to us,' and he parted from them as though they had been lifetime friends.

When they went on towards Omonia Square, an ashen twilight lay on the streets. As the evening deepened, the atmosphere seemed to shift from despair to dread. There had been no announcement. Vourakis had said that telephone communication with the front had broken down. So far as anyone in Athens could know, there had been no change of any kind, yet as though the enemy were expected that night, there was a sense of incipient panic, impossible to explain, or explain away.

The School building had been shut for Easter week. Guy expected to find it empty but the front door lay open and inside half a dozen male students were moving furniture, despite the protests of the porter, George. Flushed by their activity, they gathered round Guy shouting: 'Sir, sir, we thought you had gone, sir.'

'I haven't gone yet,' Guy said, putting on an appearance of severity.

'Sir, sir, you should be gone, sir. The Germans will be here tomorrow. They might even come sooner, sir.'

'We'll go when we can. We can't go before. Meanwhile, what are you up to?'

The boys explained that they intended taking the School furniture into their homes to prevent its seizure by the enemy. 'It will be safe. It will be yours, sir, when you come back. We'll return it all to you.'

Three more students appeared at the top of the stairs carrying a filing-cabinet between them. Those at the bottom, shrill with excitement, began shouting up instructions and a small, dark youth with wide eyes and tough black hair, came panting to Guy, his teeth a-flash, crying: 'To me, this very day, an admiring fellow said: "Kosta, you are to make suggestions *born*."'

Guy insisted that operations should cease for that evening. 'Tomorrow,' he said, 'you can take what you like, but just at the moment I want to sort out my belongings.'

The departing students shook him by the hand, exclaiming regretfully because he must go, but for the young there was piquancy in change, and they went off laughing. It was the only Greek laughter the Pringles heard that day.

George, the porter, his grey hair curling about his dark, ravaged cheeks, gripped Guy's hand and stared into his face with tear-filled eyes. Guy was deeply moved until he discovered that this emotion had nothing to do with his own departure.

George had replaced a younger man who would now be returning from the war. 'What is to become of me?' he wanted to know. 'He will turn me into the street.' George had his wife, daughter and daughter's two children in the basement with him. The School was their home; they had nowhere else to go. *Kyrios Diefthyntis* must write a letter to say that George was the rightful possessor of the basement room.

Guy was disconcerted by this appeal because the old porter knew his appointment had been temporary. 'What of the young man who has been fighting so bravely at the front?' he said.

The porter answered: 'I, too, fought bravely long ago.'

Guy suggested that the problem be referred to Lord Pinkrose, and the old man gave a howl. Everyone knew that the Lord Pinkrose, a mysterious and unapproachable aristocrat, never came near the School. No, *Kyrios Diefthyntis*, with his tender heart, must be the one to act.

In distress Guy looked to Harriet for aid but she refused to be involved. Guy wanted only to give, leaving to others the much less pleasant task of refusing. In this present quandary, she decided, he must do the refusing himself.

She said she would wait for him in the sanded courtyard. When she left the building, she saw Greek soldiers walking along the side road and went to the wall to watch them. They were coming from the station. She had some thought of welcoming them back, but saw at once that they were not looking for welcome. Like the British soldiers she had seen on the first lorries into Athens, these men, shadowy in the twilight, were haggard with defeat. Some were the 'walking wounded', expected to find their own way to hospital; others had their feet wrapped up in rags; all, whether wounded or not, had the livid faces of sick men. They gave an impression of weightlessness. Their flesh had shrunk from want of food, but that had happened to everyone in Greece. With these men, it was as though their bones had become hollow like the bones of birds. Their uniforms, that shredded like worn-out paper, were dented by their gaunt, bone-sharp shoulders and arms.

One man seeing her watching so closely, crossed to her and said: '*Dhos mou psomi*,' and as he came near, she could smell the disinfectant on his clothing. She could only guess what he wanted. She opened her hands to show she could give him nothing. He went on without a word.

When they reached the main road, most of them stopped and looked about them in the last forlorn glimmer of the light. Some of them stood bewildered, then one after the other they wandered off as though to them one direction was very like another.

After they had all gone, Harriet still leant against the wall staring into the empty street.

The civilian image of the fighting man was much like that of the war posters that showed the Greeks in fierce, defiant attitudes, exhorting each other up snowbound crags in pursuit of the enemy. Now, she thought, she had seen them for herself, the heroes of Epirus.

She had been told that many of the men had no weapons, yet, like riderless horses in a race, they had gone instinctively into the fight. Starving, frost-bitten, infested with lice, stupefied by cold, they had endured and suffered simply because their comrades endured and suffered. The enemy had not had much hand in killing them. The dead had died mostly from frost-bite and cold.

The men she had seen, the survivors, had undergone more than any man should be asked to undergo. They had triumphed and at the last, unjustly defeated, here they were wandering back, lost in their own city, begging for bread.

University Street, when the Pringles walked back, was unusually bright. The raids had stopped – an ominous sign – and the café owners, knowing the end was near, had not troubled to put up their black-out curtains.

With faces lit by the café lights people could recognize one another, and Guy and Harriet, stopping or being stopped by acquaintances, were told that the Thermopylae defence was breaking. The Germans could arrive that very night. What was there to stop them? And the retreat went on. The main roads were noisy with the returning lorries. At times, passing through patches of light, they could be seen muddy as farm carts, with the men heaped together, asleep or staring listlessly at the crowds. Stories were going about the retreat itself. The returning soldiers said it had been carried out amidst the havoc of total collapse. Driven from Albania, the Greeks had found only one road open to them. The others were held by the Germans. The remaining road, which ran west of the Pindus, was choked with retreating men, refugees, every sort of transport – broken-down cars and lorries, tanks that had lost their treads, the ox waggons which had carried Greek supplies to the front, mule trains, and the hand carts and perambulators of the civilians. The whole densely packed, chaotic and despairing multitude was constantly bombed and machine-gunned by German aircraft.

Some Greeks had been cut off in Albania; some British were cut off in Thessaly. For the British now passing through Athens the important thing was to cross the Corinth canal before the bridge was blown up or taken by enemy parachutists. The English residents, beginning to lose faith in authority, told one another that if next morning there was still no sign of an evacuation ship, then they had better jump the lorries and go south with the soldiers who hoped to be taken off by the British navy at ports like Neapolis or Monemvasia. This was a rake-hell season that called for enterprise. If authority could not save them, then they must save themselves.

In the upper corridor of the Academy, the wash-room door opened and Pinkrose came out, wearing his kimono with the orange and yellow sunflowers. Guy hurried after him, trying to speak to him, but Pinkrose went faster. Guy called: 'Lord Pinkrose,' but Pinkrose, shaking the door-handle in his haste, pulled his door open, entered and shut it sharply behind him.

Alan Frewen had remained at the office for a second night. Ben Phipps had not been seen or heard of. There was still no news of a ship for the English, and no news of anything else.

Something woke Harriet at daybreak. She jumped up and went to the window: the Major's Delahaye was standing in the drive and Toby Lush was rearranging the luggage in the back seat.

Guy was asleep, his face pressed into the pillow, his shoulder lifted like a wing over his ear. He might have been defending himself against attack, but in this icy light he looked exposed and defenceless.

Knowing she would not sleep again, Harriet put on her dressing-gown and returned to the window to see what was happening outside. Toby had gone inside and was now carrying out the canvas bag in which Pinkrose transported his books. Pinkrose followed with the blankets from his bed. Neither of the men spoke. Though he appeared agitated, Pinkrose maintained silence, moving with a purposeful caution that reminded Harriet of Ben Phipps about to bury his victim in *Maria Marten*. The manner of both men suggested that they were engaged on a secret operation. She would have said they were making a get-away, if there were anywhere to go and anything to go on. As it was, she rejected her suspicions as a sign of strain. Pinkrose and Toby had no more chance of getting away than the Pringles, yet when the car drove off, she felt deserted. The plans that had sustained them the previous night had lost their allure. It might already be too late.

A mist was rising over the garden. Less than two months had passed since she had watched Charles walk away between the lemon trees and it had seemed then that life was just beginning. For a long time she had seen herself passing unscathed through experience, but experience had caught up with her at last. In the comfortless chill of early morning, she could believe that life was coming to an end.

The telephone rang in the passage. Guy seemed heavily asleep but at the first lift of the bell he sprang up as though he had been on guard.

'This'll be it,' he said and he pulled on a cardigan without undoing the buttons.

The telephone was answered. A knock came on the door and Harriet opened it. Miss Dunne stood outside in a pink dressing-gown and pink fur slippers, hands stowed away in pockets. As the door opened, her gaze lit inadvertently upon Harriet. then sped to the safety of the cornice. Her whole stance conveyed the importance of her message: 'You're to go at once to the Information Office.'

'Is there a ship, then?'

'It looks like it. Each person is allowed one suitcase. Not more.' Miss Dunne's own personal importance had a tinge of magnanimity that made Harriet wonder if the Legation had felt some guilt about its stranded nationals.

'Are you coming with us?' Harriet asked.

'Oh, no!' Miss Dunne took a step away at the suggestion and explained that some of the Legation staff would have to go on the ship, but for persons like Miss Dunne there were other arrangements.

The Pringles set out with one suitcase and the rucksack full of books. Their other possessions and books were put into a wardrobe. 'We'll get them again when the war's over,' Guy said. They went to the main road hoping to find a taxi, but in the end walked all the way to Constitution Square where the uncomplaining English had formed an orderly queue to await transport to the Piraeus. Those who had found taxis had gone on ahead. The others would be taken by lorry.

Mrs Brett at the front of the queue called down to Guy and Harriet: 'This is exciting, isn't it? We're going to be evacuated.'

'Surely you don't *want* to go?' Harriet said.

'Of course not. Percy's grave is here; naturally I want to stay; but, still, it's exciting to see the world. And we're going to Egypt where the news is good. We keep capturing places in Egypt.'

An old coal lorry swept into the square with Ben Phipps standing up in the back. 'Who's next?' he called as he jumped down, and Miss Gladys Twocurry in her green coat and Miss Mabel in her plum came out from the Information Office and closed the door behind them. Miss Gladys, guiding her sister across the pavement, looked flustered as though she felt herself at a disadvantage. Maybe she had expected to receive some sort of preferential treatment as a result of her attendance upon Pinkrose. Instead, here she was getting into the lorry like everyone else. Miss Mabel, hauled and pushed, was hoisted up and seated on a piece of luggage where she sat mumbling bitterly about the coal-dust on the floor.

When the lorry went off, only seven people remained to await its return. Ben Phipps joined the Pringles, his eyes jumping about with joy at his authoritative position. He slapped his hands together but gave no explanation of himself until Guy asked where he had gone the previous day.

'I can a tale unfold,' he said. 'Where do you think I went? Where did little Benny go, eh? Little Benny went to the Piraeus to have a looksee-see, and what did he see-see? He saw two ships astanding by, waiting to take Major Cookson and all Major Cookson's friends and valuables to some nice safe place. And Benny wasn't alone. Who did I meet down there but the old padre nosing around. He'd had the same idea. So we joined forces. We explored every avenue, we left no stone, we bloody well pushed our way into everything and everywhere. And there were these two old vessels tucked away in a corner: about the only things down there intact. We managed to find one of the stokers who said they'd been chartered by an English gentleman. He didn't want to say more but we put the screws on him, the padre and me. And who was this English gentleman? None other than the bloody Major. A lot of his stuff was already on board. He'd been preparing for weeks. He and his friends were going to travel in comfort, with all their possessions. "Right!" said the padre, "we'll see about this," and back we went to the Legation. The padre, I'll say it for him, was magnificent. He said: "I demand that every British subject and every Greek who is at risk as a result of working for the British, shall be given passage on those ships." Our diplomatic friends were not at all happy about it. The Major had chartered the ships. What about his rights? – the rights of the moneyed man?'

'Private property, eh?' said Guy.

'Private property – you've said it. But the padre, dyed in

the wool old Tory though he is, was having none of it. He said human beings came first. He refused to move until our F.O. friends agreed that the ships would be held until every British subject was on board. As soon as the Major heard what was going on, he tried to speed up his departure. He meant to sail at daybreak, but when he got down to the Piraeus he found the ships were being held by the military.'

'Is he coming with us?'

'Oh, yes, he won't be left behind; he'll travel with the hoipolloi, but I'm told he's hiding in his cabin. In fact the gallant Major's already feeling sick.'

Guy shook hands with Ben, delighted by the Major's defeat. 'A victory for human decency, a victory for human rights,' he said. Ben was eager in agreement but watching him dancing in vindictive triumph, Harriet wondered what would have happened had Ben Phipps not quarrelled with the Major. Supposing he had been among the privileged few invited to save themselves on the Major's ship! Hatred, she saw, was a considerable force; and Ben was likely to go far.

She had once been ambitious for Guy, but saw now the truth of the proverb that the children of darkness were wiser than the children of light. Guy, with all his charity, would probably remain more or less where he had started.

The lorry returned and the last half-dozen fugitives climbed on board.

It was Good Friday. The town was in abeyance but already the inhabitants were abroad, wakeful and restless in their apprehension.

Ben Phipps said: 'The pro-German elements are out in force,' but the Greeks who waved to the lorry as it passed looked the same as the Greeks who had wandered about last evening in the despairing twilight. And there were soldiers among them.

Ben Phipps nodded at them furiously. 'The whole Greek army's been sent back on leave. It's another act of sabotage. Papademas says it's been done to save them from the futile slaughter of a last stand; but if they'd joined our troops at

Marathon, they could have accounted for a good few Germans. Now, the bloody Hun'll walk in.'

As they came on to the long straight Piraeus road which shone empty, in the morning sun, Harriet said: 'I suppose Alan Frewen's already on board?'

Ben Phipps shook his head: 'Nope.'

'No? Then where is he?'

'On the way to Corinth, I imagine. He wanted a car, so I sold him mine. When he saw the evacuation all set, all ticketyboo, he shoved his dog into the back and drove off.'

'But where is he going?'

'Don't ask me. He was in a hurry to get over the bridge before someone blew it up. That's all I can tell you.'

'So he intends to stay in Greece? Can he survive down there?'

'Can he survive anywhere? He's the sort that starts heading for the high jump the day they're born.'

'And the dog will starve,' said Harriet.

'Good God!' Ben Phipps gave a yelp of laughter at her absurdity and she, turning on him angrily, said: 'And you let him go! You even sold him a car . . .'

'I suppose he can do what he likes?' Ben Phipps blinked at her in injured astonishment. 'If he wants to go, it's not my job to stop him.'

'No, you're not your brother's keeper, are you?'

Ben Phipps laughed, too angry to speak.

Harriet, thinking disconsolately of Alan, the lonely man who had loved Greece and the Greeks, and could not leave them, stood up to take a last look as they passed the villa and the Ilissus and the little wood, whispering: 'My poor cat.'

A woman sitting behind her in the lorry said: 'We left our dogs. We hadn't time to do anything but turn the key in the lock. We took the dogs to a neighbour who promised to look after them. "They'll be here when you come back," he said.'

Her husband said: 'Better to have shot them. At least we'd know what became of them.'

She said: 'Oh, Denis!' and her husband turned on her:

'Don't you realize what's going to happen here?' he said. 'Can't you see what's in store for these people?'

No one said anything more till they stopped at the docks.

In the whole of the great basin there were no objects standing upright except the cargo boats *Erebus* and *Nox*.

The sky was a limpid blue; the water beneath it black with wood scraps. Out of this dense, black, viscous surface poked the masts and funnels of sunken ships, a tangle of wreck and wreckage, lying at all angles.

The harbour buildings, burnt or blasted, lay in fragments. Among the smoked rubble, broken glass and charred ravelment of wood, green things had taken root. The Piraeus already seemed an ancient ruin, reaching again towards the desolation that covered it for eighteen hundred years after the Peloponnesian Wars.

The *Erebus* and *Nox* alone had colour: they were red with rust. They had been used for the transport of Italian prisoners and, according to Ben Phipps, were 'not only derelict, but filthy'.

Guy said in a cheerful voice: 'Thalassa! You said you felt safe because the sea was near. Well, here we are!' but Harriet could not even remember now why the sea had seemed a refuge.

English soldiers had been detailed to help the passengers on board. They had already hoisted the Major's Delahaye and packing cases on to the deck, and carried up the baggage belonging to the Major's guests. The single suitcases of the uninvited were treated as a joke.

'That all you got?' they said when the small pile of luggage came off the lorry. 'Didn't let you bring much, did they?'

Some of the recent arrivals were still on the quay. The Pluggets were getting out of a taxi. Mrs Brett and Miss Jay were watching for the Pringles and, catching sight of them, Mrs Brett came striding towards them in a fury of indignation, shouting: 'What do you think! That Archie Callard is up there insulting everyone that comes on board!'

The Pringles had forgotten Archie Callard who, surprisingly

enough, had not been flown off to join some daring desert group but had been loitering all the time, unoccupied, at Phaleron.

'What do you think he said to Miss Jay?' said Mrs Brett.

Miss Jay, whose vast bulk had shrunk until her flesh hung like flannel over her bones, said crossly: 'You've said enough about it, Bretty,' but Mrs Brett was determined to say more: 'He said: "Women should be painlessly put down when they look like Miss Jay."'

Ben Phipps laughed in delight: 'Did he, really! Come on. If we get a squeak out of him, we'll deal with him.'

They went forward prepared for Callard who was leaning over the gunwale with Dubedat beside him, but he let the Pringles and Phipps pass without a word. His eye was on Plugget, who came behind them. 'They're all coming out of their holes,' he said. 'Here's that drip Plugget. His wife's family put him up for twenty years. Now he's saving his own skin and leaving them to starve.'

Plugget, pushing his wife importantly ahead of him, gasped, but said nothing. A little later, when she stood at the rail over-looking the quay, Harriet found him at her elbow. His wife's parents stood below with their unmarried daughter, an elderly girl who held herself taut with a look of controlled despera-tion, a suitcase at her side.

'Isn't she coming with us?' Harriet asked.

'No,' said Plugget with decision. 'She wanted to come but when she saw the old folk in tears, she didn't know what to do. My wife thought she ought to stay. I thought she ought to stay. Her duty, I told her.'

'Poor thing! What will become of her?'

Impatient of Harriet's pity, Plugget said: 'She'll be all right. You can't take everyone. Think of me landed with two women!' Turning his back on the forlorn spectacle of his rela-tions-in-law, he said: 'You people found anywhere to sleep?'

The main cabins had been taken by the Major's party and most of the deck was covered by his possessions. Any space left had been occupied by earlier arrivals. Guy and Phipps had gone off in different directions to see what they could find. Guy had at once been caught up in conversation by his many acquaintances, and it was Phipps, with his indeflectable, inquiring energy, who came back to say there was a cabin empty on the lowest deck.

Guy, Mrs Brett and Miss Jay were called together, and the party went down into a darkness heavy with the reek of oil and human excretions. Every outlet from the lower passages had been boarded up to prevent the escape of prisoners and Plugget, who had come after them, put up a complaint: 'If we're torpedoed, we'd never get out of here,' but he kept at their heels until they came to the narrow three-birth cabin next to the engine-room. Inside he at once took command:

'You two ladies here,' he said, slapping the middle bunk. 'Pringles on top. You're young and agile. Me and the wife down here. The wife's not strong. Right?'

No one contested this arrangement, but Guy asked: 'What about Ben?'

'The floor suits me,' Phipps said. 'It's cleaner.'

The bunks, without mattresses or covers, were wooden shelves, sticky to the touch and spattered with the bloody remains of bugs.

'Like coffins,' said Mrs Brett. 'Still, it's an adventure.'

Peering about in the glimmer that fell from a grimy, greasy, ochre-coloured electric bulb, she said: 'We might try to get the dirt off this basin.'

Miss Jay pulled out three chamber-pots caked with the yellow detritus of the years. '"Perfum'd chambers of the great,"' she said. 'We'll send these up to Cookson.'

While these activities went on, Toby Lush appeared in the doorway with a commanding frown. When he saw who was inside, his manner faltered: 'I was keeping this cabin,' he weakly said.

'What for?' Phipps asked.

'The Major might need a bit extra storage space. Or he might, f'instance, want something unpacked, and I thought . . .'

'If the Major has any request to make,' said Phipps, 'send him to me.'

Toby Lush put his pipe into his mouth and sucked. After an interval of indecision, he said mildly: 'Glad you got on board all right.'

'Were you expecting us?' Harriet asked.

'Hey, there! Crumbs!' Toby shielded his face in mock alarm. 'You aren't blaming me, are you? Not my fault; nor the old soul's, neither. The Major made his arrangements. He didn't consult us.'

'You knew nothing about it?'

'Well, not much. Anyway, here you are. Nothing to grumble about. I suppose you were told to bring food for three days?'

'We had no food to bring.'

The air-raid warning sounded. 'More magnetic mines,' said Toby and, giving an exasperated tut, he made off as though he meant to deal with them himself.

'Don't want to be trapped down here,' said Plugget. He hurried after Toby and the others went with him. They reached the main deck as the guns, upturned on the quay, started up like hysterical dogs. In the uproar women seized their children and asked what they should do. There was a shelter on the quay but as the passengers ran to the companionway, Dubedat shouted from the boat-deck: 'We're leaving any minute now. If you get off the ship, you'll be left behind.'

Bombs fell into the harbour, sending up columns of water that brought a rain of wreckage down on the ship. The passengers crowded into the corridors of the main deck where the nervous chatter and the cries of children caused Toby Lush to put his head out of his cabin: 'Less noise there,' he commanded. 'You're disturbing the Major,' and withdrew before comment could reach him.

At noon, in the midst of another raid, Dobson drove on to the quay, bringing the Legation servants to the ship. In his light, midge-like voice, he shouted to Guy: 'We'll meet in the land of the Pharaohs.'

'Good old Dobson,' Guy said emotionally as the car turned on the quayside and started back to Athens.

'Perhaps now we've had his blessing,' Phipps said, 'we'll be allowed to embark.' But the sun rose hotly in the sky, the reconnaissance planes came and went, and the *Erebus* and *Nox* remained motionless at their berths.

A taxi-load of students came to say farewell to Guy. They shouted up to the boat that the Prime Minister, Koryzis, was dead.

'How did he die?' the passengers asked, feeling no surprise because there was nothing left surprising in the world.

The students said: 'The German radio says the British murdered him.'

'You don't believe that, do you?'

They shook their heads, believing nothing, knowing nothing, buffeted and confused by the drama of existence. Other Greeks drove down to the Piraeus, their eyes bleared with sleeplessness and tears, bringing with them the tormented nervousness of the city. The English asked again about Koryzis. The Greeks on the quay, doomed themselves, shook their heads, mystified by a death that was too apt an ingredient of the whole tragedy.

To those on board, not knowing when they would sail or whether the ship would survive to sail at all, the afternoon shifted about like a disordered vision. They could only wait for time to pass. The only event was the appearance of a man selling oranges. Despite Dubedat's warning the women hurried ashore to buy, for there was no drinking water on the ship.

The Acropolis could be seen from the boat-deck. Harriet went up several times to look at it. Seeing it glowing in the sunset, she thought of Charles, scarcely able in memory to distinguish between his reality and her private image. She had condemned Guy's attachment to fantasy but wondered now if fantasy were a part of life, a component without which one could not survive. She saw Charles catching the flower and thought of the girls who had given flowers, not only as a recognition of valour but a consolation in defeat.

The hills of the Peloponnesus, glowing in the sunset light, changed to rose-violet and darkened to madder rose, grew sombre and faded into the twilight. The Parthenon, catching the late light, glimmered for a long time, a spectre on the evening, then disappeared into darkness. That was the last they saw of Athens.

Some time after midnight the engines of the *Erebus* began to throb and shake. Ben Phipps, on the shaking floor of the cabin, said: 'We're about to slip silently into the night.' The ship groaned and shuddered and seemed about to shatter with its own effort. Somehow it was wrenched into motion.

Next morning, when they went on deck, they saw above the southern cloud banks the silver cone of Mount Ida. On one side of the *Erebus* was the *Nox*; on the other there was a tanker that no one had seen before. The tanker, its plates mouldering with rust, was as decrepit as its companions, yet the three old ships had their dignity, moving steadily forward, unhurried and at home in their own element.

Most of the passengers took the pace as fixed and immutable, but Ben Phipps and Plugget, having conferred together, went to the First Officer with the demand that it be increased. They were told that the convoy must conserve its power for the dangerous passage past the coast of Cyrenaica.

Phipps, who had now established his authority over Plugget, went round the ship, his energy unimpaired by a night made sleepless by the thumping engine, the bugs, and the jog-trots of cockroaches and blackbeetles. Plugget felt bound to keep beside him, but Guy sat on the boat-deck, his back against a rail, and read for a lecture on Coleridge. The women, in a stupor, sat round him.

Ben kept returning to the group, trying to rouse in Guy a spirit of inquiring indignation, but Guy, refusing to acknowledge the changes and perils through which they were passing, would not be moved.

Ben Phipps had discovered that the lifeboats were rusted to the davits so there would be little hope of launching them. 'Those two boy scouts, Lush and Dubedat, are trying to organize life-boat drill. If they come up here, tell them from me the boats are a dead loss.' He went again and returned to report that there was no wireless operator on board, but he could work the transmitter himself and had talked to the Signal Station at Suda Bay.

'Nice to know we're not cut off,' said Phipps, looking to Guy for agreement and admiration. Guy, as was expected, smiled admiringly, but it was a rather ironical admiration. Harriet began to suspect that Phipps was losing his hold on Guy. When he said persuasively: 'Come and see,' Guy merely stretched and smiled and shook his head. When Phipps took himself off, Guy returned to his books. He spent the day absorbed, like a student in a library. The only difference was that he sang to himself, the words so low that only Harriet knew what they were:

'If your engine cuts out over Hellfire Pass,
You can stick your twin Browning guns right up your
     arse.'

sometimes changing to the chorus:

'No balls, no balls at all;
If your engine cuts out, you'll have no balls at all.'

Drowsy in the mild, spring wind, Harriet watched Crete take form out of the cloud. The sun broke through. Two corvettes from Suda Bay circled the convoy and let it pass. A reconnaissance plane came back again and again to look at the ships, flying so low that the black crosses were clear on the wings and some people claimed they had seen the face of the enemy. Nothing more happened. The civilian ships did not look worth a raid.

They turned the western prow of Crete, a route not much used by shipping, where the island rose, a sheer wall of stone, offering no foothold for life. Grey and barren in the brilliant light, it seemed an uninhabited island in an unfrequented sea, but during the afternoon a ship came into view: a hospital ship. It slid past slowly, like a cruising gull, and remained a long time in sight, catching the sun upon its silver flank.

As the afternoon passed, people began to rise out of their torpor and appear on deck. Among them was Pinkrose in all his heavy clothing. Feeling the heat, he began to unwrap, then, in a sudden nervous spasm, he hurried away and returned without his trilby. He was wearing instead a large hat of straw. This contented him for a time, then he felt the top of the hat and was again galvanized into action. He went off and, when he made a third appearance, had placed the trilby on top of the straw.

'Good God,' whispered Miss Jay, 'why's he wearing two hats?'

'Because,' said Phipps, temporarily back at base, 'he's as mad as two hatters.'

A very old man came on to the boat-deck trailing a toy dog among the hazards of bodies, baggage and packing-cases. Harriet sat up in surprise. It was Mr Liversage who had been her companion on the Lufthansa from Sofia to Athens. She had scarcely thought of him since and supposed he had gone on the autumn evacuation boat. Instead, here he was, jaunty as ever, with his old snub face, grey-yellow hair and moist yellow-blue eyes. The dog was an old dog, the hair gone from its worn, cracked hide, but it was as jaunty as its master.

Mr Liversage recognized her at once. 'Chucked out again,' he shouted. 'Bit of a lark, eh?'

He squatted down with the group and Harriet asked where he had been all winter. He told her:

'Cooped up indoors. Had a nasty turn; bronchitis, y'know.' He had been staying with friends at Kifissia, an elderly English couple who had looked after him well. 'Bully of them to take an old codger in. Lucky old codger, that's me. They'd a lovely home.' He described how his hostess had waked him early the previous morning, saying: 'Come on, Victor. We've got to go. The Germans are nearly here.' 'The poor girl was very brave: had to leave everything; made no complaints. "Fortune of war, Victor," she said. So we all came on the Major's boat.

Very kind of the Major, very kind indeed.' Becoming aware of Phipps standing above him, Mr Liversage said: 'See this dog! Best dog in the world.'

'Oh, is it?' Phipps bent slightly towards the old man but his eyes were dodging about in search of better entertainment.

'Collected thousands of pounds, this dog.'

'Oh, really! Who's the money for? Yourself?'

'Myself!' Mr Liversage got to his feet. 'My dog collects for hospitals,' he said.

He was deeply offended. Guy and the women attempted to assuage him but he would not be assuaged. He lifted his dog and went. Before anyone had time to reprove him, Phipps, too, was off, in the other direction.

An hour or so later the ships slowed and stopped. Word went round that they were being circled by an enemy submarine and the *Nox* was preparing to drop depth charges. As this was happening, Ben Phipps returned with Plugget in tow. He was in an agitated state and the news of the submarine was as nothing compared with what he had to tell.

'I've found a locked cabin,' he said. 'When I asked Lush for the key, he got into a tizzy. He refused to hand over. I said we'd a right to know what's inside. I told him if he didn't open up, I'd report the Major's behaviour to the Cairo Embassy and demand an inquiry. That made him puff his pipe, I can tell you. I'm collecting witnesses. Come on, Guy, now, get to your feet.'

Guy stretched himself but stayed where he was. 'I bet there's nothing inside but luggage.'

'I bet you're wrong. Come along.'

Guy smiled, shook his head and said to Harriet: 'You go.'

Bored now and ready for distraction, she rose and followed Phipps, who gathered more witnesses as he went.

When they reached the main corridor, Phipps strode past the Major's cabin and shook the next door. Finding it still locked, he gave it a masterful kick, shouting: 'Open up.'

From inside the Major's cabin, Archie Callard's voice rose in anguish. 'This is too tedious! Do let little Phipps "open up".'

The Major answered: 'I don't care what he does. All I want is to get off this damned ship.'

Toby, snuffling with defeat, came out and unlocked the door. The interior was dark. Ben strode in, plucked aside the black-out curtains and revealed a store-house of tinned foods.

'Just as I thought.' he said. He swung on Toby. 'The rest of us have eaten nothing for two days. There are children on board and pregnant women. This stuff will be distributed: a tin for everyone on the ship.'

Toby ran back to the Major's cabin. His voice high with obsequious horror, he cried: 'Major, Major, they're taking the stores.'

'God save us,' said Phipps. 'Listen to old Lush sucking up to the head girl!'

Harriet returned to the boat-deck with a tin of bully beef. The tins distributed, Ben Phipps came round in a comic coda, sharing out the Major's toilet rolls.

'Here you are, ladies,' he said as he gave three squares of paper to each. 'One up, one down and a polisher.'

'What about tomorrow?' Miss Jay asked.

'Tomorrow may never come,' he cheerfully replied.

The sun was low. With her head against the rail, watching the lustrous swell of the sea that held in its depths the hues of emeralds and amethysts, Harriet thought of Charles left behind with the retreating army, of David taken by the enemy, of Sasha become a stranger, of Clarence lost in Salonika, of Alan who would share the fate of the Greeks, and of Yakimov in his grave.

Not one of their friends remained except Ben Phipps; 'the vainest and the emptiest', she thought.

It seemed to her there would always be a Phipps, one Phipps or another Phipps, to entice Guy from her into the realms of folly, but Ben Phipps had almost had his day. Guy's infatuation was waning; and, when he had seen through Ben's last conceit, Ben would go elsewhere for attention.

If Guy had for her the virtue of permanence, she might have the same virtue for him. To have one thing permanent in life as they knew it was as much as they could expect.

Crete was still visible, shadowy in the last of the twilight, a land without lights. That night the race began. The ship's old engines pummelled into speed, her timbers cracked and rattled, and the passengers, clinging to anything that gave handhold, lay awake and listened. At daybreak the uproar slackened: the danger was past.

Their first thought was for the companion ships. They went up on deck to see the *Nox* and the tanker moving quietly on either side. The three old ships had survived the night and their journey was almost over.

The passengers had awakened in Egyptian waters and were struck by the whiteness of the light. It was too white. It lay like a white dust over everything. Disturbed by its strangeness, Harriet felt their lives now would be strange and difficult.

Someone shouted that land was in sight. She put her hand into Guy's hand and he pressed her fingers to reassure her.

She said: 'We must go and see.' Leaving Greece, they had left like exiles. They had crossed the Mediterranean and now, on the other side, they knew they were refugees. Still, they had life – a depleted fortune, but a fortune. They were together and would remain together, and that was the only certainty left to them.

They moved forward to look at the new land, reached thankfully if unwillingly. They saw, flat and white on the southern horizon, the coast of Africa.